SCHOOL FOR STINGERS

Caroline lifted her skirt, and rubbed her ridged buttocks, almost fully bared by the skimpy thong. 'You might have found another way to test me, miss,' she said ruefully, 'although I can't say I'm sorry to have been beaten.'

'Hurt much?' said Miss Chew sympathetically.

'It smarts awfully, miss, but I can cope with it, and I'm proud.'

'Spoken like a true Radegundian,' said Miss Chew. 'I like the way you repaired your knickers – illegal by the way – without a fuss. Now, I have in mind a different form of further education for you. It is a sort of, ah, finishing school, near St Ives, in Cornwall – so romantic – run by a dear cousin of mine, Mistress Laetitia Frubbin, for girls aged between eighteen and twenty-one. The emphasis is on discipline, and the acquisition of truly ladylike qualities in marriageable young girls.'

By the same author:

BELLE SUBMISSION
BELINDA BARES UP
CAGED!
CHERRI CHASTISED
CONFESSIONS OF AN ENGLISH SLAVE
THE CORRECTION OF AN ESSEX MAID
THE GOVERNESS ABROAD
THE GOVERNESS OF ST AGATHA'S
THE HOUSE OF MALDONA
THE ISLAND OF MALDONA
THE CASTLE OF MALDONA
THE DISCIPLINE OF NURSE RIDING
GIRL GOVERNESS
LACING LISBETH
MISS RATAN'S LESSON
NURSES ENSLAVED!
PEEPING AT PAMELA
POLICE LADIES
PRIVATE MEMOIRS OF A KENTISH
HEADMISTRESS
SANDRA'S NEW SCHOOL
SKIN SLAVE
SOLDIER GIRLS
THE SCHOOLING OF STELLA
THE SMARTING OF SELINA
THE SUBMISSION OF STELLA
THE TAMING OF TRUDI
THE ENGLISH VICE

SCHOOL FOR STINGERS

Yolanda Celbridge

nexus

This book is a work of fiction.
In real life, make sure you practise safe, sane and consensual sex.

First published in 2005 by
Nexus
Thames Wharf Studios
Rainville Road
London W6 9HA

www.nexus-books.co.uk

Typeset by TW Typesetting, Plymouth, Devon

Printed and bound by Clays Ltd, St Ives PLC

ISBN 0 352 33994 2

Contents

You'll notice that we have introduced a set of symbols onto our book jackets, so that you can tell at a glance what fetishes each of our brand new novels contains. Here's the key – enjoy!

 cp (traditional)

 cp (modern)

 spanking

 restraint/bondage

 rope bondage/hojojutsu

 latex/rubber/leather/enclosure

 fem dom

 willing captivity

 medical

 period setting

 uniforms

 sex rituals

1

Caned on the Bare

'Eighteen years old,' said Caroline Letchmount, bitterly, 'and to have to wear this silly bloody uniform, like some brat in the lower fourth, and wait in front of the beak's study, pretending to be penitent, when I've done nothing wrong at all. At least, not really. Is this the twenty-first century or the seventeenth? And it's only a week till the end of term. Then, I can burn this hateful uniform. See if I don't! I won't have to dress like a . . . a *girly*, ever again.'

She looked up, wrinkling her nose, at the ancient gilt-framed portrait of Lady Arabella Warchant, smiling severely above her ruff and thrusting her full breasts into prominence, above a pile of books and a crook-handled cane, cradled in her lap. Beneath the portrait, a scroll carried the school's motto: '*Semper fessae immaculatae*'.

'Well, it's the same for me, Caroline,' said her best friend, Persimmon Pipp, sniffily. '*I* don't complain. The beak is firm, but fair, and you must admit, we were caught rather in flagrante.'

The tall corn-blonde Caroline, hair daringly sweeping past her shoulders (not *quite* in harmony with school rules), had a few inches in height on her chestnut-haired friend, yet both girls perched coquettishly on heels as high as they could get away with at St Radegund's, with seams down the back of their dark-blue nylons (a grey area in the rules) and their school uniforms indeed looking rather skimpy, as they clung to heavily swelling breasts and full, ripe buttock pears – Caroline's above long coltish legs, with a horse-rider's gap between her thighs. Caroline gazed longingly through the mullioned windowpane at the fields and coppices of Wiltshire, the fluttering white slips of bare-legged girls at netball and the birds and bees, going merrily about their business – *they* weren't awaiting a ticking-off, or worse, from the beak.

'Bulstrode was snooping,' said Caroline vehemently. 'She's a damned lesbo, like all the bloody pres, and she's no business to be peeking in the showers. It's not as if we'd be smoking, is it?'

'I suppose not. We smoke behind the bike shed.'

'I mean, it's rather wet in the showers.'

'That's true.'

'Everyone knows that after gym, a girl feels a bit fruity, and . . . well, you know.'

'Still, it was a lovely wank, wasn't it?' said Persimmon coyly. 'Worth getting the cane for.'

'That's awfully sweet of you, Pers,' said Caroline, patting her friend's bottom, snugly nestling under the pleated grey St Radegund's uniform skirt. 'But I don't think anything is worth getting the cane for. I'm sick of Miss Chew and her beastly cane.'

'Perhaps she'll just give us a talking-to. We're due a careers talk, aren't we? Perhaps she won't . . .'

Voomp! Persimmon's words dried, as, from the oak-panelled door of Miss Chew's study, came the muffled swish of a cane stroke on cloth. She bit her lip.

'Now see what you've done,' Caroline said, making a moue. 'You said caning, and caning it shall be.'

Voomp!

'She'll be taking a dozzie,' said Persimmon glumly.

The two girls held their breath.

Voomp!

'Wonder who it is?'

'Angie Stroud, I expect. I know Latimer caught her smoking this morning. She's got extra knickers on, by the sound of things.'

Voomp!

'She's taking her time, the rotter,' Caroline said, rubbing her nyloned thighs together, under her short pleated skirt, which showed just a glimpse of bare thigh, stocking-tops and sussies. 'I say, Persimmon . . .'

'Yes?'

'Doesn't the thought of beastly Ange getting her bum whacked make you feel a bit fruity?'

Persimmon giggled. 'It does, rather. Those high and mighty pears wriggling! We must sit on her, for a bum inspection in dorm, and make her show us her stripes.'

'We've time for . . . you know,' Caroline murmured, licking her pearl-white teeth.

Persimmon gaped. 'A wank? Here?'

'Wouldn't it be a jape? My downstairs is ever so tingly.'

Persimmon's tongue plopped out over her lower lip. 'I'm game if you are, Caroline. You know I can't resist your gorgeous quim, and that fabulous mound. So big and ripe, like a melon, and smelling just as sweet, when I . . . you know, sniff it.' Persimmon blushed happily.

'All right, then, let's,' Caroline purred.

Primly, the girls lifted their skirts, each revealing the tops of their blue nylon stockings, the blue garter straps and sussie belt, and the white cotton knickers beneath, tightly enclosing the plump pubic hillocks. Persimmon wore standard bikini panties, but Caroline's were in a narrow thong cut, the gusset wet with seeped fluid at the folds of her gash, prominently outlined under the thin fabric.

'You *are* fruity,' murmured Persimmon, sliding her fingers into the front of Caroline's panties. 'And what luscious, rule-breaking knickers! They're so tight on your gourd! Just as well the beak won't see them.'

Her fingers penetrating Persimmon's knickers, Caroline caressed the girl's bare bottom, before sliding her fingers around the haunch, to squeeze the flaps of Persimmon's swelling, hairy gash. Holding their skirts up, with legs parted, the two girls frotted their naked quims, the lips and clitties rapidly becoming tumescent. Wet, sucking noises emerged from the writhing panties, as the cloth stained and moistened from their seeped come.

'Yes, that's it,' Caroline panted. 'Wank me hard, Pers. Gosh, it's good.'

'Mm . . . mm . . .' gasped Persimmon. 'Oh, my nubbin's going to explode! Your twat's so gorgeous, Caroline – that pube hillock, so huge outside, and the slit so lovely and tight inside.'

'I was made that way,' Caroline panted. 'Girls joke that I've an extra fesse, or an extra titty, between my legs.'

'Well, it's super. Can you get your fingers inside me?' gasped Persimmon. 'Ooh, yes. That's good.'

Caroline pushed two fingers inside the girl's slit, sliding her fingernails across her hard wombneck, while flicking the engorged clitoris with her thumb. Persimmon, meanwhile, had three fingers in Caroline's own gash, and was thrusting vigorously, slicing Caroline's swollen, extruded clitty with her thumbnail, so that Caroline gasped aloud, buckling at the knees.

'We'll drip onto the floor,' said Persimmon.

'Who cares? This is fun.'

The 'voomp' of Miss Chew's cane continued faintly, beyond the oaken door.

'Oh, yes,' Caroline groaned. 'I'm on fire! I'm going to come any second . . . wank me, Pers, wank me harder . . .'

'Me too,' gasped Persimmon. 'Can't you feel how wet you make me? Gosh, Caroline, you're the best wank chum I've ever had. Such a fabulous huge clitty! Do my twat, do me till I burst . . .'

'Ooh . . . I'm nearly there –'

Suddenly, the door sprang open, and Miss Chew's immaculate blonde coiffe bobbed before them.

'Nearly where, Caroline?' she asked pleasantly.

Blushing crimson, the two frotting girls pulled fingers from twats and hands from panties, smoothed down their skirts and hid their dripping fingers behind their backs. They hung their heads, not answering the headmistress, whose smile froze to ice. Miss Chew raised her arm for

Angie Stroud to stumble past, sobbing and rubbing her grey-skirted bottom. When Angie had disappeared down the 'punishment corridor' that led to the assembly hall, Miss Chew ordered both Caroline and Persimmon to attend her, in her study. The girls sheepishly entered the sanctum, with its perfume of books, leather and old, polished wood.

They stood before her gleaming oak desk, beside the leather sofa whose worn top attested to its service for generations of errant St Radegund's girls. Outside, the gardens and playing fields shone bright and green in the June sunshine, which dappled the headmistress's study through her mullioned windows. Miss Chew seated herself at the desk, beside the bookcase, half of which was without shelves, but accommodated a rack of dangling wooden canes, all sparkling with polish. The girls stood, red-faced, hands behind their backs, and their heads lowered. Miss Chew made an arch of her fingertips in front of her breast.

'Show me your hands, both of you,' she snapped.

Trembling, the girls held out their hands. Sunlight glistened on their come-soaked fingers. Miss Chew pursed her lips, and sighed.

'You are very naughty girls,' she said, enunciating crisply, as if they were hard of understanding. 'And on such a nice summer afternoon!'

In the distance, there was a crack of stick on ball, and a cry of 'Well played!'

Miss Chew's ripely curved body shifted in her chair, with a squeak of nylons, as she crossed her thighs, pulling her skirt hem up a little to ease the movement. Her dress was as near as possible to the St Radegund's girls' uniforms, as she frequently explained: white blouse and striped tie, short grey skirt – though tightly clinging to her full haunches, and unpleated – and black shoes, except that Miss Chew favoured nylons of different colours from the standard blue. Today, her nylons were a delicate peach.

'Both of you lift up your skirts at the front and show me your panties,' she ordered.

Shivering, the girls obeyed, Caroline being careful to show only the gusset, swelling at her quim hillock, and not the high-cut sides of her thong.

'Well!' exclaimed Miss Chew, with a click of her tongue. 'I see disgraceful stains. You are both sopping wet. You have been diddling – in front of my study, beneath the portrait of our foundress! What would Lady Warchant have to say?'

She picked up a piece of paper and scanned it.

'Prefect Bulstrode reports that she caught you doing just that – playing with each other – in public, in the showers, after gym,' she said sternly. 'So, that's what you are here for in the first place, and now you outrageously compound the offence by repeating it. I don't suppose you are going to deny it.'

'Please, miss,' Caroline said, 'the showers aren't *very* public. We didn't know that Bulstrode was spying on us, and I submit that our offence was no worse than a girl playing with herself, after lights out. I know it is an offence, but if no one sees, then, surely . . .'

Miss Chew shook her head.

'. . . and, as for just now, well, I – we – were so nervous, waiting for punishment and everything, that we must have lost control and wet ourselves.'

'That's it,' said Persimmon. 'If we had our hands in our you-know-whats, it was because we were positively *aghast* at how much we'd peed.'

Miss Chew stared at them, lip curled, in stony silence.

'With the, um, strain of waiting, you know, for punishment,' Persimmon mumbled, grimacing.

'St Radegund's girls do *not* lose control and wet themselves,' said Miss Chew. 'And the liquid on your fingers is not pee. Furthermore, your fingers, Caroline, were in Persimmon's panties, while yours, Persimmon, were in Caroline's. You have failed to persuade me you are innocent of – to call a spade a spade – blatantly masturbating.'

Caroline and Persimmon flinched.

'Well, we may have tickled each other a bit, miss,' Caroline blurted. 'It's the hot weather, it makes a girl . . .'

'Ticklish,' said Persimmon.

'Don't make matters worse by dissembling,' snapped the headmistress. 'You would serve yourselves better by making a clean breast of it. Were you mutually masturbating?'

'Yes, miss,' the girls mumbled in chorus.

'On both occasions?'

'Yes, miss.'

'We're very sorry, miss,' blurted Caroline.

'Oh, no, you're not,' said Miss Chew, smiling thinly. 'At the moment, you are rueful. After your punishment, that is when you'll be sorry.'

She reached for an ancient, leather-bound volume on her bookshelf, her hand brushing the canes as she did so and making them jangle.

'It may surprise you to know that I overheard your remarks outside,' she said, her smile pleasant. 'Very perceptive of you, Caroline, to compare the seventeenth century with this one. As senior girls, you should know by now that I consider the seventeenth century infinitely superior to the abhorrent twenty-first. A passage from the diary of our dear foundress may illustrate the good sense, love of learning and decorum which reigned amongst ladies in those happier days.'

She began to read: ' "Today inflicted vapulation with the birch of a dozen strokes on the bare posteriors of Emily Crookmuir, Sarah Gobbins and Virginia Hawkes, for the crime of stealing apples from the orchard. The girls took their punishment well, although Emily squealed betimes, and I had to admonish Virginia not to cry like a booby. Their naked buttocks coloured prettily under my sheaf, and squirmed in a manner pleasing to behold. I took it upon myself to deliver the strokes in distinct and separate sites of the posteriors, for, although strokes delivered overmuch to the same weal may increase the pain and remorse of the penitent, there is subtler rue in beholding her naked hindquarters adorned by a veritable tapestry of purple and crimson, as reproach against feminine vanity. I repeated to my wayward girls that a lady's nates must be well used to the birch or whip if she is to get a gentle and loving husband, for no husband is a true man that does not oftentimes whip his wife soundly. It is for this reason that I resist the monstrous fashion of lady's underdrawers, an impious sort of silken breeches worn beneath the frocks, for pure vanity, albeit the fashion comes from the court of our dearly beloved monarch, the second King Charles, perhaps under the continental influence of his noble Portuguese consort. A girl's loins must feel the fresh air, and her buttocks must aye be naked and ready for the skirtlifting, and the merited vapulation with birch or quirt, if she is to blossom into a virtuous housewife, and pay attention to her sewing, harpsichord and Italian grammar. The friction and stimulation of garments worn pressing the privities can only inflame that addiction to which all girls are inclined, namely to practise the solitary vice of self-admiration, by touching, feeling and rubbing said privities, for carnal pleasure. Yesterday, applied a dozen with the leather quirt of four tongues with brass roundels, to the bare hindquarters of Hester Dollity, for that very crime, she being found in the outhouse, her skirts up, and her fingers inside her *caverne inférieure.* She burst into tears, with her posteriors flaming in goodly fashion, and swore she would never repeat her offence. I believe her no more than I believe any maid, for they are all, vain creatures, fond of lewdly rubbing themselves, until their queyntes are wet, and must be whipped naked for it, and whipped again, for that is why we females have been provided with plump, soft and round posteriors, as both the scene of our female wickedness, and the site of chastisement therefore." '

Miss Chew sighed, with a beatific smile, and put aside the book. 'Things have changed slightly – we wear knickers these days, and beatings are with the cane, generally on the skirt, pyjama bottoms, nightie or panties, but our dear foundress was so right, as always. As long as girls are girls, they will give in to lustful temptation – they will masturbate.'

'You are going to cane us, miss?' Caroline's voice quavered.

'Why, of course. Surely you knew. It certainly isn't the first time. Throughout your school career, Caroline, you have been caught fighting other girls, or smoking. Always wrestling, punching, and – I shudder to think – like some dreadful tomboy.'

'Yes, miss,' said Caroline sheepishly. 'Why, only last month, you gave me six stingers on the knickers, and it hurt like the dickens. It was almost like being bare.'

'I recall it was not for smoking. You saw fit to translate a passage from the Greek for Miss Pertwee, "*Hoi polemioi koptan ta dendra en te naso*" – "The enemy are cutting down the trees in the island" – as "The Greek boys are snogging the girls on the beach". An unmpardonable impertinence. Sauciness in a girl leads, of course, to stripes on her bottom. That was after a holiday in the Aegean, I believe.'

'Mummy and Daddy took me to Samothraki at Easter, miss,' said Caroline, blushing.

'I trust your parents are well. I understand they are abroad at the moment.'

'Er, yes, miss.'

'I had a whole dozen,' Persimmon said shrilly, 'in March, on my gymslip. That hurt too, miss.'

'As it was supposed to – you borrowed Angie Stroud's best knickers, then returned them stained in a most beastly way, and quite spoiled. Now, as it's your last term, and I hope your last offence, and you really *should* know better, and this double offence of masturbating is *particularly* shameful, I feel I have no choice but to make your canings . . . rather special.'

Caroline and Persimmon shuffled, eyeing each other nervously, then the rack of canes, then the beaming face of the headmistress.

'Special, miss?' said Caroline.

'Yes, I'm going to give you twelve strokes each.'

Both girls drew sharp breaths, but not *too* sharp, for it was going to be a dozzie, after all – that was bearable.

'At the same time, miss, or one after the other?' Caroline asked.

'Oh, I think one after the other. Each will have to watch, as the other takes it, and I imagine each of you will prefer to go first.'

Miss Chew stood, and her fingers rifled through the rack of canes, finally selecting a thin three-footer, with a crook handle of gleaming yellow ash. She flexed it, revealing its suppleness, then thrashed the air, making the cane whirr. The girls paled. Miss Chew picked up her desk telephone, and murmured briefly.

'After you, Persimmon,' Caroline said.

'You go first. I don't mind.'

'No, honestly,' Caroline insisted.

'Well, all right,' Persimmon said gratefully. 'Thanks. How shall you take me, miss?'

'Over the sofa,' said Miss Chew. 'But I've asked prefects Bulstrode and Latimer to join us, as witnesses.'

Caroline's jaw dropped.

'It has to be quite clear that you accept your punishments, and in good grace.'

'Why, miss, we're Radegundians!' Caroline blurted out.

Miss Chew flexed her cane, rubbing the springy ashplant under her chin. 'I am going to cane your naked bottoms,' she said softly.

The room was silent, save for the ticking of the grandfather clock, and the gulps of the two errant girls.

'No, really, miss – on the bare?' Persimmon gasped.

'On the bare,' said Miss Chew.

'With that?' Caroline said, more as a statement than a question.

'With this,' the headmistress replied, smiling grimly. 'It is quite my hardest and most painful instrument. Angie Stroud before you took twelve, it's true, but only with the willow, and on her skirt – it would only have been a sixer, but I knew perfectly well the silly girl had extra knickers on. You girls shall have no knickers at all. I believe neither of you has taken a school caning on the naked bottom before?'

The girls nodded, blushing crimson.

'Caning on the thin pyjamas or gymslip is almost as painful,' Miss Chew purred, 'but it is the shame which makes a naked beating almost unbearable. Cloth provides a minimal protection for the skin, but a greater one for the heart. When it is stripped from a girl, her modesty is stripped also, her most intimate portion exposed, crimson and wealed, for others to see – as if immodest wealing of her flesh is itself vile behaviour. How well our foundress understood our female minds.'

There was a knock on the door, and the two burly prefects, Bulstrode and Latimer, entered, smirking, and stood by the sides of the punishment sofa. Miss Chew ordered Persimmon to remove her shoes, and take position. Trembling in her stockinged feet, the girl bent over the sofa, resting on her elbows, and grimaced, as Miss Chew lifted her skirt, unclipped her garter straps from her lacy stocking tops, and smartly ripped her white cotton panties down to her knees. She unfastened the whole sussie belt, and placed it on her desk. Persimmon's big bare bottom shone, goosefleshed and shivering, like twin moons. Her legs, slightly parted, revealed the heavy lips of her naked gash dangling between quivering thigh flesh and wreathed in the heavy, tangled fronds of her come-wet pubic mane.

At a nod from Miss Chew, Bulstrode dropped to a crouch, pinioning Persimmon's ankles, and forcing them wide, so that her panties stretched to breaking between her thighs, and her full bare quim was exposed, pink and glistening; while Latimer grasped her arms, pulling them up and away from the sofa, so that Persimmon was held taut, with her belly taking her weight. Miss Chew deftly placed a rose-patterned Wedgwood chamber pot on the carpet, beneath Persimmon's gash.

'Can't be too careful when it's a bare-bottom beating,' she said.

'Ooh . . .' Persimmon squealed, wriggling helplessly.

'It is for your own good, Persimmon,' said Miss Chew, taking position above the crouching Bulstrode, opposite

Caroline, who stood, hands clutched behind her back, gaping at her pinioned friend. 'This will hurt your poor bottom abominably, and it will be much easier for you to take it if you cannot wriggle too much. Are you ready and willing for punishment?'

'Y-yes, miss,' gasped the straining girl.

'Good. Then I'll begin. I shan't have to order you to watch, Caroline, shall I? No girl's eyes can stray from the spectacle of another's bottom striped, especially if she hasn't witnessed bare-bottom punishment before. You *haven't* witnessed it, have you?'

'I might have done, once or twice, miss,' said Caroline, shifting uncomfortably.

'And where might that have been, pray?'

'Well, you know . . . in dorm, miss, sometimes, if a girl is getting up everyone's nose, if she's snoring, or something, we give her a spanking. Someone sits on her face, and we pull her pyjamas off, and spank her with our hands, or perhaps slippers.'

'On the bare, then?'

'Yes, of course. We call it a "snore spanking",' Caroline said, with a nervous laugh. 'A girl doesn't half wriggle, miss. And her bum – I'm sorry, bottom – looks quite nice, all pink and blotchy.'

Placing her feet apart, in a fencer's stance, Miss Chew lifted her cane above her shoulder. 'Then we may consider this a snore spanking, only a little more muscular. Let's hope you find your friend's bottom quite nice, when it's coloured by my rod.'

Persimmon's eyes flashed angrily at Caroline, before shutting tight, in a grimace of agony, as the cane lashed her naked buttocks. Vip! Her stretched body shuddered violently, in the grip of the two prefects, as a thin crimson welt appeared on her bare fesse flesh.

'Uhh!' she gasped, her eyes moistening.

Vip!

'Ooh!'

Vip!

'Ahh!'

Etched in a tapestry of stripes, Persimmon's whipped bottom wriggled and squirmed quite fiercely, with tears flowing openly down her cheeks. Vip!

'Ohh!'

At each stroke, her teeth clenched, followed by a slack-jawed gape, as her buttocks writhed. Caroline's eyes were glued to her friend's squirming bare, and she rubbed her thighs together, hoping that her nylons would not squeak, as moisture began to soak her panties; they did not squeak, in fact, for her quim juice was oiling them. Miss Chew's breasts bounced, her arm muscles rippled and her thighs quivered under her clinging skirt, as she flogged, cruelly spacing the cuts on the eight seconds, for maximum smarting. Past the sixth cut, Persimmon's breasts were heaving rapidly, as she panted in pain, and her moans came as hoarse animal cries from her belly. The two prefects leered, licking their teeth, as their tethered victim squirmed. Vip!

'*Urrgh* . . . oh, miss, I can hardly bear it,' Persimmon said, sobbing.

'But you must.'

Vip!

'Ooh! Ahh!'

The lips of Persimmon's cooze were winking, swollen and red, and their wreath of tangled pubic hairs glistened darkly, as come seeped from her gash. Caroline's face flushed scarlet. She gasped: Persimmon was juicing under cane! Her own slit was tingling, nubbin throbbing, and flowing with come, as she gazed on the blotchy red pears of wealed skin that were Persimmon's croup. While Persimmon's body shuddered, legs and back jerking rigid at each cane cut, her buttocks wriggled, clenching madly, like crimson sea polyps lashed by the tide. Vip!

'Ooh! Oh! Oh!'

A jet of golden pee sprang from Persimmon's quim. It steamed long and noisily, spraying Bulstrode's face and blouse, while the main flow splashed into the chamber pot.

Caroline could not suppress her smirk at Bulstrode's bra, clearly outlined by her blouse, sopping with pee.

'Just you wait, bitch,' snarled Bulstrode, sotto voce.

Persimmon's face convulsed with tears. 'Oh . . . oh . . .' she wailed.

Vip! The cane lashed the wet tops of her thighs, and she howled. 'Ooh! Ahh!'

Two more strokes, one to the top bum, and one on the vertical, right inside the stretched buttock cleft, and the caning was over. The last stroke laid a thick red stripe between Persimmon's fesses, and, released by the two prefects, she hopped up and down, knickers bobbing at her ankles, as she frantically rubbed her bare bum, holding the cheeks wide. With the shaking of her loins, drips of fluid sprayed from her flapping gash lips.

Her eyes met Caroline's, and Caroline blushed deep, frightened that her own wet panties would somehow show beneath her skirt, or that there would be drips down her nylons, and embarrassed at the tingling in her clitty, and moisture in her quim, from watching her best friend's bare bum wealed. The knowledge that her bottom was next to be exposed naked and caned filled her with awful apprehension, and a strange welling of desire in her tummy, for the wank, interrupted by Miss Chew, had not brought her off. Her nipples tingled, erect, and Caroline hoped their swollen plums did not show through her bra and blouse, for she had always been teased about her extra-large nipples, even when they were soft.

'Time for you to take your shoes off, Caroline,' said Miss Chew.

'Oh . . . yes, of course.'

Persimmon was fumbling to restore her sussies, and her crying had calmed to an occasional snuffle. She looked at Caroline with her red eyes gleaming, and licked her lips. Caroline removed her shoes, and bent over the sofa, still warm from Persimmon's belly. The chamber pot glinted, half full of Persimmon's pee. Caroline braced her stockinged feet on the floor and, knowing what was to come, with tight lips, flicked up her skirt and undid her garter straps, then her sussies. Quickly, she rolled her panties to her knees, and raised her naked bottom high.

'Just a moment,' said Miss Chew, twanging Caroline's panties against her thighs. 'What are *these*?'

'A thong, miss,' said Caroline, shivering.

'Quite against school rules,' rapped Miss Chew. 'They wouldn't cover a gnat's bottom, let alone that – *impressively* – large peach of yours. Disgraceful – low class – a St Radegund's girl! You'll take an extra three strokes for this outrage, Caroline.'

'Y-yes, miss,' Caroline blurted out, seeing Persimmon's teeth flash in a leer.

The prefects grabbed her: Bulstrode at her stockinged feet, and Latimer pinioning her wrists, and stretching her spine quite painfully. Caroline gritted her teeth, with her fully exposed bare bottom quivering higher than her head. Bulstrode forced her legs apart, and the air caressed Caroline's naked vulva, with its tell-tale drips of come plinking in the piss-filled chamber pot.

'This will hurt far more than a snore spanking,' said Miss Chew. 'You saw what I did to Persimmon's bottom, and you've three extra cuts to take. It's those last horrid few, I find, that make a girl lose control. Are you ready? A whole fifteen strokes of my cane, nice and slow, on your delicate bare bottom, Caroline. Just *think* how it will hurt.' She smiled.

'I'm ready, miss,' said Caroline defiantly. 'I'm not that delicate.'

2

Fighting Females

Vip! The first cut took Caroline in mid-fesse, and pain seared her, like liquid white-hot fire. A lump came to her throat, she gasped, and her buttocks clenched tight. Bulstrode had her pinioned by the ankles, with her legs wide apart, in a wheelbarrow position, while Latimer stretched her arms and belly taut, with Caroline's weight taken by her tummy, on the sofa back, hot and moist from Persimmon's beating. Her thong panties were stretched so wide, she worried the elastic would snap. Vip! Her body jerked rigid, bottom clenched and squirming, as the cane lashed her tender top bum, with a horrid dry slap. Her eyes moistened with tears, as her teeth bared in a rictus. Vip!

'Ohh,' Caroline moaned.

The cane, on naked flesh, seemed the worst and most unendurable pain. It was not just the shame of a bare-beating, although that was certainly part of it, but the absence of even the thinnest cloth to protect her from the scald of the cane cuts. A caning on knickers, or pyjama bottoms, or gymslip, any thin shield – *anything* – was preferable to the dry slap of wood on bare skin. Vip! Her flogged bottom smarted, throbbing with the agony of the strokes, and it was impossible for her croup not to wriggle and squirm like a booby. Four down, and eleven to go – Caroline's brain, churning in agony, could not imagine enduring another eleven of these fearful stingers. And the waiting was the worst part: as the seconds ticked away, the smarting rose to full throb, then, just as the pain began, mercifully, to ebb – vip!

'Ah!'

Miss Chew laid a cut right across her bare thigh backs; Caroline's gorge rose, and she bounced, wriggling frantically, like a netted fish. Vip!

'Ooh!' she gasped.

'You're taking it quite well, Caroline,' panted Miss Chew, 'but do try not to spoil it with girly squeals, eh? When chaps are caught masturbating, they must bare up and take it like the true English schoolgirls they are.'

Through tear-blurred eyes, Caroline saw Persimmon, grinning, as she watched her friend's bottom blotch with weals. Vip!

'Ooh,' she moaned, in a ragged wail of despair.

Yet the hideous smarting of the first strokes was mellowing into a warm glow, where pain seemed not far from a strange pleasure – she had to think, in order to identify it as pain, and not just extreme, and unspecified sensation. Caroline became aware that her swollen clitty was actually tingling harder; that the flow of juice from her writhing cooze had increased; and that there were faster drips of come from her gash flaps, falling into the piss-filled chamber pot. Vip!

'Ah! Ooh! Ah . . . ah . . . no!' she squealed, and not from the scalding smart of the cane, for Bulstrode's fingers were tickling her stockinged toes.

Persimmon saw this cruel torment, and giggled, but either Miss Chew did not see, or did not care. The caning continued, slower now, with intervals of ten or eleven seconds between strokes, while, all the time, Bulstrode tortured Caroline with the insidious tickling. Caroline's feet wriggled, toes curling, along with the constant squirming of her flogged nates. Vip! Caroline's whole body jerked, with her legs shuddering rigid behind her squirming bare bottom, and her breasts bobbing frantically in their skimpy bra cups. The tickling sent waves of electricity up her spine, churning her spinal nubbin, the little node of pleasure, nestling atop her bum cleft, with her clitty seeming to respond to the hateful caress of her nyloned toes. Come plinked rapidly from Caroline's gash lips, and she was *sure* everyone was looking at her shamefully juicing twat.

'My,' said Miss Chew, 'I've never seen a chap shake so much under a basting. You're wriggling like a netted minnow, Caroline.'

Vip!

'Ooh! Miss, I've never been caned so hard,' Caroline said with a sob.

'Well, only another three. Bottom up, girl.'

Caroline's tummy was bursting. She needed desperately to pee, but must *not* give way . . . she had taken a whole twelve strokes on the bare, and, somehow, survived. Miss Chew was right. Another three would be easy-peasy. The agony in her flogged bottom spread, encompassing her thighs and spine and cunt basin, her dripping twat and tingling clit, and the warm, juice-spewing wetness of her quivering slit. Vip!

'Oh, oh, yes,' Caroline panted, as a strange ecstasy took hold of her loins and belly, as if her cunt were a sponge, with the cane squeezing her bum and clit, to wring liquid pleasure from her.

Vip! The cane took her squarely in her parted bum cleft, tickling her anus bud and the lower lips of her cunt. Her body convulsed, with a loud ping, as her thong panties snapped, and flew into Bulstrode's face.

'Ooh . . . ooh . . . ahh!' Caroline gurgled. 'Yes . . . don't stop!'

It can't be . . . I'm going to come!

Vip!

'Ah . . . ah . . . *ahh*!' Caroline howled, shaking her head from side to side, mouth drooling agape, and her body shuddering, as her throbbing, gushing quim exploded in orgasm.

'Well! That's the job done,' said Miss Chew. 'At least you didn't wet yourself, Caroline. Or *did* you?'

She peered into the chamber pot, now filled to the brim, with an oily sheen of come on the surface of Persimmon's pee.

'You were almost at breaking point, I think,' said Miss Chew, stroking her cane. 'I believe I may congratulate myself on a job well done – and thank the prefects for their valuable aid. After the shame of bare-bottom chastisement, a girl won't get caught masturbating again.'

'Yes, miss,' said Caroline, sobbing. 'Thank you,' she said to Bulstrode and Latimer, but not without a savage wink, and momentary baring of her teeth, at Bulstrode.

Released, Caroline stood, shaking, and, with an agonised wince, rubbed her wealed nates, until she had stopped trembling enough for her to fumble with garter straps, and pull her sussies on tight. A knot in the waistband of her panties provided temporary repair, and she slipped them over her wealed bum, before securing the garter straps to her stocking tops. She and Persimmon curtsied together, to perform the traditional Radegundian ritual of thanking the mistress for their floggings, then to sign their names in the punishment book, the latest in a series of volumes, recording all Radegundian punishments back to Lady Warchant's time. Miss Chew dismissed the prefects, and told the caned girls to remain, adding that she supposed they would prefer to stand.

'There is the matter of your future careers, when after completion of this term,' she said. 'You, Persimmon, I understand, are intent on joining the Royal Navy?'

'Yes, miss – as an ensign on HMS *Gunsight*, at Plymouth.'

'In that case, I need not detain you. Boat Brigade CPO Thorogood will deal with it.'

Persimmon curtsied again, and opened the door. Turning to Caroline, with fervent movements of her fingers, she indicated that she was ripe to complete her interrupted wank. Caroline smirked, and Persimmon understood, giving a jealous pout, that Caroline – the jammy sod! – had already come, under cane.

'Now, Caroline,' said Miss Chew, 'what is to be done with *you*? Despite your keen intelligence, I fear your exam results show slackness, and you would not achieve a place at any university. Moreover, I understand that your parents are temporarily, ah, short of the necessary cash.'

'Mummy did say in her last letter that there were certain liquidity problems,' said Caroline.

'From Brazil?'

'Paraguay. They travel a lot, on business.'

'Hmm,' said Miss Chew, pursing her lips. 'In any case, a so-called university is no place for an English lady, these days. A degree in television studies or computer games is scarcely an aid to moral development. You are destined for better things. I am glad I had occasion to cane you naked, for it proved you a girl of spirit.'

Caroline lifted her skirt, and rubbed her ridged buttocks, almost fully bared by the skimpy thong.

'You might have found another way to test me, miss,' she said ruefully, 'although I can't say I'm sorry to have been beaten.'

'Hurt much?' said Miss Chew sympathetically.

'It smarts awfully, miss, but I can cope with it, and I'm proud.'

'Spoken like a true Radegundian,' said Miss Chew. 'I like the way you repaired your knickers – illegal, by the way – without a fuss. Now, I have in mind a different form of further education for you. It is a sort of, ah, finishing school, near St Ives, in Cornwall – so romantic! – run by a dear cousin of mine, Mistress Laetitia Frubbin, for girls aged between eighteen and twenty-one. The emphasis is on discipline, and the acquisition of truly ladylike qualities in marriageable young girls.'

'I'm not sure I want to get married, miss,' said Caroline.

'Quality counts, whatever the actual result,' said Miss Chew. 'A lady prospers in this world by being feminine, and enslaving men to do her bidding. So it always was, and shall be. Men strive, and ladies enjoy! Bed, books and board at Furrow Weald are free, and students are actually paid a wage, just as in the navy. It's just right for you, Caroline. In your circumstances, I shouldn't turn it down.'

Caroline promised to give Furrow Weald her consideration, and Miss Chew assured her that, if she kept her nose clean for the rest of the term, she would put in a good word with her cousin.

'If you *must* masturbate,' Miss Chew said, 'and I know all girls must, well, for heaven's sake, be a clever chap, and don't get caught.' She smiled, and winked. 'By the way, Caroline, you don't really think me a rotter, do you?' she said, as Caroline was leaving.

'Oh! No, miss.'

'That's good,' said Miss Chew, placing her hand under Caroline's skirt, and stroking her hot bottom. 'Because I couldn't have caned you bare bum, if I didn't like you. And, unfortunately, I shan't have another opportunity to see those magnificent buttocks wriggle.' She looked out the window, at summer in Wiltshire, to hide her delicate blush, then resumed. 'I must confess, Caroline, that you would have disappointed me, had you left St Radegund's without giving me an excuse to cane you on the bare. I'm quite a connoisseur of bottoms, having the occasion to chastise so many, and yours is quite the most voluptuous I've ever seen – meaty, smooth, rounded, in short, a prize peach. However, the foundress, in her wisdom, decreed that any girl taking over twelve strokes on the bare could not be whipped for another se'ennight. Today's Saturday, and last day of term is next Friday, so you just slip in under the wire. You aren't going to be a naughty girl, I hope.'

'I'll do my very best to behave, miss, honestly,' Caroline said.

Caroline departed, and the door clicked shut; Miss Chew bent down, to sniff the sofa, still moist from Caroline's loins, and the brimming pot of pee and girl come. She settled in her comfortable armchair, parted her peach nylons, and flicked up her skirt, revealing her pantiless cooze basin, the shaven hillock gleaming alabaster smooth, and the slit red and inflamed beneath a bulging, extruded clitty. Placing a wad of tissue beneath her cunt, Miss Chew began to masturbate, rubbing her clitty, and prising open her gash flaps, to caress the wet walls of her pouch, until a trickle of come seeped from her gash, down her quivering perineum, onto the tissues. She reached to her desk, and removed a framed photo of the sixth form in their gymslips, with Caroline and Persimmon squatting, fresh faced and thighs bared. Miss Chew stroked her shaven, smooth cunt gourd, tickling and caressing the soft skin, before sliding to the wet gash beneath. Gazing at the photo, and sighing in contentment, she masturbated for several minutes, until her belly quaked, and drool seeped from her lips, as she groaned hoarsely in orgasm.

The coarse, gritty soap gave little lather, but it was quite exciting, as Caroline soaped her nipples, over and over, with the sandy pressure drawing the bulbs stiffly erect, and sending shooting stars of pleasure down her spine, into her rapidly swelling clitty. She stood nude before the cracked mirror, in the senior girls' washroom, and was thankful to have it, surprisingly, to herself. The washbasins were supposed to be for face and hands, but Caroline decided that the floor was such a mess, anyway, that she could indulge herself just this once, before stepping into the rusty, gurgling cold shower. She slopped soapy water all over her naked body, turning to admire the panoply of dark crimson weals laced across her bare bum. She reached down, wincing, as she touched one of her hardest and crustiest ridges; in the minutes since her beating, the weals had stiffened remarkably. Touching her bum welts gave her a new, lovely thrill, much more special than examining her red stripes after a caning on gymslip or panties. These welts were the real thing, from a proper naked caning.

I can't believe I came, under cane! But come I did, in a fabulous, exploding orgasm, like no other . . .

She examined herself in the glass: big pink nipples, swollen to strawberries, on the full, jutting golden breasts, quivering, as she gently tweaked and slapped them; flat, strong belly, and delicious – quite abnormal! – tiny waist, swelling to wide hips, rippling slabs of curved thigh muscle, and tapering into long, coltish legs, with her long, dainty feet mincing beneath her, the slender toes curling, as if anticipating further tickles. Her cooze mound must be abnormal, too, so big and softly curving, a real swollen gourd, under her jungle of hair, so that girls accused her, enviously, of having a third bum flap in front. Coquettishly pirouetting, she scrutinised the taut pears of her bare buttocks, ripely swelling and flawless, save for the garish pattern of welts and ridges from Miss Chew's cane. She gasped, touching the welts one by one, caressing them, as she would caress her clitty, during one of her routine wanks.

Gosh, I'm so lovely . . . I could eat me up, lick me to pieces. I wish I had a cock, so I could fuck myself . . .

She shivered, thinking of the Greek boy, on the beach at Samothraki, his massive stiff cock plunged in her wet cooze, his hard bare body slamming against her titties and thighs and belly, his mouth licking her, biting her, and his wonderful hot cream spurting at her wombneck, so copiously, she thought it would never stop; then, the next cock, and the next, as her bum writhed on the wet sand, and her twat exploded in come after come . . . and Mummy never guessed! Or, did she? *She could have been watching, from behind a sand dune.* The thought of being watched, fucking, made Caroline shiver. Then, after opening her thighs and slit to cock after stiff cock, under the Greek sun – returning to Wiltshire, and St Radegund's, and gymslips and the smell of girl sweat and pee, and onions and cabbage and carbolic soap! Small wonder a girl had to wank off several times every day, just to stay composed.

Licking her lips, Caroline began to finger her stiffening clit, while caressing her croup weals and twisting to look at her bottom in the glass. She had promised to do her best not to be naughty, it was true, and she *had* done her best. It wasn't her fault if a few moments of looking at her nude body, and caned bottom, proved that her best just wasn't good enough. It was an extra-special thrill, wanking off so blatantly, when anyone might come in and see. Well, let them see . . . let them look, and enjoy a wank themselves. Pretend we're on that lovely cock-rich Greek beach . . .

She parted her thighs, and slid her fingers, with a wet, slapping gurgle, up and down the lips of her pussy. Come trickled down her thighs; she scooped it with her palm, and slapped it on her mouth, breasts and titties, rubbing her wet fingers in a slashing motion, from her neck to her luxurious forest of pubic curls. She began to claw her bum weals, gasping, at the sharp, dizzying pain, and slap herself hard on the buttocks.

Her fount was a torrent of gushing come. She lifted her left foot, and wedged it on the washbasin's rim, opening her gash lips. Thumbing her clitty, she pushed two fingers into her slit, then a third, and a fourth, gasping, as her cunt lips were stretched like rubber. Her fingers slammed in and out of her cunt, nails slicing her wombneck, as she caressed her raw, caned bottom flesh, with sharp little spanks, waggling her fesses in the mirror, and her teeth bared in pleasure, as she watched her hand slapping the naked bum flesh, reddening the skin between her welts to a new, blotchy pink.

She began to gasp, her panting breath frosting the looking-glass, as her clitty throbbed with electric pleasure, and her fingers squelched in her twat, with loud gurgling sucks. Her belly heaved, as she pinched and slapped her tingling nipples, raking her titties with sharp nails, and thrilling, as the pain seared her.

'Oh . . . oh . . . *yes* . . .' she panted hoarsely.

Her claws raked her smarting cane welts, and she spanked her bottom harder and harder, gasping and groaning, until her cunt petals fluttered, her wanking fingers were drenched in a hot flood of come, and her bum and cooze shuddered, in a fabulous orgasm.

'Whew!' she gasped, withdrawing her fingers from her slit, with a sticky plop.

'My, but you *are* a mucky tart,' a girl sneered.

Caroline whirled round, her face reddening. It was Bulstrode. The prefect leaned against the door jamb, resting one foot on her knee, and with her arms folded. Her face wore a nasty leer.

'Another caning offence, I believe,' she said. 'You beastly frigger.'

'Don't you call me names,' Caroline retorted.

'Report to the beak's study tomorrow morning at eleven,' Bulstrode ordered.

'Shan't!'

The prefect paled. 'Insolence! A bare-bum offence! Miss Chew shall hear of this. That's more strokes for your filthy wanker's bum – and naked.'

Caroline stood with her legs apart, fingering her wanked cunt, and grinning at Bulstrode. 'In your dreams, you lesbo cow,' she sneered.

'What! You bitch!'

'Foundress's rules say I cannot be caned before another se'ennight, and term's over before then, so up yours!'

Bulstrode's face flushed in rage, then calmed, and her lips curled in a smile. 'That means I've a week to make your life hell,' she hissed.

Caroline yawned, stretching her rippling biceps and thighs. 'You try, Bulstrode,' she purred, 'and I'll make a meal of you. Beat you to a sorry pulp. I mean it. I won't have a lesbo slut spoil my last days at school.'

'You'll regret that,' snarled Bulstrode.

'Shall I? Let's square off then, if you're man enough – oh, sorry, I mean girl enough.'

'I could thrash you one-handed,' Bulstrode blurted, her face dark red.

'Tomorrow, in the showers, then, before lunch. Twelve noon, suit you? Bring your own witness as second. Girl on girl, no holds barred. Deal?'

'You *will* regret it,' said Bulstrode, with a leer. 'It's a deal.'

That night in bed, Caroline masturbated twice to ensure a sound sleep for the morrow's combat. She was rewarded with a healthy, dreamless slumber and, when she appeared at the showers, with Persimmon as her second, she was skipping and bouncing, fighting fit. Under her gymslip, her body felt lovely and slithery, coated entirely in Vaseline, on

Persimmon's advice, to give her the edge in wrestling. Her long blonde tresses were securely knotted in a ponytail, and her fingernails were trimmed to razor sharpness by Persimmon's nail file.

Bulstrode appeared, in her own gym kit, and was flanked by Latimer, in full prefect's uniform. Latimer hung a cardboard KEEP OUT sign on the door, and locked it. Wordlessly, the two combatants stripped off their gym-slips, socks and shoes, and, when they were nude, Bulstrode's lithe, muscular body – the product of the gym rat's ceaseless workouts – also gleamed with wrestling oil; her fount was shaven smooth, and her sandy hair cropped to a brush. Her powerful buttocks and thighs, though smaller than Caroline's, rippled with whipcord muscle. Persimmon said they should all four be nude, otherwise two clad girls in the showers would arouse suspicion, and Latimer grudgingly agreed. In seconds, the four girls stood naked in the wide shower enclosure, with the two combatants strutting forwards, to toe the imaginary line.

'Graeco-Roman wrestling, ladies,' said Latimer, 'with no holds barred, except eye gouging. Agreed?'

Caroline and Bulstrode nodded, with Bulstrode blatantly ogling Caroline's abundant pubic mane, its fronds dangling lush between her parted thighs, below the lips of her quim, and extending up her belly almost to her navel, with her twat mound a bulging mountain covered in silken fleecy jungle. Persimmon turned on four of the shower heads, explaining that it was for verisimilitude. Bulstrode looked at Latimer, awaiting the signal to start; Caroline seized her chance, and leapt forwards, to headbutt the girl's nose. Bulstrode squealed, and staggered back, with Caroline kneeing her in the cunt, and leaping on her, clawing at her breasts with her sharpened fingernails.

Bulstrode's thighs rippled, as she held her ground, grabbing Caroline's hair, and twisting it, while bringing her own knee up between Caroline's legs. Caroline squealed, as the girl's thigh slammed her cooze, with their oiled bare bodies slithering against one another, and tried to push

Bulstrode away. Bulstrode grabbed Caroline's pubic thatch, and pulled hard, lifting the flesh away in a balloon from the pubic bone. Caroline screamed, and her fists began to pummel Bulstrode's face, until the bigger girl chopped Caroline's nose, sending her reeling, then lowered her head, to bite ferociously on Caroline's nipples. Both bodies glistened with sweat, oil and the spray of the hissing showers.

'Ah! Ah!' Caroline screamed, flailing, and delivering ineffectual punches to Bulstrode's face and breasts.

Caroline wriggled in agony, sagging down to the wet floor, with Bulstrode wrenching her pube hair, and biting savagely on her breasts. There was a loud slap, as Caroline slipped and her buttocks crashed onto the floor. Bulstrode flipped her over, and began to gouge at the cane welts on Caroline's arse; Caroline screamed repeatedly, as the dark crusts were opened by the prefect's fingernails. Bulstrode crouched over Caroline, her naked gash swaying above Caroline's face, as Bulstrode pinioned her, knees crushing her forearms, and the bigger girl's face sank towards Caroline's open cunt. Caroline howled, as Bulstrode sank her teeth into Caroline's gash lips, and began to chew.

Her body wriggled like a speared fish under Bulstrode's weight; suddenly, Caroline's arm slipped free, and, with a rigid forefinger, she stabbed Bulstrode in the bumhole, pushing her sharpened nail a good few inches inside the tender channel, and clawing at the anal walls. Bulstrode shrieked, rearing up and trying to twist, but Caroline wriggled from under her, and, with her finger still jabbing Bulstrode's anus, kicked her in the face, then in the titties.

Bulstrode went down, and it was Caroline's turn to attack the other girl's cunt. She seized Bulstrode's feet, and twisted hard, eliciting a squeal of pain, then forced the girl onto her back, with her legs grotesquely twisted. Caroline did not repeat her opponent's mistake of presenting her bare bum for attack; rather, she kicked Bulstrode's cunt rapidly, several times, her toes clawing at the exposed clitty, before diving between the girl's thighs, and fastening her teeth on the gash flaps, biting savagely, with Bulstrode writhing, in screams of agony. Caroline got her teeth round the clitty and began to bite fiercely. Bulstrode wriggled, thumping the floor, and crying 'No! No!'

'Submit?' said Persimmon.

'No!' moaned the tortured girl, flopping and heaving in the wet. 'Uurgh!'

Steaming golden piss jetted from her cunt, splashing Caroline's face, and then a string of dungs, like tiny marshmallows, plopped from her writhing anus. Caroline removed her dripping face from the girl's soiled cunt, and, still twisting her ankles, began to methodically kick her titties and face. Bulstrode writhed helplessly, offering no resistance, as Caroline squatted, with her foot on Bulstrode's face, and started to bite her nipples, belly and soft inner thighs. Howling, Bulstrode squirmed in her own slime. The prefect's body glowed with crimson bite marks from Caroline's teeth. Caroline rose, and spanked the girl's breasts, raising the flesh to a mass of puffy red blotches, with the girl wriggling helplessly and exhausted. Then, she began to slap Bulstrode's face, jarring her teeth.

'Submit, you bitch,' Caroline said, panting.

'Urrgh . . . urrgh . . .' Bulstrode drooled. Piss dribbled from her cunt.

'For pity's sake, submit for her, Latimer,' cried Persimmon. 'Your girl is out of it.'

Latimer refused, saying that only Bulstrode herself could submit. The girl's body was no more than a sack of meat for Caroline to play with. Methodically, teeth bared, she set about torturing her helpless opponent. Clawing, biting, spanking and gouging, she elicited whimpers and groans, but no resistance, from the weeping Bulstrode. She spanked the girl's cunt, bit savagely, spanked again, then prised the gash lips apart with her fingernails, and stretched them to huge envelopes of flesh, while her big toe prodded Bulstrode's tortured clitty. She turned the girl over, and, with her face pressed in her pool of pee and dung, administered a heavy hand-spanking to the girl's wet, squirming buttocks. She stood, taking aim, to deliver savage kicks to cunt, titties and face. Caroline's own breasts bounced, as she panted in the exertions of her torture. Bulstrode wept, sobbing wretchedly, as fresh blows rained on her bruised body. The showers hissed water over both naked girls, but neither seemed to notice. Caroline stood back.

'Won't submit?'

'Ahh . . . no . . .' Bulstrode panted. 'Ahh . . .'

Come slimed her thighs, as it gushed from her tortured cunt. Bulstrode was juicing under her punishment. Caroline lifted her leg, and delivered a bone-crunching kick to Bulstrode's quim.

'Oh! Oh! Yes . . . *ahh*!' gasped Bulstrode, as her bitten belly shuddered, come spurted from her slit, and she moaned in orgasm.

A key rattled in the lock, and the door of the shower room opened, to admit Miss Chew.

'What's this?' she called. 'A KEEP OUT notice on my shower baths? I've never heard the like of it – oh!'

Her hand flew to her mouth, as she espied Caroline, her foot wriggling inside Bulstrode's squirming cunt. Caroline withdrew it, to stand, hands on hips, and gasping for breath, as the sweat poured from her heaving breasts. At her bruised purple cunt lips, a clear trickle of come sparkled in the fluorescent light.

'I trust someone can explain?' the headmistress said icily, as Latimer helped the groaning Bulstrode to her feet.

Persimmon and Latimer at once began to speak, until Miss Chew threw up her hands.

'No, don't bother to explain,' she said. 'I can see quite clearly. My, Bulstrode, you have taken a pounding. I'd have thought twice before engaging that tigress Caroline. I suggest, Latimer, that you take Bulstrode to surgery straight away. Are you in need of treatment, Caroline?'

'No, miss,' blurted Caroline, wiping her lips. 'I'll be fine.'

'Grand girl. It's a caning offence, of course, and merits a sound bare-bottom thrashing. I mayn't cane you, Caroline, nor you, Persimmon, under foundress's rules, for I've already dealt with your bottoms yesterday.'

Caroline and Persimmon exchanged smirks.

'But someone's buttocks must wriggle, for this outrage, so I *shall* cane you two, since this counts as public masturbation,' she thundered at the gaping prefects.

'But, miss –'

'Did you attain orgasm, Bulstrode?'

'Yes, miss,' Bulstrode mumbled sheepishly.

'Then you will both report to my study after breakfast, tomorrow morning.'

3

Gorgeous Animal

Caroline was waiting outside Miss Chew's study the next morning, quite early for her appointment. She sat on the red leather banquette, as footsteps padded up the punishment corridor. It was Latimer and Bulstrode, the latter grim-faced and covered in sticking plaster. She scowled at Caroline, then knocked on Miss Chew's door. It opened at once, and Miss Chew summoned the errant girls inside.

'What? You're here so early, Caroline? I told you to come at . . . well, it doesn't matter. Stay there. I shan't be a jiffy.'

Caroline got up, and pressed her ear to the door. She heard mumbled voices, and Miss Chew's sharp command, quelling argument. Then sighs, the lovely rustling of skirts raised and panties lowered, and the sharp vapulation of Miss Chew's cane – on bare skin. Vip! Vip! The strokes lashed on the five seconds. Caroline licked her lips, and, breast heaving, slid her fingers inside the waistband of her skirt, into her panties, through the jungle of her pubic fleece, and found her wet cooze. Vip!

'Ooh!'

Vip!

'Ah!'

Caroline's fingers tweaked her sopping gash flaps and stiff clitty, and she masturbated, listening to the delicious slap of cane strokes on the bare. Twelve strokes fell, punctuated by groans, gasps and bleated moans, and, almost at once, the second set began. Vip!

'Urrgh!'

Vip!

'Oh! Oh!'

That sounded like Bulstrode. Caroline wanked off rapidly and efficiently, timing her climax to the final lashes of Bulstrode's caning, and clamped her teeth shut, to stifle her groans of pleasure. That made two diddles, including her normal, drowsy wake-up wank, and it wasn't even time for elevenses! There was something about corporal punishment, about caning *on the bare*, that made a girl wet – the wriggles, the tears, the lovely slap of wood on naked flesh, and, the giddy thing was, it was exciting even if it was a girl's own bum taking the punishment.

Caroline regained her seat, in time to witness the two miscreants leave Miss Chew's study, red-faced, sobbing, and rubbing their bottoms. Grinning, Caroline let her hand linger in the waistband of her thong to show Bulstrode that she had enjoyed a lovely wank, and received a dirty look in return; she responded by making a face, and blowing a quiet raspberry. Miss Chew ordered Caroline into her study.

'Sit down, Caroline, if you can, after yesterday's tickling,' she said, smiling broadly.

Caroline thanked her, and perched her bottom gingerly on the edge of the sofa.

'I had to get that piece of business out of the way,' said the headmistress. 'My, aren't girls frolicsome at the end of term! I imagine you're glad you took your beating yesterday.'

'Yes, miss, I am glad, although not, perhaps, for the reasons you think. It was exciting, in a strange way, to be caned *au naturel*, just as it was exciting, I must confess, to listen to those bullies squirming and groaning, as you lashed their bottoms naked.'

'Exciting?' said Miss Chew, her eyes agleam. 'I do hope you weren't diddling again?'

Caroline took a deep breath. 'As a Radegundian, I must tell the truth at all times. Yes, miss, I masturbated. I've . . .

I've come to understand that bare-bottom caning actually excites me. I may be unusual, but I'm not ashamed to admit it.'

'Well! Your honesty does you credit, Caroline, and, no, you are not at all unusual, but punishment *is* in order.'

'I am aware of that.'

'By foundress's rules, you're clear, although – publicly fighting yesterday – you do merit the cane. Perhaps I am wrong, to favour you so – it is my failing, to favour girls of exceptionally beautiful fesses.'

'I wonder what the foundress had to say about that, miss,' said Caroline, in the jocular tone of a schoolgirl who was *almost* an Old Radegundian.

Miss Chew blushed. 'She does have something to say,' she murmured. 'Although I called you here on other business, we can look at it, if you'd like.'

'Yes, please, miss,' Caroline said, crossing her legs, with a slither of nylons. 'I'm awfully curious.'

Miss Chew stared at Caroline's nylons, the skirt riding high, with a sliver of garter strap and pale thigh visible over Caroline's lacy stocking tops. She smiled shyly, then bit her lip, and reached nervously for the heavy leather-bound tome. She flicked it open, coming at once to the page desired, and handed the book over to Caroline.

'It's not somehing I normally show the girls,' she blurted, 'but, since you're nearly an Old Radegundian . . .' She shrugged, then leaned forwards over her desk, cupping her chin in her fingers, and staring intently into Caroline's eyes.

Caroline read aloud: ' "Girls being lustful, vain creatures, their bare nates are mete for whipping at all times, not to cure them of their vices, for girls are by their nature incurable, but to show them that vice is properly accompanied by pain, and that lustful desires must be paid for by proper striping of the posteriors. What, though, of the mature mistress in whose charge the girls be, who allows herself to remember her own girlish wickedness? Such vixens are not ashamed to have favourites amongst the girls, with whom they sport in dalliance, playing the same lewd games of kissing, fondling the exposed body, and rubbing the privy parts, crimes which the mistress should dutifully chastise, not enjoin. Even if these foul contraventions are in the desire, rather than the doing, the crime is no less. Buttocks must be wealed for villainous thoughts, as much as for villainous deeds. I apprehended Mistress Pigsney, charged with instruction in lute, dulcimer, spinet and the Italian language, disporting with young Cleribel Blower, both ladies with skirts undone, and quite naked in their hinderparts, where they were stroking, kissing and fondling each other in a wanton manner. Each strumpet played with the other's queynte: Mistress Pigsney's queynte being shaven bare, in the manner of harlots, whilst Cleribel's was adorned by a dainty paucity of virginal sprouts. Their fingers were betimes busy in their nether holes, in imitation of the foul vice of sodomie. I birched Cleribel two dozen on her bared buttocks, bent over and secured by ropes at her wrists and ankles, and with her skirts tied up in a bag over her head, while Mistress Pigsney fluttered and seemed near to fainting at the girl's screams and wriggles. I informed Mistress Pigsney that her own punishment was to come, at which she grew very pale, and babbled somewhat. Before the assembled mistresses, I had her divest herself of all her stays, stockings, bodice &c, which took a goodly time, and she babbling all the while. She being stark naked was bound upright by legs and belly, to her own spinet, with a knot in her hair fastening her to a ceiling beam, so that she was obliged to remain erect for her punishment. I further obliged her to entertain us with melodies on the lute, held to her breast, while I awarded her four dozen cuts of the birch, on her naked posteriors, the chastisement proceeding at leisurely pace, as the company wished to enjoy said music. After her lashes, her hindquarters presented a savage aspect, as of a rainbow, and she fell to her knees, beseeching my forgiveness, which I willingly granted, upon her oath to forswear singular attachments to schoolmaids. She then joined the company in toasting His Majesty King Chas, and his Portuguese Lady, with a glass of madeira wine." '

'Lustful desires must be paid for,' Miss Chew whispered. 'I did say punishment was in order.'

'Yes, miss. But since my bottom is exempt . . .'

'*Someone* here must be caned. Since it cannot be you, there is only one choice.'

Their eyes met. Caroline's lips made a circle, and her eyes widened. Miss Chew nodded solemnly.

'Before a favoured girl leaves St Radegund's,' she murmured, 'I want her to know me, truly – to think fond thoughts of me – to understand that I am a girl, like all of you, with the same hopes, dreams . . . and desires.'

She rose, and selected from her cabinet the same whippy ashplant that she had used on Caroline's bottom, the day before.

'It's never easy,' she gasped. 'But when I saw you thrash Bulstrode – so cruel, so vicious – I *knew*. You, Caroline, of all girls, must understand me, I think.'

'Yes, I understand,' Caroline whispered.

Miss Chew handed Caroline the cane, then smiled impishly. 'I haven't got a lute, or a spinet,' she purred, 'but I have got some Madeira.'

She rose, opened a cabinet beside her cane rack and took out a crystal decanter and glasses. Her hand trembled slightly, clinking the heavy glass stopper, as she opened the decanter, and filled two wine glasses. Standing by the caning sofa, they clinked glasses, and drank.

'We should really have a biscuit with our Madeira,' Miss Chew said, frowning.

'No matter, miss, I had a hearty breakfast,' Caroline responded.

'Gosh, thanks. Do you like your wine?'

'Super.'

'We can have another glass. There's plenty of time,' said Miss Chew, fingers tapping on the worn sofa back. 'You're not in a hurry, are you?'

'I have two free periods, before Latin, miss,' said Caroline.

'Good, good.' Miss Chew refilled their glasses. 'I mustn't get tiddly.' She giggled.

Caroline lifted the cane, and rubbed it against her tongue, very close to Miss Chew's face. 'Why not?' she said. 'It might help.'

'Now, Caroline, don't tease.'

'I'm not teasing, miss. Let's be frank. You want me to cane you – even though it will hurt terribly.'

'Only if it pleases you, Caroline.'

Caroline stamped her foot. 'That's not an answer. You *want* me to cane you. Yes or no?'

Blushing, Miss Chew hung her head. 'Yes,' she whispered. 'You've no idea how much. I'm *longing* for you to cane me.'

'On your naked bottom?'

'*Yes*. Oh, *please*.'

Caroline glanced at the framed photo of the sixth form, with herself in gym kit, showing her curving thigh flesh. She smiled at Miss Chew, who blushed deeply, but smiled back.

'Yes, well,' the headmistress blurted, 'we do understand each other, don't we?'

Caroline licked her lips. 'All girls masturbate, that's what you said to me, miss, and I think you are the naughtiest girl of us all.'

'I – yes, I don't deny it,' murmured Miss Chew. 'Will that increase my punishment?'

'Most certainly,' Caroline said, draining her glass, and nodding for another.

Miss Chew served her.

'I've decided to cane you very hard,' Caroline said. 'I've been caned often enough, and am coming to understand the mysterious pleasure, for both the punisher and the punished. I can't remember a time when I didn't masturbate, but it is after being caned that I masturbate most heavily. Sometimes I wank off non-stop, for hours, with that smarting glow in my bottom. The same occurred after I'd spanked some luckless girl in dorm. I'd think of her bum, all red and wriggling, and I'd wank, and wank! I've spanked many girls, or slippered them, but never caned before. And I mean to enjoy every minute of it. That fine bottom of yours – begging your pardon, miss – it's too delicious not to be caned.'

'How flattering. Thank you,' Miss Chew simpered, sipping her Madeira rather nervously.

'You admired my bottom,' Caroline said sharply, 'and I shall return the compliment – the hard way.' She lashed the sofa back with her cane, raising a cloud of dust, and Miss Chew paled. 'There is something so beautiful about a girl's croup, isn't there?' said Caroline dreamily. 'The only way to express that beauty is to cane the buttocks naked.'

'True,' Miss Chew said. 'To cane, or be caned, the beauty is the same. It makes a girl feel truly a girl. It's . . . ineffable.'

'A good word,' said Caroline. 'I learnt it in Miss Pertwee's class, when she accused me of ineffable arrogance, for swanking my bum! Now, to business, miss. How many strokes do you deserve? You flogged me fifteen stingers, but I shall be far more generous.'

'Of course.' Miss Chew gulped, swallowing the last of her Madeira. 'I fully expect . . . we have plenty of time . . . with pauses between sets, I can bear . . . oh . . .'

'Two dozen? Three?'

'Oh, Caroline, give me my whipping, I beg you. Just, please don't make me say it.'

'Say it!'

'At least a hundred,' Miss Chew whispered.

'Don't joke.'

'It's no joke. Caroline, you're only at the beginning of this, and don't fully understand. A set of twelve, *very fast* – then, a minute's rest – another set – rest, and so on. The croup reaches a plateau, where the stingers seem like kisses.'

Caroline gasped, as her clitty tingled, and sudden moisture spurted from her quim.

'Bare up,' she whispered.

Miss Chew slipped off her shoes, and stood in cerise stockings, while rolling her skirt up over her fesses, tucking the skirt hem into her belt, so as to bare the sussies and full buttocks, an inch over the dimple at top bum. The shaven pubis gleamed white, and Caroline smiled.

'No panties, miss? A caning offence.'

'Absolutely.'

'I think I'll have the sussies right off, if you please.'

Miss Chew obeyed, unfastening her black garter straps and belt, until her buttocks shone quite nude.

'And you're shaven, down there . . . it's awfully pretty. Perhaps I'll do the same.'

'It is quite the fashion – but that pubic jungle of yours is so *sauvage*, a symbol of the tigress within. Shall I bend over the sofa?'

'Unless you'd prefer to touch your toes, like a boy.'

'No, a girl needs support.'

Miss Chew licked her lips. 'I'm rather nervous. I have the feeling you're really going to make me squirm.'

Caroline smiled, saying nothing, but tapping the sofa back with her cane. Miss Chew lowered her belly onto the leather, propped her hands on the cushions, and stood, with her legs straight and trembling, slightly parted. Caroline ordered her to spread wider, and stand on tiptoe, to elevate her bum. Miss Chew obeyed, biting her lip. The full extent of her gash was revealed, the perineum and anus quite naked of hairs, and the cooze lips swollen like gleaming tubers, on the soft skin between her thighs. The gash flaps were red, like the nylons, and glistened with wet. Caroline lifted her cane over the woman's proffered buttocks.

'Shall we begin?' she purred.

'I suppose so. I'm a bit scared.'

Vip! Vip! Vip! Caroline's biceps rippled, as she lashed three hard strokes in succession, across the milky-white fesses, which coloured at once, in three red slash marks. Miss Chew's buttocks clenched hard, and began to squirm, while her legs jerked rigid, and she trembled on her quivering tiptoes. Taking breath, Caroline followed with another three – breath – three more – breath – and three, to finish the first dozen. The whole application was over within seven seconds.

'Oof! Ouch! Ahh!' Miss Chew gasped, red-faced, as her buttocks wriggled fiercely and tears glistened at the corner of her eyes. She wiped her eyes, then rose, grimacing in pain, and rubbed her blotchy pink bottom, making a face at Caroline. 'My, that was quick,' she said.

She did knee bends, then pranced around the carpet, stamping her feet, and all the while rubbing her weals.

'Oh . . . oh . . . gosh!' she panted. 'It hurts so. Those were *awfully* tight. You're a beast, to cane so hard.'

Caroline waited until her grimaces and panting calmed, before ordering her to resume position. 'That was only the first dozzie,' she said, wiping the sweat from her brow. 'It's not over yet.'

'It isn't, is it? I'd rather hoped you would forget,' said Miss Chew, smiling ruefully.

Once more, she spread her buttocks, Caroline's target now plentifully striped, and the whole fesse flesh suffused with a pink blotchy glow. Vip! Vip! Vip! – breath – the flogged bum squirming – the full dozen applied in triple strokes, within eight seconds. Caroline was learning to place her cuts: some delivered from close up, requiring an extra-hard slice, so that a full ten inches of weal was applied to the skin; others, from further back, with a powerful wrist-flick, so that only an inch of cane tip smacked, gouging a shorter but deeper welt. Set over, Miss Chew's face was a wrinkled mask of agony, her tears streaming visibly, as she groaned, rising, to rub her wriggling flogged fesses.

The weals had multiplied and darkened, so that scarcely an inch of unmarked buttock remained. Welts were beginning to harden and crust, and Miss Chew winced, as she rubbed them. She danced in front of Caroline, weeping and kneading her fesses, all the while wheezing in a hoarse pant of agony. Her quim glistened with droplets of come, seeping from the flapping lips, down her thigh, to moisten her stocking tops. Her armpits were glistening sumps of sweat, as were Caroline's. Scanning the woman's livid bare, Caroline rubbed her thighs, feeling them squelch with an insistent seep of come from her tingling cooze.

'I think you'd be more comfortable if you took your skirt and stockings clean off,' Caroline said.

'Is that an order, miss?'

'Yes.'

The headmistress stripped, until she was completely naked below her blouse, which she knotted under her breasts. Still rubbing her buttocks, she made a face at Caroline's order to resume position, but obeyed without protest. Caroline's fingers brushed the hot skin of her victim's bum.

'Mmm,' Miss Chew mewled, wincing.

'I'll need sunglasses,' Caroline said. 'Your bum is glowing like a furnace.'

Vip! Vip! Vip! The third dozen was complete in six seconds. Caroline's blouse and nylons were soaked in sweat.

'Ooh! Ahh! Ooh!' shrieked Miss Chew, her face crumpled in agony, and frantically squeezing her bruised, squirming croup. 'Oh! Gosh, Caroline, I never dreamed it would hurt like this. You *are* a tigress.'

'Who'd have thought a headmistress liked being caned,' mused Caroline.

'No! That's just the point,' she said sobbing. 'I hate it. Can't you see my bottom squirming? I abhor pain, but . . . but I must have it. Please don't ask why, for I scarcely know myself.'

Drool trickled from the corners of her lips, her eyes were wide and wild, and her big conical titties rose and fell, in her hoarse panting. Caroline took her by the nape, and pushed her back into position. With the tip of her cane, she flicked the woman between the thighs, until they were parted wide enough for her satisfaction. The cunt bubbled with come, streaking the inner thighs. Caroline wiped the outer cooze lips with a fingertip, which she held, shiny wet, before Miss Chew's eyes.

'You're juicing, miss.'

'I can't help it, Caroline. You are so fierce.'

'You'll want a wank, I suppose.'

'Oh, please. May I?'

'Not yet.'

'Beast! Yet, so wise, dear Caroline. It's only by bare-beating that girls really become friends.'

Vip! Vip! Vip!

'Ooh! Ouch!'

'Do you really wank off, looking at the photos of us girls in our gymslips?'

'Yes . . .' Miss Chew groaned.

Vip! Vip! Vip!

'I suppose you masturbate after caning girls, too?'

'Yes . . .'

Vip! Vip! Vip!

'Oh! Ah! Gosh, that's cruel!'

Miss Chew's whipped buttocks squirmed, their dark welts and ridges wriggling like eels on the red, flogged skin.

Vip! Vip! Vip!

'Ooh! Oh! Oh!'

'There, that's four dozen, *so* far. I'm getting all sweaty, so to be more comfortable, with your permission, miss, I'd like to take off my blouse.'

'If you wish.'

Miss Chew slumped on the sofa, head hanging, and weeping tears and drool, while her bottom writhed, and her gash glistened with cunt slime, dripping down her thighs. Caroline unbuttoned her sweat-moist blouse, and bent to unbuckle her shoes. She looked at the caned headmistress, inert, save for the twitching of her bum, and, swallowing hard, unfastened her skirt. She slid it off, and stood in bra and panties, sussies and stockings, cradling her cane.

Beneath her bra, her nipples were erect domes, and her thong gusset was lividly stained with oozed come. Caroline touched herself on the clitty, poking under the wet cloth of the panties, and gasped, as a shock of pleasure coursed through her body. Her fingers caressed her erect nipples through her bra, pinching and squeezing, so she gave little gulps of delight, then slid down her back, and under her panties, to the ridges of her cane weals. Caroline moaned softly, as she caressed her bottom. She parted her legs, and lifted her cane high. Vip! Vip! Miss Chew's fifth dozen began.

A change came over Caroline's victim. Her bottom continued to clench at each flurry of cuts, but the movements of the churning buttocks were not a frantic convulsion, trying to escape the pain, more a pretty winking, as if gratefully taking the stroke, and inviting more. Miss Chew's gasps and squeals became a constant, crooning lullaby of pain.

'Have you reached your plateau, miss?' Caroline asked, lowering her cane after the sixtieth stroke.

'Yes,' groaned the headmistress. 'Can you tell? Oh, thrash me, Caroline, hard as you can. I've never known, nor needed, such pain.'

Come drooled from her sex, dripping into her stocking tops, all the way to her stockinged ankles, with her cerise nylons glistening wet. Caroline's skin was beaded with sweat; pursing her lips, she unclipped her bra, and flung it aside, letting her massive, gleaming breasts spring free. Then she unfastened her sussies, ripped down her panties, and stepped out of them.

'Ahh . . .' she moaned, placing her fingers inside her sopping cooze, and wanking her clitoris with half a dozen tweaks.

Nude, but for her stockings, and with her hand twitching between her thighs, Caroline recommenced the caning. Vip! Vip! The squirming bottom blossomed in welts, like myriad dark fronds.

'Uhh . . . Uhh . . .' gasped Miss Chew. 'Yes . . .'

Caroline masturbated harder and harder, dripping with sweat, and with come squelching from her wanked cunt.

After the sixth dozen, Miss Chew no longer rose to hop in agony, rubbing her fesses, but lay like a rag doll on the sofa, wriggling and moaning. The pauses between sets grew shorter, Caroline maintaining her wank, as she lashed the welted bare with savage cuts. Her breasts bounced and wobbled, dripping with sweat, as her fingers tweaked her throbbing clitty, and her belly began to convulse.

'Uhh . . . uhh . . .' she panted.

At the eighty-seventh stroke, Caroline gritted her teeth, as orgasm flooded her, and come squirted copiously from her writhing, slippery cunt. Miss Chew looked round, her face crimson and contorted in pain.

'Caroline,' she gasped, 'wank me off, I beg you.'

Caught in flagrante delicto, Caroline started, but made no attempt to disguise her masturbation.

'Silence, bitch,' she snarled, and continued to cane.

Vip! Vip! Caroline began to stroke Miss Chew in the arse cleft, lashing her full on the anus bud, and with the cane tip slicing the pendant cunt flaps. Come seeped from Miss Chew's pussy.

'Ouch. Ooh. Gosh, that hurts. At least let me be naked,' Miss Chew moaned.

Caroline paused, while the headmistress fumbled with her top, sloughing off her blouse, and releasing her taut, conical breasts from their cerise bra, to quiver naked beneath her, as her bottom jerked under the blistering cane strokes. Her nipples were hard and erect, capping her full teats like huge, squashy mushrooms. Vip! Vip! Vip!

'Ooh! Ooh . . . I *must* wank . . . oh, sweet Caroline, please!'

'That's nine dozen,' panted Caroline hoarsely. 'I haven't finished with you.'

'Let me wank. I'm almost there. Oh, please, let me wear your panties, Caroline. Let me wank off into your panties.'

Caroline thrust her thong panties over Miss Chew's feet, slid them up her nylons, and clamped them tightly across her cunt basin. The narrow thong left the buttocks totally exposed, save for the string, snaking in the arse cleft, and

Caroline resumed caning the exposed arse pears, wanking hard, while her victim vigorously masturbated her dripping wet cunt.

'Oh, yes! I'm coming! Oh!' cried Miss Chew.

Almost at once, her body stiffened, convulsing, as she climaxed; yet she continued to masturbate, as Caroline's cane lashed her. After eleven dozen strokes of the cane, Caroline, firmly masturbating, said the beating was complete. Her body sizzled with electric pleasure, as her wanked sex throbbed and juiced, fluttering towards a new come. Miss Chew's bare bottom was a glowing moonscape of pits and ridges and purple welts. Groaning, she rose, and flung herself to the floor, to kneel before her chastiser. She pressed her lips to Caroline's stockinged feet, and began to lick them.

'Thank you . . . thank you . . .' Miss Chew snuffled. 'Oh, Caroline, my tigress, let me worship you.'

She rose, clamping her face to Caroline's cunt, rubbing her nose in Caroline's drenched pubic forest, and taking hanks of hair between her lips to chew them.

'Such monstrous fleece. And so luscious a hillock. A beautiful big drinking gourd. You *gorgeous* animal,' she moaned.

Caroline pressed Miss Chew's head into her belly, parting her thighs wider, and gasping, as Miss Chew's tongue found and parted the lips of her pussy. Miss Chew's throat gurgled, as she drank Caroline's juice, and her tongue began to flick the stiff clitty, until her lips enclosed the whole cunt, and she was gnawing, sucking and kissing the throbbing nubbin. Her hand was between her thighs, masturbating herself with slow, luxurious strokes, through Caroline's soaked panties, dripping beads of come onto the carpet.

'Uhh . . . yes . . .' Caroline groaned, squeezing her own nipples. 'Mm . . . don't stop . . .'

She pushed up her left breast, took her engorged nipple into her mouth, and began to bite and suck, as Miss Chew gamahuched her cunt, her hands clutching and stroking

Caroline's bare buttocks. Miss Chew's flogged bottom was high; perching on one leg, Caroline stretched out her foot, and began to scratch the bum welts with her sharp toenails.

'Mm!' Miss Chew gurgled, her mouth full of Caroline's sex. 'Mm! Mm! *Urrgh* . . .'

She masturbated to a second, rapid climax, and, as she shuddered in orgasm, her teeth gripped Caroline's clitty, so that Caroline's belly, too, heaved.

'Yes, lick me, oh, do me, wank me, fuck me with your tongue, I'm coming . . . Oh! Oh! *Ooh*!'

The two females panted, convulsed in their spasms, with come flowing from each wanked cunt. They remained motionless, for nearly a minute, until their sobs and gasps were muted to contented sighs. Miss Chew rose, embraced Caroline, and kissed her full on the lips. Caroline tasted her own come on the woman's mouth, and their slippery tongues met, inside Caroline's mouth. They French-kissed for over a minute, until their mouths parted with a sucking slurp.

'Well!' gasped Miss Chew. 'I've never had such a beastly, vicious, utterly adorable caning. Caroline, my dear, promise you won't be a stranger when you are an Old Radegundian?'

'I'd like to, miss,' Caroline replied, 'but I still don't know what I'm going to do, or where I shall be.'

'And Furrow Weald?'

'It's a possibility, of course.'

'I think it's more than that,' Miss Chew sighed. 'That's really why I summoned you.'

Still wearing Caroline's panties, she sat bare-breasted at her desk, wincing, as her bottom touched the seat. She opened a drawer, and, removing a sheaf of papers, she waved the top one.

'A bank cheque,' Caroline said, frowning.

'For your last two terms' fees, inclusive of bed, board, equipment, travel tickets and so on – rather a large sum. Signed by your mother, and drawn on the Citizen New Century Bank, in the Cayman Islands.'

'It didn't bounce, I hope.'

'It didn't have the chance to bounce. You see, there is no such bank.'

'I . . . uh . . . there must be some misunderstanding, miss.'

Caroline stood nude before the headmistress, blushing, hands behind her back, and her head hung low. Miss Chew perched a pair of rimless spectacles on her nose, rustling the papers against her big bare breasts.

'These papers are from Messrs Machin and Sooke, solicitors, of Richmond-upon-Thames. You have been accustomed to spending the school holidays at your family home on Richmond Hill, I believe?'

'Yes . . . well, it's not exactly my family home, miss. You see, Mummy isn't actually my mummy. She was previously married to my daddy, Sir Piers Letchmount, only he wasn't my daddy, really, because he was previously married to my real mummy, and so my daddy today isn't my real daddy, either. It's a bit complicated.' Caroline shrugged helplessly.

'Just so,' said Miss Chew. 'Well, it seems that your home on Richmond Hill is no longer your home, either. The bailiffs have seized it, along with everything else. To put matters bluntly, Caroline, it seems you are homeless and penniless. Furthermore, the police might well wish to interview you, concerning the whereabouts of your, um, parents, with the distinct possiblity, as you are over eighteen, that you might face accusations of conspiracy. A less understanding headmistress might well deliver you up.'

Caroline began to cry. 'Oh! What am I to do?'

'Signing on for a year's training at Furrow Weald doesn't seem a bad option. It would mean I could tear up this dud cheque.'

'Would you?'

'Of course, my dear. I have the papers for Furrow Weald right here. All they need is one signature.'

She extended a fountain pen and, wiping away her tears, Caroline signed.

Miss Chew clapped her hands. 'That's settled. You'll go straight to Furrow Weald after end-of-term assembly. I do envy you. You'll have such a super time. Mistress Laetitia Frubbin provides everything a girl could wish for.'

'I don't know how to thank you, miss,' Caroline said, snuffling.

Miss Chew rose, and snapped the waistband of Caroline's thong against her tummy. 'Look,' she murmured. 'My panties are a blatant infringement of St Radegund's dress code. That merits a spanking, Caroline, at the very least.'

Caroline bared her teeth. 'My pleasure, miss,' she said.

4

Furrow Weald

'Corporal punishment is never given, or taken, lightly,' said Mistress Laetitia Frubbin, refreshing Caroline's cup with tea.

'No, mistress,' said Caroline.

'However, you have carefully read your enlistment contract,' said the mistress, 'and are aware that corporal punishment is an integral part of discipline here at Furrow Weald.'

'I – er – yes, of course, mistress.'

Caroline supped her tea, rather warily, and nibbled on a ginger biscuit.

'We like to keep a girl on her toes.'

Mistress Frubbin brushed an imaginary strand from her immaculate coiffure, and smiled at her own joke. Ten years Caroline's senior, she wore a brown silk business suit and cream blouse, the skirt quite short, over cream nylons. Her blouse was open to the third button, revealing a well of smooth bare breast, on which nestled a string of gleaming pearls. She swept her manicured hand across the oil portraits and photographs framed on the wall of her study; beyond, through the panoramic window, stretched the vast acreage of Furrow Weald, the eponymous giant rampart, or weald, shielding it from gaze, and the cliffs, where the Atlantic breakers crashed on Cornish sand. Girls, tiny figures, marched on the parade ground, ran round the perimeter, in gruelling single file, or played hockey and netball. Caroline saw that the game players wore short gymslips, while the parading girls were in military uniform, or nude – apparently as punishment – and the runners were all in the nude.

'Here you see some of our most successful old girls,' Mistress Frubbin said. 'Alice Dittle, personal assistant to the billionaire Mr Eamonn B. Fitzsimmons, of New York; Sarah Moon, now the Countess of Longiligne; Emma Nickerson, retired to the Bahamas, with her inheritance of millions, from the late Sheikh of Al-Hoceima . . . and so on. All girls who have made themselves irresistible to an illustrious male, and reaped the benefits. I hope to see your portrait there, one day, Caroline.'

She sipped, put down her cup with a tinkle, and scanned a sheaf of papers.

'I have your file here,' she said. 'Miss Chew recommends you most warmly, which is why we have made a place for you – there is a long waiting list. It seems you are quite a rumbustious character, Caroline.'

Caroline blushed. 'Oh, I wouldn't know, mistress.'

'Fond of fighting, it seems.'

'Sometimes, I got into scraps with other girls, when they were pinching my tuck, or something. I couldn't help it.'

'We like rumbustious characters,' Laetitia said. 'Our job is to channel that spirit to ladylike ends. I shall put you down for boxing. You'll like that – we fight in the nude, except for gloves, boots and socks, of course. You *are* accustomed to athletic nudity?'

Caroline said that in St Radegund's school sports, the girls always swam without costumes.

'Quite so. Later, perhaps, the all-in wrestling, which is in the full nude. I'm sure you'd like that – pounding a naked bruised girl into submission, eh? It is quite wonderful, how girls can turn into savage beasts, when they are naked together, and bent on hurt. Obedience and submission, Caroline, that's the thing in life. Total obedience makes the complete lady. Your file is marked with a gold star. Do you know what that means?'

'No, mistress.'

'A silver star means a girl is used to corporal punishment, on her clothing, while a gold star means that you have been caned on the full bare. Hence, we have no need to mollycoddle you. Some girls come here with scant experience of corporal punishment, and we must break them in gradually, with spankings at first, then light canings, until they are ready to bare their bottoms for true, rewarding punishment. You are fortunate, Caroline, to skip those first steps.'

'I am?'

'Beating on the bare buttocks is more than punishment,' said Laetitia, staring dreamily out of the window. 'It is a sacrament between caner and caned, to awaken the flogged maid to the beauty of her hindquarters, and her true femininity. I do admire your costume, Caroline.'

'Thank you, mistress.'

Caroline wore her best maroon linen skirt, very short, over black nylons – despite the summer heat – with maroon stilettos, a white blouse and a white linen jacket. Her skirt rode up, showing bare thigh, and a hint of black sussies. Laetitia drained her teacup, and stood, pearls bobbing on the full breasts, tightly constrained by her clinging blouse. She rubbed her hands.

'Well. Get your clothes off, please, Caroline.'

'I beg your pardon, mistress?'

Laetitia frowned. 'Are you questioning an order?'

'I . . . no, but . . .'

Laetitia opened her rosewood cabinet, and Caroline gasped. Inside hung a rack of canes, leather quirts and metal devices with buckles, straps and screws, which made Miss Chew's equipment seem mild. The mistress noted Caroline's alarm, smiled icily, and snapped the cabinet shut.

'Once, and once only, a new maid may hesitate before obeying an order from her superior. Since you are a new maid, Caroline, at this moment, every Wealder is your superior. The first words to a Wealder's lips are "Yes, I shall obey." Got it? That was your one go. I shall not repeat the order.'

Flushed and trembling, mouth agape, Caroline undid the top button of her blouse. Laetitia put her hands on her hips, and scrutinised Caroline, rather coldly, pursing her lips.

'Hurry up, Caroline,' she said. 'We haven't got all day. Matron will examine you, of course, and your prefect inductress, Miss Valcul, I believe, will show you to your room, and get your kit organised, but it's best a maid starts at the beginning.'

Caroline's blouse came off, and she fiddled with her bra, until the cups bounced from her naked breasts, which jumped up, with the big nipples swelling pertly. Laetitia smiled, nodding approval.

'Thirty-eight, I'd say, with a C cup?'

'Forty, actually, miss,' Caroline blurted, crimson with shame, 'and a D.' She undid the fastener of her skirt, and unzipped it.

'No good blushing, girl,' said Laetitia. 'New maids go nude for their first two weeks, you see. Then, they wear what we call "girly kit". After your basic training, you'll do your exams, and, one hopes, qualify as a senior. Your inductress will explain everything, and do her best to ensure you have a nice time. Come now, strip off.'

Caroline's skirt slid off, and she bent down to unbuckle her shoes. Her bare breasts bobbed beneath her ribs.

'My, you are a splendid wench,' said Laetitia. 'It's in your file, of course, but dear Miss Chew does tend to exaggerate. I can't wait to see your bottom.'

The stockings slid down, sussies were unclasped, and, finally, Caroline stepped out of her thong panties. Laetitia sucked her breath.

'What a tremendous thatch! Swivel, please.'

Caroline turned, showing her bared buttocks.

'Yes, the croup is quite superb, still with a faint blush from your last caning by Miss Chew. And such lovely long legs. Thighs delightfully muscled . . . my cousin wasn't exaggerating in the slightest. Your pubic mound! So ripe and swelling, like a girl's breast, it's quite the pièce de résistance. Such a pity the thatch will have to go, for it is so marvellously savage. I've never seen one quite so big, why, it almost reaches your divine belly button, my dear – it must be that scrumptious big pubic mound. However, that's the way we do things here. New maids are in the nude, until they are strapped in – that is, acclimatised – and, all girls are pubically shaved. A smooth gourd is so tasty, and you'll just love it. Then you'll learn the school anthem – "Bare up, Furrovians, bare up and obey!" – oh, you'll be so happy. Now, I trust you are ready for your initial beating.'

'My what?' Caroline gasped. 'I mean, yes, mistress, I shall obey.'

Laetitia clapped her hands. 'That's my girl. Every inductee takes a welcome whopping, to start her on the pennies ladder.'

'Please forgive me for not understanding, mistress,' said Caroline, nervously glancing to the punishment cabinet. 'You are going to cane me, when I haven't done anything?'

'It's precisely because she hasn't done anything that a new maid takes her whops. A girl's bare bottom is the most tempting thing in creation, and a girl must pay the price of being a temptress.'

'I shall obey, of course, mistress, but it doesn't seem awfully fair.'

'Exactly. Life is not fair. At Furrow Weald, you shall learn that. Of course, I am not going to cane you. I only cane maids who *have* done something. You are going to cane yourself.'

Caroline's jaw dropped.

'Don't look so surprised. Honour canings are a fact of life here.'

Laetitia reached under her desk, and withdrew a rod of stiff black rubber, about three feet long. She flexed it, bending it right back, then let it spring straight.

'This is a self-baster, and you'll be issued with your own, which you must guard most carefully. You will now cane yourself a dozen, on your bare bottom. As you will see, the springiness of the baster allows a good, and very painful, wrap-around stroke, by flicking the wrist. Please bend over your armchair, with your legs spread.'

Caroline obeyed, bending over the worn leather chair back, and accepted the rubber cane. 'I've . . . I've never done this before, mistress. I feel a bit silly.'

'Not even practised spanking youself with a hairbrush, while masturbating?'

'Well, yes, a few times. Most girls have done that.'

'This is the same, only more painful. I shall watch, but not comment. You'll go straight to Matron for your medical, and she will evaluate your stripes, awarding you a score from one to ten, which will count towards pennies on your account. There is no money here, but you may earn pennies and shillings for dutiful deeds, and spend them at the tuck shop, on the little treats we girls like so much. A maid with a negative balance in her chequebook earns an immediate and very severe flogging, to put her back in credit.'

There was a soft knock at the door, and Laetitia bade entrance. A slender, rather willowy, girl appeared, her flat blonde hair draped over her shoulders and large, pointed breasts – like fashion models in old photos from the 1960s – with her legs shiny in white nylons, over laced-up brown shoes. She wore a pleated brown skirt, over large buttocks that jutted boldly from her lithe frame, a black blazer with cream piping and a white blouse, with a pink and lemon striped tie. Clipped at her belt, a yellow wooden cane nestled in her skirt pleats, under her blazer.

'Good afternoon, mistress,' she began, then espied Caroline's raised bare bum. 'Oh – if you're not finished –'

'Stay, Vicca. This is the new inductee, Miss Caroline Letchmount. Caroline, this is prefect Vicca Valcul. No, don't rise.'

Caroline looked round, smiling uncertainly, as the prefect stared open-mouthed at her buttocks.

'Gosh,' said Vicca, 'I see I've arrived at a sensitive moment. How awful of me! Well, bare up, Caroline – you seem an awfully nice maid, with a gorgeous bottom, if I may say so. I hope you don't mind my watching, and I'm sure we'll be good friends.'

'So,' said Laetitia, 'you may commence your self-basting, Caroline, remembering that the harder you cane yourself, the more pennies you earn.'

Caroline lifted the quivering rod high over her bare bum. Gritting her teeth, she flicked the handle, and winced, as the rod leapt like a beast, to lash her bare bum hard. Vip!

'Oof!' she gasped, clenching her buttocks, as pain seared her naked flesh.

'A little less of the squealing, Caroline,' said Laetitia.

'Gosh, mistress,' blurted Vicca, 'in fairness, that *was* a bit of a stinger. Look at her stripe.'

Vip! Caroline gasped, but did not cry, as she lashed herself the second stroke. Vip! The third started her buttocks squirming; the rubber rod made her bum smart abominably. Vip! She began to pant, hoarsely, as the pain blossomed across the whole naked croup.

'Don't slacken, Caroline,' said Laetitia.

'She's a grand girl, mistress,' said Vicca Valcul, in a breathy voice.

Vip! Tears moistened Caroline's eyes, and her gorge rose, as she lashed herself in one of her existing welts.

It was hard to aim the strokes; one flick of her wrist, and the rod flew into action, to land with crushing force on her exposed bare. Her face burned with shame and distress, as she felt both girls' eyes on her flaming bottom.

I must look a right booby. Well, I'll show them.

Lifting her arm, she brought it down hard, flicking her wrist at the last moment, and slapping the rod between her buttocks, in her arse cleft, with the tip flogging her bumhole and lower cunt lips.

'Ooh!' she moaned, as tears flooded her eyes.

'Good *show*,' said Vicca.

Vip! Caroline's legs began to tremble violently, as the welts smarted on her bare, but she forced herself to flick the rubber harder and harder, flogging her bottom unmercifully, until, panting and wriggling, she had completed her twelve. Vicca clapped her hands a few times, and said the maid did herself like a trouper. Caroline rose, panting, and wiping the tears from her eyes, then rubbing her sore fesses, with a gasp of surprise at the depth of her welts.

'Yes, that was not unimpressive,' Laetitia murmured. 'It is very difficult to deliver a stroke with full force to your own bottom, but you got very close. Well, straight to Matron with you, Caroline. Gather up your things – they'll be kept in the storage room, until you have permission to wear them.'

'I'm so glad Caroline is joining us, mistress,' cooed Vicca. 'She's such a brave girl. Come on, Caroline, we'll see if Matron won't put some nice zinc ointment on those stripes.'

She showed Caroline out, into the bare-boarded corridor, redolent of polish, musty wood, and the sweaty perfume of girls' bodies. Caroline's face was creased in pain, and her hands ceaselessly rubbed her wealed bottom. The door slid shut.

'I never thought I could hurt myself so much,' Caroline said.

Vip! Vicca's cane lashed her full across the naked breasts.

'*Ooh*!'

'Speak when spoken to, bitch,' Vicca snarled.

Vip!

'Ahh! Stop! What did you do –'

Vip! A third cut took her right on the nipples.

'Oh! Oh! That hurts!'

Vicca's hand dived to Caroline's cunt basin, and wrenched her pubic fleece by the roots, twisting and opening her gash lips, which squirted wetness over her thighs.

'Ouch!'

'You dirty slut,' sneered the prefect. 'Look at that pussy-juice. You're wet from a few weedy cane strokes. And look at that pube-gourd. Like a bloody marrow between your smelly thighs, or a third bloody arse pear.

You're a real apewoman, and no mistake. Another stinking sub. Knees up, slut, and follow me at the double. Hup!'

Caroline began to run on the spot, then lurched in pursuit of her inductress. 'Please, miss, whatever do you mean?' she asked.

'You're a sub – we get a lot here – like being caned and shamed, need a thrashing to wank off. I'd cane your beastly arse blue, except Matron would think you basted yourself, and award more points.'

Vip! She whirled round, and delivered another ferocious cut to Caroline's titties, causing her to drop her bundle of clothing. Caroline stopped running, and bent to pick her things up, but this launched a paroxysm of fury from the slender Vicca, who thrashed Caroline across her bare back.

'Bitch! Hup! Hup! You dropped them, you lose them. Filthy slut. Hup! Hup! Get those knees up. Hup!'

Caroline wobbled, but rose to her feet, clutching only her handbag. She started to cry, but after wincing, from two more fierce stingers to her bare teats, which looked like two red, bouncing jellies, she staggered after the prefect, arms pumping, knees up, and hitting her flogged breasts as they bounced. They passed two girls, Caroline's own age, in pleated miniskirts, with white shirts, black shoes and white fluffy ankle socks, and each with a self-basting rubber cane swinging from her waist. Caroline heard the girls giggle behind her, with a whisper of 'new slut'.

'Juicy bum . . .'

'Lush boobs, and a twat like a football . . .'

'Cane the bitch raw . . .'

'Wank all over her . . .'

Crying and panting, with her flogged titties heaving, Caroline followed Vicca Valcul's swaying bum, tight under her clinging skirt, and heard the whistle of the prefect's cane, swishing the air. They passed a common room, where girls in uniform shrieked merrily in front of the television, showing *Up Your Raspberry*, where Britain's top television personality, the odious Frank Funn, awarded prizes to girls who humiliated themselves, fighting in mud, tearing at each other in catspats while squatting on the lavatory, and other horrid stunts. How depressing, that Furrovians liked such rot! Vicca sneered that there was no way a worthless harlot like Caroline could pass basic training, and her exams, and become a senior maid.

'What are you?' she snapped.

'A worthless harlot, miss,' Caroline responded.

'Your file says you're fond of scrapping. Well, slut, I'll give you a scrap. I'll kick your cunt in, and bite your titties off, and that big thick twat gourd too.'

Caroline, according to Vicca Valcul, would be like most of the new maids, worthless sluts and boarding-school tarts, full of poncy self-esteem, who took a few months of basting, then ran away, or were flogged off the estate, never to return. Vicca was her best friend – her only friend.

'What are you, Caroline?' she spat.

'A worthless slut, miss . . . a boarding-school tart, miss.'

Vip!

'Ooh!' Caroline squealed, at another cut across her bare nipples.

'And what am I?'

Vip!

'Ahh! My best friend, miss,' Caroline gasped, through her tears.

'Don't you forget it,' snarled Vicca Valcul.

Caroline sighed in relief, when they got to Matron's surgery. Still running at the double, she heard Vicca coo, in her sweetest little girl's voice: 'The new maid, Caroline Letchmount, for you, Miss Tongue. She's an absolute darling, and you'll love her. I know I do.'

The matron, Miss Emily Tongue, was a serenely handsome lady of about thirty years of age. Her swelling breasts and croup were tightly encased in dazzlingly starched whites, with white rubber bootees and apron, and her glossy brown hair was neatly curled under her nurse's bonnet. She cast an approving eye over Caroline's naked body, and licked her lips.

'She's had her self-basting?' she asked Vicca.

'Yes, Matron.'

'More than that, by the looks of things. Those titty weals are fresh.'

'The new maid was resistant to discipline, Matron.'

'Of course.'

Miss Tongue reached out and squeezed Caroline's breasts, pinching the nipples quite hard, in a manner Caroline did not think entirely medical. The matron looked down to consult her notes.

'It says you have a history of fighting and unruly behaviour, Caroline. Well, it might earn your bum a few stripes, but it'll be useful for survival here. You've had tea?'

'Yes, miss,' Caroline said. 'With Mistress Frubbin.'

'Good. At Furrow Weald, we believe a maid must always get her tea. Well, let's get a look at your basting. Hop on here, please.'

Miss Tongue indicated a sort of operating table, large enough for two people, and covered in white rubber. Caroline climbed on, and lay on her tummy, with the rubber cold and clammy against her skin. Miss Tongue prised her thighs apart, and began to prod her bottom, clawing her bum weals, perineum and soft inner thighs. Caroline's fesses twitched.

'Ouch!' she said.

'Yes, you've basted yourself quite well,' said Miss Tongue. 'I shall award this ten points. Admirable, young lady. A little zinc ointment for your weals.'

Caroline relaxed, sighing, as the matron's supple fingers rubbed cool ointment into her bottom, her fingers straying well into her anus, tickling her, although Caroline had no weal in *there.*

'We proceed to your medical. You may lie as you are.'

Caroline gasped as a glass thermometer poked right into her rectum; then, Miss Tongue thumped and squeezed her shoulders, spine and legs, twisted her feet, wrenching each toe, bent the legs back, and finally removed the thermometer. She ordered Caroline to turn over and lie on her back.

Vicca watched, arms folded and sneering, as Miss Tongue examined the inside of Caroline's mouth and nose, shone a light into her eyes, examined her hair roots, and felt her titties and tummy, poking hard. She mashed Caroline's cunt hillock, wrenching her pubic fleece, with a whistle of admiration, saying she had never seen such abundant thatch, nor such a swelling twat mound.

Donning rubber gloves, the matron plunged a finger into Caroline's cooze, and Caroline wriggled as the hard finger reamed her wombneck; the finger was followed by a second, until Miss Tongue had Caroline's quim distended by all four fingers. Her thumb began to knead Caroline's clitty, which rapidly stiffened, with Caroline gasping, as her pussy became wet.

'An unusually prominent and responsive clitoris,' Matrion said, 'and your quim is a heavy juicer. I take it you masturbate a lot?'

'Well, yes, I do,' Caroline said. 'But that's normal, isn't it? I mean, all girls wank off.'

'I am not here to apportion blame or innocence,' snapped Miss Tongue, 'simply to observe medical facts. Would you say you masturbate, on average, once a month, once a week, or once a day?'

'Usually, three or four times a day, miss,' murmured Caroline sheepishly.

'An average masturbatress, then,' announced Matron brightly. 'You shall feel at home here, Caroline.'

She withdrew her gloved fingers, wet with Caroline's juice, and making a gurgling plop, as wetness oozed from the swollen gash flaps. Stripping off her gloves, she donned a fresh pair, and inserted a finger into Caroline's anus, pushing it hard into the rectum, and beyond, with Caroline wincing, as Matron touched her colon. Miss Tongue inserted a second, and a third finger, stretching Caroline's anus most painfully, and the three fingers spent over a minute reaming the inside of her bumhole. Caroline grimaced, blushing, as come flowed from her cooze, with Vicca Valcul staring straight at her vulval opening. At last,

Miss Tongue pronounced herself satisfied, and withdrew her fingers in a rush, which made Caroline gasp – the ticklish thrill was just like doing a row of dungs, and made her cunt spurt faster.

The matron depressed a lever with her foot, and Caroline started, as the surgical table hummed downwards towards the floor, until she lay at knee height. Vicca stepped forwards, brandishing a three-foot wooden pole, with holes at each end. She snapped the ends open, and deftly cuffed Caroline's ankles, locking her in the restraint, with her feet parted wide, and her quim spread.

'That's a surgical hobble,' said Miss Tongue, smiling. 'You'll see why it's advisable. Now, raise your legs as far as you can, Caroline.'

Caroline obeyed, holding her feet straight up over her quim, while Miss Tongue took her wrists, and strapped them with a buckle to the ends of the hobble bar, beside her ankles. Caroline rocked gently backwards and forwards, her weight on her top buttocks and spinal nubbin. Licking her teeth, Vicca leered at Caroline's fully exposed cunt basin, anus and bum cleft, stretched taut.

'Would you please shave her, Vicca?' said Miss Tongue.

Soap, a shaving brush and hot water were fetched, and Vicca applied a cut-throat razor to Caroline's lathered cunt fleece. Caroline winced at her deliberately harsh strokes, but marvelled at how quickly her proud fleece disappeared. Vicca made sure to shave every inch of her pubis and perineum, scraping right up to her gash lips and anus, so that, within minutes, Caroline's cunt basin was naked and gleaming smooth. Vicca pinched her shorn hillock, saying it was a monster. Miss Tongue stroked the swelling cunt mound, and agreed.

'Now I must peg you,' the Matron said. 'We need your peg size, for the maids' showroom.'

She fetched a tray, containing a selection of stiff black rubber tubes, standing upright and shaped like male sex organs. They ranged from quite dainty to monstrous. Caroline's eyes widened, and her mouth gaped, as Matron chose quite a slender one, and coated it with shiny lubricant jelly from a tube. She lifted the cylinder from its peg, and pressed its tip to Caroline's anus.

'This is a one-incher,' she said. 'You should have no trouble with it.'

Miss Tongue pushed the rubber cylinder into Caroline's anus, and Caroline groaned at the pain.

'Just relax your sphincter,' said Matron. 'Let the tube into your rectum. It's only an inch thick. Imagine how big your dungs are!'

Caroline tried to obey, and gasped as the slender rubber tube penetrated her, right to the arse root. Matron began to slide the tube in and out, with a squelching sound, its tip slamming the hard opening to the colon. Caroline wriggled, gasping at the pain.

'There, that's not so bad, is it?' said Miss Tongue.

'N-no, miss,' Caroline blurted, her eyes misted by tears. Her wrists and ankles rattled her hobble bar.

'Splendid!' said Matron, withdrawing the tube, with the same giddy tickling as before, and the same sudden spurt of come from her cunt, as it left Caroline's anus.

She felt her come trickling down her thigh backs and buttocks, and *knew* Vicca could see it.

'I think we can skip the one-and-a-half,' Matron said, 'and try a two-incher. It might be a tiny bit uncomfortable at first, but it's pretty much the standard model for most maids.'

She took another cylinder, much longer and thicker, and slopped it with jelly, then quickly penetrated Caroline's anus. Without much pressure, it slid into her rectum, and thudded at the arse root.

'Why, that's splendid!' cried Miss Tongue.

She repeated the reaming, sliding the tube rapidly in and out of the bumhole, with squelchy, squirting noises of jelly, while Caroline's cooze seeped copious come. Caroline gasped hoarsely, her legs jerking rigid on her hobble bar, and her fingers clenching and unfolding, with her face a grimace of pain. Vicca said that the maid was juicing like a right slut.

'Language, Vicca dear,' said Miss Tongue mildly. 'I'm awfully pleased the maid is juicing, for it shows mettle. Do you think she'd go to two-and-a-half?'

'I'd take her straight to three, miss,' said Vicca laconically.

'Gosh, I can't remember the last maid who took a full three inches, but I suppose you're right. Her anus and rectum dilate wonderfully.'

'I'd even volunteer,' said Vicca. '*You* know.' She smirked at the trussed girl.

'Have you had much experience of anal penetration, Caroline? asked Matron. 'Your compliant rectum suggests you have.'

'Miss?' Caroline gasped, as Matron selected an enormous rubber tube, thick as a girl's wrist, and as long as her forearm, with curious rubber straps hanging from an extra, thumb-like protrusion at its base.

'I mean, have many boys fucked you in the bumhole?'

'No, miss!'

'She's lying,' said Vicca with a snort. 'Let me do her, Miss Tongue. And if she's not, then it will be a pleasure to break in such a juicy morsel.'

'Very well,' said Miss Tongue, her eyes bright.

Vicca unzipped her skirt, and took it off, then stepped out of her panties. She tied her blouse at her ribs, and stood with her jutting buttocks and shiny, shaven pubis nude. Matron helped her strap the three-inch-thick rubber tube to her pubic mound, where it stood out like a boy's stiff sex organ, with the little thumb poking inside her cunt flaps at her glistening wet clitty. Vicca cupped her hand at Caroline's open gash, and took a palmful of her pussy juice, with which she anointed the gleaming hard rubber shaft. She positioned herself over Caroline's gaping loins, the tip of the massive tube at Caroline's anus bud.

'No, please . . .' Caroline gasped faintly.

'Chin up, Caroline,' Matron chirped. 'Just think, I can award you an extra two points – that's twopence – so, after your buggery, you'll have a whole shilling!'

5

New Bitch

'Ahh . . .!' Caroline groaned, as the huge rubber dildo penetrated her anus.

Vicca's hard flat belly knotted with muscle, her buttocks clenched and her stockinged thighs rippled, as she slammed the dildo hard into Caroline. Three inches of black rubber disappeared in Caroline's bumhole, lips stretched to bursting; then five, and suddenly, with a grunt from Vicca, her bare-shaven cunt gourd slapped on Caroline's upended buttocks, as the rubber disappeared all the way up her bumhole. Caroline panted and groaned, tears streaming from her eyes, and her face wrinkled in agony.

'Oh,' she moaned. 'You're hurting me.'

'Yes,' Vicca panted, as her hips squirmed, slamming the giant dildo into Caroline's tripes, as she began to bugger the helpless trussed girl.

Caroline writhed under her fierce buggery, squealing and sobbing, yet unable to take her eyes from the horrid black rubber thing, penetrating her intimate body – *fucking my bumhole!* – her belly convulsing and thighs quivering, and the spurts of come from her shaven cunt, which looked so exposed, and strangely exciting. Her belly felt split to bursting, as the monstrous thing poked her, yet beneath the pain was a gorgeous sensation of fullness in her tummy, and a yummy tickling in her anus and rectum, despite their dreadful stretching. Her thigh backs and fesses were glazed in cunt juice. Vicca's cooze, too, was drenched in come, as the little rubber thumb winked in and out of her swollen wet gash flaps, tweaking her distended clitty. Vicca's tongue hung out, as she fucked, with drool coursing down her chin, from her slack, trembling lips.

'Gosh, this is good,' she panted, buttocks pumping, as she buggered the squirming girl. 'This tweaker on the dildo is ever so thrilling, miss. I'm trying not to come too soon.' Her blouse was drenched in sweat, with her bubbies bouncing.

'I think Caroline might come,' said Miss Tongue, 'judging from her flow of juice. She's quite a fountain! It reminds me, I haven't had my afternoon wank yet. I was going to have it with my cup of tea, but this is too exciting.'

Coolly, Matron lifted her skirt, showing her white nylons and sussies denuded of any knickers. Her smooth shiny pubis swelled between the garter straps, with the big red cunt lips fattened and glistening with come. Caroline gaped. The matron placed her fingers to her cooze, and quite casually began to frig her clitty, as though it were no more unusual than . . . than . . .

Than being buggered by a girl with a strap-on dildo.

Moaning, Caroline began to thrust her buttocks in the rhythm of her buggery, slapping her thighs against Vicca's, both girls dripping with sweat and cunt juice. Miss Tongue began to pant, and placed one foot up on Caroline's heaving belly, exposing her full cooze, with the cunt lips stretched wide around the glistening pink flesh.

'I mustn't wet my nylons,' Miss Tongue said. 'You are a rather exciting girl, Caroline. I hope you're enjoying your buggery.'

'Ooh! Ahh! It hurts so, miss,' Caroline panted.

'That's not what I asked. You're juicing rather a lot, so you must be enjoying it. I know I am. My nubbin's really throbbing.'

Caroline's eyes flicked from the monstrous shaft penetrating her arse to the matron's deftly tweaking fingers, pummelling her erect clitty, and drenched in pussy juice. Panting, she thrust her bum up to meet the invading dildo, and suck it deeper into her rectum.

'Oh . . . oh . . . yes . . .' Caroline gasped. 'Fuck me, do me hard . . .'

'Good girl,' said Miss Tongue.

Drips of glistening come trickled from her cunt onto Caroline's tummy.

'I'm nearly off,' panted Vicca.

Matron wanked faster. 'Yes,' she gasped. 'Let's come together. Caroline too . . .'

Come oozed from Vicca's cunt, and from Matron, as she masturbated vigorously over Caroline's squirming belly. Caroline felt her tummy bursting with pain, which was awful wrenching pleasure at the same time. Her cunt basin began to twitch and heave, as electric pleasure tingled in her spine and clitty.

'Please, miss . . .' she gasped.

'Yes?' groaned Matron.

'My nubbin . . . please . . . I need . . .'

'A helping hand? Oh, all right.'

Still masturbating her own cooze, Miss Tongue reached down and began to wank Caroline's throbbing, erect clit, with Vicca's belly slapping the back of Matron's hand, as she fucked Caroline's anus.

'Yes!' Caroline squealed. 'Oh, yes! I'm coming!'

'Ah . . . ah . . . ahh!' shrieked Vicca, come pouring from her tweaked cunt.

'Oh! Oh!' pouted Matron, her titties heaving. 'Ooh . . .'

The three girls gasped together in loud orgasm. Caroline's was the longest and noisiest, and, when her belly's heaving ebbed, a stream of golden steaming piss spouted from her gash onto Vicca's cunt and belly, and spraying the linoleum floor.

'Oh! I'm sorry,' Caroline moaned.

'You fucking bitch,' snarled the prefect. Seizing her cane, she began to thrash Caroline's belly, breasts and thighs. Vip! Vip!

'Ahh! Don't!' Caroline shrieked, as her bubbies flapped.

'You slut! You pissing trollop!'

'Language, Vicca,' murmured Miss Tongue.

Vip! Vip! The flurry of cane strokes striped Caroline's naked skin in angry welts. Vip! Vip! Dildo bobbing at her gash, Vicca lashed between the thighs, directly on the anus and cunt. Vip! Vip!

'Ooh!' Caroline shrieked, writhing madly, with her ankles and wrists slamming against her hobble bar.

'Take that!' hissed Vicca, 'and that!' as she whipped Caroline's spread pink cunt flesh, spraying piss and come.

Tears flowed down Caroline's cheeks, red with anger and pain, as her bottom frantically squirmed in a vain effort to avoid Vicca's cane. The cane sliced her bum cleft, her cunt, thighs and the soles of her tethered feet, which had Caroline jumping and curling her toes in agony.

'Ooh! Ahh! I'm sorry,' she squealed. 'Oh, it hurts! Please stop, oh please.'

Miss Tongue licked her teeth, smiling, as her fingers slopped in her wet cooze, frotting her clitty. Vicca refused to stop. Her thighs and cooze dripping with Caroline's piss, she flogged the helplessly trussed girl, until Caroline's gasps became shriller and hoarser, and come spurted from her writhing cunt in shining driblets.

'Oh . . . oh . . .' she moaned, her belly heaving under the cane's lash. 'Oh . . .'

'I do believe the maid is coming again,' said Matron, masturbating vigorously.

Vip! Vip!

'Oh . . . yes! Ohh . . .' Caroline shrieked, as come poured in a glistening torrent from her flogged cunt, and she convulsed, once more, in climax.

'Oh! Yes! Good! Ooh . . .' gasped Miss Tongue, as she wanked herself off to a second spasm.

Vicca put down her cane, and unstrapped her dildo. 'I *knew* the bitch was a beastly sub,' she panted.

'But a gorgeous one,' said Miss Tongue. 'I've just had my after-dinner diddle as well.'

After a further application of zinc ointment to her bruises, Caroline marched, at the double, to her new room. They passed through winding corridors, up and down flights of spiral stairs, until Caroline was quite dizzy, and sure she would never fathom the mysteries of this inscrutable house. Everywhere was that familiar school smell of soap, leather, wood, dust, pee and girl sweat. Several times, they encountered girls alone or in a gaggle: some in pleated miniskirts, ankle socks and buckle shoes; some superbly dressed, in an aura of lovely perfume, with nylons of various hues, and gold necklaces or brooches; some, evidently schoolmistresses, in mortar board and gown, sensible skirts and shoes, and plain blouses, clinging tightly to their breasts; some fully nude, like Caroline. All carried canes at their waists, and all eyed Caroline's whipped, zinc-smeared body with pursed lips, or little smiles of admiration.

'Your welts show you can take it,' said Vicca, in a surly tone. 'That gets you respect, bitch. You're a cert for the Stingers.'

Caroline had neither time, nor breath, to question that puzzling remark, before they came to a corridor of cells with wooden doors, and Vicca pushed open the door marked with the number 34. It had no lock, and swung back and forth on spring hinges. The room was small, about nine feet by fifteen, but bright and airy, with a large window, looking out from three floors up, on gardens, arbours and playing fields, with the foam-capped sea visible at the horizon, beyond the weald. There was a metal bunk bed, with crisp white linen sheets folded on the mattress; an armoire; a washstand with cups, jugs and crockery; a wooden table and chair; and an enamel chamber pot peeping underneath the bed on the linoleum floor. Beneath the window was a curious wooden frame, with straps and buckles, like a vaulting horse, but curving upwards in an arch, the size of a human body. In the corner, to Caroline's surprise, was a compact refrigerator, beside an array of brushes and cleaning things. Vicca ordered her to make her bed, paying especial attention to her hospital corners, then left her to it.

Wrinkling her face from time to time, for the pain in her buggered bumhole was still acute, Caroline set to making her bed. She had just finished when Vicca returned, leading a tall girl with rosebud lips, her raven hair piled in a bun, wearing a blouse and short skirt like Vicca's, but without the striped tie, and with the blouse undone to the third button, baring ripe tan breast flesh. Her arms and legs rippled with muscle; she wore a whistle round her neck, and at her waist, a yellow cane like Vicca's.

'Attention, new bitch,' snapped Vicca, and Caroline stood smartly to attention.

Vicca announced that the muscular girl was Submistress Bronwen Bellibone, Caroline's floor mistress. Bronwen glanced at Caroline's made bed.

'Oh! This bed won't do,' she said, looking out of the window, then casually overturned the mattress, and ripped apart the sheets and blankets.

Caroline's face fell.

'Miss Valcul is your guardian prefect,' she said crisply. 'She takes care of your doings in school, while I am in charge of you here on your floor. The latrines are at the end of the corridor. At morning bell, you assemble there for shit, shower and shave, then wank parade. Wank parade last thing at night before lights out. If you masturbate in private, you must fill your come pot, decant it into your bottle, and place it in the fridge, for collection. Girl come is a prized product of our retail division – but you don't concern yourself with business matters.'

She opened the fridge to reveal a jug of iced water and a dark-green stoppered bottle, its label reading CAROLINE LETCHMOUNT – VULVAL JUICE.

'In your armoire, you will find your girly kit, wrapped up, until you pass your basic training and become a schoolmaid. You must not tamper with it or I'll flog you. You will find your wash things and punishment panties, also your self-basting cane, to be worn, strapped at the waist, at all times off my floor. New bitches go nude, as Miss Valcul has explained, and, frankly, in this hot weather, you are to be envied. There are thirty maids on my floor, and I haven't time to listen to your whinges.

You'll keep your room swept, and your whipping horse polished. Any smuttiness or untidiness, and I'll flog you. Any horseplay or noise, and I'll flog you. No visitors in the rooms, unless for the express purpose of mutual masturbation, and no talking after lights out, or I'll flog you. Anything at all I don't like, and I'll flog you. At supper bell, you line up with the other new bitch nudies, *after* the maids and schoolmaids.'

She put her face inches from Caroline's and pinched her cheek, leering, to bare her pearl white teeth. Then, she tapped Caroline on the buttocks. Caroline winced.

'I don't like blondies, and I'm sure I don't like *you*, new bitch. That is all for the moment.'

She turned sharply, with a click of her high heels and a wiggle of her shapely bottom pears, tightly swollen under her miniskirt, leaving Caroline and Vicca alone. Vicca watched, as Caroline remade her bed.

'Please, miss?'

'Yes?'

'What does "stingers" mean?'

'Some depraved girls join gangs, although it's beastly, and against the rules. There are two gangs, the Stingers and the Swanks. Steer clear of them. Gang membership earns a maid quite unthinkable punishment – public whipping, for starters, and then much worse.'

'And what are punishment panties?'

'Sort of chastity belt, and horribly uncomfortable, as you're certain to find out, new bitch,' answered Vicca. 'Enough questions. You'll want to rest, I suppose, until supper.'

Tipping over Caroline's made bed, she walked out. Sighing, Caroline set to work again, and, when the bed was finished, flopped, exhausted, for a nap. She dozed, dreaming of Persimmon's wealed bottom, and Miss Chew's tongue licking her cunt, and awoke, in the shadow of a girl.

'Wanking already,' the girl purred.

Caroline started, to find that her hand was on her twat, her clitty stiff, and her come flowing.

'I'd better join you,' said the girl. 'Mustn't disobey the rules, eh? We've plenty of time for a wank before supper. Turn over a little, so that I can feast my eyes on your bottom. It's already the talk of the school.'

Rubbing her eyes, Caroline showed the girl her bottom, parted slightly, with the shaven slice of her quim lips revealed.

'Golly, yes, that's a corker. Such lovely weals. And on your titties and slice, and everywhere. You poor darling. You've been spotted, you know, frogmarched by that bitch Vicca.'

The girl was wearing a pleated brown miniskirt, white nylons and blouse, with gleaming brown stilettos, and a brown and yellow tie. She lifted her skirt, and, pushing aside the gusset of her white nylon panties to expose her gleaming cunt lips and shiny, hairless cooze mound, began to masturbate.

'Gosh, that's good. I've been too busy to diddle since this morning. I'm Aaliz de Brest, by the way.' She spelled the name.

'Caroline Letchmount.'

'Yes, I know.'

'Aren't you a prefect, miss?'

'Yes, but shush. Not on Bronwen's floor.'

Aaliz put a finger to her lips. Her sex flaps writhed under her nimble fingering, with her swollen red clitty bulging between thumb and fingernail. Caroline licked her lips, and pressed her own clitty, which was beginning to throb and tingle; watching Aaliz's fingers squelching her naked cunt, Caroline began to wank off. Their eyes met, and both girls smiled in complicity.

'Isn't a maid supposed to wank into her come pot?' Caroline asked.

'Oh, yes. I'd forgotten. Do you want . . .?'

Still masturbating, Aaliz reached for a glass jar from the top of the fridge, and handed it to Caroline, who sat up and tucked it beneath her quim lips, wedged in her bum cleft. Come from her wanked cunt, which Caroline was stroking with vigorous up-and-down slaps, began to spurt into the pot.

'You've got the knack already,' said Aaliz. 'You're one of us. I say . . . I'd like to kiss you. Would you mind?'

'No,' Caroline panted, 'I'd like that.'

'I'm almost off, you see, and it's so sweet to come when you're kissing,' Aaliz said, then pressed her lips to Caroline's.

Penetrating Caroline's mouth, her tongue met Caroline's, and the two girls drooled in a firm, sucking kiss, as they frigged.

'Mm . . . mm . . .' Aaliz groaned.

'Urrgh . . .' Caroline gasped.

'Mm! *Mm* . . .!'

'*Ahh* . . .'

They writhed in orgasm, drool flowing from their kissing lips, as come flooded from their cunts. Caroline held up her come pot, astounded that it was half full.

'Gosh,' Caroline said, as their lips parted, with a smack – mwah! – 'I've come and wanked so much today! Yet still, I feel I want more.'

'That's why you're here,' murmured Aaliz. 'You're a heavy juicer, girl.'

Caroline went to the fridge, and unstoppered her come bottle, carefully pouring in her glassful of come, and laughing as it tinkled in the bottle.

'What a fabulous, jealous-making bottom,' crooned Aaliz. 'I could – I could – oh, but there isn't time. Tell you what, there's something very important I want to discuss with you. Why don't I visit you after lights out? We'll have all our time for – *you* know – if you'd like to, that is.'

'I'm not sure I do know,' Caroline replied.

'Well, a proper cuddle – both of us nude.'

'A lesbo pash?' Caroline blurted.

'Heavens, no. We're not lesbos, are we? That's unthinkable. Just a super-hot cuddle. Surely you've done that.'

'Yes,' said Caroline, thinking of Miss Chew, 'I suppose I have.'

'I mean, if there were boys around, things would be different. We can sneak out for a seeing-to from the coarse fellows in Trelashen village, or flower pickers from St Ives, if you like *that* sort of thing –' she sniffed '– but otherwise we girls must pleasure ourselves. It's the Furrow Weald way, and it keeps us wet for when our dream chap is going to pick us from the showroom.'

She kissed Caroline again, then licked her nose, which made Caroline giggle.

'Are we on?'

'Yes,' Caroline said.

'Right-ho. See you after lights out, then. By the way, don't talk to anyone about my visit, and don't greet me at supper, or I might have to cane you.'

Caroline felt like a shower, as the zinc ointment, though marvellously weal-soothing, was greasy, while the sweat and come from her wank with Aaliz compounded the slippery feeling. Taking a rather fetching shower cap of pink rubber from her armoire, along with a towel and her purse, she padded along the corridor towards the gurgles and smells of the washroom. The chamber was large, with all facilities open to view: showers, washbasins with mirrors and a row of toilet seats, side by side, over a gurgling drainage runnel. There was only one other girl in the washroom, a luscious, big-titted black girl, who squatted in the centre of the toilet row. Caroline nodded, smiling, and decided that she did need to pee and dung, and before she could decorously select a discreet position, the black girl patted the seat next to her.

'Take a pew,' she sang.

Anxious to follow Furrovian etiquette, Caroline slid her buttocks onto the seat next to the ebony girl. It was impossible to ignore the girl's massive breasts, smooth and creamy as black silk, and jutting firm as cannon balls, topped with hugely domed caramel nipples. Nor, close up, could she fail to admire the girl's extra-large buttocks, voluptuously full and curved, leading to wide, rippling thighs, parted on the toilet seat, so as to display her satin-shaved pubis, and the glistening pink meat inside the dark cooze folds. Her clitty stuck up like a little pink thumb.

'Hello, chum,' said the girl, flashing her dazzling white teeth.

Caroline felt a stab of worry if her teeth were white enough. She brushed twice a day, as she had been taught, but was it enough? At once, her fingers unconsciously crept to her bottom, and she winced, as she touched her cane weals. Was her bottom *firm* enough . . . ?

'I'm Merilee Caine,' said the ebony girl.

'Caroline Letchmount.'

'Just arrived?'

Caroline nodded.

'I've been here a week. It's absolutely frightful. Full of damn lesbos.'

'What about these gangs, the Stingers and Swanks?'

Merilee rolled her eyes. 'Hush, maid! It's a flogging offence just to *mention* those. Now, I expect you want a good wank.'

Caroline blushed. 'Why, no, that is, I've just had one.'

'Please yourself,' said Merilee. 'You don't mind if I do myself? You've such a fabulous bod, such lovely welts – sorry, but they *are* lovely – I'll be off in no time.'

Whistling, Merilee put her fingers to her gash, and began to masturbate, pausing every so often to let a stream of piss clatter into the runnel, and then tensing her belly, as dungs plopped from her anus.

'That's better.' She sighed. 'Now I can enjoy a jolly good frig.'

Caroline, too, sighed, as pee hissed from her opened cooze. 'Yes,' she said, 'there's nothing like the pleasure of a good pee.'

'Nothing?' said Merilee, arching her sculpted eyebrows. 'I can think of something.'

Caroline giggled, and told Merilee all about her day's experiences, her self-basting, and her sore bumhole, though she left out the visit from Aaliz de Brest. Merilee did not volunteer, or had no opportunity to volunteer, much information about herself, save to cluck sympathetically, and assure Caroline that all new bitches went through the same.

'Are you sure you won't join me in a diddle?' she purred.

Caroline scanned the black girl's *fabulous* body.

'Oh, all right then,' she blurted, blushing, as she slid her fingers down her tummy to her piss-wet cunt flaps. She began to wank her clitty, licking her lips, as pleasure made her spine tingle, and her nubbin stiffen and throb.

'You've a gorgeous gourd,' Merilee said, with her eyes on Caroline's pulsing bare cunt mound. 'I've never seen one so big. It's like an extra bottom.'

'Oh, they all say that,' gasped Caroline, her cooze dripping come, as she wanked hard. 'It's a blessing or a curse, I don't know.'

'Definitely a blessing,' Merilee replied. 'Titties, arse pears, gourd, a wonderful cosmic harmony.'

'You can touch, if you like,' Caroline murmured.

'Why, thank you.'

The girl's soft fingertips caressed the mons, above Caroline's masturbating fingers. Soon, they slipped down to the gash, to enlace Caroline's, and Caroline's right hand slipped between Merilee's thighs, to wet themselves in her copious juice. She touched Merilee's erect clitty, and Merilee jumped, with a shrill whistle.

'Whew! *That's* nice,' she said.

There was a loud plop, as a stream of dungs spurted from Caroline's bumhole.

'Ooh, that's nice too,' Caroline said.

'You *are* a tease.'

'Mm . . . don't stop.'

'No. Mm . . .'

'Ooh!'

'Ahh!'

The girls brought each other off simultaneously, their cunt juices splashing into the flowing runnel. Merilee sprang to her feet, and pulled Caroline by the wrist, into the shower. Caroline gazed on the bare black body, the coltishly long legs, the flat, narrow belly, the ripely jutting bum pears, and the huge, quivering titty flans, topped with the outrageously big, stiff nipples, like twin cathedral domes. She laughed as Merilee opened the shower tap with a flick of her titties, and eagerly responded as the black girl began to soap her soaking body.

She lathered Merilee's back and buttocks, then soaped her titties, squashing and kneading the massive bulbs, while Merilee grinned, licking her teeth. The two girls pressed their titties and cunt mounds together, their arms snaked, locking them in a tight embrace, and Caroline's lips swooped, to kiss Merilee's, in a long, sucking clasp of tongues. She felt Merilee's fingers at her bum cleft, stroking her weals, then tickling her anus bud, and penetrating her with a fingertip.

'Ooh,' she moaned, her buttocks clenching, to trap Merilee's invading finger. 'I like that. Have we time for another . . . you know?'

She pressed Merilee's firm velvet buttocks, mashing their wet cunts together, and found Merilee's bumhole, slipping a finger inside the hot moist elastic of the anus.

'That's the one good thing about this place,' Merilee cooed. 'They want us to wank off, to keep us hot all the time, for the showroom, and such. That's why we have to bare up so much. Bare-beating makes a girl hot to wank. And it makes her bumhole ticklish, so she needs arse-tupping. It's scientifically proven. Mm . . .'

Her slippery body writhed against Caroline's, breasts slapping wetly, as Caroline kissed her hard.

It's just like snogging a boy, except Merilee is heaps lovelier than any boy . . .

The bell rang for supper.

'Cripes, we're out of time,' said Merilee. 'Tell you what, I'll come to your room after lights out, and we can have a lovely cuddle. OK?'

'I'd love to,' Caroline began, 'but –'

'That's fixed, then. Come on, we mustn't dawdle, or it's a thrashing. I'll show you the ropes in the refectory. Guzzle as fast as you can – you won't like it.'

They dried off, and Caroline dashed to her room, to hide her purse under her mattress, and get rid of her towel. She lined up with the other naked new bitches (as Caroline couldn't help calling herself), behind maids in short shoulder-strapped tunics, over nude bodies, with white socks and gym shoes, maids in blouses and miniskirts, with white ankle socks and buckled shoes, and maids in diverse frocks and frillies, with shiny high heels. Merilee whispered that those were maids, junior maids and schoolmaids, or seniors. Caroline remembered she was still wearing her shower cap, then saw that a few other girls, those with long tresses, also had white or blue rubber caps – not Merilee, whose luxurious tight curls clung to her scalp in a gleaming helmet. As the senior girls began to shuffle into the landing, and down the wide stone staircase, Bronwen Bellibone swaggered towards the new bitches, swishing her cane, and the line of nude girls was cowed to silence.

'Talking, Merilee?' she hissed.

'Please, miss, a mosquito bit me,' Merilee mumbled.

'Really? Like this?'

Vip!

'Or this?'

Vip!

'Or this?'

Vip!

Merilee winced, grimacing, as three stingers lashed her directly on the nipples, leaving wide pink streaks across her ebony breasts. The other ten or so girls looked away.

'What about you, bitch?' she snarled at Caroline. 'Think your pretty pink cap will protect you from mosquitoes?'

Vip! Caroline gasped, as a stinger seared her naked buttocks, landing just in one of her most crusted and painful weals. Tears leapt to her eyes.

'N-no, mistress,' she mumbled, head hung low, and longing, but not daring, to rub her smarting bottom.

Bronwen ordered them to cross their hands at the top of their buttocks. All, including Caroline, obeyed, and Bronwen passed down the line, snapping plastic handcuffs on each girl's wrists. This done, she threaded a rope through the loop in each pair of handcuffs.

'Anyone else for mosquito stings?' Bronwen guffawed. 'No? Off to the trough, then, sluts.'

She tightened the rope with a jerk, and led the tethered girls to their meal.

6

Face Rider

Bare bottoms flicked by Bronwen's cane, the new bitches shuffled into the refectory. Above them, at high table, sat Mistress Frubbin, with her schoolmistresses and school-maids, served by waitresses in frilly French maid costumes, with wine, silverware and crisp linen napery. Below them, in the body of the oak-raftered hall, sat the maids and juniors, with uniformed prefects at the head and foot of each table, while other prefects patrolled the aisles, canes swinging. One of them was Aaliz de Brest, but she ignored Caroline's glance. Frilly maids passed, with trolleys of steaming soup, meats and potatoes, and every girl seemed to scoff heartily, the rafters ringing with shrill chatter. Other maids, responding to cries of 'Fill me, bumpkin!' poured from jugs of beer, and Caroline thought it quaintly mediaeval.

Right before the kitchens and serving hatch stood a long wooden trough, with a post at each end. Bronwen ordered the new bitches to stand before the trough, and hitched each end of their tethering rope to a post.

'Kneel, sluts,' she barked, and the maids obeyed.

Caroline knelt, with her arms thrust painfully above her back, in strappado, by the taut rope fixed to her handcuffs, and her face pushed almost into the trough.

'Slop, bumpkin!' Bronwen cried.

A sullen maid in a brief frilled skirtlet, showing her knickers, and black fishnet stockings, hobbled on high heels from the kitchen, bearing a large pot. She emptied its contents into the top of the trough, passing down its length, to scatter the stinking food equally amongst the tethered maids. At once, there was a noise of gobbling, as the girls plunged their faces in the trough, and ate voraciously. Caroline wrinkled her nose; the trough was full of congealed soup, bits of meat and fish, half-munched vegetables, stale bread and potato peelings, or anything that a normal cook would throw away. Vip! She winced, squirming at a horrid stinger from Bronwen's cane, that took her right in her spread arse cleft.

'Better eat, slut,' Bronwen snapped. 'Any slop you leave will still be here at breakfast.'

Caroline realised she was hungry; all her orgasms had given her an appetite. She lowered her face, recoiling at the impact of a cold, soggy onion on her nose, then took a deep breath, pressed her face deep into the muck, and began to swallow. There was something fishy, something meaty – ugh! It was too horrible to think about. She turned, to see Merilee gobbling. The black girl raised her dripping face and flashed her teeth in a grin, which gave Caroline the encouragement to continue. She had to fend off the faces on either side of her, their snouts invading Caroline's territory, so that eating became a battle.

More slops arrived, as tables were cleared for pudding, and Caroline was distracted by a turmoil at the far end of the hall. One of the slop bumpkins had spilled something; Aaliz de Brest wrenched her hair, and forced her head into a full tureen of soup (or maybe custard). She ripped off the maid's skirtlet and flimsy knickers, and caned the bare bottom a good dozen lashes, very fast, with a tap–tap–tap. The maids cheered, and even the girls at high table turned to laugh and raise their wine glasses. When the caned girl was released, gasping for breath and scarlet with tears, she rubbed her wealed fesses, groping for her skirt and panties, while maids pelted her with bread rolls. Caroline was the only new bitch who even bothered to observe the shameful punishment, and it meant she had to eat extra fast to get her share of the jam pudding and custard, now dropping into the trough. With the other bitches, she licked the wooden surface clean, realising that her belly was pleasingly, if not tastily full.

Darkness was falling, and new bitches slept at darkness, to rise with the dawn. Caroline was tired, and oddly pleased at her full belly – a small victory over the system – despite the ache in her arms. Bronwen marched her bitches back to their floor, passing, on the way, the video lounge, where another group of junior maids chortled at a taped *Up Your Raspberry*. The unctuous Funn, and his horrid sidekick Greta, leered, as prize-hungry girls in their undies wrestled in mud pools, or were buried in sand, smeared with honey and assailed by flies; the losers, those voted off by the telly audience, were further humiliated by loud raspberries from the survivors, and kicks up the bottom from Greta.

Caroline shuddered, thinking that maybe there were worse places than Furrow Weald, and if the reward of submission to discipline, scarcely worse than at any English girls' boarding school, was her launch into society as a complete English lady, then perhaps there were few better places. Comforted by this thought, she docilely lined up with the others, in front of their cell doors, and masturbated, cup under quim, for Bronwen Bellibone's evening wank parade. Sneaking glances at Merilee's naked body – and with Merilee sneaking glances at *her* – Caroline was one of the first to fill her cup with come, and heave in orgasm, after which she was excused.

She flopped naked into bed – new bitches not being supplied with nighties – listening to the lash of Bronwen's cane on the bottom of the hapless maid who was last to climax. Smugly assuring herself that it was never likely to be her, she drifted off to sleep, as the lights on the corridor went out, with her hand caressing her bare bottom, no longer throbbing, but with the ridged weals almost quaint and friendly. Her tummy felt all warm and cosy, after her evening wank. What a sensible idea. Despite the ever-present menace of strokes, it was certainly not a bad rule, which actually *encouraged* a girl's basic instinct to diddle as much as possible. She dreamed happily of more wanks tomorrow, and the next day, and ever after . . .

Moonlight beamed through her open window, as a pinch of her thigh awakened her. She sat up groggily, and threw her sweaty sheet aside, to see a tall figure in silhouette.

'It's me, Aaliz,' whispered the intruder. 'You hadn't forgotten?'

'Why, no, Aaliz,' Caroline mumbled. 'How pretty you look.'

The prefect wore a diaphanous lime-green nylon shortie-nightie, with her cane strapped to her bare waist underneath, its tip poking under the high frilly hem.

'Sweet,' she cooed. 'Well, here I am.'

She slid her nightie over her head, and lay down, nude, beside Caroline. They embraced, the cane pressing into Caroline's cooze, and Aaliz gave a little laugh, saying it was second nature to wear one's cane at all times.

'It's a gutta-percha ferule,' she said proudly. 'The most painful, for the most senior prefects.'

She unstrapped it, placing it within easy reach on the bedside table, and pressed her lips to Caroline's mouth. Breasts squashed together, they kissed passionately, tongues slurping, and hands exploring their nude bodies.

'We must be careful,' Aaliz whispered. 'If Bronwen Bellibone catches us, my prefect's rod means nothing *here*.'

They squatted cross-legged, nipples touching, and leaned forwards to kiss. Aaliz's toes tickled Caroline's spread gash flaps, poked inside the slit, and began to frot her clitty. Gasping with pleasure, Caroline did the same, and got her big toe inside Aaliz's pouch, waggling and slicing the wet cunt walls, and mashing the girl's distended nubbin. Cunt spurting come, Aaliz slithered closer, and stroked Caroline's shaven cooze gourd, already wet with cunt-juice. They straightened their bodies, and pressed them together in slippery embrace, fingers exploring wet gashes, while their tongues slurped and lips sucked, in squelching kisses, that had drool dripping from their chins onto their squashed titties. Aaliz gasped, as Caroline's fingers penetrated her.

'Yes,' she moaned, 'fuck me, Caroline.'

Her own fingers began to dance on Caroline's throbbing, stiff clitty, making Caroline's legs scissor, as she gasped at the shock of electric pleasure. The girls masturbated, with Aaliz's thumb and forefinger tweaking Caroline's nubbin, while Caroline jabbed Aaliz's wombneck with three fingers pressed together, and sliding easily up and down the wet slit, her sharp nails slicing the swollen clitty on the downthrust. Aaliz's cunt basin writhed, slapping against Caroline's belly, as the prefect moaned, with a low gurgle deep in her throat.

'Oh . . . it's so good . . . where did you learn to do that?'

Caroline answered with another hard, extra-sloppy kiss, her tongue penetrating Aaliz's throat. As she wanked Caroline's clitty, Aaliz's palm cupped Caroline's gourd.

'Oh, you're so big . . . I must . . .' Aaliz groaned.

She removed her hand from Caroline's lathered twat, and, slithering down the bed, pressed her mouth to the gash flaps, licking and sucking, while her lips chewed Caroline's clit, like a lolly.

'Urrgh,' Caroline gasped, pulling Aaliz by the toes.

'Oh! Don't tickle,' murmured Aaliz, her voice vibrating through Caroline's cunt.

Caroline did tickle the girl's toes and soles, which had her writhing and jerking, her teeth biting Caroline's clitty in short, teasing nips, while her nose rubbed the smooth, swelling orb of the cunt gourd. The girls gamahuched, face to twat, and toes entwined in each other's hair. Aaliz pulled Caroline on top of her, and Caroline tongue-fucked the girl's cunt, pausing to suck and bite the stiff clitty, while Aaliz drank the juices from Caroline's gash, writhing on her face. Caroline sucked up Aaliz's pussy juice, swallowing it, and finding it tasted quite nice.

'Fuck me,' Aaliz moaned, over and over. 'Fuck me.'

Caroline panted, as her belly convulsed. 'I'm nearly there,' she gasped. 'Ooh, yes . . . how about you, Aaliz?'

'Nearly,' rasped the wriggling girl. 'Fuck me hard, fuck me.'

'Ahh!'

'Ooh!'

'Ah! Ah!'

'Oh! Yes!'

Aaliz's fingers clawed Caroline's bum weals, making her bum buck, and her twat slap Aaliz's face, as both girls groaned in gushing spasm.

'Gosh, Caroline,' Aaliz moaned into Caroline's cunt, 'would you . . . I mean, I need you to . . . I'm so shy . . . oh, would you . . .?

'Anything,' Caroline gasped.

Aaliz's fingers groped for the gutta-percha ferule, and thrust it into Caroline's hand.

'You want me to *cane* you?' Caroline whispered.

'Mm-mm,' Aaliz murmured.

She wriggled away from Caroline, without looking at her, and raised her buttocks at a crouch, while burying her head under Caroline's pillow.

'Cane my bare bum raw, my sweet,' she crooned, in her muffled voice.

Caroline's fingers stroked the springy little cane. 'Gosh,' she blurted, 'this is hard. Are you sure I won't hurt you?'

'That's the idea, silly. Please, hurry, make my bum smart. I've been longing for it. But it's difficult, as a prefect, and as – well, you'll see.'

Caroline planted her feet well apart on the floor, and lifted the heavy little flogger over Aaliz's buttocks, straining upwards, as if pleading for the lash. Between the fesses peeped the bare cooze slice, streaming with wetness, which streaked the girl's quivering thighs. New come soaked Caroline's own gash, as she planted a kiss to the virgin white buttocks, and began to masturbate.

'I'm in a mood to hurt you,' she warned.

'Yes, please.'

'That bum's too lovely.'

'Flatterer. Hurt me.'

Caroline raised the ferule. Vip! She sliced it hard across mid-fesse, raising a long pink weal. The bottom shivered, and there was a gasping bleat from under the pillow. Caroline's hand gently tweaked her throbbing clitty, fingers squelching in the come flowing from her gash, as she lifted the cane again. Vip!

'Mm.'

Vip! The pale buttocks were churning, clenching and wriggling, with pink stripes showing livid. Vip!

'Mm.'

Vip! Caroline lashed the girl straight in the bum cleft.

'*Ooh*!' Aaliz's face, streaked with tears, emerged from her pillow. 'That wasn't fair!'

'Stop snivelling, bitch. You asked for it, remember?' Caroline snarled.

As she licked her lips, at the sight of the helpless buttocks, quivering under her lash, Caroline's fingers vigorously masturbated her cunt, spurting copious come down her thighs. Vip! Vip! Two more strokes took Aaliz in the bum cleft, the ferule stroking the anus bud, with its tip slapping her wet pendant cunt flaps, and her bottom squirmed madly.

'Ooh! Ooh,' she gasped, beneath the pillow. 'Don't stop.'

Vip! The cane lashed her top buttock. Vip! Caroline sliced her fleshy underfesses, at the thigh tops, and began to weal the thighs, lower and lower. Aaliz's bum and thighs wriggled furiously, a deep, moaning wail came from beneath her pillow, and her head thumped the mattress. Vip! Vip! Caroline began to work on her tender haunches, which striped deep and quickly, with a paroxysm of squirming from the whipped girl. Vip! Vip! Caroline's fingers squelched on her rigid clitty, which throbbed, as come gushed from her wanked cunt, while Aaliz's cooze also poured come over her thighs. Vip! A cut took Aaliz between the gash flaps, slapping the clit.

'Ahh! Oh! Oh!'

'You haven't said how many strokes you want,' Caroline panted.

'It's up to you, mistress. That's the beauty of it. I'm helpless in your power. I love it when you call me "bitch" – don't you like caning my bare? Seeing it writhe?'

'Yes,' Caroline gasped, wanking fiercely. 'Yes, I do.'

'You cane so well, so cruelly, as if born to it. That's why –'

Vip! A cut across the mid-fesse, in an existing weal, made the buttocks writhe.

'Ouch!'

'Go on, bitch. Why what?'

'I'm here to recruit you . . . for the Stingers.'

'A gang,' Caroline hissed.

'We prefer "maidband".'

'I thought you *liked* me.'

Vip! Vip!

'Ooh! Ouch! Yes, I do, sweet Caroline. That's exactly why –'

Vip! Vip!

'Ahh!'

Aaliz's head peeped from the pillow. She wiped tears from her face, which was wrinkled in agony. 'Don't stop caning me, mistress. Oh, please! I beg you, wank your sweet twat, as you watch me squirm for you.'

Her hand darted to her sopping cunt, and she began to wank quite furiously. Vip! Caroline caned her hand off the gash flaps.

'You'll wank when I say, bitch.'

'Oh! Yes, mistress.'

Vip! The caning continued, with the flogged bum an increasingly dense tapestry of welts, and the patches of pale, unbruised skin disappearing under crimson, while Aaliz gasped her explanation. The Stingers and Swanks were deadly enemies, their rivalry going back to the very foundation of Furrow Weald in the seventeenth century. Originally, the games were harmless – Stingers were submissives, who liked to bare up for the rod, and Swanks were dominants, who liked to administer it. Those early distinctions had blurred. Stingers were supposed to be subs, but needed whippers, to pleasure them, while the Swanks needed subs within their own ranks, to practise on. If a gang member trapped an enemy, her duty was to flog the maid's bottom to ribbons, until the maid was so sore, she couldn't walk. Both maidbands needed subs, who could willingly take such punishments, and dominants, to inflict them. In sum, Swanks were *basically* dominant, and Stingers *basically* submissive.

'I'm no sub,' Caroline growled.

'Are you sure? Darling, all girls are submissive at heart. You have shown wonderful bravery under bare-beating.'

Vip! Vip!

'Ooh! Oh!'

The moon shone directly on Aaliz's writhing bare arse globes, streaked black, blue and crimson, the welts dancing like a rainbow in the pale gleam.

'A girl has to take the cane, at St Radegund's, and keep a stiff upper lip.'

'But you can switch, like a true goth – you thrashed Miss Chew, just as sweetly as you're caning me,' Aaliz said.

'How do you know?'

'Our maidband has its intelligence service.'

Vip! Vip! Masturbating hard, Caroline lashed the buttocks with all her strength, determined to make Aaliz pay for her cynical treachery.

'Ooh!' Aaliz squealed, fesses wriggling. 'I'm sure I won't recognise my bum, afterwards. It's glorious – the best caning I've ever had. Please join the Stingers, Caroline. We get extra tuck and cash, and exeats to go to St Ives for lovely fudge teas and real Cornish pasties. Mistress Frubbin, like all mistresses before her, must tacitly accept maidbands' privilege, and it's all *totally secret.* You'll be able to go straight to junior maid, and have your own gutta-percha ferule, I promise. That's an immense privilege. And –'

Vip! Vip!

'Ooh!'

'And what?'

'We can sneak out along the weald, to Trelashen village, and meet *boys*.'

'My own gutta-percha ferule?'

'Of course. I've taken forty-seven strokes – I've counted – just imagine thrashing a Swank's beastly arse, or the loving canes your own bottom will enjoy.'

Vip! Vip!

'Ooh!'

'I'm not sure the cane should be loving. Wank yourself off,' Caroline commanded.

As Aaliz masturbated, with a few deft strokes, to a gushing, shuddering orgasm, Caroline flicked her clitty twice, and exploded in her own spasm.

'I'm in,' she panted. 'I'll be a Stinger.'

There was the creak of a door, and footsteps padding in the corridor.

'Quick,' hissed Caroline. 'Hide in the armoire.'

Still rubbing her wealed bottom, and groaning softly, Aaliz sprang to her feet, and darted to the armoire, leaving a telltale spray of come on the linoleum. Caroline thrust Aaliz's nightie and ferule under her bed, lay down, and feigned sleep. Just as the armoire door clicked behind Aaliz, Caroline's cell door swung open, and a tall body entered, bare black breasts bobbing, and ebony skin glistening in the moonlight.

'Hi, Caroline,' said Merilee Caine.

'Merilee, you startled me,' said Caroline, sitting up.

Merilee pulled the sheet from Caroline's naked body. 'Did I? You're all sweaty, girl.'

'I must have been dreaming.'

'Of me, I hope,' Merilee said, sitting on the bed beside Caroline, and parting her thighs wide. 'From here, your twat looks good and juicy. And that gorgeous gourd on top.' Her slender fingers opened the lips of her cunt, showing Caroline the wet pink slit flesh. 'I'm juicy too, Caroline, thinking of your gorgeous bottom.'

Caroline smiled coyly, wiping a hair from her brow. 'Mine is scarcely as gorgeous as yours,' she murmured.

'Let's find out,' said Merilee, sliding on the bed, beside Caroline, and embracing her tightly, with their breasts pressed together.

'Oh!' Caroline gasped. 'You're crushing me.'

'Not yet,' whispered the black girl.

Caroline reached down, and pulled the sheet over them.

'Modest?' Merilee laughed.

'Someone might see.'

'The man in the moon? It's too hot for modesty.'

The sheet crumpled to the floor, and the girls writhed in nude embrace. Merilee kissed Caroline, in a long, wet tongue-probe, while her fingers squeezed and teased Caroline's stiffening nipples.

'Ooh, that's lovely,' Caroline gasped.

She broke away from Merilee's kiss, and squirmed down to the massive black teats, where she filled her mouth with Merilee's right nipple, and began to lick and suck. Her tongue and teeth danced on the big fleshy dome, while Merilee pressed her head to the teat.

'Suck me, bitch,' Merilee crooned. Caroline sucked the nipple powerfully, and Merilee began to wriggle, gasping. 'Mm! It's good.'

Caroline's hand slid down Merilee's writhing back, to the top of her bum cleft, and began to caress the firm arse globes, while Merilee squashed Caroline's face into her teats. Caroline found the quim, gushing come, and slipped her fingers an inch inside, thumbing the huge stiff clitty, and making the black girl jerk, yelping.

'Oh! Yes!'

Caroline's finger crept down the perineum, and tickled the anus bud, then penetrated the bumhole, and began to probe. Merilee clawed Caroline's nape, crushing her nose and mouth into her massive breasts. Her thighs flailed, as Caroline's finger reamed her anal elastic, then plopped out, to tickle the stiff clitty.

'Yes! Wank me, you sweet bitch,' Merilee gasped.

Caroline felt two firm palms on her bottom, the nails caressing and clawing her bum welts. Her cunt spurted come; she groaned, and bit Merilee's nipple, hard. Merilee yelped.

'Ooh, you bitch,' she gasped, her strong fingers parting Caroline's gash flaps and stabbing inside.

Caroline's bum and cunt basin wriggled on the impaling fingers, as Merilee found her throbbing clitty, and began to pinch and rub. The two girls gasped, writhing in mutual masturbation. Suddenly, Merilee broke free, wrenching her buttocks from Caroline's fingers, and sprang up, to plunge her cunt, with a wet smack, on Caroline's face.

'Urrgh!' Caroline squealed, as Merilee's squashing buttocks began to churn powerfully, crushing her face, with squelchy plopping gurgles from her cunt spurting come into Caroline's mouth.

'Love me, bitch,' Merilee commanded.

Caroline's hands pressed Merilee's arse pears to her face, while Merilee reached back, her outstretched fingers clamping Caroline's gushing cunt, and masturbated the wriggling maid with one hand, the other squeezing and clawing Caroline's titties. Caroline tasted warm pussy juice, her nose pressed to the silky smoothness of the black girl's cooze hillock.

'What a fabulous gourd,' Caroline gasped. 'So big and black and creamy, like a lovely pudding.'

Merilee's rippling thighs clamped Caroline's head, while she ground her buttocks into her face, pressing her quim lips and extruded clitty into Caroline's mouth. She wriggled, so that Caroline's face was squashed by her anus, and Caroline got her tongue an inch inside the tight bumhole; then, she moved up, to press Caroline's face with her wet, fleshy cunt, so that Caroline fastened the black girl's clitty between her teeth, and began to chew, while sucking the juice that cascaded in heavy spurts from Merilee's slit. Caroline gurgled, as she drank the black girl's copious come.

'I want you to be mine, Caroline,' said Merilee. 'I'm your face rider. Are you my bitch, maid?'

'Mm . . . yes . . . mm,' Caroline groaned, her buttocks slamming the bed, as the black girl frigged her sex.

Caroline's squirming bum slithered in the pool of her own come, while her hair was drenched with Merilee's pussy juice, which was dripping down her face. Merilee began to moan, her breath a harsh rasp, and her titties bouncing, as she rode Caroline's face. Her fingers pinched Caroline's clitty and Caroline squealed.

'Mm . . . mm . . . I'm going to . . .'

'Yes!' Merilee cried. 'Suck me, bitch!'

'Mm.'

'Oh, yes!'

'*Ahh! Ooh!*'

'*Urrgh! Mm!*'

Their cunts spurting come, the two girls exploded in climax. As Caroline writhed in her orgasm, Merilee swivelled, and, with her quim still pressed to Caroline's mouth and nose, plunged her own face between the lips of Caroline's wanked cunt. She gurgled, drinking Caroline's come, and making Caroline's twat spurt *more* come. The black girl kissed and licked her clitty, until Caroline moaned anew, knowing she was going to climax *again.* The flow of come into her own mouth, from Merilee's pussy, was unabated, with the thrashing of the meaty black buttocks making her think Merilee had not even stopped coming. The two girls writhed, bodies slippery with come and sweat, until Caroline gasped, her spine electric with pleasure, and spurted a wash of pussy juice into the black girl's greedily sucking mouth; as the waves of pleasure shook her, Caroline heard Merilee noisily swallowing her come, and whimpered at the explosive force of her new orgasm.

Merilee slithered loose and, at once, the girls were in each other's arms, cuddling and kissing, each girl's face smeared with the other's come. Quims and titties pressed, with hands cupping bare slimy buttocks, they licked each other's faces, giggling softly.

'I *am* yours, Merilee,' Caroline gasped.

Merilee put a finger to her lips. 'Sshh,' she whispered. 'This is top secret.'

'I'm listening,' Caroline whispered back. 'Stroke my bottom, Merilee. I love your fingers on my bum weals. They are so lovely and sensitive – it's quite true that bare-bum caning leaves a girl hot.'

Merilee giggled. 'That's what my cousin Clive says. He's corporate hospitality director for FernandOil, in San Fernando.'

'Where's that?'

'Off the coast of West Africa. It's where I come from. Very rich. Lots of oil and cigar tobacco.'

'How exciting!'

'It is . . . for certain girls.' She caressed Caroline's bum weals. 'I want you to join us,' she said. 'Our maidband, the Swanks.'

'You, a gang girl, Merilee?' Caroline gasped. 'But you've only been here a week.'

'I was recruited straight away – I can't say by whom – and I get a shilling for new recruits. But that's not the reason. I want *you*, Caroline – your bottom and cunt to be *mine*.'

'So that you can cane me?'

'That fabulous bum begs for stripes.'

'I'm not a sub,' Caroline blurted. 'At least, I don't think so. But you are so dominant, Merilee, like a cruel, sleek panther. I . . . I long to submit to you.'

'I know about you thrashing Miss Chew,' Merilee whispered, 'and that beastly prefect, Bulstrode. You can be a tiger. Maybe you're a goth, a girl who can switch from sub to dom. Just what we Swanks need.'

'It seems everyone knows more about me than I do.'

'That's any girl's fate. Join us, Caroline. There are oodles of perks and treats.' Licking Caroline's ear, she stroked her tingling fesses.

'You want me to cane you, don't you?'

'Oh! Yes. You're making me so wet.'

'Say you're a Swank.'

'I'll join,' Caroline moaned. 'I'm a Swank. There. Now please cane me . . . mistress.'

'I shall. Is your self-baster in the armoire?'

'Yes. I mean, no!'

Caroline's hand flew her lips. Already, Merilee was opening the armoire.

'What's this?' she hissed.

'Ooh! Ouch! You're hurting me!' cried Aaliz, as Merilee dragged her by the hair from her hiding place.

The black girl scanned the floor, spied Aaliz's leaked come, and then kicked her nightie and cane from under the bed. 'A pair of damn lesbos,' she spat.

Caroline blurted that she needed to pee, and Merilee scornfully pushed the chamber pot towards her. While Caroline squatted, filling the pot with a torrent of steaming pee, Merilee, teeth bared in a snarl, ripped Aaliz's lime-green nightie to ribbons, and pushed the whimpering girl face down on the bed.

'So you fucking lesbos have been playing caning games,' she sneered. 'Well, this is no game.'

She knotted Aaliz's ankles and wrists together, then wadded the rest of the nightie into Aaliz's mouth, as a gag. Aaliz squirmed and squealed, while Merilee lashed her with her own gutta-percha ferule.

Vip! Vip!

'Urrgh! Mm!' the flogged girl squealed, as her welts darkened in new livid blotches of purple.

Vip! Vip!

'Mm!'

Vip! Vip!

'Mm!'

Caroline gazed at the sinuous grace of the black girl's nude body, thigh, arm and buttock muscles rippling, and breasts bouncing, as she caned Aaliz's wriggling bottom, lifting her arm high, before lashing the wealed bum flesh. Aaliz's eyes were wet with tears, her face scarlet, and her bound wrists and ankles jerked helplessly. Drool streamed from her nightie gag, as she wept and squirmed, bleating at each pitiless lash of the cane. Caroline stared at the flogged bum, licking her lips, as she squatted on the chamber pot, spurts of come mingling with her piss. After over a minute's flogging, Aaliz's buttocks were criss-crossed with weals.

Panting, and dripping sweat, Merilee wrenched Caroline's hair, and lifted her off the pot, her cunt still spraying pee. She forced Caroline to kneel, buttocks up, and tied her wrists at her bum cleft, then pushed her face into the brimming chamber pot. Merilee held Caroline's head down, with a bare sole pressing her nape. Vip! Vip!

'Urrgh!' Caroline gurgled, her head immersed in her own pee, as the cane lashed her bottom.

Vip! Vip!

'Mm!'

Vip! Vip!

'Ooh!'

Bubbles sprang from Caroline's mouth, to foam the surface of the piss, as her head thrashed underwater, banging the sides of the chamber pot. Aaliz, groaning and snuffling, gazed at Caroline's squirming bottom. Vip! Vip! The smarting pain was dreadful, worse than anything Caroline could imagine, and her lungs burst with the effort of holding her breath. Yet her clitty tingled and, in this deepest humiliation, she felt new come spurting from her cooze and trickling down her thighs. After two dozen rapid cuts, Merilee wrenched her head up, and she spluttered, gasping.

'You're juicing, bitch,' the black girl snarled. 'Maybe you're not such a goth – a beastly sub!'

'No . . .' Caroline wailed, before Merilee pushed her face once more under the pee, and recommenced her caning.

Come poured faster from Caroline's cunt, as her caned bottom quivered. Aaliz no longer whimpered, but was rubbing her thighs together, and frigging at Caroline's shame. That made Caroline's clitty throb harder.

Caned and shamed by a gorgeous naked black girl, while my friend watches, wanking off at my pain . . . why do I love it so?

The strokes went past fifty, and her cunt basin was all warm and tingly and throbbing. Vip! Vip! Merilee pulled her face from the chamber pot, and stuck her big toe between Caroline's cunt flaps, for a contemptuous mashing of her stiff clit.

'Ahh! *Ahh*!' Caroline squealed, as orgasm flooded her.

Merilee's own thighs were wet with copious come, dribbling from her naked slit. Her massive shaven gourd pulsed, like a bellows. She ripped the binding from Aaliz's ankles, and pulled her to her feet, then, holding her hair, kicked her bottom several times.

'If I thought you were one of those filthy Stingers, you wouldn't be *able* to walk,' Merilee snarled, kicking Aaliz out the door.

Wailing, Aaliz began to hobble, still weeping, gagged and wrist-bound. Merilee lifted Caroline, and embraced her, kissing her full on her piss-soaked lips.

'Oh, please love me, Merilee,' Caroline said, sobbing. 'Cane me, ride my face . . . I'm your bitch.'

'I'm surprised you don't thirst for revenge on *my* bottom.'

Caroline's eyes flashed. 'But I do,' she hissed. 'I'll have it. I'll cane that lovely black arse raw, one day.'

'That's a good Swank,' Merilee said. 'Perhaps we'll teach you to vanquish your submissiveness, and let the tigress out.'

Mwah! She kissed Caroline again, with a long, sensuous stroking of her smarting bottom, before slipping out the door. Caroline flopped back onto her bed, drenched with sweat and girl come, and fell into a warm satisfied doze.

Gosh, I'm a gang girl – twice!

Was she a Swank or a Stinger? Only by caning Merilee's ebony buttocks would she find the truth.

7

Swank Flogging

Caroline confidently adapted to the routine of a new bitch; even without the eventual perks of maidband membership, she would finish her basic training and wear proper school uniform. Furrow Weald *was* a proper school: gruelling hours of Latin, arithmetic, French, Italian, cookery and deportment, in the classroom, where the new bitches crouched nude at the front, and where the gowned and capped mistresses did not hesitate to punish infractions by even the most sumptuous senior schoolmaids with a severe caning. It was satisfying to watch a snooty senior lift her fine skirts and lacy pastel undies, for six or twelve stingers on the bare – even though a new bitch risked having her own bottom lashed for smirking.

The day began before dawn, when Bronwen Bellibone rooted the slumbering new bitches from their beds, to stand before their cell doors for wank parade. While they were filling their come pots, Bronwen inspected their refrigerated bottles, replacing filled bottles with empties. Wanking off was a hygienic ritual, to be practised as often and vigorously as possible, rather like brushing teeth, changing into clean undies, and – well, going to the lavatory; like those, it was not something you did everywhere, or all the time, and, like dunging, it was mentioned in ribald or coy tones – 'I've just had an absolutely *monster* wank!' or 'I feel *so* much better after my diddle.' Masturbation was to keep a maid 'hot', or 'fizzing', or 'regular'.

Morning wanks over, the girls marched at the double to the washroom, where they dunged, then shaved their quims, legs and armpits, while showering in freezing water. Afterwards, they trooped to the end of the corridor, and waited, shivering, while the junior maids were roused, nude, for their wank parade, last to awaken being the senior schoolmaids, who were excused morning masturbation. At last, they marched to the breakfast trough, where they gobbled scraps of bacon fat, egg, stale bread and sausage, the trough being flooded, finally, with tea dregs, and the thirsty girls drank it dry. Above them, the slop bumpkins would gossip about the Trelashen village boys, who sounded a rampant and lustful rustic crew, and singularly well-endowed, if the slop bumpkins' boasts were to be believed. 'My jamhole don't half hurt' and similar remarks made Caroline tingle with curiosity.

Three hours of lessons followed, with lots of homework given for after-supper prep, and then an hour's gym before lunch. All maids, senior or junior, exercised in the nude, and the exercises included netball, swimming, vaulting and soft-glove boxing. After luncheon, the maids had an hour's nap, during which they were expected to masturbate privately. Then, there was military drill, like gymnastics, performed outside, in the nude, save for straps, belts, packs and agonisingly painful hobnail boots. Each maid had her locker, in the changing room, where she kept her military kit. The new bitch battalion trained separately from the junior maids and schoolmaids, although, from Caroline's observation, the drill was as punishing for all.

Most important were the canvas straps of her harness, into which she had to buckle herself before drill, with Sergeant Pimella Plumply cracking her cane, until the straps were so tight, a maid could hardly breathe. The canvas had to be dazzling white, achieved with painstaking application of smelly blanco. The webbing harness enclasped a maid's torso, squeezing the breasts up and out, criss-crossing across back and belly, to pass across the buttocks and inner thighs, framing the exposed quim. The tightness of this restraining harness enforced proper posture, with arms rigid, as any sloppiness made it chafe abominably during marching.

The drill was more than marching; at any moment, they had to run on the spot, or drop, for twenty press-ups, with lashes of Pimella's cane on bare buttocks for any maid whose arms did not straighten fully, or whose titties did not squash flat onto the ground. On pain of a parade-ground flogging, sloppy or recalcitrant maids could be 'flagged': having to march with the stem of a red punishment flag inserted in the anus, and holding the flag at ninety degrees to the buttocks, requiring a vigorous pressure of the sphincter, as well as the discomfort of the wooden pole nudging the arse root. Or, a girl might be 'bricked': having her nipples fastened in clamps, from which heavy bricks were suspended; clamps and bricks might also be applied to her cunt flaps, stretching them grotesquely.

Early on, Caroline witnessed a drill flogging, and vowed never to earn one. The offender, a ripe-titted blonde named Emma Spivey, had to stand in a star shape, legs apart, with arms lifted and spread, and her torso bent forwards at 45 degrees precisely. Sergeant Plumply delivered a 'two bob' – twenty-four strokes of her gutta-percha ferule – to the maid's splayed bare buttocks and, during the punishment, Emma was not permitted to squeal or squirm, or the set would be repeated in full. Caroline watched Emma's fesses colour and weal, the pink turning to crimson, on the quaking bare skin, and could not restrain a flow of juice from her pussy, trickling down her thighs, but thankfully missing her white harness straps. She was not the only maid whose cunt moistened, watching the vicious caning.

After her chastisement, Emma had to march in boots without socks, and wear 'mushroom panties', for the rest of the drill, and the day. Pimella ordered her into the adjoining woods to gather mushrooms and, when the maid returned with two handfuls, Pimella squashed these into the gusset of her rubber punishment panties, until the mushrooms were a horrid brown pudding. Pimella sprinkled cayenne pepper onto the mess, and pulled the panties up very tight over Emma's crotch, fastening them with a tiny padlock, as the girl's face wrinkled in distress. The slimy filling both inflamed and stimulated the cunt, so that a girl longed for the relief of a wank, except that punishment panties contained a hard thimble, forming a cupola over the clitoris, and making it impossible to touch.

It was a relief to strip off the military kit for cross-country runs, in the full nude, save for running shoes and socks. The runs took the maids around the vast acreage of the Furrow Weald estate, and along the weald itself, where they were at last permitted to scamper down the tortuous cliff paths, past mysterious caves and crevices, to Furrow Weald's private beach, for a splash in the Cornish surf. Sergeant Plumply would permit favoured maids – including Merilee, the undoubted drill champion – to 'fall out for a smoke', rewarding them with a cigarette from her own silver case. When Caroline, pleasantly astounded by the distinction, began to stammer: 'Oh! Um, I don't . . .' her lithe, petite marching mate, Samantha Gouge, elbowed her and flashed a warning frown. Caroline took the cigarette, and let Samantha show her how to smoke it; when it was her turn to inhale, she found it a little giddy-making, but strangely soothing – like being a real soldier.

The hardships of drill, trough and constant summary beatings, gave the new bitches a rather subversive camaraderie. Emma swanked, for a while, on the strength of her bottom's new bruises, but in truth, no new bitch possessed unwealed buttocks, and Merilee assured Caroline that the senior maids had to bare up just as much, only in private, with their welts shrouded by panties and skirts. Word had gone round of Caroline's thrashing Aaliz de Brest – a prefect! – and she found she enjoyed respect from the other maids, and even from prefects Cynthia Cunnell, Victoria Brounbirch, Alice Wellbed and Mandy Tuppe. When they summarily caned her – 'dumb insolence' being the usual excuse – they murmured: 'Awfully sorry about this.'

Vicca Valcul, however, took every opportunity to order a slow self-basting, as shameful as it was painful. The occasional 'sixpence' or 'shilling' – summary beatings from Bronwen, or any other prefect who felt in the mood, were not so bad, as the prefects dealt their strokes quickfire, with a sixpence lasting, at most, three seconds. The strokes were over, even before a maid's gorge had time to rise, or her bum to wriggle, or her tears to flow – that came after, when she could rub her weals at leisure.

Usually, Caroline rushed to the 'bog' to wank off, where her comrades would eye her wealed bottom with lustful sympathy, often joining in the wank. When Vicca applied her own cane – always a shilling – she took her time, letting the pain of each stroke sink in for several seconds, before applying the next, with Caroline squirming in agony – always where lots of girls could see and titter, or even blatantly wank off. She was glad to be caned in the nude, for she had no stockings to stain with the come that *always* spurted from her sex, as her bum danced bare under strokes.

The tuck shop was open for fifteen minutes every day, but with scant warning, so that a knot of girls thronged the narrow serving hatch, with most having to leave disappointed. Cane-wielding prefects patrolled, licking their lips, and it was rare that scuffling maids left without a caning on the bare, rubbing their wealed bums, while tears dripped over their precious sweets, clutched to the breast. Caroline got to the tuck shop on her fourth day, with maids, in uniform or nude, making way for her, and discovered herself quite rich: various snack bars or fizzy drinks cost only a penny or halfpenny.

She depleted her shilling credit, buying enough to gorge, but keeping several aside in her armoire for a rainy day. The tuck shop did not sell cigarettes, but there were always maids well supplied, including Merilee, and there was a black market in cigarettes: some maids sold them for tuck-shop credits, in the form of written IOUs – perfectly legal – or else for cuddles and cane strokes. A girl might spend the night with a predatory amorist, like the impish, shameless Samantha Gouge, to emerge with well-chewed quim and titties, and two or three smokes.

Merilee explained, during her nightly wanks with Caroline, that the slop bumpkins from the village were the source. She promised that Caroline's initiation to the Swanks would be soon, mysteriously blaming 'formalities' for the delay. Aaliz promised the same, for the Stingers, and made the same excuse. Caroline ensured that their lustful visits did not overlap. She wasn't sure which chum she preferred – Merilee, the superbly physical, or Aaliz, with her sentiments and 'pash', as well as her need to be caned with her own gutta-percha ferule, which Caroline frankly enjoyed, the more so, as Aaliz promised her a ferule of her own, after her intiation to the Stingers. Yet, she enjoyed Merilee thrashing *her* bum, riding her face, and the lovely wank afterwards. And now, Samantha Gouge demanded they be best chums! It was so confusing.

Samantha was appallingly outspoken. Hard as wood, with firm young titties and buttocks jutting from a lithe, whip-muscled body, she boasted openly about how many boys had been up her bum, and how many girls she had wanked, and how many cane strokes her firm, unshreddable leather bum had taken. Samantha *liked* being caned.

'How could you?' Caroline asked. 'I know a girl has to be caned, for her own good, but liking it . . .?'

'We all do,' said Samantha. 'I admit it, that's all. That's why we're here. When the pres cane *us*, they are really begging *us* to cane *them*.'

They sat nude on Samantha's bed, sharing one of Caroline's snack bars, with fizzy lemonade, and a smoke. Samantha's chocolate-smeared fingers stroked Caroline's cunt gourd.

'I'm hoping to get into the Stingers,' Samantha prattled, 'and then I'll be able to bare up, and order my sessions, like a true sub.'

Caroline did not mention her own forthcoming initiation, nor her enrolment in the Swanks as well. She did murmur that she thought the Stingers weren't totally submissive, but Samantha scoffed that the Stingers were *massive* subs, who liked to be caned until they just came and came. Both girls were enjoying a free period, sandwiched between Latin and Fine Arts, and the hot sun beamed on their sweating bodies. Caroline stroked Samantha's bottom, marvelling at the corrugated pattern of weals, seemingly built into the naked flesh.

'My very first bare-bum caning, I knew I wanted it.' Samantha giggled. 'I wanked off three times in a row, touching my welts. I was so thrilled and proud to be beaten.'

'But why?'

'The feeling of power. A sub is really in control, making others work to flood her body with lovely sensation. Pleasure or pain, it is sensation that counts, and the thrill of yoking your body to another's will. You control that will.'

Her fingers dabbled at the opening to Caroline's cunt. 'You're pretty wet,' she murmured. 'Let's wank off.'

'Gladly, Samantha, but don't you want me to cane you first?'

Samantha crouched on her bed, buttocks up and spread. She fingered her gushing twat, and began to moan for her 'five shillings', so Caroline lifted her rubber cane and lashed her sixty strokes. The tight muscled bum pears danced, as red weals overlaid the marks of previous floggings, with Samantha's squirms seeming to beckon the cane, until a lattice of pretty crimson ridges overlaid the entire croup.

Samantha did not squeal, but gasped and gurgled quite loudly, with hoarse pants, as come gushed from her cunt, and gave a little whinny whenever Caroline delivered an upender, lashing the cunt lips and taut bum cleft. At an especially harsh cut, she said 'Ouch!', with a little coo of admiration. Caroline's own quim was a torrent of pussy juice, with her clitty well extruded from the swollen flaps, and she masturbated cautiously, intent on saving her climax for Samantha's lips and fingers.

'Oof! That was good!' cried Samantha, after the sixtieth stroke. Eyes bright, she licked her teeth, while sensuously rubbing her bottom. 'You're beautifully dominant, Caroline,' she purred.

'Oh, I don't know.'

'A goth, then. Mm.'

She writhed, as Caroline's lips suddenly kissed her cunt, mwah! Samantha's fingers slid deep into Caroline's slit, poking hard, with her nails slicing the wombneck, and Caroline wriggled, her lips sucking and drinking the juice from Samantha's twat. The girls squirmed into position, and gamahuched, each with her face between the other's legs, drinking her come, and sucking and kissing her wet cunt. Caroline's buttocks parted to admit Samantha's finger into her anus; two, then three, fingers slid inside her bumhole, filling her rectum, with Caroline moaning softly and her buttocks squeezing the painful, tickling invader. She replied in kind, penetrating Samantha's elastic anus with her own fingers. Gasping and whimpering, the slippery nude fricatrices stabbed colons, fingers reaming the hot slimy bum space, until both gurgled in long, shuddering orgasm. Samantha clasped Caroline's ear with her mouth.

'Tell you what, Caroline,' she whispered, licking her fingers, 'let's start our own maidband. We could call it the goths. We can spank and wank and cane as much as we please, with our own rules and everything.'

'Just the two of us?'

'Well, I'm sure others will join . . . Gertrude Seaman, Vapula McCloskey, Peggy Droule, Sarah Hogplum, Emma Spivey, Janet Petardo . . .'

'You've certainly made friends amongst the new bitches.'

'My bum makes friends,' said Samantha. 'They aren't all new bitches, either. Janet Petardo's a schoolmaid.'

'Well, I never! Have they all . . .?'

Samantha patted her glowing wealed fesses. 'Yes! I'm such a . . . such a slut, no one can resist my arse. They are appalled, but enticed, knowing how much flesh has been up my twat and bumhole. What will make the goths special is . . . boys! All those juicy Cornish hunks in Trelashen are just waiting to bum girls who are gagging for it. They'll pay in cigarettes! I know that from the slop bumpkins.'

'Bum us?'

'Of course. It's the Cornish way. You *have* been bummed, I take it?'

'Well . . . sort of.'

'Isn't it super? A stiff hot cock pounding your rectum to pieces and squirting all that lush sticky spunk up your tripes? *So* wank-making.'

'I . . . I can't disagree,' Caroline murmured, heart pounding, as a new spurt of come wet her cooze. 'Maybe it's time my bumhole made some friends.'

It was the drowsy free period after luncheon. Merilee sat on Caroline's face. Caroline lay on her bed, legs spread, while Merilee gently, teasingly, spanked her open cunt with stiff fingers. Occasionally, she lashed the cooze extra hard, making Caroline groan, wriggling, as she drank the black girl's come, with her hands clasping and kneading Merilee's bare buttocks. Her erect clitoris protruded from her spanked cunt flaps, and Merilee would pause in the beating, to bend forwards, take it in her mouth and suck it like a wet pink lollipop, making Caroline squeal, writhing, with her cunt gushing come.

'It's tonight,' Merilee said. 'Your initiation into the Swanks. Nine o'clock sharp.'

'Mm,' Caroline moaned into the black girl's cunt folds, crushing her face.

Merilee gave her instructions: how to sneak out of school and make her way to a cave above the beach, which Caroline had seen many times. Orgasm interrupted her; as the black quim spewed pussy juice over Caroline's face, Merilee slammed her mouth onto Caroline's bruised cunt, and took the whole vulva between her lips, sucking Caroline to her own shuddering spasm.

'It's short notice,' Caroline said, as they embraced, tongues slopped together.

'You'll see. Not a word, mind.'

'Of course not. But I haven't a thing to wear.'

Merilee laughed. 'You're supposed to be nude.'

'Oh. Am I going to be whipped?'

'You'll *see*,' Merilee insisted, kissing Caroline's nipples, before getting up to go. 'It's a test. Something you've never done before, to see if you have the arse for it.'

'How do you know I've not done it?'

'We've checked.'

Caroline tingled with excitement throughout afternoon drill, supper and prep. Aaliz begged for a wank visit and a caning, but she fended her off with the excuse of a headache. Aaliz sulked, and Caroline thought she would really have to do something to control the increasingly submissive prefect, who now called Caroline 'mistress' and herself 'slave' – except, how did she control an avowed submissive? Caroline pouted, complained about her tardy admission to the Stingers, threatening Aaliz's own bottom with stripes for the delay, and bit her lip, as the girl's face lit up at the threat.

Naked, but for gym shoes and socks, Caroline made her way down the cliff path to the cavern. There was a crescent moon, and ample starshine to light her passage. A faint glimmer shone from inside the cave, and she entered, stooping, in a long narrow corridor of rocks and scree, gradually widening, until she emerged into a large cavern, whence the light issued. The rock walls were adorned with oil lamps, casting a smoky glow on a circle of girls' nude bodies, over a dozen in number. One of the bodies was black and unmistakable as Merilee's, yet Caroline neither gave nor received a sign of recognition. The girls were completely shaven, save for one, who had a luxuriant forest of auburn pubic fronds, covering her lower belly to the navel and hanging well below her cunt lips, together with lush armpit foliage, straggling over huge bare bubbies, like gleaming sixteen-pounder gunshells.

All of their faces were concealed by shiny black rubber masks, with holes for eyes and mouth, and each girl held a long cane at the ready. In the centre of the circle stood a large oblong slab of rock, resembling a butcher's chopping block. On it knelt a boy, in jeans and T-shirt, with his hands behind his back, and his face leering somewhat scornfully. He was not bound, yet his attitude seemed a mixture of shame and defiance.

'We have a live one,' intoned the girls, and Caroline curtsied, not knowing what else to do, before realising they meant the boy, not her.

'Let's get on with it, girlies,' sneered the boy. 'I can take anything you dish out.'

The girl with full pubic hair, whose cane had a silver top, stepped forwards, and slapped the boy's face with her palm.

'Ouch!' he squealed. 'That hurt.'

'Silence, worm,' she snapped. 'You will hurt a lot more before dawn. Your wretched bottom is the sacrifice to our new sister.'

She handed Caroline her cane. 'You must prove yourself worthy of Swankhood,' she said.

Caroline's quim spurted juice at the awful, thrilling knowledge. *I'm to cane a boy on his bare bottom.*

'Repeat after your sisters the sacred oath of the Swanks.'

The girls began to chant: '*Sacred be our rods, to chastise the nates of our enemies*.'

Caroline, alone, repeated the sermon.

'No croup shall be left unwealed, and no coynte shall remain dry, as we flog with scourges of righteousness.

'Males shall wriggle under our female wrath, and their bodies shall forever bear the marks of our pleasure.

'Girls who are traitors shall scream their lungs out, as their fesses take stripes a hundred hundredfold. Not coyntes, nor bubs, nor bellies, nor backs shall be spared the bruise of our canes.

'Cruelty! Cruelty! The Swanks rule forever more!'

'This miscreant merits severe chastisement,' said the befurred girl. 'His fate is in your hands.'

'Wait a minute,' whined the boy, looking at Caroline. 'It's in fun, right? A game to impress the Trelashen scrubbers with my spanked bum.'

Caroline scrutinised him. He was no older than herself, with soft skin and a cherub mouth, rather dishy, in a slender, almost girlish way. His hair hung lank over his forehead, and she resisted the impulse to brush it back for him. His very dishiness made her cunt tingle and juice at the prospect of beating him. She tapped the rocky floor with her cane.

'This is no game,' she said sonorously. 'You are here to pay for your crimes.'

'It's no crime to have a peek at birds with their kit off,' he protested, then leered. 'I think I saw *you*, miss, the other day, playing your army games. I couldn't forget that arse, nor those titties.'

'You cheeky swine,' Caroline hissed. 'Strip, this instant.'

'What, everything?'

'Everything. I shall flog you in the full nude, boy.'

'What if I refuse?' he asked insolently.

Caroline looked at the masked faces. Everyone expected her answer. 'You shall be subdued, trussed and flogged ten times your tariff,' she declared, 'then covered in dung, and set loose to return home in naked shame.'

The boy looked uncertainly at the ring of nude girls, their hostile eyes and rippling muscles; he gulped. 'All right, I'll take your punishment, miss. Those Trelashen sluts would cut me off the nookie trail if I came back without any marks on my arse.'

'Stand and disrobe, worm,' thundered Caroline, swishing the air with her heavy, springy cane, in a fearful whooshing sound that made the boy pale.

He obeyed, hesitantly unbuckling his belt, and slithering out of his clothing, until he stood nude before the girls. Caroline licked her lips at his taut, muscled bum, just begging for stripes, and his really quite massive tool, dangling uncertainly beneath his huge ball globes, and with a little tremor that indicated the beginning of an erection.

Seeing Caroline's eyes on his cock, he put his hands behind his back, parted his legs, and stood, insolently thrusting his balls and cock forwards. The cock stiffened a little more, and rose from the ball sac.

This is so super! A naked boy in my power, with a yummy stiffening tool, and he must take my punishment, as some kind of manhood test. Gosh, that cock really is a monster. I'll punish him for possessing it!

Caroline sprang onto the rocky dais, to face the boy. She flicked the tip of his stiffening cock with her cane, then pressed the cane to his balls.

'You wretched filth,' she hissed. 'You dare to insult pure ladies with your beastly male body? It is not just your bottom I can flog. Get rid of that horrid erection at once.'

The cock swelled further.

'I . . . I can't, miss,' he mumbled, staring at Caroline's heaving bare breasts. 'You're far too sexy.'

'Flattery won't work,' she sneered. 'I shall have to flog you till your tool is soft. Turn round, bend over and touch your toes.'

Shivering, the boy obeyed, presenting Caroline with his taut arse, and the balls swaying beneath the bum cleft. She prodded the balls with her cane.

'Cock soft, remember, boy,' she said. 'It'll be four shillings, that is, forty-eight strokes.'

'*Forty-eight*!' he exclaimed.

'You have agreed to take punishment on the bare.'

'Yes, but –'

Now it is *five* shillings. No squealing or wriggling, or you get the cut over. *You are in a woman's power.* Understood, worm?'

'Understood, miss.' The boy groaned.

The circle of girls moved closer to the dais, with several, including Merilee, putting one foot up on the table top, and baring their quims. Caroline knew from their eyes, behind the masks, that they were grinning lustfully. She lifted her cane high – there was a sigh from the masked maids – and she lashed the rod with full force on the boy's arse. Vip!

'Urrgh!' he cried, his buttocks clenching tight, as a long pink weal flared on the bare flesh.

The maids cooed. Caroline pressed her breasts, to stop them bouncing, then lifted her cane for the second. Vip! The fesses tightened once more, and began to wriggle, the bum cleft clenching hard, and the balls wobbling quite violently. His back rippled, glistening with sweat. Caroline licked her lips, pushing her bouncing titties back, and lashed the boy once more. Vip! His breath came in a low, harsh rasp. Vip!

'Uhh!'

Vip!

'Uhh!'

Vip!

'Uhh! Uhh!'

His bum was colouring nicely, with red weals darkening to puce, criss-crossing the buttocks – by now, squirming healthily – in what Caroline judged a pleasing pattern. Vip!

'Ooh,' he whistled.

'Careful, boy,' she panted. 'What is your name, by the way?'

'Jabez Prestellen, miss.'

'You're doing nicely, Jabez. Don't spoil things with silly girly squeals.'

Vip! He suppressed his moans, as Caroline took the beating past a dozen, and she stopped worrying about her flapping titties. They *would* bounce! Her body poured with sweat, and she was aware of a ticklish squelching between her thighs, as her cunt drooled come. Her clitty was up and throbbing, and as she gazed on the boy's flogged bare arse, pleasure thrilled her. Around the whipping scene, the Swank girls caressed spread quims, sighing in delight, as they masturbated. Vip! The boy clutched his toes, rocking backwards and forwards on the balls of his feet, with his legs jerking rigid at each cut to the fesses. He squirmed violently, as Caroline began to stripe his haunches, until his whole croup, from spine to thighs, was a blotched pattern of deep welts. Vip! Caroline sauntered around him;

the boy's face was scarlet, dripping tears and sweat, yet his sex organ was fully, monstrously erect! Caroline gasped at the huge fleshy pole, quivering against his belly.

'Jabez, you disappoint me,' she said, trying not to let her hand fly to her pulsing clitty and bring herself off, at the sight of the massive cock. 'Your organ is disgracefully stiff.'

'I'm sorry, miss,' he whined. 'I can't help it. I've never been beaten by a girl before.'

'Something tells me you like it.'

'No, miss, honestly! It's awful.'

'Your cock says you lie, Jabez.'

'Please don't be cruel, miss.'

'But girls must, just as worms must wriggle.'

Merilee nodded; her fingers were all the way up her slit, stabbing fiercely, while her thumb mashed her swollen clitty. Juice streamed from the winking cunt mouth, over her glistening ebony thighs.

Vip! Caroline lashed him across top buttock.

'Oof!' he squealed, wriggling.

'That cut over, Jabez. You understand.'

'Yes, miss.'

'And no silly baby squeals, from now on.'

Vip! Vip! Caroline settled into the fierce rhythm of her caning, aware of her wanking comrades around her, and her own powerful longing for masturbation. Unsure of the etiquette, if the actual whipper might wank off or not, she kept her fingers away from her quim, although her clitty begged to be touched, and it was impossible to hide the streams of come sparkling on her legs, right down to her toes, which were all squishy and slithery. She could hear the slap of his cock on his belly, as he jerked at each stroke, and drooled over her chin, wanting to take that monstrous engine between her lips, into her throat, and eat it, balls and all.

It's not fair that boys should have such lovely, wicked things. But at least a girl has her cane, to punish them for it.

The gasps of the masturbating Swanks grew louder, with several maids' bellies convulsing in orgasm, though they did not stop frigging. Vip! Vip! Caroline took the caning past three dozen, then four, with Jabez squirming, as his bottom blackened with deep, puffy welts. Far away, the ocean breakers softly crashed, over the hoarse panting of girl whipper, whipped boy, and drooling fricatrices. The flogged boy's wealed bottom and straining muscles glared luridly in the flickering light of the oil lamps, making him seem more elfin and helpless with each stroke to his bare. Caroline wanted to eat his arse, his balls and stiff cock: all of him! Vip! At the sixtieth stroke, she laid aside her cane.

'There,' she said, 'it's done.'

She wiped her mouth of drool, and slapped her thighs, but it was hopeless to try to stem her flood of come. Jabez rose, his face glazed with tears, and rubbed his bottom. His cock was shivering and erect, bell end purple and exposed, facing Caroline, who could not take her eyes from it.

'You hurt me, you fucking bitch,' he hissed. 'I'll have you.'

8

Nude Combat

'Stop!' Caroline shrieked. 'That hurts!'

The naked boy wrenched her hair, grabbing her wrist, and twisting her arm behind her back. Despite his cherubic features, he was strong, with whipcord muscle. He kneed her in the cunt, and she doubled up, groaning and helpless, as he forced her down onto the table top, with the rock scratching her squashed titties. Her legs flailed, until he got his knee between her thighs, parting them, while pressing her face to the rock.

'Stop! No! Help!'

The masturbating Swanks panted. Caroline wriggled, squealing, as their come-soaked hands grasped her ankles and wrists, holding them apart, while the boy mounted her.

'Stop him! Help me! What are you doing?' Through eyes blurred with tears, she saw ebony hands holding her wrist. 'Merilee, don't. I'm one of you.'

'Not yet, Caroline,' Merilee purred. 'Be patient.'

'But the brute is hurting me.'

Jabez grasped Caroline's hips, and drew her wriggling bottom up towards him. Smack! Smack! He began to spank her, very hard.

'Ouch! Ooh! That hurts.'

'Nothing to what's coming, bitch,' the boy hissed.

Smack! Smack!

'Ooh!'

Smack! Smack!

'Oh! Ahh!'

The fast spanking continued, until Caroline's squirming bottom was burning with pain, and she had taken over a hundred slaps.

'Oh, Merilee,' she said, sobbing, 'tell the boy to stop spanking me, please.'

'Stop spanking her, boy,' Merilee ordered.

The spanks stopped; Jabez pulled Caroline's buttocks higher, opening them wide.

'What –' Caroline gasped, then felt the monstrous swollen bulb of his cock nuzzling her anus.

'No!' she screamed. 'Not that!'

Jabez chuckled.

'Ahh!'

The tip of his obscenely huge cock cleaved her anal bud, poking inside.

'Oh! No! Stop!'

'You're a three-incher,' said Merilee. 'You can take him.'

Waves of pain seared Caroline's anus, as the massive tool continued to penetrate her. Jabez thrust vigorously, his cock wrenching her anal elastic, with Caroline shrieking and sobbing, her body squirming, yet clamped by the boy's weight, and the firm, pitiless grip of her friends. His hips slapped her bare bum, in a powerful thrust, that made her gurgle, as her gorge rose, and his cock filled her rectum, sinking inside her, until his balls were squashed on her buttocks. She writhed, impaled on his fleshy spear, with his swollen cock tip probing the entrance to her colon. Moist with her copious arse grease, his cock began to slide rapidly in and out of her rectum, as he began to bum fuck her, each brutal thrust of his cock piercing her anus anew, and his bulb slamming her tender sigmoid colon.

'Stop, please, I beg you,' she groaned.

'That's a stupid thing to say,' Jabez said, panting.

His cock made a sucking, plopping noise, as it squelched out of her anus, before plunging in again. The boy's power seemed merciless, his strength inexhaustible, as Caroline squirmed, gurgling with agony, under the fierce, slamming buggery, which rocked her whole pain-wracked body. Pain radiated from her tortured bumhole, and it seemed that her whole self was nothing but a giant rectum, filled with a flaming ball of agony.

'You're cruel,' she said, sobbing.

'Ain't I just?' Jabez panted. 'It's all you city girls understand. You need proper bumming, afore you're a real Cornish maid. See, your arse is starting to twitch up.'

'No!' Caroline squealed. 'You're beastly. I hate you. I've never been hurt so much.'

'Then you're enjoying it,' gasped the buggering boy.

Caroline's buttocks were beginning to rise, and meet his thrusts; under her squirming cunt, a lake of come dripped, soaking her thighs and gourd. Her clitty throbbed, drubbed on the coarse rock.

'Ooh . . . ooh,' she moaned, slapping her buttocks against his balls. 'Oh, you bastard. Do me, then. Fuck my bum hard, you filthy swine.'

The cock stabbing her colon became a warm enemy, comforting her tummy, filling her with vicious male heat.

'I'm helpless,' she drooled. 'Fuck me, spunk in my bum, shame me, hurt me . . .'

Around her, the Swanks cooed, gasping, as they vigorously wanked off. Jarring pleasure seared her spine, as the cock reamed her arse root, and her clitty throbbed, scraping the table top.

'Ooh . . . ooh . . . yes . . . *ohh*!'

Caroline wailed, gasping, as orgasm flooded her buggered tummy. Chuckling and panting, Jabez continued to bum fuck, with his massive tool squelching in Caroline's oozing arse grease. She slammed her bum upwards, to slap his belly and balls, as her rectum squeezed his cock, milking him.

'Come on,' she said, 'fuck me, you filthy brute, give me that spunk in my tummy.'

She heard Merilee gasp and shudder in wanked climax. Clenching her buttocks extra hard, she trapped his cock at her colon.

'Spunk in me, boy, I command you,' she hissed, squeezing his cock with tight wriggles of her bum.

She felt the massive bulb, reaming her rectum, with his tip at her sigmoid colon – her clitty scraped rock, and she whinnied, as another orgasm washed over her cunt and belly. Grunting, Jabez freed his cock, and recommenced a furious ramming of her rectum, now so lubricated by her arse grease, that the dripping cock slid in and out as easily as a monstrous oiled piston. The pain of her spanked bottom, and the agony of her tripes' penetration, merged into a fiery pleasure.

Samantha was right, sensation is all.

She rubbed her throbbing, erect nipples on the hard rock, and gasped, as pleasure seared her, from clitty to nips, with the cock pounding ecstacy in her bumhole. A drop of hot cream from Jabez's cock spurted into her colon.

'Fuck me. Spunk in me,' she panted. 'I want *all* your spunk.'

She squeezed hard, the tender skin of her bumhole feeling and caressing every fold, ridge and protrusion of his cock. He grunted harshly, as a flood of hot spunk washed her colon, filling her tripes with his come.

'Oh! Oh . . . *yes*,' she groaned, drool sliming her face, as her belly erupted once more in climax.

Gasping in their own orgasms, the girls cheered.

'Now you're a proper Swank,' said Merilee. 'A real dominant maid.'

Gosh! If this is dominance, what awaits me at the Stingers?

Caroline had butterflies in her tummy, as she climbed naked into the boxing ring, for her first fight. Her opponent was Judy Tinsell, a superbly muscled brunette, with long, rippling thighs, a tightly packed arse, and hard, conic titties, over a belly that was a washboard of muscle. The Swanks' secret sign, left hand opened at the thigh, with thumb pressed to palm, was impossible to make with boxing gloves on, and even if Judy was a sister Swank, it would scarcely do her any good. The band's watchword was that secrecy counted above all advantage.

Judy was the winner of several fights, but was smaller than Caroline, only just, and Ermine Floss, the boxing mistress, decreed them equal, although Caroline was a light heavyweight – 'only because of your bum and titties', she quipped cruelly – and Judy a middleweight. Caroline had only seen Judy in pleated skirt and blouse, and thought her lithely attractive – possibly, an interesting wank partner – but now that Judy scowled, in the nude, her rippling muscles seemed quite menacing. Each girl wore white fluffy socks and red boots, with shiny red leather gloves; Caroline's long hair was tied behind her in a ponytail, while Judy's sleek, cropped boxer's mane had no need of restraint. Miss Floss – Ermine, as she liked the maids to call her – was referee.

'Let's have a good clean contest, maids,' she bubbled, 'and remember the rules – punches to the body, slaps to the face.'

Boxers were forbidden to use head punches; instead, they might slap their opponents with the palms or backs of their gloves. The bell rang, and Caroline advanced from her corner, not fast enough, for Judy shot forwards, and delivered a double slam to Caroline's titties, the searing pain knocking her back, then followed up with two crashing slaps to Caroline's cheek, which sent her reeling groggily to the ropes. Her arms flailed, managing to connect with Judy's left breast, but Judy stormed in, fists flashing in a flurry of jabs to Caroline's belly and nipples. Judy's body shielded Caroline from Ermine's gaze, and her belly punches dropped to the gourd, where Judy landed several agonising blows to Caroline's cunt.

Caroline doubled up in pain, as Ermine pulled Judy away. She had only moments to regain her balance, and put her fists up, before the next attack. This time Caroline, maddened with pain and anger, lunged forwards, and stopped Judy with a massive punch to the belly, followed by two uppercuts to the breasts, and a double slap, hammering Judy's face. Judy swivelled, and Caroline leapt, to pound her bare arse with punches. Judy squealed in protest, but Ermine grinned, and advised that bum-punches were within the rules. Panting, the girls faced off, their cheeks and titties red with slaps, trading punches, until the end of the first round.

In the second, Caroline held her own, getting the measure of Judy's lightning attacks, taking the punches, and waiting until she could knock the smaller girl sideways with one of her own sledgehammers. Judy always sought Ermine's blindside, to viciously pummel Caroline's cunt, and the dry slaps of her gloves turned to wet, squelchy thuds, as Caroline's cunt began to drip come. Caroline responded with low blows of her own, her glove wetly slapping the big swollen lips of the girl's cunt; Judy's gash, too, glistened red and wet beneath her heaving shaven gourd, and both girls fought with nipples erect.

Judy's prancing style meant that her thighs were often apart, as she danced around Caroline, so that Caroline was able to aim several uppercuts between her thighs, slamming the gash flaps, and making Judy groan and stagger. The slugging match continued through the third and fourth rounds, with Caroline swaying, a punchbag, and used to the rain of jabs from the sweat-scented leather. Her body glowed with bruises, and her titties hurt awfully, but Judy's, too, showed evidence of pain, with her hard titty-bulbs bruised crimson, and several livid welts to the belly and quim. Both girls panted, tongues hanging out, and their chins wet with drool. Their teats and bellies glistened with sweat, and, as they danced, come sprayed from their punched cunts.

The pace slowed, each fighter circling the other, looking for an opening, and now Caroline's rarer, but harder, punches had the edge on Judy's ferocious flurries. Caroline slapped Judy's cheek, spinning her head, then followed with a double uppercut to the titties, a hard right to the belly and two vicious uppercuts to Judy's cunt. Tears appeared in Judy's eyes, and she bared her teeth in a rictus of pain and anger. Caroline raised her glove to slap Judy again; then, with the warm spurt of come from her cooze, swept aside her guard, and, mockingly, bared her breasts to the tough smaller girl. Judy seized her chance, knocking Caroline to the ropes, with a cascade of jabs to the nipples.

Caroline bounced off the ropes, straight onto Judy's left to her groin, and jackknifed in pain. Judy thumped her back, and mashed her titties at the same time, her glove grinding Caroline's nipples against her ribcage. Gasping, Caroline careened into Judy, clasping her, and feebly hitting her buttocks, while the smaller girl's gloves danced in a ballet of agony all over Caroline's breasts, belly and cooze. Caroline clutched tighter; both cunts met, pressed in a wet embrace, with come flowing over their rippling thighs. At last, she stumbled back, arms limp, and allowed Judy to hammer her entire torso, flopping like a rag doll. Thwap! Thwap! The leather slapped Caroline's breasts, titties and belly, with fierce slams to her sopping cunt.

She staggered, and fell to her knees, with Judy standing over her, cooze an inch from Caroline's pain-wracked face, and continuing to slap her cheeks, while thumping her breasts with her knees. Miss Floss bounced, bright-eyed, her frilly skirtlet fluttering, to show her crisp white panties stained with come. She did not stop the fight, not even when the battered Caroline slumped, with her face against Judy's quivering cunt. Caroline's lips were on the girl's cunt flaps. With Judy's gloves raining blows to her back and titties, she began to lick the girl's extruded stiff clitty, and suck the oozing pussy juice. Judy gasped, her blows faltering, and Caroline was able to push her away, and stagger to her feet. She still made no effort to protect herself from the battering, and went down again, on her knees.

This time, she clasped Judy's buttocks with her gloves, and began to slap hard, with her face pressed to the girl's juicing gash. Caroline's lips squelched in the flood of come from Judy's cooze flaps, and her throat gurgled, as she swallowed it, while her lips sucked Judy's erect nubbin.

'Ooh . . . ooh . . . yes . . .'

Judy began to moan, her blows no more than swipes, as Caroline tongued her cunt. Caroline suddenly rose, aimed, and delivered a savage right hook, straight to Judy's clitoris. Judy toppled, and stayed down, writhing, with come spurting from her gash, to puddle the canvas. Caroline put her boot on the girl's heaving titties, and squashed viciously, making Judy writhe and moan. Ermine Floss began the count.

'Ah, one, ah . . . ah, two, ah . . .'

At 'ah, ten, ah . . .' with Judy still groaning under Caroline's boot, she proclaimed a knockout, and lifted Caroline's hand in victory.

Back in the changing rooms, the girls stripped off gloves and boots, and dived together into the shower.

'Quite a scrap, eh, Judy?' said Caroline, soaked under the freezing spray.

The vanquished girl glowered. 'You fucking bitch,' she snarled. 'You cheated.'

'I *beg* your pardon?'

Judy grabbed Caroline's hair, wrenching it from the scalp and knotting it around her fist. Caroline squealed, as she was forced to her knees.

'You're not so tough, with the gloves off, slut,' Judy hissed. 'That was a dirty trick, licking me like that, and . . . you know, getting me hot.'

'I couldn't help –'

'Well, you can finish the job, bitch.'

Judy pressed Caroline's face to her cunt, opening her thighs, so that Caroline's tongue could penetrate the wet pink slit. Caroline's nose nuzzled Judy's shaven quim, as her lips fastened on the quim flaps, and her tongue entered the gash. She began to gamahuche Judy, tonguing her clit with long, firm strokes.

'Ahh . . . yes,' Judy gasped. 'That's good, bitch. Wait till I get you in Graeco-Roman wrestling, no holds barred. I'll spank that lovely arse raw. Wank off, as you tongue me.'

'Yes,' Caroline moaned, 'yes.'

Judy's come spilled down Caroline's chin. With her right hand cupping Judy's bare buttocks, Caroline's left hand slid to her own cooze, and masturbated her throbbing clitty.

'I wanted to come so much, as you belted me,' she panted.

'I know you did, you fucking sub bitch,' said Judy. 'Don't stop – oh, your tongue's *so* good. You really *are* a sub.'

Judy lifted her left leg, and clasped her thigh around Caroline's neck, with her toenails clawing her back. Caroline drank Judy's copious come, then gasped, as a sudden hiss of steaming pee took her unawares, splashing into her face and mouth.

'Drink my pee, slut,' snarled Judy.

Mouth gaping, and wanking faster, Caroline swallowed the acrid golden pee, mingled with cunt juice. After several seconds, the flow of pee abated, and she recommenced tonguing Judy's swollen clit, drinking the torrent of come flowing from her cooze. Judy's belly began to heave.

'Yes . . . ooh . . . yes,' she gasped.

Caroline's teats quivered, the nipples straining stiff, as she masturbated her gushing cunt.

'Uhh . . . uhh,' she moaned.

The girls came together, each yelping, as their bodies twitched in orgasm. Caroline did not resist, as Judy squatted, squashing Caroline's titties on her knee, and began to spank her buttocks. Slap! Slap! The spanks echoed above the shower spray, with Caroline's bum flans pinking, then reddening, as Judy's palm etched spank marks from her thighs to haunch to spinal nubbin.

'You love being spanked,' Judy panted.

'Yes, I admit it. But I love spanking as well.'

'And caning. You caned Aaliz de Brest on your very first day here.'

'She begged me to.'

'So you're a nicey-nicey,' Judy sneered.

'I try to be nice.'

'Ready for another wank?'

'Gosh, yes.'

Judy released Caroline, who straightened, and grabbed Judy by the cunt, fingernails clawing the clitty and slitmeat.

'Ouch!' Judy squealed.

Caroline flipped her over, and began to spank her on the bare. Slap! Slap!

'Oh. Stop. You fucking bitch,' Judy moaned, her bum wriggling.

Impaling Judy's cunt on her fingers, Caroline spanked her buttocks to crimson. Judy squirmed, groaning and gasping, as her clitty thudded against Caroline's forefinger. Slap! Slap! A new flood of pee soaked Caroline's wrist.

'Oh, I'm sorry,' Judy whimpered.

Caroline parted her thighs wide, bending Judy's arm back, so that her fingers could penetrate Caroline's slit and wank her off. Spanking and masturbating, the two naked girls cooed, writhing, until they exploded in new orgasm. Squatting over the pinioned girl's face, Caroline released a hearty stream of piss, right into Judy's mouth.

'Swallow, bitch,' she purred; moaning, Judy obeyed, her throat bobbing, until she had swallowed all of Caroline's copious pee.

Gasping and rubbing her bottom, Judy rose. Caroline smiled at her.

'Let's be friends,' she said.

'Yes, let's.'

'Would you like to join our new maidband?'

'New? The Swanks or Stingers? Poo! I've no time for silly games.'

'This one isn't silly. We're called the goths. We are very, very cruel, and . . . we have boys. Nice boys, who know how to serve a lady, in every way, and who aren't too timid to bare their juicy male bums for thrashing, nor their cocks to bum us.'

Judy licked her lips. 'Go on. You're making it up.'

Caroline *was* making it up, but the idea seemed sound.

'Who's in it?'

'Samantha Gouge is my co-foundress.'

'That whore!' cried Judy.

She embraced Caroline, kissing her full on the lips, with their wet nipples and cunts squelching.

'Boys for bumming?' Judy asked.

'Oodles. Hot Cornish cocks to pound your tripes.'

'Count me in.'

At her next cuddle with Samantha, Caroline explained her idea. Samantha, sitting on Caroline's face, agreed eagerly.

'Boys,' she said, 'that's the key. There's one in Trelashen, Jabez Prestellen, a real stud. He bummed me once, outside the back door of the sweet shop – *and* fucked my cunt. His balls are absolutely brimming with cream.'

Sworn to Swank secrecy, the frowning Caroline could not reveal her acquaintance with young Jabez, but she made sure to thrash Samantha's bottom extra hard with her rubber cane, although it only made the girl gurgle in pleasure. It was agreed they should make an evening reconnaissance patrol into Trelashen.

'Why not cover St Ives as well?' Samantha enthused. 'There are loads of artists who live there, and they'll pay good money to paint girls in the nude.'

That, too, was agreed.

'This is absolutely secret,' Samantha whispered, though there was no one else to hear her, 'and I swore I wouldn't tell anybody, but as part of our ladylike training, Mistress Frubbin sort of introduces us to generous gentlemen, if you know what I mean. Some of them like to watch girls undressing, or in the nude, or fighting. They drink our come – a bottle of girl come costs more than vintage champagne! Some of them even get to . . . well, you know . . . bum us.'

'For money? But that would be illegal. Wouldn't it?'

'Why do you think our holes are pegged when we enter Furrow Weald? You see, there are lots of rich people and celebrities living in Devon and Cornwall, and they can get up to mischief down here that they wouldn't dare to back in London. Not just from this country, either. Compliant maids – really compliant – can strike it rich, and we've nowhere else to go, have we? I'll bet you're an orphan.'

Caroline thought of her parents, on the run. 'As near as dammit,' she said glumly.

'I'm an orphan – we all are. That's why we're chosen, for maximum *compliance.* Nymphos, subs, lesbos, with no ties, nor shame – slaves to pleasure.'

'But I'm none of those things,' Caroline protested.

Samantha licked her lips, then bit Caroline's left nipple very hard; Caroline moaned, and pressed the girl to her breast.

'You *will* be,' murmured Samantha.

Mistress June Prodigal was the advanced biology mistress, and although Caroline protested that she had never taken beginner's biology – not a subject approved at St Radegund's – she nevertheless had to attend the class. It was nearly two weeks into her basic training, and, to her surprise, there were no juniors or schoolmaids present, only new bitches in the nude. They sat nervously at their desks, while Miss Cynthia Cunnell, the uniformed prefect, distributed a large cardboard box to each girl, with a rather saucy leer on her wide red lips. When Mistress Prodigal ordered them to open their boxes, there were gasps, giggles and blushes.

'These, maids, are latex replicas of the *phallos*, or male sex organ, and you will be glad to hear they are very much larger than life size.'

The maids tittered, some with groans of feigned disappointment.

'You will have learnt by now that a Furrow Weald maid must be submissive. A girl's role in life is to submit to a male, and give him pleasure, in order to get what she wants from him. Since the pleasure brain of the male resides largely in his sex organ, it is essential to know the correct way to manipulate this ungainly, but vital, appurtenance. You will find that these models, fashioned with the very latest German technology, are accurate in every detail. I have my own model here, and you will please pay attention. Later, you shall take and keep your *phallos*, and no doubt use it for masturbation. With proper caution, and due modesty, you may replicate every operation of the male sex organ in your various apertures.'

Mistress Prodigal ordered the maids to pay close attention, as she began to caress the tip of the flaccid rubber tube; it stiffened, swelled, and came to life, until it was standing in monstrous rigidity, a good two feet in height, and three or four inches in girth. Her fingertips gliding over the sex organ, she fluently instructed them in the sensitive areas of frenulum, corona and glans, prepuce and balls, the two huge rubber orbs at the base of the monster. It was the maids' turn to try, and they followed her movements, squealing with delight, as they roused their organs to erection, until every maid sat, stroking a huge stiff rubber cock. The teacher showed them the correct method of drawing the prepuce right back, either rapidly, with an abrupt shock, or slowly and sensuously, in order to tickle the naked neck of the glans.

'You will notice that the organ seems to throb, as the male approaches his pleasure,' Mistress Prodigal said. 'At that time, it may be appropriate to apply labial suction. A girl's warm, wet throat is a fine approximation of her nether holes – either of them.'

Her head swooped, as she took the giant tool between her lips, and slid down, then eased back, until her lips and tongue were tickling the peehole. She repeated the movement, keeping her lips nuzzling the balls, and her throat working, to squeeze the cock shaft. The maids giggled, fumbling and shy, but soon, every maid was energetically masturbating her own tool. Caroline's twat was wet, as she stroked and sucked the giant cock, scarcely able to get her lips round its massive girth.

I wonder . . . my bumhole . . . gosh, it would be such a thrill if I could . . .

Suddenly, Caroline squealed, as a blob of white cream appeared at the peehole of her cock. She rubbed the cock harder, and pressed her lips to the glans, taking it fully into her mouth.

'Urrgh . . . urrgh,' she gurgled, as a massive flood of hot sweet cream spurted into her mouth.

'Well done, Caroline,' said Mistress Prodigal.

Soon, every girl had brought her cock to spurt, and was squealing in glee, as the sticky confectioner's cream splashed her face and hands. Caroline swallowed every drop of cream, its sweetness like a liquid meringue. The teacher explained that the balls must, of course, be refilled before every frotting – she suggested condensed milk, or, for the more affluent, dairy cream – and, if a maid was really thirsty, she could cheat, by squeezing the balls hard, although it was unwise to do that in real life. The rubber cocks would remain rigid for a long time after ejaculation, although, again, this was rarely the case in real life, one reason why intelligent girls were adept at masturbation. At the end of the class, she blew her girls an air-kiss.

'Mwah! Happy practising with your new toys.'

Caroline scampered to her room, and, having no cream, filled the balls with honey from her tuck jar. Positioning herself in front of the looking glass, with one foot up on the table, she gazed at her cunt, opened the lips, and began to masturbate, while stroking with her other hand the flaccid rubber cock. Before long, her cooze was dripping, and the cock erect. Pursing her lips, she calculated the girth – four inches at *least* – and inserted the tip in her cunt, where she began to frot her throbbing stiff clitty. After some minutes, she pushed further, gasping, as her twat stretched to bursting, and began to poke the shaft up and down her pouch, slamming her wombneck. Come dripped from her distended cunt flaps, as her belly fluttered, and a climax approached.

Panting, she withdrew the rubber cock from her cooze, with a squelchy plop, and turned, baring her bottom to the looking glass. She parted her cheeks as wide as she could, and, slopping her hand into her wet cunt, anointed the rubber cock with come. She poked into her anus, and greased herself there, as well, although her hole was already wet with arse grease. Taking a deep breath, she relaxed her sphincter, and pushed the cock tip against her anus. It wouldn't go in – she reamed her anus bud, shivering, at the tickling pleasure stabbing her clitty and spine – until, with an extra hard push, the giant rubber tool penetrated her. She gasped at the sharp pain, but continued to push, wrenching her anal elastic, until she cried out, as the cock slid right into her rectum, filling her to bursting. She panted hoarsely, scarcely able to breathe, at the agonising pressure in her tummy, yet rammed the rubber tool as far as it would go, until its tip tickled her colon. Her cunt streamed with come and, as she wanked off her clitty, she pushed the tool up and down in her rectum. The tool squelched, dripping with come and arse grease, and squeezed her slit flat.

'Oh,' she gasped, slamming it harder and harder into her tripes. 'Oh, that's fabulous.'

Honey spurted from the bulb of the cock, washing her sigmoid colon in hot stickiness. Her belly aflame with pain, she sliced her clitty with her thumbnail, and orgasmed at once.

'Yes! Oh . . . oh!'

Her door opened, and Aaliz de Brest came in.

'Good news, Caroline. The Stingers – tonight – my gosh, whatever are you doing with that dreadful thing?'

Caroline plopped the tool from her anus.

'You got *that* in your bumhole?'

'You'll get it in yours, bitch,' Caroline snarled, 'if you don't get your panties down.'

Trembling, Aaliz obeyed. 'I've never seen you so . . . so *dominant*, Caroline.'

'Bend over, you impudent slut. Spread your arse – cheeks wide.'

Aaliz presented herself for spanking, with come oozing from her twat. 'You scare me, but thrill me,' she whimpered. 'Please don't be too harsh on my bum – oh, I mean, please do.'

Caroline rubbed the the dripping rubber cock back to full hardness, then raised it over Aaliz's bare buttocks. Whap! She lashed the fesses, raising a jagged pink welt.

'Ooh!'

Whap!

'Oof!'

Whap!

'Ouch! Oh! Oh!'

Aaliz's naked bottom squirmed, as weals multiplied on her quivering bum skin.

'I love your bum, Aaliz,' Caroline panted. 'No matter how hard you clench the cheeks, there's such a lovely little tremor of the flesh after the skin is slapped – a shiver right through the bum meat, and up your legs and spine. That's why a beating must always be on the *naked* buttocks.'

For over five minutes, Caroline spanked the wriggling, sobbing maid to crimson with the stiff rubber cock, and throughout the spanking, as Aaliz's welted bare bum squirmed and wriggled, the cock remained rigid. *As if it does have a brain!*

9

Smarting Fesses

Caroline sneaked out of school, the moon gleaming on her nude body, and padded across field and coppice, following the directions for her intitiation to the Stingers. There could be no mistake, as it was the only house in view, and she found herself knocking on the door of a twee little pebble-dash bungalow, with a garden of roses and honeysuckle, and a pleasant view of the ocean, at the farthest end of the Furrow Weald estate. Aaliz de Brest opened the door, and hugged Caroline. Aaliz was wearing a flimsy shortie-nightie, in sheer, transparent turquoise nylon, clinging rather wetly to her naked breasts and croup, and with a lovely flounced frilly hem. Aaliz looked so *right* in frillies!

'So glad you came,' she said. 'The gang's longing to meet you. It's sort of a pyjama party, only, as new girl, you won't need any pyjamas.'

Caroline wiped her wet feet on the welcome mat, and followed Aaliz into the drawing room, where a gaggle of girls in nighties lounged in armchairs. There were tea things and plates of biscuits. Mistress Ermine Floss stood to greet her.

'Welcome to my humble abode,' she said.

Caroline gasped, for there was Judy Tinsell! Her sister goth-to-be . . . was this some kind of trap? She thought – hoped – she saw Judy wink complicitly at her.

'I expect you'd like some tea. Judy, would you?'

'Thank you, Mistress Floss.'

The mistress tut-tutted. 'Ermine, please. We are all Stingers together, Caroline, and soon, you will be one of us.'

So she *was* in the right place. She recognised some of the maids: Vapula McCloskey, Sarah Hogplum, Emma Spivey, and the senior schoolmaid Janet Petarda, pompous as could be. Judy Tinsell poured Caroline a cup of tea and offered her the plate of biscuits. Perched in an armchair, Caroline took her tea, and helped herself to a rich tea and a custard cream, not wishing to appear greedy. The chatter took up again around her, mostly school gossip – complaints about the rigours of drill, prospects for the forthcoming 'peg party' and giggling speculation as to which depraved maids had a lesbo pash – with no mention of Caroline's intitiation into a secret society. Perhaps this harmless tea party *was* her initiation. She drained her teacup, accepted a refill from Judy, and helped herself to another custard cream.

'You are perhaps surprised that a mistress heads the Stingers, Caroline,' said Ermine Floss, 'when maidbands are technically unlawful.'

'A little, mistress – I mean, Ermine,' Caroline replied, after brushing crumbs from her lips.

'We are a sort of watchdog, you see, to ensure that Furrow Weald does not depart from the founder's rules. Mistress Frubbin is an admirable leader, but sometimes remote from daily doings. Maids can be tempted away from our Furrovian ethos of pure submission, by many impure forces – boys, for example. There is another, sinister maidband, called the Swanks –' Ermine shuddered '– whose filthy practices include consorting with boys, to the shame of all Furrovians. They are anonymous, as befits their shady lusts, and communicate by absurd secret signs, while we Stingers bare our faces and bottoms –' the girls giggled '– without fear. You have, of course, received your school dildo, Caroline?'

'My – oh, yes.'

'And you use it frequently to masturbate?'

'Why, yes,' Caroline said, blushing.

'Anal as well as vulval?'

'Mostly anal.'

There was a ripple of admiring murmurs.

'Good. You must understand that a male is all cock and balls, and *only* cock and balls. To her own advantage, a proper maid must – on the *proper occasion* – submit to thrashing, bondage and cock impalement, but not to his wiles and smiles.'

'Bondage?' said Caroline nervously.

'Don't be alarmed, it's part of any normal girl's . . . well, you'll see.'

Ermine Floss rose, her gossamer nightie rippling over her naked body, the titties, belly and thighs as ripe as a teenager's, with a bum as firm and proud as Caroline's own. Her buttocks bore numerous faded weals.

'Come, maids. It is time for us to enjoy Caroline's initiation as a new Stinger. Follow me to the dungeon.'

Judy held Caroline's arm with rather unnecessary tightness, as they descended to the cellar, which was a vast chamber lit with small red carriage lamps, and a sponge floor.

'Do you like it, Caroline?' said Ermine. 'I knocked through, you know.'

'It's very nice.'

The chamber was darkly shadowed by mysterious machines of supplice, all straps, spikes, thongs and buckles. Caroline shivered, her titties sprouting goose pimples, and the nipples stiffening, while a seep of come filled her cunt. She squished her thighs together, finding them damp.

'The floor is real sponge, from the Aegean – Samothraki, actually. Do you know it? An adorable island, with such obliging young men. We Stingers are awful for dripping girly juices everywhere, during our spank sessions, so sponge is a necessity. Here you see our wrestling mat, gibbet, rack, flogging frame and stools: everything a girl could want for submissive spanking fun.'

'Is that to be my initiation?' Caroline asked. 'You are going to spank me? If so, I'm quite ready.'

The girls eyed her, leering, with little shiny patches of come at the crotches of their flimsy nighties, and the transparent fabric poked upwards by erect nipples.

'There is a little more to it,' said Ermine. 'Our enemies, the Swanks, are beastly cruel, and if they take prisoners, they resort to the vilest tortures to extract confessions. It follows that a Stinger must be able to withstand such tortures.'

Caroline went pale, yet felt a spurt of come wet her cooze.

'You *do* want to be a Stinger?' said Aaliz.

'Of course.'

'Because if you refuse your initiation ordeal,' Ermine purred, 'then we must assume you are a Swank spy, and torture you anyway.'

'It seems I've no choice,' Caroline said with a sigh.

'That's the spirit,' said Ermine.

Caroline stood, trembling, and then wrinkled her face in pain, as two heavy candlesticks were clamped by tight pins to her swollen nipples. Almost flush with her breasts, the candles came up to her collarbone. Several girls were already openly masturbating, and licking their lips, as they eyed Caroline's bare body, pristine, but for the faded ridges of previous beatings. The girls wriggled their cunt basins, wanking themselves through their nighties, the nylon sopping with shiny come. Breasts bouncing under the heavy candlesticks, Caroline stepped into a flogging frame, like a slender guillotine, without the blade. Judy, with a whispered apology, grasped Caroline's mane, and wrenched it tight, then knotted it around the top crossbar of the guillotine, so that Caroline was obliged to stand on tiptoe.

Ermine pressed Caroline's wrists together, and pushed them between her thighs, lashing the wrists together at Caroline's thigh backs, with the cord extending around each thigh, so that Caroline had to stoop, with her back at an angle, and her hair wrenched by the roots. Ermine explained, with some pride, that this position – a Stinger speciality – was a compromise between the naval strung suspension, suitable for whipping the vertically stretched back, but not so much for buttock punishment, as the fesses were too clenched, and the old school 'bend over' position, suitable for caning the tautly stretched buttocks, but curving the back overmuch, with less ease of access. In this position, the pain to her wrenched hair would keep Caroline from wriggling and shaking too much, while both back and buttocks were exposed for maximum flogging pain.

'Comfortable?' she asked.

'No,' Caroline gasped, eyes moist with tears.

'Good,' said Ermine, rubbing her hands. 'Let the ordeal begin, and I want to see every maid's fingers diddling wet!'

'Yes, leader,' chorused the girls.

Judy lit the candles atop Caroline's bare breasts.

'Please, Ermine,' Caroline gasped, 'mayn't I know how many I'm to be flogged?'

'Why, no, Caroline,' said Ermine, stroking Caroline's bottom. 'That is the beauty of total submission. A sub knows nothing. Your pain, your fear – they are what make our wanks so thrilling.' Her fingers crept between Caroline's cunt folds, making Caroline's bum wriggle, with a sticky wet sound. 'Like a true sub, you are thrilled, too, my dear. We must make your ordeal extra painful.'

'Oh, no, please . . .' Caroline moaned. 'Ooh!' The first drips of hot candle wax scalded her nipples. 'Ooh . . .' she moaned. 'My breasts hurt.'

There were gasps of excitement from the wanking maids, who rolled their nighties up and knotted them under their breasts, to leave their cunts and bums naked for action. Ermine stepped back, and placed her fingers between her legs. Caroline sobbed, her face wet with tears, and her mouth a rictus of pain, as her titties piled with searing hot wax, solidifying on her nipples, before flaking off in a crust, leaving the nipples bare for the next scalding droplet.

'As part of the fun,' said Ermine, 'you'll have a secret code word, that no one will know except Judy. If you reveal the code word, your punishment will stop.'

Judy pressed her lips to Caroline's ear, and whispered. Caroline nodded. At Ermine's command, Judy lifted a three-foot cane, of dark, springy rattan wood, over Caroline's trembling bare buttocks. Vip! The cane lashed the naked fesses; Caroline twitched, groaning, and her flogged bum clenched hard around the broad pink stripe. Ermine joined the other girls in vigorous masturbation of her cooze and clitty. Vip!

'Ooh!'

Vip!

'Ahh!'

Caroline's beaten fesses squirmed.

'You should really save your squeals, Caroline,' said Ermine, 'for there's worse to come.'

'Oh, Ermine, it hurts so dreadfully. I can't imagine anything worse,' Caroline said, sobbing. 'My bum's on fire.'

Vip!

'Ahh!'

Caroline's head began to shake, straining at her tautly bound hair, which prevented her body from wriggling, or doing more than shudder on the spot. Judy slipped off her sweat-soaked nightie, and began to cane in the nude. Vip! Caroline's buttocks squirmed, livid with fiery red weals, darkening to crimson, but she kept her stance on tiptoe, with her hair pinning her to the flogging spot. The fingers of her hands, poking between her thighs, twitched madly, while each stroke of the cane made her breasts bounce, spraying hot wax over the seared teat flesh.

'Oh! Ooh! It's so cruel . . .' Caroline panted.

'Indeed,' mused Ermine, as her fingers squelched within her gash flaps. 'Strung, naval style, with arms up, gives a maid the release of slamming and wriggling against her bonds, but when the rope is her own hair, there's not much she can do to express her pain, which makes it all the more frustrating.'

Vip! Caroline's crimson fesses squirmed tight.

'Although your bottom does wriggle rather deliciously,' purred Ermine, her fingers wanking noisily in her sopping cunt.

Vip! Vip! Judy flogged her bottom with rapid, skilful stingers, wealing the whole quivering expanse of bum flesh, until Caroline's arse was a rainbow of weals. The tally of strokes mounted steadily, Caroline's face scarlet and pain-wrinkled, with drool pouring from her gaping mouth, and lolling tongue, while sparkling clear come wet her cunt and quivering thighs. Vapula, Emma and the others gurgled with pleasure, as they wanked off, and the haughty Janet Petarda had Sarah Hogplum bent over before her, grasping her hips, while she buggered her anus with a huge black strap-on dildo of gnarled rubber, lubricated with the groaning victim's arse grease. Sarah's moans of distress competed with the dry whack of Judy's rattan on Caroline's bare, yet Sarah's quim, like Caroline's, was a glistening torrent of come, and her clitty protruded stiff and shiny from her winking cunt lips.

'Ooh! Oh, please, mistress . . .'

'Ermine.'

'Ermine, surely my bum's had enough?'

'After a mere three dozen? Tut tut! Lay it on harder, Judy, please.'

Judy complied, and Caroline's whimpers turned to screams, as the awful rattan thrashed her between the bum globes, right on her anus and dripping cooze flaps. The wood made a dreadful wet slapping thud on the come-soaked perineum and squishy gash flaps, and Caroline's bum jerked uncontrollably, as come poured over her palms, trapped between her wet thighs.

'Unless you'd care to confess the secret password?' Ermine murmured.

Vip! Vip!

'Urrgh! No . . . no matter how my bum smarts, I can't betray the Stingers,' Caroline said, sobbing.

Ermine stepped in front of Caroline's tear-glazed face, thrusting her belly forwards, so that Caroline could observe her masturbate. Her fingers squelched inside her dripping quim, with her thumb mashing the bright red nubbin, stiffly erect and distended well beyond the vulval lips.

'Doesn't it excite you, Caroline, to know that I, and other maids, are wanking off, at your pain?' she whispered.

Caroline began to cry. 'Yes, you know it does,' she said bitterly. 'Oh! I admit it, I'm a sub . . . a Stinger!'

'Not yet a Stinger,' panted Ermine, squeezing her stiff red nipple domes, as she wanked. 'Not yet.'

After sixty cane strokes to her buttocks, Judy lowered her rattan, and began to masturbate furiously. Emma Spivey approached, with a quirt of long rubber thongs held between her teeth. Ermine said Caroline's bare bottom was as pretty as a Cornish patchwork quilt, and it was time for the cat. Caroline groaned, as Emma lifted the scourge above her bare back. Thwap! The thongs bit deeply into Caroline's shoulders, slamming her head against her trussing rope of hair.

'Ahh!' she cried.

Thwap!

'Ooh!'

Thwap!

'Ahh! Ohh!'

'Worse than a bum-caning?' asked Ermine.

'Gosh, yes,' Caroline gasped.

'Then you're ready to confess.'

Thwap! Thwap!'

'Ooh! Never!' Caroline said, shaking her head.

Thwap! Thwap! The scourge flogged Caroline all across her naked back, until the flesh was criss-crossed with deeply gouged welts, crimson, turning to purple. Caroline's helpless body was jolted back and forth and sideways, as the heavy rubber thongs, two inches thick, lashed her unprotected skin. After several minutes of whipping, her back and buttocks formed an unbroken tapestry of weals. Janet Petarda buggered another whimpering girl, her dildo now stabbing between the buttocks of Judy Tinsell, who wanked herself off, as her bum squirmed under her bugger's slamming thrusts.

Other girls masturbated singly, or in pairs, using dildos to penetrate the cunt, while their teeth bit their own nipples, or those of a wank chum. Sarah Hogplum embraced Vapula McCloskey, kissing her full on the lips, their tongues slurping, while their bellies slapped, with one end of a double-pronged dildo dripping from each girl's cunt. Ermine wanked alone, thumbing her clitty, with thighs parted, and manipulating a rubber arse plug in and out of her anus. Emma's big titties bounced, as she flogged Caroline, and, sometimes, Ermine removed her come-smeared fingers from her cooze, to slap and tweak Emma's nipples, bathing them in her come. Caroline's breasts were streaked with the searing hot candle wax, which crusted and fell, as her titties shook under flogging, leaving vivid red bruises on the breast meat.

'Ready to confess, Caroline?' panted Ermine, as her arse plug squelched in and out of her rectum.

'Never,' Caroline spat.

Her face turned, twisted in agony, to the smiling Ermine, her own face scarlet, and her wanked cunt gushing come.

'How I hate myself. Whipped bare, as a helpless piece of girl meat,' Caroline said with a sob, 'yet my quim is wetter than yours, mistress. Oh, bother! I *like* it.'

'That's the spirit.'

Her back took sixty lashes of the scourge, until Ermine nodded that it was time to proceed to the next stage of her initiation.

'You're doing awfully well,' she said.

Vapula and Janet untied Caroline's hair and wrists, and permitted her to stand, groaning and wincing, as she rubbed her whipped bottom and back. Emma held up a looking glass, and Caroline craned to look at her flogged flesh, bursting into a flood of tears, as she saw her whole naked rear criss-crossed with savage weals.

'Please, Ermine, I need to pee,' she said.

'Of course you do, dear,' Ermine said. 'It's all that tea. Only number ones?'

'I think so.'

Ermine gave Caroline a huge chamber pot, as big as a standard lavvy bowl, and the girls watched, while Caroline squatted and released a powerful jet of steaming hot piss into the bowl. Giggling, each nude girl in turn squatted to pee, until they had all voided, and the bowl was brim full of golden acrid liquid. Janet wheeled forwards a wooden platform, with handcuffs at each end, and a hump, two feet high, in the middle; from it, Aaliz retrieved a basket of fruits and vegetables, while Emma unrolled a bulky fireman's hose of black rubber tubing. Trembling, Caroline allowed the maids to wrap her in the rubber tubing, fearfully tight, first one leg, then the other, but leaving her buttocks and cunt bare, before sheathing her belly and face, with the titties naked and squashed to hard, bursting bulbs of flesh. Caroline groaned and gasped, protesting that she could hardly breathe, until the rubber wrapped her head, with her mane poking out as a topknot, shrouding her completely, save for a breathing hole at her nose.

'Mm . . . mm,' she moaned, as she was bent backwards over the humped platform, legs spread, cunt and anus exposed, and thighs straining, with her ankles and wrists cuffed to the ends of the board.

Aaliz positioned the brimming piss bowl under her, and immersed Caroline's head. 'I'm awfully sorry,' Aaliz murmured.

Caroline wriggled wildly, air bubbling from her nostrils through the piss, but was helpless to escape her bonds.

'You must hold your breath for one minute, Caroline,' Ermine said, 'while the whip is applied to your bubbies and quim.'

Vapula lifted a short rubber quirt of thongs a foot in length, and positioned herself over Caroline's quim, while Sarah took a cane, twenty inches long, and stationed herself over Caroline's bubbies. At a signal from Ermine, they began to whip the bound girl's privities, with Caroline heaving and wriggling at each lash to her helpless cunt and teats. Vip! Vip! The flogging tools cracked on her skin, while the piss seethed with bubbles around her rubber-sheathed head.

Her whipped cunt squirmed, the red slit meat glistening with come, which drooled down her quivering rubber thighs. The swollen lips assumed a dark crimson colour, bruising and puffing, with the flogged clitoris itself standing stiff and livid under the lashes of the quirt. Sarah worked on every inch of the bare titty flesh, stinging the nipples again and again with her cane tip, then lacing the areolae, and the enclosing teat skin, until Caroline's entire breasts were mottled red with a criss-cross of sharp weals. After a minute, Ermine pulled her head from the chamber pot, and Caroline gasped and spluttered, shaking her piss-soaked hair.

'Ready to confess, maid?' asked Ermine.

'No,' groaned Caroline, her voice muffled by her rubber gag.

'Then we'll try the fruit basket. Let her taste some fine Cornish produce.'

Caroline's head was once again immersed in piss, while Emma stuffed two ripe peaches into her cunt. Aaliz seized the cane and began to lash Caroline's breasts, while Vapula whipped the open cunt, until the peaches were reduced to dribbling mush, and, between whip strokes, the maids took turns to apply their lips to Caroline's gash and suck the peach pulp from the drooling whipped slit. Next, it was a banana, then a pear, then grapes, and an apple, all whipped to pulp, and sucked by the eager maids, flicking their lips and tongue on Caroline's clitty, as they swallowed come-soaked fruit mush, with Caroline brought up at minute intervals to draw breath. Her whipped bubbies were now a livid purple, with Aaliz, her face scarlet, wanking off feverishly as she caned her friend's naked breasts, with specially vicious attention to the bruised, erect nipple domes.

'It really hurts me to do this,' Aaliz blurted. 'But Stingers must enjoy hurt.'

Vip! Vip! At each cane stroke, the flogged teats quivered like jellies. Each time Caroline surfaced, she refused to end her torment by giving up the secret password. Her bruised cunt dripped with come and fruit mush; Janet strapped on her dildo thong, and fitted a huge sharp carrot, seventeen inches by five, as prong, and then began to fuck Caroline's cunt with it. Caroline's head banged the sides of the chamber pot, under the swirling piss, as her cunt basin writhed under the onslaught of the giant vegetable, and the girls wanked vigorously, looking at the come squirting from her flogged, fucked cunt, to trickle down the rubber sheathing of her thighs.

With a plop, Janet withdrew the carrot from Caroline's cunt and, with Judy holding apart the buttocks, poked it hard into Caroline's squirming anus. She thrust powerfully, and the carrot disappeared right to Caroline's colon, with Janet's pubic gourd slapping Caroline's buttocks, as she bum fucked the trussed girl. Vapula resumed whipping Caroline's cooze, the flashing rubber thongs lashing a hair's breadth from Janet's belly, as the senior girl fucked Caroline's arse. Caroline's anal elastic tightened around the carrot, squeezing it, until Janet withdrew, the orange tube mauled to dripping shreds, clammy with Caroline's arse grease. Snarling, Janet replaced the spoiled carrot with a marrow, bigger and thicker than the carrot, and with a gleaming rounded tip.

'She'll never take it,' Aaliz gasped.

'She'd better, the fucking slut,' sneered Janet.

Janet strapped on the marrow, oiled it with come from Caroline's come-spuming cunt, and rammed it into the writhing girl's distended anus. The girls gaped, wanking hard, and Aaliz continued to cane Caroline's titties, as the marrow filled Caroline's anal elastic, thrusting deeper and deeper into her rectum, until its entire green bulk vanished inside Caroline's body. Panting, Janet began to fuck her, with strenuous slamming thrusts, while Caroline's belly bulged under its rubber tubing. Every time Caroline's head was wrenched up, dripping piss, she took several deep breaths, but wasted no time in bleating, concentrating instead on getting a lungful of air to last her next minute's torture.

Before each immersion, she ritually refused to admit the password. After several minutes' buggery, Janet's marrow was reduced to pulp by the suction force of Caroline's anus, and she replaced it with an outsize corncob. Buggered fiercely for minutes, Caroline's bumhole squashed that, too, to mush. Her rubbered legs were a torrent of come, sluicing from her whipped cunt, and, as Vapula's lash descended, Caroline thrust her bare cooze upwards, to meet the thongs. Her clitty was swollen and extruded, shivering like a tulip in the breeze, as the rubber thongs whipped it. Caroline's flogged breasts heaved up and down, the nipple plums stiffly erect, and quivered under Aaliz's caning.

'Oh! It hurts me so much,' gasped Aaliz, masturbating.

Come streamed from Aaliz's wanked cunt, as she flogged Caroline. Sarah and Emma wanked each other, spanking bare bums, while their kissing mouths deep-tongued. Ermine was squirming, with little squeals and moans, and wanking her own clitty, as Judy rammed her arse plug in and out of her rectum, while spanking her fesses. As Caroline's arse squirmed under fierce tooling, Vapula's quirt continued its rain of lashes to her deeply striped cunt mound, the thongs licking hard inside the wet red slit meat. Vip! Vapula delivered a savage blow, which missed Caroline's cunt, and caught Janet's belly, just as her tool, a giant cucumber, plunged into the bound girl's anus. Red marks sprang up on Janet's tummy.

'You fucking bitch,' she snarled.

Janet ripped her cucumber from Caroline's anus, and sprang at Vapula, felling her with a punch to the breasts, then leaping on top of her, to kick her belly and cunt, and claw at her nipples.

'You pig!' Vapula screamed, and kneed Janet between the thighs.

Janet fell against Aaliz, knocking the cane from her hand.

'You fucking rotter,' hissed Aaliz, wrenching Janet's hair by the roots, and delivering a kick to her nose.

'Ouch! Let go!' Janet moaned.

Judy kicked Janet between the legs.

'Maids, maids!' cried Ermine.

'Stay out of this, bitch,' said Emma, busy frotting Sarah's drooling cunt.

'How dare you!' Ermine blurted, lashing Emma's bare bum with her cane.

'Why, you –' Sarah snarled, kickng Ermine in the quim, then throwing herself on the naked mistress, savagely biting her bare breasts.

Ermine squealed, and fell into the scrimmage of fighting girls. The room was a mass of thrashing nude bodies, echoing with squeals and groans, as cunts were kicked, breasts clawed, feet bitten, noses ripped and bumholes gouged. Caroline raised her head from the chamber pot.

'Wait!' Janet cried, withdrawing her fingernails from Ermine's anus. 'That's the bitch who should suffer!'

'She started this,' agreed Vapula, releasing Sarah's nipples from her teeth.

'Let's not be too cruel,' squealed Aaliz, panting and writhing, as Emma's teeth chewed her wet cunt lips.

'Wait . . . please,' Caroline whimpered, as she was stripped of her rubber cocoon, untied from the flogging frame, and hurled naked and bruised to the sponge matting.

As one, the Stingers hurled themselves upon her, biting, punching, kicking and gouging, while Caroline sobbed, thrashing under savage blows. Her hand was between her legs, bathed in a pool of spurting come, and, as her whipped body shuddered under kicks, punches and scratches, she wanked off vigorously.

'Yes,' she gasped. 'I deserve it.'

Janet had a spear of broccoli jammed in Caroline's cunt, and Emma used stalks of rhubarb to fill her bumhole, while Aaliz fucked her mouth with a flowering courgette. Caroline's fingers danced on her swollen clitty, as she masturbated faster. Ermine squatted and pissed on her face, while Sarah peed on her flogged breasts, Judy bit her wealed buttocks and Vapula crouched low over her belly, to slime her tummy with a rapid plop of dungs. Caroline's tortured body slithered, writhing, in a lake of come and steaming piss, her buttocks slapping the come-soaked sponge, as the girls took turns to fuck her, until the fruit basket was empty.

'Yes, do me,' Caroline moaned. 'Shame me, hurt me, maids.'

Each girl, masturbating her clit and tweaking her bare nipples, squatted over Caroline's mouth to dribble steamy piss for her to swallow, and obliged Caroline to lick her to orgasm, while swallowing all her piss and come. Emma and Aaliz kissed wetly, as Caroline's tongue flickered over their cunts and bumholes; Ermine wanked off, her bum bitten by Judy (who admitted she *loved* biting girls' naked bottoms), and bit Vapula's titties, with her finger poking Vapula's anus, as Vapula squatted over Caroline's face, with the tongue mashing her clit; Caroline masturbated, moaning and writhing, as she frotted her own clitty, her bum squirming in the spongy piss and, as the orgasming Janet's come poured down her throat, she gurgled: 'Oh! Oh! *Ahh*! Yes! I'm coming!'

Come spewed from her wanked cunt, as her belly heaved, and her thighs rippled, with hot climax flooding her body. As the naked tribadists disengaged, Caroline was left, writhing on the sponge and crooning in ecstacy. She gave a gasp of relief, as a powerful jet of pee steamed from her cunt, splashing the feet of her tormentresses. Panting, she rose, to crouch low and lick all the bare feet dry of her piss.

'Congratulations, Caroline,' Ermine panted. 'You are a true submissive, and one of the Stingers.'

'Oh, goody!' Caroline cried, hugging Aaliz, and all the other nude girls in turn. She gave a little squeal of pleasure as Judy poked her index finger into her anus, right to the knuckle.

'No hard feelings?' asked Ermine.

'Well,' Caroline said thoughtfully, 'my fesses are smarting just a little.'

'Then you are definitely one of us!' cried Judy. 'Even though you *said it*.'

'Said what?'

'The secret password.'

'Oh?' said Caroline. 'I was having such a lovely, super time – crushed and shamed and peed on and caned, and *everything*! – I don't know *what* I said.'

Judy smiled, and scratched Caroline's wealed bare bottom, making Caroline wince, then grin bravely.

'You said "Yes, I'm coming." That's the secret password.'

10

Wet Pink Panties

'My,' said Matron Emily Tongue, 'whoever gave you such a dreadful basting, Caroline?'

Her hands kneaded Caroline's naked buttocks, smearing them with cool ointment.

'Why, um, Miss Vicca Valcul, Matron,' Caroline replied, crossing her fingers for fibbing.

'Your bum and titties, and back as well? It wasn't just a cane from the looks of things.'

'I was rather cheeky, miss, so I was whipped with the leather, too.'

'Well, it's in the rules. But your titties – they look rather scalded. And what's this – teethmarks on your bum?'

'Well . . . it was another girl, miss. We were fighting – from my file, you know my reputation as a hellcat, which is quite unfair – and this other girl threw a lighted candle at my bubbies, and then bit my bum, so Miss Valcul caned us both for fighting, and whipped me for biting.'

'I thought it was for cheek.'

'Uh . . . that, too.'

'And wasn't it the other maid doing the biting?'

'Well, I must have done more than her.'

Caroline's crossed fingers were beginning to ache.

'If I didn't know it was nonsense,' Matron said sighing, 'I'd say you'd been in some horrid initiation ritual for one of these absurd maidbands, which I expect you've heard of, Caroline? Take my word, they don't exist. They are just a way for wicked maids to frighten others into doing them favours – playing wanking games, or fetching them cigarettes from uncouth boys in Trelashen. I imagine your unnamed opponent was Judy Tinsell – she *is* a hellcat, and many's the time she's been caned for bum-biting. She likes to sneak up on girls asleep, whip up their nighties, then bite their buttocks really hard. If the girl is sleeping on her back, Judy will even bite her gourd, or twat lips.'

'She – the girl I can't sneak on – did that, too, miss,' Caroline blurted, opening her bruised cooze flaps, with a wince.

'My, so she did.'

'I put some cream on, and I wanked and wanked an awful lot – you know how a girl has to wank after a really hot spanking.'

Matron nodded, stroking her chin.

'I used my come as ointment for my bum weals, which helped a bit, but even so, I didn't sleep very well, so I thought it best to come to surgery.'

'I see. Vicca certainly doesn't appreciate cheek, and, as you are her special ward, I suppose she must be harsher on you than the others.'

'I *did* merit chastisement, miss,' said Caroline, eyes closed, and beaming, as the wonderful cool cream soothed her smarting welts.

'My special lotion will have you right as rain in no time,' said Emily. 'It has zinc ointment, seaweed, Cornish herbs, and, oh, one thing and another. It's specially for maids, you see.'

'I'm curious. What else, besides herbs?'

Emily laughed. 'Curiosity and the cat, maid.'

'Oh, go on.'

'It'll cost you a favour.'

'All right. Tell me.'

Matron blushed.

'Gosh,' she murmured, 'I'm a bit shy. Normally I wouldn't dream of being so bold, but, Caroline – that bottom of yours, and those bubbies, and that absolutely *fabulous* gourd above your cunny lips, I can hardly resist eating you up. I've had my breakfast wank, and that normally carries me till luncheon, but the very sight of your nude bottom – your whole body! – makes me frightfully wet. How *did* you get such a huge cunny bulb? It's like an alp, above your thighs, and in perfect counterpoint to the gorgeous swelling of your bottom – I mean that one highlights the beauty of the other. I have certain . . . artistic leanings, and you'd be perfect as an artist's model.'

'I was made that way, miss,' Caroline said. 'As for my twat gourd, why, some beastly girls call it a camel's foot. But I'm determined to be proud of myself.'

'Do you find me pretty, Caroline?' murmured Emily, coyly. 'I put on my best nylons and panties and things, and my laciest sussies this morning, and even a little rouge on my nips – I don't know why – a little bird must have told me you were coming.'

'I think you are very lovely, miss,' Caroline replied gravely. 'How could I think otherwise, with such an adorable touch to my bottom?'

'Look,' said Emily, lifting her short white rubber skirt.

She was wearing pink nylons, with lacy tops; under her white rubber singlet, unzipped almost to her nipples, lacy pink bra cups pressed her teats upwards, swelling together in two bulbs of bare flesh; her tight pink thong panties were sopping wet at the gusset, which clearly outlined her engorged cunt lips.

'One of the secret ingredients in my ointment is come,' she whispered thrillingly. 'Not girls' come, but . . . you know, boys' spunk. Don't ask me where I get it – well, I might tell you, if you are extra nice to me, and do me the special favour I want.'

Emily whispered in Caroline's ear; Caroline giggled.

'Spank you on the bare bottom, miss?' she said. 'Why, it will be my pleasure.'

'You really, truly mean that?' said Matron, blushing crimson.

'I'll prove it to you,' Caroline replied. 'I've been wondering lately if I'm becoming too submissive – I know that's the whole point of my training, and I love it – but spanking a delicious bare bum will sort of balance things.'

'It's the other way round for me,' Emily said. 'As matron, I must be stern, though I long to submit to pain, and the shame of a glowing spanked bottom, like a normal girl. When I masturbate, you see, I spank myself with my hairbrush, and I dream of a really hard bare-bum spanking from a strong hand – it's not easy to ask for what I crave, since a matron is supposed to be an authority figure. But all girls crave spanking, don't they? I mean, every one of us, no matter what her station in life, wants to bend over and bare up, for that luscious warm smarting you get when your bare bum clenches and squirms, with super cracks on your unprotected skin, as your legs jerk at the bum-drubbing, and each spank makes your toes curl. But I'm getting a little ahead of myself.'

Panting and bright-eyed, Emily licked her lips. 'You promise to spank me *really* hard?'

'Promise.'

'Gosh, you're making my twat seep. I'd best get my panties off, then. My, they are soaking. How embarrassing ... your lovely body has got my twat and knickers so frightfully wet.' She began to roll down her pink panties. 'We're all little girls at heart, aren't we?' She giggled. 'And there's something awfully nice about teasing, when you lower your pink panties inch by inch to show your bottom just as pink, so you can't see where the panties stop and the spanked bum starts.'

'Pink is such a gorgeous colour,' said Caroline. 'I wish we maids were allowed to wear pink with our school uniforms – when I get my uniform, that is. Although I'm getting used to being in the nude all the time.'

'Yes, it's healthy and fun, isn't it?' said Emily, rolling her knickers further down. They made a sucking noise, as the gusset detached from the cooze lips, and the lacy pink triangle of the thong dripped cunt juice. 'Bumweals heal sooner, with the fresh air. But I know where you can wear pink knickers – in fact, where you are asked to, and stockings and sussies as well, just like mine. Pink makes a girl feel so . . . so girlish.'

'Where?' asked Caroline.

'Spanking first,' said Emily, tapping her bottom, with her rubber skirt making a squishy sound, as she rolled it tightly over her back. 'Then we'll see.'

'Would you prefer to touch your toes, miss, or bend over my knee?' Caroline asked.

'Since you're the spanker, you must be in charge,' Emily replied. 'It's so much more fun that way. But I'd prefer to be bent over your knee, and feel my twat rubbing against your bare thigh. You'll get awfully wet with my come, I promise.'

'Very well, miss,' said Caroline, frowning. 'You will kindly bend over my thighs for a bare-bottom spanking.'

'Oo-er,' mumbled Emily, looking suitably scared. 'Must I, miss?'

'You must,' Caroline snapped. 'You've been awfully naughty. Look at your pink panties. They're sopping wet – an absolute disgrace. You may leave them round your ankles to stop your legs flapping, as I spank you, for I promise I'll really make your bum squirm.'

Caroline stood, watching Matron's wet thong slither down her nylons to her ankles, and test-slapped the back of the leather armchair. Matron blanched. Caroline perched on the chair, and invited her to take position, spreadeagled over her thighs. Moving awkwardly, with her panties at her ankles, Emily hobbled forwards, and plumped her belly and twat on top of Caroline's thighs, which she had pressed together and raised to make a platform. Caroline pushed Emily's head down, with her hair brushing Caroline's bare feet, and her face squashed against her shins. She made Emily part her thighs, until the panties' elastic was fully stretched at her ankles, so as to reveal the fullness of her naked cunt and perineum, with the wrinkled brown prune of her anus peeping coyly amid the taut skin of the bum cleft. Already, Emily's fesses were quivering, and come oozed from her swollen gash flaps. Caroline raised her arm high, over the buttocks. Smack! Without warning, she brought it down hard on mid-fesse, leaving a pink palm print on the skin.

'Oof!' Emily gasped, as her buttocks jerked.

Smack!

'Uh!'

Smack!'

'Oh! That's hard.'

Smack! Smack! Smack!'

Caroline dealt three savage spanks in quick succession, turning her varied palm prints to a deepening red, and making Emily's buttocks clench tight.

'Ooh!' Emily squealed.

Smack!

'I don't –'

Smack!

'– want *any* –'

Smack!

'– noise –'

Smack!

'– out of you –'

Smack!

'– bitch!'

Smack! Smack! Smack!

'Uhh . . . uhh.'

Gasping, Emily wriggled her flaming red bottom, her ankles wrenching at her panties and her legs jerking rigid at each furious spank to the helpless fesses. Her breath came in agonised pants, in a low, whining rasp, as drool dribbled from her lips, tightened in a rictus of pain, and her cunt lips seeped shiny come over Caroline's bare thigh. Smack! Emily's spanked buttocks clenched tight, before resuming their agonised squirms.

'You asked for a spanking and, by gosh, you're going to get one,' Caroline gasped, her titties bouncing, as she spanked, and her clenched thighs all squishy with the come that was beginning to pump from her own tingling, turgescent cunt.

Smack! Smack! At each spank, her thighs pressed her stiffened clitty, jolting her tummy with waves of pleasure. Emily panted, her face banging against Caroline's feet, and her titties squashed on her thighs. Her breath rasped hoarsely. Smack! Smack!

'You see, miss,' Caroline panted, 'I have to look at that bold bottom, wriggling and squirming at me, *quite naked*, and I take your immodesty as a personal affront. How dare you –'

Smack!

'– show your naked bum to me –'

Smack!

'– so shamelessly?'

Smack! Smack! Smack!

'Ooh! Ahh!'

'You may speak,' Caroline gasped, wriggling her thighs against her throbbing clitty. 'I want to hear why your beastly bare bum deserves punishment – you naughty –'

Smack!

'– horrid –'

Smack!

'– maid!'

Smack!

'*Ahh*! Yes, Miss Caroline, anything you command.'

Sobbing, Emily stammered that beneath her matron's starch and rubber beat the heart of a trollop, a slut, an absolutely vicious little girl. Caroline kept up the spanking, her nipples and clit throbbing stiff, with her cunt gushing more and more copiously, as she listened. Emily explained that she had once been married, when only seventeen, to an immensely rich man over twice her age.

'He showered me with luxury,' Emily said. 'We travelled all over the world, but it didn't take me long to realise he was a cruel and beastly pervert. For the sake of luxury, I followed his whims, and even, to my shame, grew to enjoy them.'

Smack!

'Ooh! He liked to spank me, you see, and I didn't mind that, for any girl loves her bare bum spanked, even though most of us are too coy to admit it. He caned me on the bare, really viciously, and that, too, was a pleasure, for amid my pain, I had the joy of submission, and frequently was flogged to orgasm, without the slightest touch to my clitty – although sometimes, the cane tip would slice between my cooze lips, which gave me a real tingle.'

Smack! Smack!

'Ouch! Then he caned me in bondage, hobbled, with my feet and hands tied, while other girls watched, or strapped in a harness, like a pony, or sheathed in plastic film from head to toes, and I grew to like being so deliciously humiliated. He made me watch while other girls sucked his cock, or else he buggered them, with my face inches from his cock squelching in and out of the girl's anus, while one of his cruellest sluts flogged me, gagged ith my own pee-wet panties, and strapped in bondage, with a sjambok or rawhide whip. The sjambok hurts awfully, and it's worse when you are tied head to foot and can't wriggle. We went to Africa a lot, for he had a thing for African girls, and liked to watch a black beauty, in the nude, whipping or caning me, with her gorgeous black titties bouncing up and down like big firm footballs, and her fingers opening her pink wet slit, as she wanked herself over my squirming bum . . . liked also for me to watch while a black girl, or several, birched *his* bare arse, and I wanked him off between my toes.'

'You *are* a vicious beast,' Caroline said, her cunt slopping come all down her quivering legs. 'Were you birched, too?'

Smack! Smack!

'Oof!' Emily gasped, her crimson bare fesses squirming hard. 'Yes, I was. The kiss of the birch is worse than any cane or whip – its dry crackle is exquisitely painful, on the completely naked buttocks, and we don't birch here at school because it becomes addictive. Once a girl has been birched on the bare a few times, has known the utter pain and shame of a naked birching, no other punishment is so pretty, or so gasp-making.'

Smack!

'Oof! Under my husband's tutelage, I became adept at giving and taking the birch, usually on the naked bottoms of black girls, but sometimes to girls in Venice, or Paris, or San Remo, or wherever we were. I flogged hard, knowing my bum would be next to suffer, a sort of vengeance in reverse, and my husband always made me masturbate as I whipped the girls, just as he encouraged them to masturbate, as they thrashed *me.* When I myself was whipped unbound – proud that I could take the strokes without bondage – and my hands were free, I was always obliged to masturbate, as my bottom squirmed, with one hand wanking my twat, and the other pinching my bare nips.'

'Did you enjoy it?' murmured Caroline.

Smack!

'Ooh! Yes! I came and came, masturbating while thrashed – and I loved to wank off, and feel my thighs all slippery, with come squirting from my twat, as I striped a luscious black bottom, nude and squirming under my cane or birch.'

The spanking Caroline's thighs were slippery with come.

Smack! Smack! Emily's glowing bare bum wriggled violently.

'Ouch! Ooh! That's so lovely, miss. My husband fancied himself an art lover, and liked me to pose as a nude model for artists in Paris and places like that . . . and I loved showing off my body. But he didn't content himself with *poses plastiques.* I had to do *poses élastiques* as well, meaning, not just static, but active tableaux, *peinture gynécologique*: where I was painted – with my buttocks wealed crimson by a sound flogging – under fucking or buggery, or sucking my husband's cock, usually as one of several cocks in succession. Painters, especially French and Italian, are a randy lot, I assure you, and didn't limit themselves to depiction, but got their smocks up, with their bare tools stiff underneath, and participated willingly. "Leda and the Swan" was one favourite theme, with different chaps pretending to be the swan, or "The Judgement of Paris", with three or four girls showing off, vying for the favours of the young prince, by stripping off their veils, masturbating before him, or doing lesbo things: wanking each other off, clit sucking and titty squeezing, without forgetting hearty bum or titty spankings. We would have to wrestle in the nude, too, no holds barred and whipped on bum and teats if we halted in a clinch. That could be so painful – far worse than bare-breasted boxing.'

Smack! Smack!

'Ooh! Yes! You're really hurting me now. But, you know, Caroline, for really super pain and shame, and the most fantastic comes, a girl has to be bum-fucked by a cruel lover, with a sex organ so huge, it seems to burst her tummy in two. And for total humiliation, he pisses on her face and bum.'

Smack! Smack!

'I can imagine,' panted Caroline. 'How *awfully* wet-making.'

'It is! My husband liked to fuck me in the bumhole, which suited me, for it's much more painful and satisfying for a maid to be used that way, than in a normal sloppy twat poke, unless the male is really well hung. In a hard anal swiving, even a modest sex organ can stimulate that voluptuous pain and pleasure we girls crave. My husband's cock was average, so he liked to bugger me, which pleased me, of course, but preferred me to "ride the bicycle", that is, sit on his lap, and squeeze his cock between my naked thighs, pumping them up and down as if riding a bike, until he splashed his spunk all over my legs and belly. He liked me to watch and masturbate, as African girls cycled him, and if I was a good girl, he would lick my clitty while one black girl's thighs milked his cock, and another, below, sucked his balls. Also, I gave him tit wanks, because my bubbies are rather big, and brought him to spunk over my nipples, which I would push up to my face and lick dry, or a toe frot, between my feet, where I made him spunk all over my toes, then bent my legs, and licked up his sperm. Never mind what some silly girls say, hot spunk tastes yummy!

'Most of all, he liked to watch me buggered and twat fucked, often at the same time, by enormously hung black boys. Some of them, in Africa, have organs that have to be felt to be believed, Caroline! My husband was quite a good painter himself, and he loved the contrast of the velvet skin with pink cooze flesh, shining wet inside a girl's twat, or the lovely red of an exposed and buggered anus against a girl's ebony buttocks. He made lots of paintings of me, in the nude, of course, with my bum striped as red as my cooze, and a black cock cleaving my bumhole, often with one equally huge plunged to the balls in my pink wet cunny. To feel *two* massive stiff cocks filling you at once, Caroline, while your bum smarts from a thrashing – it is just so, so come-making. Those African boys' bodies have such lovely, hairless velvet skin, rippling with muscle, and enormous balls, so full of cream.

'Some of them are circumcised, Timbuktu style, as they call it, that is, the entire skin of the cock peeled away, so that the tool is a shiny smooth carapace, like ebony mother-of-pearl. Also, the glans gets very hard and knobbly, so that when it's swollen stiff, it's like a beautiful ridged dildo, reaming my clitty or rectum, or slamming right at my sigmoid colon. I would orgasm again and again, as I felt a huge jet of spunk wash my colon, from a giant black shaft of hot cock meat. My husband liked to remind himself, and me, that a girl is no more than a spunk receptacle and sex animal, meat for spanking and fucking and bumming. The more brutal their fucking – the more my whipped bottom writhed, and I screamed in agony, at a black boy's buggery – the more it pleased my husband, for, as I was bum fucked, I wanked him off to spunk, with my breasts, the soles of my feet, my big toes, or even my armpits.'

Smack! Smack! Caroline's rigid fingers spanked Emily in the arse cleft, slapping her anus and cunt lips.

'Ooh! That hurts.'

'So it should. You rotten strumpet, you're making my twat juice quite shamefully.'

Smack! Smack!

'Ooh! Beast!' the wriggling girl squealed, as Caroline spanked her right on the cunt, releasing a spurt of come all over her fingers.

Caroline put her hand to her mouth and licked Emily's come from her fingers.

'But it's awfully good for me,' Caroline said. 'Perhaps a maid can become *too* submissive, and I'm worried that I love Furrow Weald a little bit too much.'

'Submission is necessary,' Emily gasped, 'to find a buyer – I mean, suitor. You have to be pegged – the suitors expect that, and, with your three-incher, you're bound to snare a lovely rich fellow.'

'You mean . . .'

Smack! Smack!

'Ooh! There's no harm in confiding. Suitors choose a maid for her aptitude in anal sex. On peg day, you must squat on your peg, with the size marked, while you chat and flirt, and try to hook a fellow. You'll get a man with a huge tool, you lucky girl. But a maid mustn't forget her dominant side, for it's a rare male who doesn't relish a bare-bum thrashing from a maid turned vixen.' Emily giggled. 'Especially if she wears pink. Men find it a turn-on, and so do girls, of a certain nature. A fully nude dominatrix is always acceptable, and often, so are black stockings, bare titties and tight rubber basque, with an agile riding crop, but pink is always exciting. It symbolises a spanked bare croup, wet cunt meat and stiff nips – a submissive girly turning deliciously, and surprisingly, nasty.'

Smack! Smack! Caroline delivered two more hard spanks, which made Emily groan, and her cunt squirt come.

'Well, your croup has been jolly well spanked enough,' said Caroline crossly. 'You've wet my thighs, and made my slit all wet, so it's time to make amends. Down on your knees, bitch, and lick me off.'

'I'm matron,' protested Emily. 'I should give the orders.'

Slap! Caroline struck her across the face.

'Not when you are my bitch,' she hissed. 'Obey!'

'Yes, mistress,' Emily whimpered.

Panting, and red of face and croup, the matron slid to the floor, and knelt between Caroline's open legs. She pressed her face to Caroline's dripping cunt, and took the engorged clit between her lips.

'Mm,' Emily moaned, as she began to lick the wet cunt flaps, chew on Caroline's swollen nubbin and slurp her gushing come, swallowing the pussy juice, with little gurgles in her throat.

Caroline moaned, too, her belly quaking; she held Emily's head pressed tightly to her quim, as her fingers squeezed and pinched her gamahucher's erect nipples, thrusting against their rubber blouse. Emily writhed at the painful caress, getting her whole mouth around Caroline's cunt, and sucking hard, with squelching noises, as she tongued Caroline's throbbing stiff clitty. Caroline sank to the floor, upended her fricatrice, and plunged her nose and mouth into Emily's wet cunt, so that the two girls embraced, thighs squeezing heads, as they gamahuched with moans and gurgles. Caroline's rigid tongue poked Emily's sopping slit, while rasping on the stiff nubbin.

'Oh, do me,' groaned Emily. 'It's so good.'

She sucked on Caroline's gash and clitty, while her nails clawed Caroline's creamed bum welts, making Caroline's buttocks jerk.

'Drink my come, bitch,' panted Caroline, scraping her fingernails on the matron's hot spank bruises.

'Yes . . . oh, you're hurting me,' Emily gasped. 'Yes . . . oh, I'm going to come . . .'

Her throat bobbed, drinking Caroline's come, as it spurted from Caroline's cooze and drooled down Emily's chin. Caroline directed Emily's hand to her stiff nipples, which Emily squeezed and tweaked.

'That's so good,' Caroline panted, 'you're bringing me off, bitch.'

'Yes . . .'

'Yes . . .'

'*Ohh!*'

'*Ooh!*'

Both girls exploded in orgasm, with come gushing from their sucked cunts, into each other's mouth. As her climax ebbed, Caroline, still clutching Emily's face between her thighs, gasped, as her twat released a heavy spurt of piss, right into Emily's mouth. She released all her piss, while Emily gurgled anew, swallowing the acrid golden fluid; when the spurt had finished, Caroline ordered the matron to lick the puddle from the floor, and Emily obeyed, bum up, while Caroline gave her further, scornful spanks. Emily whinnied, licking the linoleum dry, and masturbating her cunt, as her spanked bottom wriggled.

'It's a pity these gangs – maidbands – are just a myth,' said Caroline casually, 'otherwise maids together could have such fun – playing games of submission and dominance.'

'Yes, I've heard of such things,' Emily replied. 'How naughty!'

'Suppose there were such a band – let's call it the goths – taking it in turns to spank and be spanked, and – you know, *pretending* to be lesbos – would you like to join?'

'Gosh,' Emily bubbled. 'It sounds heaps of fun. But playful maids can still have fun. How would you like to come to St Ives with me this afternoon? It's for art class – a very good painter friend of mine, called Pris Frocker. She specialises in the nude, male and female.'

'Impossible,' said Caroline. 'I have military parade.'

'Poo! I'll give you a matron's exeat. You'll earn a few shillings, as an artist's model, you know. And – I'll let you into another secret, if you promise not to tell – it's Pris who supplies me with boys' spunk for my ointment. She pays her male models by wanking them off, you see. It's the very best Cornish spunk.'

'All right, then, I'll come.'

'It's so exciting when you call me bitch,' Emily said dreamily. 'It reminds me of my husband. Well, I'm glad that's out of my system. Confession is so good – like a spanking of the soul. Now we can go to St Ives, and enjoy ourselves.'

'But I'm still a new bitch in the nude – I haven't a thing to wear,' Caroline protested.

'You don't mind dressing in one of my rubber nurse's uniforms?'

'Of course not. It sounds rather naughty.'

'Then I'll pick you up in my car after luncheon.'

11

Spank Magnet

'Why, Merilee!' Caroline cried. 'What pretty pink panties!'

''Lo, Caroline,' said the ebony girl, somewhat coyly, but with an impish flash of her big white eyes. 'I'm not wearing panties. I'm in the nude.'

'But your bottom . . .'

Merilee nodded to Miss Pris Frocker, the celebrated painter of St Ives, a pretty tourist town, smelling of sea, Cornish pasties, fudge and oil paints. Miss Frocker was flexing a rubber-soled tennis shoe. As her artist's smock, she wore a paint-spattered rubber apron, knotted above her breasts (as firm and shiny and pointed as high explosive shells, Caroline thought), and extending to just above her bare knees, and was nude underneath, apart from tennis shoes without socks. Her back, bottom and legs were bare, crossed only by the strap of her apron, at her spinal nubbin. Miss Frocker cast an admiring glance at Caroline, primly sheathed in her white rubber nurse's outfit, with navy-blue nylon stockings (frilly top) and white rubber laced-up bootees.

'A new model,' she murmured. 'How thoughtful of you, Emily.'

'Her name is Caroline,' Emily said. 'She's a new bitch at Furrow Weald. She's from London – Richmond Hill.'

'Well, I'm not really from anywhere partic –' Caroline began.

'Richmond Hill,' said Pris Frocker, airily. 'Why, Frank Funn has a delightful residence there, when he can't be in

Cornwall. Quite handy for the television studios. I expect you know him, Caroline. Well, as a Furrovian, you would, of course.'

Why should I know such a creep?

Miss Frocker smiled, stroking her chin, with a toss of her long auburn mane that made her breasts shiver beneath the apron straps. The artist's bottom was a model of smooth, satin pertness, the arse globes clustered like perfect pear drops, but, while nearly as large as Caroline's own, the fesses were overshadowed by her massive, jutting breasts, slightly larger than Merilee's, and even (Caroline grudgingly admitted to herself) than Caroline's own; she estimated 44 inches at least, and certainly requiring a C cup – quite possibly a D – should Pris feel conceited enough to wear a bra, an unnecessary extravagance, with her bubs standing as firm as meaty alps. Each of her armpits sheltered a hairy forest, and Caroline wondered if her gourd was as handsomely thatched.

'Splendid,' Miss Frocker purred. 'I can never have enough pretty little girls, untamed. I rather think I am in my "pink period" – you know my fixation on the spiritual nature of young girls' bare bottoms, and pinkness seems to bring out their delicious karma. Merilee, here, is a most apt young model, and took my slippering with an intriguing hint of excitement. Her twat became quite moist, as I spanked her.'

The black girl's entire cunt basin was basted a delicate pink, from her shaven cunt to her perineum, buttocks and haunches, in the shape of a high-cut bikini bottom. Merilee had never looked so beautiful as in the warm light shining through the studio panes: long dark legs, satin smooth and shiny; the massive black teats, topped with the big brown nipple domes, stiffly erect, after her spanking; the flat, muscled belly, and the cheekily sprouting extrusion of her navel, over a pubic gourd almost as big and swollen as Caroline's own; and a waist scarcely wider than one of Merilee's rippling bare thighs, sleek and gleaming with ebony muscle.

The interplay of light and shade on the curves of her body made her nudity a painting in three dimensions, drawing the eye to the twin nodes of the buttocks and the voluptuous cunt lips, their black spanked to rosy pink, with a gleam of red wetness from the fleshy slit within, at the roll of Merilee's buttocks. As she gazed at the nude black girl, Caroline, tightly encased in Emily's rubber nurse's uniform, felt her borrowed pink panties suddenly wet with juice from her seeping cunt. Those magnificent, thrusting fesses were just made for spanking, and more – Caroline knew she just *had* to cane Merilee's naked bottom. First, she'd have to strip, for it was awfully hot and sweaty in Matron's tight rubber things, then really wrestle her, no holds barred, punish her – and take punishment herself.

Can this be love? Surely not a lesbo pash.

Merilee was so casually regal, born to command – surely, an African princess. Caroline blushed at the submissive pleasure she expected from Merilee's punishment of her bum, bubbies and cooze, Merilee's savage pearl teeth biting her – then, when both girls were whimpering with pain, she would crush Merilee's haughty face to the dirt, and whip her bare bottom with the hardest, springiest rattan cane imaginable, until the bum was gouged with welts, while Merilee thrashed and squealed, and begged Caroline to stop caning her, promising to do anything if the cruel cane would stop flogging her helpless croup . . .

When Merilee was wealed beyond weals, Caroline would hold Merilee to her promise . . . making Merilee her bitch, her *thing*, to serve her and kiss her clitty and wank her off, drinking her come, while Caroline sat squirming on Merilee's crushed face; to bare her ebony bottom for the cane, at Caroline's slightest whim; or, when Caroline was naughty, her servant Merilee would strip her, crush Caroline's face with her naked arse, wanking off, so that her come and pee filled her mistress's throat, and administer a fearful caning to her mistress's own bottom, without heeding Caroline's screams or pleas for mercy, until

Caroline's bum was shredded with welts as dark as Merilee's nipples . . .

Above all, she envied Merilee the aristocratic ease with which she pouted and minced in the nude, as though, under the African sun, nudity was as natural as the breath that made her gleaming ebony breasts swell. Caroline assured herself that she was perfectly at home in the nude, yet there was something about rainy England which required an *excuse* to be naked – a gym session, an artist's studio, or a headmistress's study furnished for caning . . . as she daydreamed of playing with Merilee, under the African sun, Caroline's panties were soaking with hot come.

'Manners, Caroline,' whispered Emily.

'Oh . . . how do you do, miss?' Caroline blurted, bending her knee in a curtsy to the haughty Miss Frocker.

'Miss Frocker is an artist of genius,' Merilee said, with rueful pride, as she pirouetted, to show off her whopped bottom and gourd, blushing pink.

Pris smiled a trifle smugly, her massive breasts heaving under her apron straps, and briefly exposing a huge pink nipple dome, whose areola seemed to spread like a squashed strawberry from the sharp central bud, before she tucked her breast neatly inside the straps.

'All art involves suffering,' said Pris. 'Since a normal girl enjoys a sound spanking on the bare, her suffering – shamed and smarting – is *spiritual.* Was yours spiritual, Merilee?'

'Assuredly, miss,' Merilee said shyly. 'My bare has never smarted quite so spiritually.'

Pris beamed. 'Then you are ready to be painted,' she said. 'That is, I shall photograph you with my digital camera, and work from your likeness.'

Caroline felt a stab of envy, at the way Merilee sprang so *easily* into lubricious postures for the artist's clicking camera: baring her bum and cunny, pinching her nipples, twat flaps and extruded clitty into stiff fleshy bulbs; pouting with her lips of face and quim; even twisting her long supple legs, so as to get her foot in her mouth, and suck her own toes, with drool spilling over the sucked ebony foot's creamy sole. Pris must be planning an awful lot of portraits of the nude ebony girl, with very few of them suitable for public display.

'It's awfully hot, miss,' Caroline said. 'Would you mind terribly if I took off my clothing?'

'Not at all,' Pris replied, wagging a playful finger. 'But only if you are prepared to model as well, in Cornish fashion.'

'A bare-bottom spanking, miss?'

'I'm afraid so.'

'Why, miss, it shall be an honour.'

'That goes without saying. I shall pass some pleasant minutes planning just how, and with what, I shall spank your bare. Merilee took a hearty slippering, and *really* squirmed when I whopped her gash. For you, miss, I have far more exquisite bottom-ticklers. Your bum shall wriggle like tops'ls in a Cornish gale.'

Caroline blushed, her cunt instantly oozing come, curtsied again, pouting, and stuck out her tongue at Merilee. She peeled off the sticky rubber skirt, panties and blouse, and fiddled with her garter straps, although Pris ordered her to leave her stockings and bootees on. Soon, she was as naked as the pouting Merilee, apart from hose and footwear, with trickles of clear shiny come seeping into her blue nylon stocking tops. Caroline made no attempt to hide the swelling of her gash flaps, the erection of her bared nipples, nor the stiff extrusion of her throbbing clitty.

'I'd say you were gagging to be spanked, Caroline,' purred Pris, unabashedly scanning her nude body. 'That croup's a spank magnet.'

Caroline blushed. 'I . . . I can't deny it, miss,' she blurted.

Why is it that a girl's nice fesses lure spankers, and the nicer they are, the more she wants them spanked?

'You shall have your wish presently,' Pris said.

'I told you she was a ripe mot,' Emily said, beaming.

Pris fiddled with her camera – lenses zoomed in and out – as she squatted, fully baring her breasts, with her apron straps creasing, and poked the camera lens, extended to its full length, right inside Merilee's twat, whose lips Merilee held open with her fingers. Merilee began to masturbate, punishing her swollen, stiff clit, as the camera clicked; she twirled and crouched, presenting her bared fesses to Pris, with her anus well extruded in the taut bum cleft. Merilee masturbated, come sluicing from her cunt, as Pris approached her anus, pushing the lense inside, and snapping, as the bumhole expanded to clutch the shiny silver tube.

'Yes,' Merilee groaned, as the extended lens, about eight inches long, disappeared up her bumhole. 'It's in my rectum, miss – ooh! My colon! How it hurts! You're torturing me, miss. It's like being buggered by a huge hard cock – a four-incher, miss.'

Of course, she exaggerated, but *had* Merilee taken cock four inches in girth? The memory of her three-incher in her own anus excited Caroline, and imagining a girth of *four whole inches* of hot stiff cock flesh – as for the length, it would be superhuman! – made her cunt spurt almost unbearably. Merilee wanked off harder, Pris buggering her with the camera lense, making a tinny buzzing sound, as the lense whirred in and out of the black girl's squirming anus. Caroline glanced at Emily, and saw the matron's fingers busy frigging her cunt, under her white rubber skirt. She, too, was wanking off!

Surely there could be no harm? Caroline was already in the nude, with come soaking her thighs and stockings. She pressed a finger to her clitty, rubbing hard, with loud squelching noises between the engorged cunt flaps, and moaned, as pleasure jolted her, with a hot spurt of come splashing from her wanked cunt. Pris squatted, buttocks spread wide, as she snapped the masturbating Merilee, and a steady drip of come glazed her parted thighs, pouring from her swollen cunt lips, beneath her big hairy gash gourd. Her massive pubic bush extended its tendrils deep below her quim, with fronds clinging to the wet cunt lips, while the enormous cunt jungle made scratchy noises, as Pris's loins writhed against her rubber apron.

Emily rolled her rubber skirt right up, and plunged her hand into her pink rubber panties, making a plopping squelchy sound, as she masturbated her cunt, squirting come through the tight panties' gusset. It seemed that Pris was the only girl unwanked, and Caroline wondered if the artist would welcome a caress, when, beneath the tight, muscular squirming of Pris's buttocks, she saw a gleaming black cylinder poked in and out of her cunt by the bum muscles. The dildo had a knobbly prong which caressed the Pris's clitty at each movement of the main shaft, a good three inches thick. Seconds later, she saw a second object – a bum plug! – winking inside Pris's anus, and Caroline gaped, for it could not have been less than three inches – her own anal tariff.

The superb muscle control of her thighs, sphincters and buttocks ensured that the twin dildos slipped in and out of Pris's holes without manipulation. Caroline got two, then three, and finally four fingers inside her slit, and wanked off vigorously, with her thumb pummelling her clitty, adding her gasps of pleasure to Emily's and Merilee's. The black girl gasped, as her belly heaved in a come, with pussy juice splashing all over Pris's fingers and camera, and shortly after, Emily's voice shrilled in her own climax, with a pool of come sloshing inside her quivering rubber panties. Caroline's belly tightened in the sweetness of her own approaching spasm – a few more flicks to the clitty would do it – when, suddenly, Pris removed her camera lens from Merilee's body, with a sticky plop, and whirled, to observe Caroline's hand deep in her cunt, with her thumb pummelling the bared stiff clitoris.

'The gel is *masturbating*!' she shrilled. 'It's the lowest of bad manners.'

'But – but – I'm sorry,' Caroline blurted helplessly.

'Caroline, as an alumna of Furrow Weald, I know what smutty sluts get up to when my back's turned. Seize her, gels!'

Emily and Merilee grabbed her by the arms, Merilee twisting her left arm painfully behind her back. Pris rose, scarlet with rage, and smoothed her apron, before slapping Caroline's face. Whap!

'Ouch!' Caroline cried. 'I thought it was all right to wank off, honestly, miss.'

Whap! Whap! Pris slapped her twice more, and Caroline began to cry.

'You *thought*, did you, bitch?' she snarled. 'In my studio, only *I* am permitted to think. And I think the slut must be properly punished.'

'Flog her bum to shreds,' said Emily.

'The harder the better,' Merilee agreed.

'Girls, take her downstairs, to the gallery,' Pris ordered.

Gleefully, her friends hustled Caroline down a spiral staircase into a cool white basement, smelling of paint, wood, varnish and the salt tang of the sea. A panoramic window, which Pris swiftly covered with velvet curtains, showed directly onto a shingle beach, with the Atlantic waves crashing only a few yards from the house. The beach was quite narrow, enclosed by rocky forelands, rising to cliffs, and Caroline saw, through her tears, that, even if she could escape her punishers, it would be almost impossible to swim or climb away from this secluded spot. The white walls of the long vaulted gallery were crowded with paintings, while the floor was occupied – Caroline's heart pounded – with gnarled wooden and metal contraptions, that could only be instruments of supplice: there was a gibbet at one end, and a rack at the other; cauldrons, flogging frames, stocks and pillories, all antique and lovingly burnished.

'Do you like it, Caroline?' asked Pris. 'It's not far from the St Ives Tate Gallery, you know, if you were to swim – which you won't – but mine is, of course, infinitely superior to that dumpster of daubs.'

Caroline whimpered. Whap! Pris slapped her again.

'Do you like it?' she hissed.

'Y-yes, miss,' Caroline said with a sob.

Pris smiled. 'Good. You have taste. So, happily, do my discerning private customers, worldwide. The photographic image, so admired decades ago, is today so ubiquitous as to be thoroughly déclassé. My clients appreciate art with the personal touch – they are the cream of what the vulgar call "celebrities", crowned heads, princes, even the president of San Fernando – an *intimate* friend of Merilee's.'

Merilee smirked. Pris's hand stroked Caroline's quivering bare buttocks, with a finger sliding up and down the bum cleft, nipping the wet cunt lips and poking into Caroline's anus. She withdrew, and pinched Caroline's pubic hillock between her two palms, making Caroline squeal.

'My, if I had gourd and arse as maginificent, I'd be wanking off, just looking at myself,' she said dreamily. 'You must pay the price of being a spank magnet, you beautiful bitch. If I didn't know you so well, I'd say you were a filthy submissive, one of the horrid Stingers gang.'

How can she know me so well? Has Emily betrayed me?

'No, miss, I swear,' blurted Caroline, with her fingers crossed. 'I'm no sub, honestly. I hate pain.'

'Then, your punishment will be so much more fun,' said Pris, leering and licking her sparkling white teeth.

She jerked her apron strap and let the garment fall, allowing her naked breasts to jut point-blank into Caroline's face. Her cunt juicing, Caroline gasped, longing to open her mouth wide and gobble up a huge pink nipple, sprawled like a great dollop of strawberry blancmange on the girl's firm, shiny breast meat. Pris smiled.

'Certain work is best done in the nude,' she said. 'Now, were you insolent, in masturbating without permission, Caroline?'

'Well, yes, miss,' Caroline whimpered, 'I suppose I was a bit forward.'

'Do you therefore accept my punishment?'

'It's not the first time I've earned a punishment for masturbating, so . . . I do accept my punishment.'

'You know I shall hurt you dreadfully. You *are* a sub.'

'No, miss!' Caroline blurted, feeling her thighs squelch, as her cunt seeped come.

'Then, you must prove it. A truly dominant gel, a member of the beastly Swanks, for example, would be unable to bear the pain I shall inflict.'

Her arms were released, and Pris, nude, but for her gym shoes, and looking like a perky (though sockless) gym mistress – particularly since her huge titties *were* bouncing merrily – took her by the hand, to show her the paintings. All were large, immaculately detailed and coloured canvases, depicting girls in the nude, for the most part, joined in intimate pleasures. Girls sucked titties, gamahuched upended, or simply smiled at the portraitist, hands frigging each other's twats, against a background of flowers or sea. Caroline swallowed nervously, for she recognised several Furrovians. Emily followed, her arm around Merilee's waist and playing with her quim, with both girls simpering at some private joke.

The pictures became harsher: now, the girls were whipped naked, chained or roped, wearing masks or branks, with their tongues clamped, their nipples and cunt flaps bricked, and boiling hot wax was poured over their naked breasts by cruelly smiling maids. Caroline recognised Pimella Plumply, pouring wax over Samantha Gouge's bare teats, while Cynthia Cunnell caned Samantha's naked buttocks with a four-foot rod, as Samantha hung by her hair, knotted to the gibbet, with her wrists bound behind her neck; Emma Spivey, her face contorted in agony, as Mandy Tuppe whipped her bare back, the flogged girl cuffed at wrists and ankles and suspended by nipple clamps, pinching the nips white and stretching her huge breasts to twice their length; Sarah Hogplum, caned bare-bum by Victoria Brounbirch, as she sucked Bronwen Bellibone's clitty; Vapula McCloskey caning sweet Aaliz's upthrust naked buttocks.

Caroline was powerless to stop the flow of come from her cunt, which had her lacy stocking tops a sopping mess and her thighs squelching aloud as she walked. The painted Aaliz crouched in a hobble that enclosed both her ankles and wrists, with her arms pressed against her belly and between her legs. Her face was ground into the beach pebbles by Janet Petarda's leather boot, while Janet masturbated, dripping come over Aaliz's hair and face. Surely, these were fantasy paintings. Yet they all looked so horribly realistic.

'That hobble looks awfully cruel,' Caroline blurted, then bit her lip, for she knew from Pris's leer that she had said the wrong thing.

'Yes,' Pris replied. 'Simplicity is always cruel.'

Caroline gasped, recognising Jabez Prestellen, standing on the beach, while a nude girl knelt before him, with his cock impaling her throat. His lips bore a smirk of male dominance that Caroline found hateful, yet shiveringly compelling. The girl clasped his buttocks with sharp claws as she tongued his swollen tool, drool trickling down her chin, onto her breasts. Her eyes were closed, as if in ecstacy. Behind her, a nude Victoria Brounbirch flogged the fellatrix on the bare back, with a quirt made of seaweed fronds studded with broken seashells, while Sarah Hogplum applied a wooden cane to her out-thrust bare croup.

Come spurted in glistening jets from the spread cunt lips of the whipped fellatrix, who was Mistress June Prodigal, the biology teacher. The next tableau showed Jabez again, this time with another leeringly nude Cornish boy. Pimella Plumply crouched, buttocks spread, on the long stocks Caroline saw not far from her; her bum was raised by the central hump, with her wrists and ankles cuffed at the extremities of the platform. Jabez buggered her bum, his tool sunk to the balls in her anus, while her face was pressed to the balls of the other boy, with her head held high by her hair, knotted to a crossbar hanging from the ceiling.

The second boy's tool was plunged to her throat, and, with Pris's admitted talent for the lifelike, the tableau seemed to move, with the girl quivering under buggery, while her throat swallowed the spunk of the fellated boy. Ermine Floss, boxing mistress and chief Stinger, appeared in the next tableau, this time fucked in the cunt by Jabez, standing on the beach, with Ermine's legs wrapped around his shoulders and her bum balancing on his cock, while the second boy, mounted on a rock, straddled her, with his cock buggering her bumhole, and a third boy, also mounted, fucked her in the mouth. Ermine's bare buttocks, sandwiched between her two fuckers, glowed with fresh cane stripes. Caroline stared intently, licking her lips, and blushing, as come spouted from her tingling twat.

'As you see, you are in illustrious company, Caroline,' Pris said, tittering at her discomfiture.

There was a groaning, sighing sound that seemed to make the white ceiling timbers shiver. Caroline decided it was the noise of the ocean outside.

The paintings mesmerised; she saw a row of nude Cornish boys, cocks erect, with Judy Tinsell kneeling to serve them with her mouth; Alice Wellbed, hogtied and buggered by the same boys, while sucking a huge, gnarled cock, dripping with arse grease, and its owner unseen; the same monstrous tool buggering Vicca Valcul, her bum striped with cruel quirt weals and her face twisted in agony, as (to Caroline's private satisfaction) the gnarled cock stretched her anal lips to several times their normal size. Samantha knelt in a gymslip and bra, licking a boy's balls, with her fingers on the peehole of his erection, which was spurting a jet of spunk high in the air, the drops falling on Samantha's extended tongue, while the gnarled cock bum fucked Samantha from the rear. Peggy Droule was stretched nude on the rack, its rollers turned by Sarah and Vapula, also nude, and masturbating with open pink cunts, the tortured girl's face bathed in tears and her eyes wrinkled shut, as she sucked the same giant cock with the unseen owner.

At the end of the gallery, the last painting occupied the whole rear wall, and was covered by a blue velvet cloth with gold tassels. Beside it was an oaken door, and

Caroline was sure she could hear the moaning of the sea, and perhaps the squawk of a seagull, echoing from the wood. Emily, following close behind, had her fingers inside Merilee's juicing twat, while the black girl's hand was down the front of the matron's rubber knickers, making a gurgling sloppy noise, as she wanked her.

'You can't see that picture,' Pris said, 'as it is already sold to a very special private customer.'

Yet, she made no move to stop Emily's come-soaked hand, plopping from Merilee's cunt, from grabbing Caroline's fingers, and making her tug on the gold tassel. The velvet drapes swung apart, revealing the painting.

'Oh! I'm sorry!' Caroline blurted. 'I didn't mean –'

Pris clicked her tongue. 'You *are* a very curious and naughty maid, Caroline,' she purred, 'and must pay a heavy price.'

Merilee and Caroline gaped, while Emily giggled impishly, and Pris, beaming with pride, played with her own nipples. The girls stared at the ranks of Furrovians – Stingers and masked Swanks; in the centre, a naked male, also masked, sat on a throne, his gnarled cock hugely erect, and body slabbed with muscle. Worshipping his cock, the trussed, crouching nude figure of Mistress Frubbin licked his balls, while the masked Pris Frocker, recognised by titties and cunt thatch, lashed Mistress Frubbin's blotched buttocks with a switch of six gutta-percha ferules.

Half-concealed by the painted throne, a nude female crouched, her bare birched by a naked girl, bum fucked by a Cornish boy, while the birched female sucked Jabez Prestellen's cock. The crouching female was Miss Chew, and her bircher, Persimmon Pipp. At the head of the Stingers crouched Ermine Floss, doubled up in agony, as a Cornish boy buggered her; beside her, also buggered, Emily and Aaliz, both heavily striped with weals. All the Stingers had scarlet faces, as they were whipped or bummed by the boys, while, across from them, the Swanks lashed the bottoms of boys hogtied for correction. Caroline's glanced switched between the nude Pris beside her, and the masked Pris in her own painting.

'You . . .' she gasped.

'Careless of you not to twig,' drawled Pris. 'I'm the maid with the cunt fur – leader of the Swanks. Cunt and armpit fur are so *Cornish*, don't you think? It was Bronwen Bellibone who brought Merilee here, just as Emily, a loyal Stinger, brought you. And of course our submissive slave Miss Chew sent you to us in the first place. Swanks or Stingers, we are all girls, and eager to help.'

There were further moans and squeals, not from seagulls, but from behind the oaken door.

'Oh! Ahh! You swine! Do me hard, you fucking bastard . . . punish me, bitch . . . hurt me . . .'

'Well, time for your chastisement, Caroline,' Pris murmured.

'Oh! You fucker! Don't stop . . . right up my fucking raspberry . . .'

The door opened, and Caroline gasped, as an erect cock emerged, its gnarled massive shaft wet with come and arse grease. *Three inches in girth . . . four . . . surely not five? That's impossible!* Beyond the hugely muscled male body, Mistress Frubbin, nude, and buttocks splayed, crouched on a brass bed, piss and come sluicing down her quivering thighs, and her bumhole wrenched horribly open. Caroline's heart pounded, as she stared at the massive gnarled cock, which she recognised from Pris's paintings, then back at Mistress Frubbin's gaping, sopping arsehole. *Gosh, you could fit a tin of peaches in there.* Laetitia's body shuddered with sobs, and tears streamed down her face, as Persimmon Pipp, wearing the summer whites, short pleated skirt and blouse of a Royal Navy girl cadet, applied pincers to her nipples and cunt flaps, licking her lips as she tightened the clamps, and making Mistress Frubbin moan in agony. The mistress's arms were wrenched behind her back in strappado, wrists cuffed to a rope tautly hanging from the rafters, while her hair was lashed tightly to the bed's headframe.

'Make me come,' she squealed, as Persimmon tightened the nipple pincers. 'The fucking bastard didn't bum me to spasm.'

'You mustn't speak so rudely of your employer, mistress,' Persimmon chided. 'I'm afraid that calls for correction.'

From her belt, she unhooked a crook-handled navy-blue cane, with a gold Royal Navy crown at the hilt. Vip! She began an energetic caning of the mistress's bare buttocks, her wrist a blur, as, with perfect control, she dealt twenty lashes in little over six seconds. Mistress Frubbin's violently squirming fesses blushed livid crimson, as she writhed, shrieking in unfeigned agony, with her big bare titties flapping wildly against her ribcage.

'Ooh! Ahh! Stop! Oh, please! It hurts so much! Please, Ensign Pipp, do my nubbin.'

Persimmon removed the pincers from the left nipple, and stuck them between Mistress Frubbin's gaping cunt flaps, where she found the clitoris, and squeezed hard.

'Oh, yes!' squealed the mistress. 'Oh, how it hurts! You fucking dirty bitch! Oh, yes, I'm coming! Oh . . . yes . . . ohh!'

She writhed in orgasm, as Persimmon wanked her clitty with the pincers, at the same time using her cane handle to masturbate her own cunt beneath her crisp white skirt. She looked up.

'Caroline! *So* nice! *Mwah*!' she cried, blowing an air-kiss. 'I've oodles of things to tell you about the navy. It's such fun, with lots and lots of lovely wanks – and I get to cane juicy boys on the bare. We girls are i/c discipline – that's why they have girls aboard ships these days.'

'Do I hear *Caroline*'s to be punished?' purred a baritone voice. 'I've waited a long time for *that* treat.'

'Oh, yes, sir – I was going to tell you – I wasn't expecting you to be finished doing Frubbin so soon,' stammered Pris. 'I hadn't forgotten.'

'If I thought you *had* – well, I've buggered that slut's raspberry to pulp, so Ensign Pipp can whip her arse and wank the horny bitch till she faints,' drawled the muscled owner of the cock, with a gleaming smile at Caroline, that had her heart aflutter. 'Caroline Letchmount, the famous spank magnet – *this* is the damsel I want to see squirm.'

'Of course, sir,' Pris said. 'Right away. Emily – Merilee – the hobble for Caroline, please.'

As the girls fetched the dreadful ankle and wrist hobble, the nude male strutted forwards, the stiff gnarled cock bobbing before Caroline's quivering titties, with a smile at her heavily juicing twat.

'Sorry I haven't time to give you girls an autograph,' said heart-throb television celebrity Frank Funn.

12

A Cut Above

Vap!

'*Ahh*! Please . . . I can't take any more.'

'Complaint is useless and demeaning, Caroline,' said Pris Frocker.

Vap!

'Ooh! Please stop.'

'But I've only just started.'

Vap!

'Ahh!'

Vap!

'Oh! Oh! It hurts so horribly!'

Eyes flooded with tears, and face contorted, Caroline thought her birching would never end. There seemed to be nothing in the world except her flogged bare bottom, her humiliation, face squashed to the floor, bum obscenely high and spread, hands tucked into the hobble between her ankles, and the pain, smarting in the squirming, pinioned fesses – her naked body was alone in a whole universe of pain. Not quite naked – her stockings and sussies still clung to her hips and thighs, and amid the agony, Caroline worried they would get ripped, or spoiled by the dribbles of come that oozed from her tortured twat.

The *birch.* It was a nightmare, worse than a nightmare. The clean sting of the cane, even the heavy slapping of leather whipthongs, were nothing, compared to the crackling caress of the birch twigs, dancing in their kiss of pain on her wriggling buttocks, as Pris Frocker lashed her. Birching was not for girls, but for boys – clean-limbed sailors, stretched nude, with their bums squirming under the bosun's lashes! *Is that what Emily does in the new Royal Navy?* The pain was like molten gold, each cut spreading its weal over her whole fesse meat, embracing her, making her seared bottom the very centre of that pain universe . . . while Pris openly masturbated, as she birched, and Merilee and matron, her *friends*, wanked off their clits, smiling at her distress.

Merilee had donned lacy white silk stockings, and sat on Frank Funn's lap, bicycling him, her ebony thighs slowly pumping up and down, squeezing his monstrous huge cock; while Emily, in her rubber nurse's costume, knelt beneath, licking his balls, from time to time taking a huge orb into her mouth and sucking on it, as on a boiled sweet. Both girls stole glances at Caroline's flogged fesses, and giggled, wanking their clitties quite blatantly as she groaned. Vap!

'Ooh!'

Vap!

'Urrgh!'

Vap!

'*Ahh*! Oh, miss, this is cruel.'

'Thank you,' said Pris. 'But you have a long way to go in submission.'

'Yes,' drawled Frank, 'the gels are queuing up to get on my show. I have to break them in first, of course, spank their arses a couple of hundred – usually, I have that saucy cow Greta do those sort of things, slap them around a bit, soften 'em up, before I give them a good bumming. If they don't boast, they're worthless. You know Greta, from the show, in the frilly pink knickers and see-through bra – my assistant, or *ars*-istant, I call her, ha ha. She's a flaming lesbo, so I have to encule *her* raspberry most days to keep the bitch in order.'

'Boast?' said Emily.

'Bend over and spread them,' Frank said, chortling. 'I only choose young juicy ones. Gagging for it, they are.

Show me a gel who ain't gagging for it *in* her arse after a hundred spanks *on* her arse.'

'Could I be on your show, Mr Funn?' chorused Merilee and Emily together.

'You *could*, I suppose,' he said, 'although a Furrovian is a cut above the rest. That's why I bought the damn place, and the Warchant school, St Wossname's, to get a higher class, d'ye see. The gels mostly go on to become, you know, beauty queens and such. Unless they get sold – *hired* – at auction. Lucky ones get to be on my *Ripe Raspberry* show, that's on the cable television, round the world. The adult channel – we don't film it in England, of course, far too namby-pamby.'

'I'm game for that,' panted Merilee.

'Me too,' said Emily.

'Well, hold your horses, gels.' Frank chuckled, lighting a cigar by flicking a match against Merilee's erect left nipple. Her white silk stockings squeezed and caressed the massive glans of his cock, protruding between her rippling thighs, like a giant shiny marrow.

'You're not bad, gel,' he told Merilee. 'You know just how to keep me humming, without coming. Yes, I could use you, and you, Matron, in that rubber gear. That birched bitch as well, I think, she's got a real submissive's arse, and she's well abject, gagging for humiliation.'

'No! It's not true!' Caroline shrieked.

Vap! Pris's birch lashed Caroline savagely between her buttocks, striking the anal bud and cunt flaps.

'Ooh!' Caroline howled, a heavy spurt of come drenching her stocking tops.

'See what I mean?' drawled Frank, expelling a plume of fragrant cigar smoke. 'Her twat's a fountain, as she's flogged. A real sub – not like my naval gel Persimmon, a born dominatrix – unless Caroline's that rara avis, a goth.'

'Some of us are,' Merilee said.

'I can always use goths on *Ripe Raspberry*,' drawled Frank, 'particularly for the action segments, you know, girlhunts, plantation punishments, babe battles and such.'

He puffed smoke, which Pris and Merilee sniffed hungrily. 'Like my corona? It's from my own plantation.'

'Ooh,' said Emily, 'where?'

'That's for me to know, and you to find out,' Frank said.

Vap!

'*Ahh*! *Ohh*!'

After thirty cuts of birch on bare buttocks, Caroline's cries of agony turned to screams, as Pris began to birch the stockinged soles of her feet, trapped in the ankle hobble. Vap! Vap! Caroline's toes curled, the feet jerking, as the birch rods crackled across the soles, rapidly shredding the nylon of her stockings, so that the birch beat bare skin. Pris masturbated vigorously, poking her twin dildos in and out of her holes, with squelching slurps, as come squirted from her cunt, dribbling over her perineum to her anus, gleaming with arse grease. Vap! Vap!

'Ooh . . . ooh . . .' Caroline wailed, 'will no one stop her?'

'That's not the point, Caroline,' chided Merilee. 'This is a test.'

Vap! Vap!

Caroline's toes wriggled in agony. 'Ahh! Ahh!'

The bastinado continued for a further twenty cuts of the birch, after which Pris laid aside the instrument, denuded to a few twigs, and took up a bullwhip. Thwap! The heavy leather tongue cracked across Caroline's bare back.

'Ooh!'

Thwap!

'Ooh!

Thwap!

'Ooh! Ahh! Please, haven't I suffered enough?'

'Give her thirty, or so, Pris, then she can ride me,' called Frank.

The whipping went on, to over three dozen strokes, leaving Caroline's naked back and shoulders a livid mass of purple and crimson welts. Pris released her from the hobble, and Caroline lurched to her feet, sobbing uncontrollably, rubbing her birched bum, and barely able to stand on her flogged soles; from back to buttocks, her whole rear presented blotched puffy skin, wealed by her floggings.

'She looks a treat,' said Frank. 'Well telegenic.'

Merilee gave way to Caroline, who perched her bum on Frank's giant cock, with his glans in her arse cleft, and the peehole nuzzling her anus. Merilee got her fist around the cock shaft – her fingertips only just joining – and guided the glans into Caroline's anus, while Pris and Emily held Caroline's arms, forcing her down on the tool.

'No, please . . .' Caroline sobbed. 'Ahh!' The glans penetrated her to an inch, wrenching her anus wide. 'Oh, that hurts!'

Pris and Emily pushed harder, and Caroline squealed, as the huge cock shaft sank a further inch inside her. 'Oh! Oh!' she whimpered.

Merilee was tweaking Caroline's clit, wanking her hard, and palming come, which she slapped on Frank's cock to lubricate it. She grasped Caroline's buttocks, pinching them with her claws, and making the girl squeal, then dragged the wealed bum down further over the cock, until, with a sudden grunt, Frank penetrated Caroline's rectum; a further push, and his huge cock disppeared into her, right to his balls, filling the rectum and ramming the sigmoid colon. He sighed happily, as her bare bum squashed his balls.

'Ooh!' Caroline shrieked, as his glans rammed her colon.

He began to thrust, from his lolling position, his balls slapping Caroline's fesses, and the cock, oiled with her come and dripping arse grease, slid wetly between the lips of her grotesquely wrenched anus. Persimmon watched from the open door of the bedroom, where she was meticulously torturing Laetitia Frubbin with pincers, nipple and clit clamps, and her naval cane: between pinches, she dealt her shuddering, whimpering victim a brisk dozen strokes on her crimson bare. Laetitia's pincered breasts bounced and wobbled, her bound hair pulled at its roots, and her arms strained above her back, fingers clasping and unclasping in a ball, with her toes curling. Heavy squirts of come soaked her thighs and swollen twat flaps.

Squatting on Frank's thighs, Caroline began to lift her haunches, drawing the cock inches out of her anus, then plunging back, to slap Frank's balls with her buttocks, as the shaft penetrated her to the arse root. Pris and Emily released her, and she leaned forwards, to gain leverage by clasping his shins, so that her thighs and croup bounced faster and faster on his slimy stiff tool, penetrating to her colon at each plunge. Frank reclined, smoking, as Caroline's flapping titties sprayed sweat, while come from her swollen cunt drooled over his balls, and down her pumping thighs. She panted and fucked for several minutes, taking the cock to her colon, and squeezing the glans with her rectum, so that each exit was slow and sucking, the cock emerging with a greasy slurping sound, right to the neck of his glans, before Caroline dropped her bum on his balls once more.

With darting fingers, Caroline wanked her own clitty, her fingers squelching in her cunt's flood of come. The others masturbated furiously, watching Caroline's buggery, and, as Frank's belly tightened and he grunted, the girls gasped, wanking themselves to come, at the sight of copious spunk splashing from the lips of Caroline's anus, while the male's bucking cock filled her rectum with sperm. As the cream filled her, Caroline gave her nubbin a flick, and exploded in heaving orgasm. Frank slapped Caroline's bottom, and she withdrew from his semi-stiff tool. He frowned at Pris, still masturbating, as she licked her lips, gazing at Caroline's welted bum and stretched anus.

'You're rather cocky, miss,' he drawled, 'for somebody who revealed my private painting, *and* neglected to tell me of Caroline's punishment.'

'Well, sir, I said I was sorry,' blustered Pris.

'That, as you know, is not good enough,' he said, rising, with his cock swinging, semi-rigid. 'You Cornish bitches are too smug by half, and need to be taken down a peg.'

'What? No! I can explain. Wait –' blurted Pris, too late, for Merilee and Emily already had her pinioned by the arms.

Caroline's face was scarlet with tears, and her teeth were bared in a sneer of vengeful hatred. She opened the door to the shingle beach, and grabbed Pris's hair. Merilee ripped the dildos from Pris's cunt and anus, and used the larger tool to spank her buttocks, with hard wet slaps.

'Oh! Ahh! Stop! Let go!' Pris wailed.

Caroline tugged harder, wrenching the hair by the roots, so that, arms twisted up her back by the other girls, Pris was dragged through the door, onto the shingle.

'Ouch! You're hurting me!'

'You've a lot further to go, you hairy Cornish slut,' Caroline hissed.

Frank watched, smoking, with his arms folded, and cock risen, as Caroline dragged the screaming Pris across the shingle, with the sharp stones bruising her cunt, belly and teats. She put her foot on Pris's neck, squashing her face in the pebbles, and began to kick her arse, forcing the thighs apart, so that her toenails slammed the girl's cunt and anus. Ragged bits of nylon stocking flapped around Caroline's thighs and ankles, as, leering savagely, she drubbed her tormentress. Flipping her over, she dragged her on her back and buttocks across the shingle, repeating the livid bruises and stripes covering her front, and kicking the squealing girl repeatedly on her titties and hairy cunt. She dragged her to the sea, and plunged her head repeatedly for a ducking of up to one minute, all the time kicking and punching her between the legs, on the belly and massive, swinging teats, which darkened with blue bruises.

'Ooh! Urrgh!' Pris spluttered, each time Caroline lifted her from the water. 'No more, please!' But Caroline slapped her face and breasts, before ducking her once more.

Merilee squatted on the beach, gathering fronds of seaweed and seashells, which she knotted expertly into a flail, and handed it shyly to Caroline.

'I hope you like it,' she said.

'Why, it's perfect! Mwah!' Caroline gasped, blowing an air-kiss to the black girl.

Emily offered a handful of wriggling crabs, which Caroline pushed up Pris's squirming twat, before flipping her onto her front, and beginning to savagely thrash her bare wet buttocks with the quirt of seaweed.

'Oh, please, not the crabs,' Pris begged. 'They hurt so awfully.'

Vap! Vap! As Caroline whipped her, the seashells left horrid little welts, blushing crimson on the squirming buttocks, pale and wet, but rapidly blotching with the weals of Caroline's furious flogging. Vap! Vap!

'Oh! Ahh! Please – have mercy,' Pris shrieked.

Caroline whipped harder. Vap! Vap!

'Ooh!

Vap! Vap!

'Ahh! Ohh!'

When the squirming Pris had taken sixty strokes of the quirt on her wet buttocks, Caroline began to flog her back, still with her mane twisted in her hand, and holding Pris's head up, with her huge titties flapping helplessly, as her bum and back writhed under the whip. Emily and Merilee masturbated, with coos of joy, as Pris's face streamed with tears. The flogged girl suddenly wailed, as a stream of piss erupted from her squirming vulva.

'Oh! Noo . . .' she moaned, as the acrid golden pee flushed a bevy of crabs from her cunt.

'Bet she loses her mud,' sneered Merilee.

Pris's anus spewed a stream of tiny brown dungs, over the pee-soaked crabs.

'The dirty cow,' said Frank, affably, with Emily kneeling to lick his balls, while Merilee sucked the matron's anus from behind her spread buttocks. 'Let's clean her up.'

He summoned Persimmon, who clapped her hands, and cried 'What fun!' as she brandished her nipple pincers; behind her, Laetitia whimpered, left bound and gagged in suspension, with her holes stoppered by navy-blue rubber bungs. Pris was spreadeagled on the shingle, with Emily, Merilee and Caroline sitting on her, Caroline's anus being above Pris's face.

'Lick me off, bitch,' she snarled, and sat heavily, crushing Pris's face beneath her bum and wet cunt.

'Mmph!' Pris gasped, as her tongue began to lick Caroline's clitty, with her nose poking the anus.

'Ahh!' she screamed into Caroline's slit, for Persimmon used her pincers to clamp a tuft of her pubic mane, and yank hard. The entire tuft came away from the gourd skin, leaving a bald patch. 'Ooh!'

Pris's mouth flapped on Caroline's juicing cunt, as Caroline ground her buttocks in the girl's face, with come pouring from her sucked twat into Pris's throat. Pris gurgled, as she swallowed mouthful after mouthful of Caroline's come, then squealed, as Caroline released a torrent of her own piss, drowning Pris in golden steaming fluid, but Pris swallowed that as well, all the time licking and poking Caroline's engorged clitty with her tongue.

'Urrgh! Urrgh!' she gurgled, squirming, despite the pressure of the girls' bodies, as Persimmon yanked tuft after tuft of her pubic mane, until Pris's cunt hillock was as smooth as if freshly shaven.

Persimmon began to work on her armpits, and a few tugs had those, too, nude and girlishly proper. As the last strands of hair vanished from Pris's body, her lips clamped Caroline's clitty; Caroline yelped, and her belly writhed, as her cunt convulsed, spurting floods of come, in massive orgasm. Frank sauntered towards the girls, and casually wrapped Pris's legs around Caroline's neck, exposing her cunt and anus. He straddled Pris, and inserted his glans into her anal bud, making her squeal and writhe, helplessly, with Caroline's bum crushing her face, and her hands pinioning Pris's ankles around her nape.

Persimmon vanished, returning, moments later, with Laetitia Frubbin on all fours, chained to a braided dog-leash by her clamped nipples and cunt lips, and the Royal Navy rubber bungs still stoppering her holes.

Laetitia smiled through the soiled panties gagging her, as she watched Frank slam his muscled body against Pris's squirming loins, in ruthless buggery. Persimmon played with Laetitia's clit, wanking her off, as Frank's giant cock split Pris's wrenched bumhole, and the squirming artist screamed and sobbed into Caroline's crushing cunt.

'Mm . . . mm . . .' Laetitia gurgled, as she was masturbated to come. '*Ooh . . .*'

With Emily and Merilee wanking themselves to spasm, Frank grunted, and buggered faster. Caroline raised her thighs a trifle, strained, and with a rapid plop-plop-plop, released a flood of dungs onto Pris's face and titties, just as Frank's cock bucked, filling her bumhole with his cream. Spunk slopped out over the lips of her squirming anus, and Pris squealed, her dung-smeared belly heaving, as her cunt sluiced come over Frank's balls, in her exploding spasm of climax. Persimmon tweaked her clitty between finger and thumb, and convulsed in her own spasm, blowing kisses at Caroline.

'Mwah! Ooh! Ooh! Mwah!'

When the entire company had refreshed themselves with a dip in the sea – Pris saying she couldn't *wait* to look at her bare twat in a mirror – they trooped back to the gallery. Pris asked them to wait, and ran upstairs, still in the nude, to return with four sheepish boys, also naked; seeing the nude females, they had rapid erections, which made them a little less sheepish.

'I haven't forgotten your spunk delivery, Emily,' Pris said.

The boys lined up; stooping, Pris clasped the first stiff cock between her massive breasts, and began to tit wank the boy, who moaned. Merilee eagerly jumped on the second boy, Persimmon on the third, and Caroline took the biggest cock of all between her naked titties, gasping with pleasure, as she felt the rigid tool and tensed balls enfolded in her soft breast flesh. She began to rub him, slowly and voluptuously, and he groaned, making an attempt to stroke her hair, but she slapped his hand away.

'Naughty boy,' she said. 'Look, not touch.'

'Oh, miss, you're cruel,' he moaned.

'Yes, and boys love it. That's why you're going to give my tits your lovely spunk.'

Only the swollen crimson of his bulb peeped from her teats, as she massaged the cock, squeezing her breasts up to engulf the glans and stroke his peehole with her nipples. Come streamed from Caroline's cunt – to wank off a boy with her teats meant such power! Pris's boy spunked first, spurting a huge jet of cream all over Pris's quivering breasts; quickly, with a wooden spoon, she scooped the spunk into a jar. The others got jars and spoons and, soon, Merilee's black breasts were covered in creamy white spunk, which she scooped into her jar, after briefly licking her sperm-smeared nipples. When all save Caroline's boy had spunked, Caroline said she was going to do something they couldn't do, so there! She turned, bent over, and took the boy by the balls, manoeuvring his cock between her outstretched buttocks, and then frotted the tool between her fesses. Her churning arse cheeks squeezed his cock, pressed in her cleft, until he spermed right against her anus, and Caroline held the spunk between her cheeks, until his load was delivered, when she opened her buttocks wide, and let the spunk plop into the waiting jar. Emily took delivery of her spunk stock with a 'mwah' of thanks to Pris.

Laetitia Frubbin presented Merilee and Caroline with big cardboard boxes. Agog, they opened the boxes, pushing aside the scented crinkly tissue paper, and found their brand-new Furrow Weald school uniforms. Eagerly, they donned school stockings and sussies, knickers, bras, pleated grey skirts and plain white blouses, admiring themselves in the mirror, at a respectful distance from Pris, who clucked with pleasure at her welted bum and shaven cooze.

'I'm a real Stinger,' she purred.

'And you're quite a Swank, Caroline,' said Frank, smoking a cigar. 'Pleasingly dominant, when you wish.'

'Thank you, sir,' Caroline said, curtsying.

Merilee and Caroline preened, in their new school uniforms.

'Fit for peg day,' Emily enthused, 'when girls present themselves at beauty auction.'

'We really are a cut above,' Merilee said.

'Don't get too cocky, or I'll cane your pink arse black again,' Caroline said.

'Ooh,' said Merilee. 'You dominant bitch.'

Caroline dripped with sweat, grunting, as her nude body writhed under the equally nude Jabez Prestellen, although his grunts were louder than hers.

'Gosh, you're splitting me in half,' she moaned, 'you're so big! You're the biggest cock I've ever had.'

'You mean it?' he panted, taking a swig of cider.

'Absolutely,' Caroline gasped. 'Oh, Jabez, you're hurting me so much! My bumhole's so sore, I shan't be able to walk straight! You're so big, so different.'

Downstairs, snooker balls clicked in the public bar of the Cockler's Arms in Trelashen. Beside Caroline, Merilee's nude buttocks wriggled on the balls of another Trelashen boy, whose tool was plunged in her rectum. Beside her, Samantha was buggered, and beside her, Aaliz.

'Hurry up and spunk in me,' Caroline panted. 'I want all that lovely spunk right up my hole.'

'Ooh,' gasped Merilee to her pumping swain, 'I've never ridden such a big one.'

'This is my biggest ever,' trilled Samantha. 'You're so huge, you're frightening! I do believe it'll burst my tummy wide open.'

'I can't believe a boy's cock could be so *enormous*,' cried Aaliz.

'Oh, gosh! Oh! Oh! Ahh!' groaned Persimmon Pipp, flanking Caroline, as the girl ensign exploded in orgasm under vigorous buggery.

Jabez began to spunk in Caroline's rectum, and she, too, whimpered, as her cunt gushed come over his balls, and she came in a slow, groaning climax. As the boys emptied their balls of spunk at the girls' colons, they withdrew, sheepishly shaking their dripping, flaccid members. Caroline grabbed the cider, and took a hefty swig, then lit cigarettes for herself and Persimmon.

'Are you sure you're all right,' Caroline said, 'about the navy, I mean?'

Persimmon inhaled deeply, blew smoke, and shrugged. 'I'm technically AWOL,' she replied, 'and I'll be birched two dozen on the bare. So what? I'm having such fun here – I can't miss peg day. Mr Funn insisted I attend.'

'Suppose someone buys, I mean, hires you?'

'I'll have to choose between my yummy new job as a slave and the navy,' Persimmon replied. 'Plenty of seagirls desert, overseas, usually, where the men have big cocks and a taste for English girl slaves – the navy hushes it up.'

Merilee gasped in climax, as her boy's spunk bubbled over her anal lips, glazing his balls, as he filled her arse with sperm. She plopped off him, gave him a playful spank on the bum, and sent him packing, with a big 'Mwah!'

'Got a fag?' Merilee said.

Caroline lit one for her.

'You're right,' said Merilee, puffing, 'we get a lot of English girl slaves in San Fernando.' She giggled. 'They like the climate, the money – and the cock. Not to mention the extremely strict discipline – so my cousin Clive assures me. English girls like corporal punishment, don't they?'

'*You're* English,' said Caroline, 'pretty much.'

'Very much,' said Merilee, smiling and running her tongue across her gleaming teeth.

'Want a tissue, anybody?' Caroline asked.

The three girls had come-soaked twats and sperm dribbling from their arseholes.

'No,' said Persimmon. 'Boys like spunking where another's already been. It's called "sloppy seconds". They smell when a girl's been fucked lots and is hot for more. It's scent hormones or something, anyway, that's why males like really *slutty* girls. Their brains sense that if lots of blokes have done us, we must be pretty good. It's also male rivalry – if our holes are full of other chaps' spunk, a bloke wants to impress us that *he* has the biggest load.'

'Same as he wants to spank our bums, to punish us for exciting him.'

'Yes. He's jealous of the gorgeous bums girls have and he hasn't.'

'The fact that we like being spanked doesn't count?'

'On the contrary, it infuriates him, so he wants to thrash us extra hard, until we *stop* liking it.'

'But we never stop liking it.'

'He wants to spunk in our bumholes because it's a squeezy tight fit for his cock, and it's so shaming, and hurts us.'

'We like that too.'

'Exactly. That's why girls always win.'

'Oh, good, here's my next one,' said Merilee, as a nude boy, cock fully erect, appeared from the changing room. He was followed by others, and all the girls, after the departure of one bugger, enthusiasticaly opened thighs and anus to the next.

'A good seven or eight bum fucks will have our holes stretched *way* tight,' Merilee panted, grimacing, as a cock speared her anal elastic, 'so we'll all be bought this afternoon. It was a jolly good idea of yours, Caroline.'

'Super,' echoed Samantha.

'Terrific,' gasped Aaliz.

The barn-like dance hall, above the pub, creaked with the couplings of the Furrovians, and the eager young buggers of Trelashen. The air stank of sweat, cider, spunk, pussy juice, and arse grease, despite a fresh breeze from the window, open onto the ocean.

'We're going to be beauty queens, and fashion models and stuff,' Caroline panted, writhing under her bugger's plunging cock, with her cigarette parked in the corner of her lips. 'Surely we won't be *slaves*?'

'Yes, we will,' said the girls, in unison.

'If you'd like to sit here, Caroline,' said Laetitia Frubbin, 'under your number. You're a three, aren't you?'

'Yes, mistress,' said Caroline proudly.

'Just remember,' said the mistress of Furrow Weald. 'You are to sit demurely, like the proper gels you are, with no touching your pegs, yourselves, or each other.'

'I'm longing for a wank, mistress,' moaned Samantha.

'*No* masturbation *whatsoever*,' snapped Laetitia. 'When the guests come in, you are to obey orders without question. Miss Bellibone is the number three team leader.'

The girls wore school uniform, shining spotless, with Aaliz, not far from Caroline, smiling at her, in her prefect's uniform, beside Vicca Valcul. Both prefects hoisted their pleated skirts, as far up their thighs as was decent, to show sussies and stocking tops, and slivers of pink panties. Caroline's panties were white, but she had the marvellous THREE sign above her, not a measly 'two'. The maids were grouped, not by rank or seniority, but by anal capacity, and the Swanks and Stingers clustered under THREE smirked haughtily. Merilee and Persimmon (deemed a definite three by Frank Funn) were there, as were Emma, Vapula, Gertrude, Cynthia, Peggy and Janet, and Bronwen Bellibone. Beside each girl, perched on her high stool, was a two-foot pink rubber dildo, her 'peg', prettily arrayed on a side table, and exactly three inches thick.

'After this morning's seeing-to at Trelashen,' Samantha said, 'my anus feels like the Cheddar Gorge, and those things look positively weedy.'

'You could fire a space rocket through my bumhole,' trilled Merilee.

'I feel someone already has,' said Caroline, smiling, licking her lips, and blushing happily.

'I do hope I'm not *too* big, you know, down there,' murmured Peggy. 'It *is* true males like a big anus, isn't it?'

'Yes,' Bronwen said. 'Men like a tight anus, but there's no point in being so tight that he can't penetrate you at all. The ideal girl's bumhole is both tight and flexible, able to delight the male by squeezing his tool, yet expand to accommodate the largest. Frank Funn, you know, when he was a wrestler, they used to call his shorts "Frank's fun pack". He's had us all – he likes to break girls in, with that *disgustingly* huge tool – so I dare say we really qualify as more than three.'

'Four,' said Caroline.

'Five,' said Merilee.

'I dream of six,' said Samantha. 'Six inches wide and . . . yards long!'

'You're a sex maniac, you are,' sneered Vapula McCloskey.

'I didn't know you were even a three, Vapula,' Samantha said, sniffily.

'Well, I am, so there,' snapped Vapula. 'Want to fight me to prove it? I wrestled Vicca Valcul to come just the other day, *and* caned her two dozzies, before I would let her get up. She's only a rotten two. I've wrestled boys, too, and caned them on their bares, then sucked and swallowed. Big boys, with big cocks. Bet you've never caned a male, Bronwen Bellibone.' She sniffed proudly.

'Not exactly,' said Bronwen. 'But I've been jolly close.'

'Spanking? Pah! That doesn't count.'

'What about the birch?' said Persimmon.

'The birch?' said Vapula, flushing slightly. 'Well, I wouldn't know. I've always beaten boys with the cane. You can't get more painful than a good whippy English ashplant. Boys don't *like* being caned, not the same as we girls do, and that's the fun of it.'

'Are you sure?' said Persimmon.

'Course I'm sure. When you've seen a boy wriggle and bleat and sob, as his bum reddens . . . gosh, I need a wank. Hope these geezers arrive soon. I'm itching to go on display, and bare up, for my new owner.'

She licked her lips, crossing her legs, with a sliver of nylon, to hoist her skirt higher. Her sliver of white knickers was stained wet.

'Cane? The *birch* on a boy's naked buttocks is more fun,' said Persimmon. 'In fact, it's positively come-making.'

'Do tell,' blurted Samantha.

'All right.'

13

Ensign of the Birch

'Well now, Ensign Warchant, you *have* been a naughty boy, haven't you?' said Persimmon Pipp, thrusting out her breasts, and pointedly stroking the twigs of her birch sheaf, to hide her nervousness, for it was the first time, after meticulous training as female disciplinary officer, that she had been detailed as chief punishment mistress.

Heather, Jenny, Robyn and Grace, the other four girl ensigns of the punishment squad, stood stony-faced, with arms folded, around the birching donkey – an oblong table, with a raised cushion in the centre for the miscreant's loins. All wore summer punishment dress of short white pleated skirt, its hem slightly lower than the dark-blue naval knickers, bare legs, white blouses, white ankle socks and canvas shoes (girls, gymnastics and punishment, for the use of). From their waists hung their navy-blue, crook-handled canes with gold crowns. Each girl ensign was to secure one of the miscreant's limbs, with Persimmon, wearing a jaunty peaked cap to denote her status (temporary, summary unlogged punishment, for the infliction of), as punishment mistress.

Holding a chalkboard, on a high stool, at the head of the birching donkey, perched the long-maned blonde Lieut Dr Sue Culpepper (who reminded Persimmon of her very best chum Caroline Letchmount), in full blues, with her navy nylons sleekly crossed, under a navy skirt hoisted well up, revealing her white garter straps over the pale firm flesh of each thigh, with a sliver of white officers' panties at her quim. She was only a few years older than Persimmon, and present, as required by ship's regulations, to supervise the proceedings, without playing any role, either verbal or physical. Hooked to her stool was Persimmon's blue cane, which she had exchanged for her standard navy birch, (breech, bare, cadets', for use on), regulations permitting a female disciplinary officer to 'sport' only one instrument at a time.

'Yes, ma'am,' said the boy, blushing, with his head lowered, and cap held between his legs, yet his eyes fearfully darting towards Persimmon's bushy birch.

A ceiling fan whirred in the wardroom, flashing its shadow on the white-painted metal bulkheads; outside the single porthole shone the grey-green waters of Plymouth Sound, lapping the hull of HMS *Gunsight*. Persimmon tapped the birch against her palm, wincing slightly, at the hard, springy twigs, but licking her lips, as she surveyed the nervous boy, in his shorts and immaculate whites. She swallowed, feeling a seep of come from her cooze, into her navy-blue cotton panties, cut as daringly high as regulations would allow, with the gusset ticklingly tight between her gash flaps. Bother! Come stained even navy blue; they'd have to be washed. Actually – it was Persimmon's secret – the panties were not navy issue at all, but came from Nick Hers, the hot Knightsbridge boutique, so washing out come stains was especially delicate. But Ensign Warchant, with his slim, muscular body, boyish curl flopping over his forehead – and most important, a ducky tight arse – *was* rather a dish, and the prospect of birching him *on the full bare* could not but wet a girl's cooze, ship's regulations or no.

'Ensign Warchant, you are aware of your sentence, handed down by the chief female disciplinary officer,' Persimmon said.

'Yes, ma'am,' he gulped. 'A . . . a birching.'

'Exactly. The new navy, aware that male recruits *need* to be efficiently punished, has reintroduced some of the sensible features of the old. As you are aware, birching became the major punishment for miscreants in the mid-nineteenth century, as it was more dignified than the cat-o'-nine-tails, and more painful than the cane. Boys used to be strapped to the ship's cannon, but today, of course, we use a less lurid, more streamlined, method. Unlogged punishments avoid all the dreary paperwork which impair our efficiency as a top-hole fighting force. You take your cuts from a female disciplinary officer and can get back to work. You have, I know, been caned before.'

Warchant grinned sheepishly. 'Why, yes, ma'am. I've often taken down my pants for a bulkhead sixer from a lady ensign – usually for getting back late from Devonport.'

'A birching is somewhat different. You have earned the standard sentence of twelve cuts –' she was pleased to see him swallow, and pale '– although the maximum is twenty-four.'

His lips pouted in a rather girlish sulk. 'It still seems a bit much, ma'am. I mean, just slipping behind the searchlight for a quick fag – how was I to know they'd have searchlight drill?'

Persimmon's nostrils flared. 'Dereliction of duty is always serious, boy,' she snapped.

'Yes, ma'am.'

'Shall we get down to business?'

'I suppose so, ma'am.'

Persimmon swished the air with her birch. 'You *suppose* so, boy? Remember that I am *in loco admiralis* here.'

He stood to attention, and saluted. 'Ensign Peter Warchant, ready and willing for punishment, ma'am.'

'That's better. Well, you'd better get your kit off. The drill for a birching is: take off your shorts, shoes and socks – I want you completely bare from the waist down – then knot your shirt high under your ribs. You may turn round, for modesty, if you like, before placing yourself on the birching donkey.'

The boy's jaw dropped.

'Well? Jump to it, boy.'

'On the *bare*, ma'am?' he asked.

'Why, of course on the bare,' Persimmon said. 'You've been caned on the bare, haven't you?'

'But, ma'am, that was only with a teazer.'

'Why should a birching be any different? You'll take twelve cuts of my birch on the naked buttocks, to be administered at intervals of not less than ten and not more than twenty seconds – unless you prefer formal disciplinary proceedings. It's black marks on your bottom, or a black mark on your record.'

He shivered. 'I'll . . . I'll take your punishment, ma'am.'

'Then strip. I'm becoming impatient with you, Ensign Warchant. Remember, time-wasting is also an offence. Your forebear Lady Warchant, foundress of St Radegund's, would not be pleased to see her descendant too timid to bare up for a flogging – *she* subjected her husband and sons to the same whippings as her serving maids and stable boys.'

'You know about our family tradition, then,' he murmured, smiling coyly.

'I am an Old Radegundian, and my own bottom is no stranger to the lash, as decreed by Lady Warchant – so I may permit myself a certain vengeful pleasure in flogging *yours*, Warchant.'

The boy turned, removed his shoes and socks, lowered his shorts and pants, then knotted his shirt high. The four girls faced away. Persimmon licked her lips at his bare arse, before she, too, faced away, but not without a glimpse of his swelling cock, a massive tube of flesh, quivering at half mast. When she about-faced, Peter was spreadeagled correctly on the table, his buttocks upthrust by the cushion, and his limbs splayed. Persimmon nodded to her four helpers, and each girl grasped a wrist or ankle, stretching him taut. Sue Culpepper offered him a chewing leather, but he refused it with a scornful wave of his head.

'I am required to advise you of your last chance to refuse punishment,' Persimmon said, her quim dripping come into her squishy wet panties.

'Oh, let's get on with it,' he drawled. 'I can't imagine a whopping from a soppy girl can be all that bad.'

'How *dare* you?' Persimmon spat, her breasts bouncing in rage, over her lacy blue scalloped bra cups (skimpy to just within regulations), beneath the tight white cotton blouse. 'For that insolence, I am empowered to apply the maximum punishment of twenty-four cuts.'

'Now wait a minute . . .'

Persimmon raised an eyebrow at Sue Culpepper, who nodded agreement.

'Twenty-four is regulation,' she purred. 'It's a shame we can't double it, for this insolent brat.'

'Well, Warchant? Are you up for two dozzies?'

Blushing, he nodded. 'I – I'll take it like a Warchant.'

The girls, knees bent, held tightly to the naked boy's wrists and ankles, as Persimmon raised her birch. *Easy now, just as in birch training – raise, lash, and caress.* She took stance, as she had been taught – legs parted and straight – lifted the birch high over her head, with arm fully extended, then, flexing her knees, brought the twigs crashing onto the centre of the boy's naked croup. Vap!

'Uhh!' he gasped, his buttocks clenching tight.

Sue Culpepper chalked her board. Persimmon let the twigs rest on the skin for a few seconds, wiping them over his bare bottom in a caress, before withdrawing the birch, straightening her legs, and lifting the instrument for the second cut. *Ah-one, ah-two, ah-three* . . . she watched the delicate mosaic of bruises visibly redden on Peter's bare bum, as she counted to fifteen, then whipped him the second. Vap! Sue chalked again; the boy's buttocks clenched tight and hard, with a long, low gasp of pain escaping his throat, and the four discipline girls pressing hard on his limbs, as his bottom, legs and back began a shuddering wriggle. Vap!

'Ooh!'

His cheeks clenched and his legs jerked rigid, as Persimmon aimed her cut to the tender tops of his buttocks, rewarded with an instant reddening of the skin, with lots of lovely small blossoms where the twigs had bitten. Only three cuts of the birch, and already almost the whole expanse of his arse was mottled pink and crimson, with some bruises darkening purple. Her cunt oozed come, and she pressed her thighs together, as if that would soak up the come in her panties, but it only made things worse, as her panties made a squelching sound, and she blushed. She could feel her clitty throbbing, swelling against her tight knickers, and began to wish she had worn a floppier pair, or better still no knickers at all, although that breach of regulations would mean her *own* bare bum for the birch. Vap!

'Ooh!'

Peter's bottom was squirming quite hard, clenching and unclenching, with his spine wriggling, as though to dissipate the pain. His face was scarlet, his breath hoarse and rasping, and his eyes moist with tears. Persimmon's cunt gushed come; she forgot all thoughts of concealing her excitement – modesty was not possible, with such delicious weals spreading on the boy's naked buttocks – and concentrated on raise–lash–caress, the 'caress' part being most satisfying, as the twigs clawed through the welts they had just raised, inflaming and deepening them. She counted to ten seconds. Vap! The boy's body began to shudder fiercely, with his welted bum darker and more livid, and wriggling like whipped jellies. The girls panted, as they struggled to control his writhing, with their knuckles white, gripping his wrists and ankles. Persimmon counted to eighteen, trying to get the optimum interval for maximum pain to seep into the boy's buttocks. Vap!

'Uhh!'

The boy began to groan, an unceasing mewl of agony that accompanied his jerking shudders, as the birch lashed his bare. Vap! Persimmon's breasts bounced heavily at each cut, settling on fifteen seconds as the best interval: she could enjoy the frantic squirming of the bum, watch it ebb and the boy's gasps soften, until, at just the right moment before his pain had vanished entirely, another cut took him, right on the same blotched weals. Vap! At each cut, little twigs flew from the birch, although it was so bushy that complete denudation, however satisfying, would be unlikely. Between cuts, she panted, sweat soaking her armpits, just as come poured from her gash to sop her soaking panties. As she birched, her skirt flew up, revealing the panties. *Thank heavens they're dark blue, or I'd be mortified by my come stain . . .* Vap!

'Ooh . . . ooh . . . ooh!'

'*Do* stop that ridiculous girly bleating, Ensign Warchant,' she snapped. 'It doesn't make my job any easier.'

Of course, when I become an officer, I can have lovely lacy white knickers and sussies, but then, if I have to flog a boy, my come stains will show. Drat! Officers like Lieut Culpepper don't administer CP – maybe I'd better remain a female disciplinary officer. Decisions, decisions!

Vap!

'*Ohh! Ahh!*'

'I warned you! Do you want a repeat cut? It's lawful, you know.'

Sue Culpepper smiled, nodding ageement. She crossed her nyloned thighs with a wet slither, revealing a flash of white panties gusset, the crisp cloth stained dark with moisture from her cunt.

'I'm sorry, I can't help it, ma'am, you slice a chap so beastly hard.'

'You think *that* was hard?'

Persimmon angled her birch, and he took the cut squarely in the bum cleft, where she could see the twigs just brushing his full, dangling balls.

'*Ahh! Oh! Oh!*'

His bum leapt from the cushion, and all the girls gasped, for his cock was fully erect! Only Sue, marking her chalkboard, seemed not to notice. The four discipline helpers blushed, Persimmon's scarlet face making her blush unnecessary, as her cunt spurted a huge splash of come into her already slopped panties. Her clitty throbbed almost painfully, sending waves of pleasure up her spine, as it rubbed against the wet panties cloth, and – after seeing that *fabulous* stiff cock and the boy's *gorgeously* bruised bare bottom – Persimmon knew she needed to masturbate. Panting hard, she waited impatiently for fifteen seconds to pass, before she lashed him again in the bum cleft. Vap! He yelped, legs jerking rigid, and his left wrist and leg breaking free of the helpers' grasp, to flail unrestrained for several seconds, before they had him once more under control. Vap! The same thing happened, with the girls fighting to keep his thrashing body still. Vap! The birch lashed his thighs, quite legally, within three inches of the lower fesse.

'*Ooh! Ahh!*' he squealed, squirming frantically, and tears glazing his face. 'You bitch! You're rotten! I'll have you! I will! You absolute bitch!'

There was stunned silence in the flogging chamber, broken only by the lapping of the waves on the hull, far below, the caw of seagulls and the sobbing groans of the whipped boy. Beneath his wriggling purple buttocks, all the girls, including Sue, saw that his cock throbbed rigid. Sue licked her lips, uncrossing her legs, and raising her skirt to fan her crotch, then letting her skirt rest, bunched almost to her waist, with her come-slopped panties plainly visible, as a pale triangle between her thighs pressed tightly and demurely together. Sue licked her lips.

'That, I'm afraid, is mutiny,' she murmured.

'I'm sorry!' blurted the boy. 'I didn't mean – it's just that my bum hurts so terribly. And that thigh cut. It's . . . it's awful.'

Sue rose, taking Persimmon's cane from her stool, formally displaying it to each girl in turn, then hooking it onto her belt. She took off her jacket, pegging it neatly, and her full breasts rippled angrily under her crisp white blouse, spotted with sweat at her armpits, where her hair tufted dark.

'Having sported my cane, I now have formal rank as acting female disciplinary officer,' she explained, 'and I trust you will have no objection, Ensign Pipp, if I take judicial charge of this case, without prejudice to your executive status.'

Persimmon nodded, and stood to attention. Sue Culpepper scribbled a chit, and ordered Grace to fetch 'number two birching tackle' from the purser's office. While Grace was gone, Sue lifted the shirt above the boy's head, and stripped him entirely naked, without resistance on his part, then walked slowly round the trembling nude boy, tapping his bum weals gently with her cane tip, and making him wince. She flicked the cane under his hip, raising it and showing the massive tube of his erect cock, snug between his belly and the birching cushion. Sue tut-tutted. Grace returned, bearing an armful of buckled rubber straps, and, with crisp instructions, Sue directed the girls to strap Peter's wrists, waist and ankles tightly to the block. A rubber girdle, ten inches wide, secured him by the small of his back. There remained a black rubber hood, with a breathing hole at the mouth.

'Now, Warchant,' Sue said, 'we are all witness to your act of mutiny. In addition, there is the – admittedly, rather ancient – offence of *beastliness.* As a doctor, I find no medical excuse for your erect cock. At eighteen years of age, you are required to control yourself.'

'Please, ma'am, I can't help it,' Peter wailed. 'I've never been birched before, by a lady . . . on the bare, you know . . . I mean, I've been used to bare-bum caning at home – my big sister took my pyjama bottoms down, and thrashed me with a two-foot ashplant, and I admit I sometimes got excited by it, but that's different.'

'I don't see how,' Sue snorted. 'Most of us girls are used to bare-bottom discipline, but don't make disgraceful exhibitions of ourselves. You've taken the teazer on your bare from FDOs, of course. Did your cock rise then?'

'Y-yes, ma'am, only I made sure to hide it.'

'Mutiny and beastliness!' Sue snapped. 'Either offence would dismiss you in disgrace from the navy – however, I may ordain a continuance of unlogged chastisement. Would you prefer that?'

'Yes, ma'am,' whimpered the boy. 'If you please.'

Sue clapped her hands. 'Very good,' she said brightly, and encased the boy's head in the rubber hood. 'Persimmon, you will please birch the miscreant six further cuts; Heather, six cuts from you; Grace, six cuts; Jenny, six cuts; Robyn, six cuts; Persimmon again, and so on, until denudation of the birch sheaf,' Sue commanded. 'The cuts, according to the mutiny regulation, to be delivered on the three seconds.'

'Oh, no,' moaned Peter, his voice a muffled drone inside the rubber hood.

Persimmon lifted the birch once more. Her cunt was really juicy, and her panties absolutely soaked by now; she wondered if she could get permission to pee, and bring herself off with an ultra-fast wank.

'According to medical regulations,' said Sue, her face slightly flushed, 'in a birching of intervals less than ten seconds, any FDO may opt to make herself completely comfortable, for optimum performance of her duty. I think you understand what I mean.'

She began to unbutton her white blouse, opening the garment, until her bra and full pale breast flesh were exposed, then stripping it off. Casually, she unhooked her bra, allowing her massive titties to spring free and naked, the nipples hard red plums atop the gleaming teats. Lush forests of glossy blonde hair sprouted beneath her armpits.

'My, isn't it hot?' Sue murmured.

She continued to disrobe, unzipping her skirt, folding it neatly, and placing it on the stool; then, snapping open her garter straps, and rolling down the navy-blue nylons, with her white, come-soaked panties the last garment to go. Sue stood in the full nude, her breasts quivering in the wind from the fan, and rubbed her bare buttocks briskly. Her full-bushed blonde twat glistened with seeping come, and her engorged clitty peeped from the swollen cunt lips. She patted her hairy cunt, like a pet, and smiled.

'*That's* better,' she said, her fingers idly brushing her swollen nubbin, peeping from her engorged wet cunt flaps.

Coyly, the four helpers rapidly shed their summer punishment uniforms, little more than gym kit, and were soon nude and barefoot. Each of their cunt hillocks – all shaven regulation shiny, like their armpits, as mere ensigns were not permitted 'underbeards' – were glazed with come from their dripping cunts. Vap! Suddenly, Persimmon, the only ensign still clad, lashed the trussed boy's bare buttocks.

'Ooh!' he howled, beneath his rubber mask.

One, two, three –

Vap!

'Oh! Oh! Ahh!'

Persimmon wished she were nude, like the others. In the corner of her eye, she saw Sue licking her drooling lips, and demurely, but obviously, wanking her exposed stiff clitty, as she gazed at the boy's squirming naked body and purple-birched buttocks. Vap! Vap! The six cuts, on the three seconds, were done rapidly; Persimmon changed places with the naked Heather, who eagerly took stance, and lifted the birch over Peter's bare bottom. Vap! Vap! The cuts continued almost without pause, and Persimmon positively *ripped* her uniform off, panting, until she stood nude beside her colleagues. Sue's teeth were bared, her eyes slits, glaring at Peter's squirming nates, as her fingers squelched inside her gushing cooze. Heather wanked off, as she birched the boy; Jenny, Grace and Robyn were masturbating enthusiastically, with come soaking their wanking fingers. Parting her thighs, Persimmon touched her throbbing clit once, and exploded in orgasm.

She was not the only girl to come; all masturbated feverishly, as the birch passed from Heather, to Grace, Jenny, and Robyn, and all convulsed, drooling and gasping in their separate climaxes. Lieut Dr Sue Culpepper wanked herself to three comes by the time it was Persimmon's turn to birch again. She took the instrument, half as bushy as it was before and with the deck covered in twigs. Vap! Vap! Her fingers stabbed her drooling cunt, as she gazed through sweat-blurred eyes at the boy's flogged bare buttocks clenching at each cut, the hips slamming into the cushion, squirming piteously, then, stretching his rubber waistband, jerking up and down, in a bizarre mimicry of fucking, but showing clearly that his monstrously stiff cock was untamed. Vap! Vap! Peter's strangled moans of agony lilted with the girls' shrill cries of orgasm, as the sweating nude girls, teeth bared and eyes glowing, birched the naked boy's buttocks, and wanked off.

At last there remained but one strand on the birch; Persimmon held it, little more than a thin cane. She dealt a savage cut, right between the boy's buttocks, in the blotched purple arse cleft, with the cane tip brushing his swollen balls, and he howled. The last birch wand snapped in two, at the force of her blow, and she masturbated herself to one more climax. Standing right above Peter, her belly quaked, as her cunt spurted come all over his wealed bum, and Persimmon was positive the pussy juice sizzled, as it slopped his flaming purple welts. Denudation was accomplished; the deck was sopping with wanked come, and each girl ensign had thighs and bare feet glistening with her cunt fluid. Peter lay, whimpering and shuddering, after the girls obeyed Sue's command to release him. Tenderly, Sue grasped his hand, and helped him to rise, with his massive cock pole still jutting over his belly.

'This ensign is still in a state of beastliness,' Sue panted, 'and, according to medical regulations, I am obliged to return him fit for duty, or else we shall all be accomplices to his offence. It calls for drastic measures.'

Sue clambered onto the table, and squatted, with her cunt inches above Peter's face. She motioned the girls to do likewise, and all five squatted over his prone body, Persimmon's cunt directly above his balls.

Pssss!

At Sue's signal, the girls peed over him, bathing his body in streaming golden liquid. Sue's own pee flowed straight into his open mouth, and he gurgled, as he swallowed her whole load of piss.

'Oh, yes . . .' he gasped, 'yes . . .'

Sue frowned. 'The shame should have softened his cock,' she said, 'but he's stiffer than ever.'

'I'm sorry ma'am,' he blurted. 'It . . . it's rather lovely, being peed on by girls.'

He stood, dripping girl piss, and smiling, as the four girl ensigns lay side by side on the birching donkey. Sue laid Peter on his back, across the girls' breasts – they gasped, giggling, at his weight – then wiped her hand between her thighs, and came up with a palmful of glistening come. She parted her buttocks, holding her anus open with her fingers, and slopped her come over the anus bud, and inside her bumhole, then slapped her cunt again, and poured a second palmful of come over his stiff tool.

'Peter,' she said, 'have you ever had sex with a girl?'

'Beg pardon, ma'am, but I don't think you have the right to ask me that,' he gasped.

'As your medical officer, I have,' she said. 'Has your cock ever penetrated a girl's vulva?'

'N-no, ma'am. I'm saving myself.'

'Or any other orifice?'

'What? You mean – why, that's disgusting, begging your pardon, ma'am.'

'We shan't disturb your virginity,' said Sue solemnly.

She squatted atop his stiff cock, with his bulb an inch from her come-wet anus bud. Persimmon's breasts were squashed by the boy's wealed buttocks, and her twat was juicing heavily, as she wriggled, feeling his delicious crusty welts caress her stiff nipples. She managed to free one arm, and got her fingers to her cooze, just as her breasts were crushed under Peter's weight, and his body sank, with Sue impaling her anus on his huge tool. He groaned.

'Please, ma'am, no . . .'

Sue squirmed, clutching his cock, and jamming its huge girth into her tiny bumhole, inch by inch, until she rose slightly, and slammed the whole weight of her buttocks on his glans, which disappeared into her anus, with the cock shaft penetrating and filling her rectum.

'Ahh . . .' Sue sighed, and began to pump up and down, while Persimmon wanked herself, breathless, as her titties were squelched by Peter's bum weals.

'Oh, ma'am, that's so good . . .' Peter moaned. 'Please don't stop . . .'

As she buggered herself on his cock, the lieutenant wanked off vigorously, with streams of her come dripping over Peter's balls, and copiously soaking Persimmon's crushed titties. Persimmon's thumb mashed her clit, as she watched Sue's naked buttocks rising and falling, with Peter's tool, slimed in come and arse grease, squelching in and out of her distended anus. The other girl ensigns were wanking off, too, and Peter's breath grew hoarse and rapid, with Sue panting, as she frigged herself to orgasm.

'Oh, yes . . .' she groaned.

'Oh . . .' Peter gasped.

'Yes, I'm coming,' Sue panted. 'Yes . . . yes . . . Ohh! *Ohh*!'

Come sluiced from her cunt, over Peter's balls and cock, and down to Persimmon's teats, with Persimmon wanking herself off to a huge orgasm, just as the boy groaned shrilly, and creamy white spunk bubbled from Sue's sucking anus lips, to drip onto Persimmon's squashed bare breasts, nipples throbbing in her climax. Bare belly churning, Sue milked his cock of every drop of sperm, then removed his tool from her anus with a loud plop, put it in her mouth, and sucked the softened cock meat dry of spunk, and her own come and arse grease.

'*Now* this miscreant is fit for duty,' she said, smiling and licking her lips.

Dressed, the naval personnel behaved as if nothing whatsoever had happened. Salutes were exchanged; Peter was beside Persimmon as he left, rubbing his bum, under his white shorts.

'I meant what I said,' he hissed.

'What?'

'You were beastly rotten, and I'll have you for it.'

'But *everybody* birched you.'

'You were the cruellest. You were the one who made my cock stiff.'

'Flatterer. You put it in Sue's bumhole, though.'

'She's a medical officer – I had to obey. It was so good to pour my spunk into that lovely tight elastic hole, but still, I feel besmirched, impure. Someone must suffer in return. It's your fault, Ensign Pipp. *I'll have you.*'

Persimmon looked at his bulging groin, and licked her teeth. She turned, raised her skirt, and parted her sopping wet knickers and buttocks to flash her bumhole.

'Promise?' she said.

14

Girl Meat

There was Furrovian champagne come for the guests – two-thirds girl come, with the school selling it worldwide for a thousand American dollars a bottle. Caroline perched, preening and pouting, thrusting up her teats, and crossing her legs seductively, tickled to be displayed as merchandise. Caviar and smoked salmon were served by junior Furrovians in French maids' costumes, with teetering spike heels, while 'CC' was poured by prefects – including Mandy Tuppe, Pimella Plumply and Victoria Brounbirch – neatly attired in their prefects' blazers, short pleated skirts and pastel nylons, with buckled shoes, and canes swinging from their belts at their haunches. The buyers were conservatively and richly dressed, and all rather shy, save for Frank Funn, who talked volubly, flanked by a beaming Laetitia Frubbin and the sluttish Greta, from his television show, who scowled, sucking on a menthol cigarette.

'Not a bad show of girl meat, I suppose,' Greta sneered. 'That one, with the big arse, needs taking down a peg.' She pointed her cigarette at Caroline.

'Big arse, tight arsehole,' quipped Frank, licking his lips.

There was a commotion, as one of the maids stumbled, and spilled some caviar; Mandy Tuppe sweetly drew her cane, and ordered the girl to lower her thong panties and touch her toes, for correction. The thong wouldn't come down, without a strain, because it was so tight; the frilly maid's black chiffon tutu required just a wiggle of the hips, to bare her buttocks completely. Mandy gave the girl six, with casual disdain, in only a few seconds. That broke the ice, and the men started to ogle the displayed girl meat; another maid spilled something, accidentally or on purpose, and took ten strokes from Victoria, with a fine show of squirming, as her naked buttocks reddened, framed by the quivering black lace sussies.

'. . . of course, sir! Any order must be obeyed,' Mistress Frubbin purred, 'for the customer is always right.'

The males' shyness gave way to a feeding frenzy, albeit a gallant one; no girl was without champagne, and, if her bladder exacted its price, a dainty porcelain chamber pot awaited under her stool. Pimella, buttocks wiggling, circulated, smiling sweetly in her skirt and blazer, bearing a dish of canes: long, short, stout, or springy. She curtsied whenever a buyer chose one, and soon every male was flexing his own instrument. They prowled, canes and champagne glasses raised, circling the perching girls, to examine breasts, lips, thighs, ankles and buttocks.

They pinched and kneaded and poked, ever bolder, lifting skirts and parting blouses. Before long, Emma Spivey had to bare up for a test caning, bent over her stool: skirt raised, head bagged, knickers at her ankles and bum bared for twelve strokes, which she took with wriggles and moans. Her champagne reward made her want to pee, so she squatted over her chamber pot, skirts raised, to tinkle noisily, with hearty applause.

Before Emma made herself proper, someone poured a glass of champagne over her shaven cunt gourd, and encouraged Gertrude to lick it up, which she willingly did, squatting before Emma's open cunt, to lick not just the champagne, but the cunt flesh as well. Gertrude's school uniform skirt was pulled up over her back to avoid spoiling it on the floor, and she exposed her knickers, which were soon tugged down, and a stroke from several gentlemen's canes applied to her bared buttocks, which clenched and reddened quite alarmingly, as the caned Gertrude slurped Emma's moist twat.

A gentleman wondered 'what was under' Merilee's skirt, and Merilee showed him; then, he wondered 'what was under' her knickers, and she showed him that, too. When he wondered what it must be like to wank such a succulent gash, she showed him, eagerly masturbating, with both quim lips held wide, and her thumb rubbing her swiftly engorging clitty, while her hand slopped in the glistening pink meat of her wet cunt.

She wanked off, until come was streaming down her thighs and her nubbin was swollen like an acorn, whereupon the gentleman wondered if Merilee knew what happened to naughty girls who were caught frigging. Little-girl innocent, Merilee popped a come-soaked thumb in her mouth, made doe eyes, and said she had no idea, and when the gentleman proposed to teach her, she assented willingly to her lesson. Bum bared, panties strung between her knees, Merilee draped herself over her stool, with her ankles and wrists clinging to the legs, as the buyer delivered a dozen slow, excruciating stingers to her naked buttocks, which squirmed in the same tortured rhythm as Merilee's hoarse gasps of pain.

Caroline felt a hand on her buttocks, smiled demurely, and parted the fesses, to allow a male's finger to poke her cleft and anus. She pouted, as the hand delved under her skirt, found her panties waistband, snapped it against her tummy, then slid inside, to finger her naked twat. Opening her thighs wide, she let the fingers progress across her perineum to her anus pucker, and emitted a soft little cry of surprise, as she was anally penetrated.

'That's never a three-incher,' grunted the buyer, as his finger slid into her rectum, up to his knuckles. 'You're too darn tight.'

'I assure you, I am, sir,' she murmured.

'Fibber!' he exclaimed. 'You know what happens to fibbers.'

Caroline glanced at Merilee's squirming bum, and was jolted by a spurt of come from her cunt, which drenched her interlocutor's hand. He smiled.

'I like a wench wet at the thought of bare-bum caning,' he said. 'Knickers down, gel, and cheeks up for my cane.'

Caroline assumed position over her stool, and did not protest when her knickers were ripped right off and her wrists and ankles strapped to her stool legs. The male began to cane her with a springy, three-foot willow rod. Vip! Vip!

'Ooh, sir! You're hurting me!' Caroline gasped, her buttocks clenching tight.

'None of that girly moaning,' he growled. 'A girl slave must take her stripes.'

Vip!

'Ouch!

Vip!

'Ooh . . . ooh . . .'

Caroline's buttocks wriggled, as her cunt gushed come, at the pain of the cane strokes streaking her naked flesh. Vip! Vip! Her clitty swelled, and she began to rub it on the seat, hoping to bring herself off. Vip! Vip! The cuts scalded her bottom, and she counted to a dozen, gasping in shock, as he continued past the twelve. Vip! Vip!

'Ouch! Ooh! Sir, I can't take any more. Oh, please stop! I've never been wealed so hard!'

Her buttocks were bruised crimson, wriggling, as she slapped her stiff clitty against the stool; Caroline endured two-dozen strokes of the cane on her bare.

'Oh! Oh, yes,' she whimpered. 'Thrash my naughty bottom, sir.'

At the last few cuts, she began to pant and shudder, with the cane whipping her to a heaving orgasm that drenched her legs in come.

'Ooh! Ooh! *Ahh*!'

Come poured from her twat, drenching her thighs, as her cunt fluttered in climax. Bouncing nimbly to her feet, she squatted to pee, and accepted her reward of champagne as her piss tinkled in the pot. No maid on the market now had a bottom unbared, titties unsqueezed, or an empty piss pot. The smack of cane, or hand, on bare bum flesh, echoed above the clinking of champagne glasses, and the shrill cries of beaten schoolgirls. Panties, bras, sussies and stockings littered the floor. Persimmon was on all fours, nude, sucking one gentleman's cock, while buggered by another's. She winked at Caroline. Scarcely had Caroline made herself decent – although she wasn't allowed to wipe her piss-wet twat – than she willingly stripped off, to join the schoolgirl fun.

Samantha slurped champagne, while squatting on her pole, her feet supporting her on the circular shelf, halfway down the pole. The dildo was plunged into her cunt. With a wiggle of her bottom, she plopped it from the slit, and impaled her anus on its come-soaked shaft.

'Three inches . . .' gentlemen murmured.

Smiling, Samantha extended her left leg straight, then the other, sinking down onto the dildo, with her full weight taken by her impaled bumhole. Then, she balanced her champagne glass on one erect nipple – a second was soon provided – and sat, legs splayed rigid, with two glasses balanced on her teats, while she masturbated her swollen clitty, with loud squelching sounds, as her come dripped into her chamber pot.

'I can do that,' Caroline blurted impatiently.

'Can you balance a glass on your shoulders?'

'Of course!'

'At the crouch, then, slut.'

Caroline crouched on all fours, and felt the cold glass sitting between her shoulders, then gasped, as her bare buttocks were parted, and a male's stiff tool teased her anus.

'Wait –' she began.

'Shut up and obey, slag,' snarled Greta, the television charmer.

'Ooh!' Caroline squealed, as the giant cock penetrated her anus, pushing, until it cleaved her rectum and the throbbing glans was mashing her sigmoid colon.

Her wine glass trembled, but did not spill. The male began a fierce buggery, ramming his cock all the way to her colon, so that each stroke slapped his balls against her trembling buttocks.

'*Urrgh . . . urrgh*!' Caroline groaned, as pain shot through her buggered bumhole, and tears flooded her eyes. 'Oh, gosh, sir, I've never been bummed so hard, or so painfully. That cock must exceed three inches in girth.'

'I'm not Donkey Dick for nothing,' he said with a chortle.

Donkey Dick – if that really *was* his name – buggered her for several mnutes, while Caroline's cunt spewed more and more copious come down her quivering thighs, yet still her wine glass balanced intact. Frowning with jealousy, Merilee crouched beside her, and began to bite her nipples.

'Ooh! Oh!' Caroline squealed. 'Stop, you bitch!'

A champagne glass was placed on Merilee's back, and a vicious little gutta-percha ferule applied to her naked bottom. Vip! Vip!

'Ohh!' Merilee moaned, her teeth biting fiercely on Caroline's engorged nips, her wine glass upright on her quivering ebony back, even as her bare bum took the cane.

Come sluiced from her twat, trickling towards the stream from Caroline's gash, and their comes pooled on the floor. Merilee took over two-dozen strokes on the bare, until Donkey Dick grunted, and spunk bubbled from Caroline's buggered anus. Persimmon crawled forwards, to plunge her face between Caroline's buttocks, and lick the spunk dribbling in her cleft. The girls were rewarded with their saved glasses of champagne come, and refills, before Greta pushed them down to gamahuche each other by request. Caroline's mouth was on Merilee's hairless black twat, and Merilee's tongue stabbed hard into Caroline's wet cunt, while the girls clawed bare buttocks, wriggling together on the floor, with Persimmon sucking Merilee's toes.

Above them, Samantha slipped up and down on her impaling anal dildo, powered by the suction of her own sphincter, and, suddenly, paused in her wank to emit a steaming jet of golden pee, drenching the enlaced naked bodies of the tribadists. Caroline moaned, swallowing Merilee's come and Samantha's pee, then squealed as Merilee bit her clitty, making her spurt a powerful jet of pussy juice into Merilee's mouth. Moments later, she pointed her arse at Persimmon, and pissed, squirting her jet straight into Persimmon's mouth. The navy girl swallowed noisily.

Merilee gurgled, swallowing Caroline's come, and reaming her erect clit with her lips, while Caroline took Merilee's whole cunt into her mouth, and began a powerful suck, with her tongue tip flicking the slimy wet clitty. After swallowing Caroline's piss, Persimmon wanked off, as she licked Merilee's toes and soles, while Vapula viciously caned Persimmon's bum with a gutta-percha ferule. There was a plop, as Samantha vaulted from her anal impalement, and fell hard on the writhing naked bodies in a wrestler's crush.

'Not fair to leave me out, you beastly friggers,' she panted.

With her tongue in Merilee's anus, she poked her big toe into Caroline's bumhole, which she began to frot, her toe slopping in spunk and arse grease, while her fingers wanked Persimmon's cunt, shuddering and juicing under Vapula's caning. Eager gentlemen gathered to watch the writhing maids.

'What sluts,' sneered Greta, flicking cigarette ash into Samantha's cunt.

'Cheeky bitch!' Samantha cried, flying at Greta and knocking her down, with a forearm to the titties.

Squatting on the nude gamahuching bodies of Caroline and Merilee, Samantha put the wriggling Greta over her knee. She ripped off Greta's skirt, tore her thong panties to shreds, then spanked her bare buttocks crimson, while Greta squirmed and shrieked, pausing to accept another menthol cigarette, which Frank kindly placed between her lips. Smack! Smack! Samantha spanked fiercely, as Greta's buttocks squirmed.

'You fucking cunt,' Greta gasped, 'you'll pay for this.'

When her bare had taken over a hundred spanks, Samantha spat on her bruised bum several times, and rubbed in her spittle, saying that Greta was a mucky tart for juicing so much. Greta's thighs, forced open, revealed her swollen hairy minge, the lips glossy with cunt juice, and the come gushing from her pink wet slit meat.

Vip! Vip! Vapula put down her cane, saying Persimmon had had her lesson; Persimmon, sobbing angrily, promptly floored her with a wrestler's dive, and began to bite and suck her quim, while pummelling her titties. Vapula writhed, screaming, until Persimmon slammed her cunt flat on Vapula's face, and Vapula began to suck Persimmon's clitoris, swallowing the come spurting from the caned girl's gash.

Samantha resumed spanking Greta, this time on the bare cunt, and erect, extruded clitty, while Greta writhed, shrieking in pain. Samantha ripped off Greta's blouse and bra.

'You fucking whore!' shrieked Greta. 'Those were from Nick Hers of Knightsbridge.'

Samantha lifted her by the pubic bone, pressing Greta's cunt to her face, and took a savage bite of her hairy quim. Greta yelped, then pissed heartily, splashing Merilee and Caroline in new pee, and wrapped her legs around Samantha's neck, begging to be sucked off. Samantha grabbed a bottle of champagne, shook it furiously and, as the foam swelled, stuck it right up Greta's anus, where the cork exploded with a loud pop.

'Ah!' Greta screamed, her belly writhing, and expelled the cork, followed by a froth of champagne, which Samantha drank greedily from the anus.

She commandeered a plate of caviar and smoked salmon from a maid with only one shoe, and rammed the pink fish and glistening black eggs up Greta's cunt. Pressing her mouth to the smeared gash, she began licking and sucking, while swallowing the cunt juice, fish and caviar that spewed from the girl's wriggling slit.

Vapula and Persimmon writhed, wrestling, hissing insults and tongue-fucking, on the floor.

'Kiss me, you fucking bitch.'

'Drink my come, you beastly twat.'

All around them, maids groaned, impaled on their dildos, or shuddering under cock and cane. The floor became a lake of girl come, spunk and golden girl piss, in which prefect and maid alike slipped and slithered. Maids moaned, wrapped in cling film, or strapped in rubber harnesses, rode piggyback on male backs, or were themselves ridden as ponies, with fierce lashes of the crop on their naked haunches, as they whinnied and bucked. One by one, the buggered or caned girls hobbled or crawled to watch the hillock of naked tribadists.

'Sir, may I join?' cried Aaliz, rubbing her bottom, bruised purple with welts from a nine-thonged cat, as she hobbled on all fours, guided by a studded leash around her neck, and masturbating her cunt with a three-inch wide dildo, while a maid's spike heel stuck in her anus, the sole slapping her wealed bum.

Her trainer assenting, she threw herself on the pile of writhing bodies, and bit flesh. Gertrude followed, then Cynthia, Peggy, Janet and others.

'I'm being crushed,' mumbled Caroline into Merilee's streaming cunt. 'Ooh . . . I'm coming! Yes!'

'*Ahh*!' gasped Merilee, as the two crushed maids heaved together in orgasm.

Their gamahuche did not cease for other cunts and bare titties, slippery with come and piss, pressed between Caroline's lips, as other toes poked her slit and anus. The pyramid of naked girls writhed like a beast alive, with groans of climax and the hiss of pee. Caroline and Merilee squirmed under the mountain of naked girl flesh, swimming in piss and pussy juice, wanking, and coming again and again. It seemed to Caroline, squashed in this warm womb of girls' bare bodies, that she would never *stop* coming. Persimmon drooled in thrashing orgasm, as Vapula chewed her clit; Vapula erupted in her own spasm, seconds later, as Persimmon raked her anus with sharp fingernails.

'Ooh!'
'Oh! Oh!'
'Ahh!'
'Yes . . .'
'Oh, yes, I'm coming!' shrieked Samantha.
'Shut up, you fucking whore,' snarled Greta, her toe up Cynthia's cunt and her fingers reaming Gertrude's rectum.
'Up yours, bitch,' panted Samantha, managing to get enough leverage for savage punches to Greta's breasts.
'Oh! Ouch! Stop!' wailed Greta, kicking Emma in the cunt.
'You bitch,' gasped Emma, slapping Greta's face, and digging Cynthia's teats with her elbow.
'Hey, you careless slut,' Cynthia snapped, her bum slapping Vapula's, and making Vapula bite Persimmon's clit.
'Ouch! You cunt!' squealed Persimmon.
'Cow,' hissed Vapula to Cynthia.
The mountain of bare bodies turned to a ferocious wrestling match, with screams and whimpers, as the naked girls kicked, bit, spat and gouged.
No . . . I don't want to be a hellcat, but I've no choice!
Caroline's fists flew, spanking bottoms, smashing girls in the cunt or titties, and clawing pink wet slit meat with her sharp toenails, until they pissed themselves, squealing and sobbing. At last, Merilee, Persimmon, Samantha and Caroline sat atop the heap of come-drenched bodies, with the crushed, bruised girls weeping and snivelling under their buttocks.
'Did I drub you by accident, Merilee?' Caroline said. 'Or you, Samantha? I'm awfully sorry.'
'Don't be,' Merilee said. 'It was super. Mwah!' She blew an air-kiss.
'I loved you punching me,' said Samantha. 'Mwah.'
'Terrific,' said Persimmon. 'Mwah.'
Caroline blew return kisses.
'Mwah . . . mwah . . . mwah.'
'You poncy fucking bitch, Caroline,' snarled Greta, wriggling from the mound of bodies. 'I'll do you.'

Caroline slapped her, with fierce punches to the face, cunt and titties, and Greta sagged, sobbing, onto Peggy Droule's crimson wealed buttocks, protruding from the pyramid, with no clue as to where the rest of Peggy was.

'Caroline?' It was Aaliz's voice, quavering from deep in the girl pile.

'Yes, Aaliz?'

'I'm thirsty. Would you pee on me, please?'

Caroline squatted, balancing on Gertrude's left buttock and Vapula's right, then pissed down Bronwen Bellibone's naked, wealed bum cleft. She heard Aaliz beneath her, gurgling, as she swallowed.

'Thank you. That was lovely.'

Persimmon, Merilee and Samantha each pissed down Bronwen's cleft.

'Oh . . . ooh . . . yes,' Aaliz gurgled. 'I'm going to come. *Yes*!'

Mistress Frubbin clapped her hands. 'Time for the auction, maids and gentlemen. Will all maids resume their places?'

'Just a minute,' said Frank Funn, reaching into the girl mound. He extricated Greta, wrenching her by her lush pubic hairs, as she squirmed and squealed.

'You'd better smarten up, cow,' he chided, 'to look after our new contestants.'

'What new contestants, sir?' she said with a sob.

'Why, Caroline, Samantha, Persimmon and Merilee,' Frank chortled. 'I'm buying them myself – droit de seigneur – and they're going to star in my show.'

'How wonderful,' beamed Mistress Frubbin.

'My reality show – *Girl Zoo*. We shoot in the wild, down in San Fernando.'

Greta, though nude, come-dripping and snuffling, passed a chain around the waists and buttocks of the three girls, snaking it through their twats. She leered, jerking them to their feet.

'We cannot forget my friend Aaliz, sir,' said Caroline, curtsying, then delving into the scrum, and dragging Aaliz out by her piss-soaked nipples.

'Thank you,' Aaliz panted, as her cunt basin was chained.

'My personal airbus is waiting at Plymouth airport, girls,' said Frank. 'You won't mind travelling nude, and chained? It'll get you into the light-hearted spirit of the show.'

'TV stars!' cried Samantha.

'Our own show!' chirped Merilee.

'It's my dream come true,' said Persimmon. 'Bugger the navy.'

'Super,' Caroline agreed.

To polite applause, Frank led his girl slaves to the door, followed by Greta, scooping up her shredded knickers and skirt.

'I'll get my revenge,' hissed Greta. '*How* you bitches will suffer.'

There were no air-kisses on San Fernando, only drudgery, pain, and heat. After a month, a year, or an aeon – it didn't seem to matter – all Caroline knew was the smarting of her whipped bottom, the ache in her buggered anus, the constant wetness of her cunt, the incessant tingling of her nipples and clitty and spine. Sunbronzed, lithe and hard-bodied, she was a female animal on heat, prepared to submit to every humiliation, in order to satisfy her lust for the lashes on her naked flesh and the fullness of cock in her bumhole.

'The game,' Frank had said, as the airbus touched down on the upcountry airstrip, 'is that you are girls in cages, naked, stripped of everything but lust. Girl slaves have neither clothes nor dignity – none of this rubbish from Nick Hers of Knightsbridge to hide your beastly female selves. You are girl meat in the raw.'

Greta flashed her boss a dirty look. 'In the game, we pretend you are slaves of a cruel, despotic master. And the beauty of it is, *you are*.'

Life on San Fernando was sweltering heat, the whip, and brutal girl guards; drudgery in the laundry, kitchens, or tobacco plantation; the cages where they slept, lusted and fought, defecating, masturbating and gamahuching in full view of Frank's leering camera crews. They lost all shame, learning fast that they never really had any; Caroline, like the rest, would give a wank display, masturbating herself to the cameras, for a handful of cashews; or make a tribadic clusterfuck with Persimmon, Merilee, Samantha or Aaliz. They named Frank's cameramen Porky, Baldy, Randy, Smelly, or Beardy, although they were combinations of all. The guards were Bitch, Slut, Twat, Hag and Cow – collectively, the 'slags' – uniformed in tight pink bra and panties, bright against their nut-brown skin, with high, rope, Grecian sandals, and razor-sharp, slave-kicking nails.

If a male wanted to fuck, cane, or be fellated, any girl slave had to obey, on pain of a whipping from one of the slags. It was rumoured that *really* bad sluts were branded on the breasts. The first greeting on arrival had been two-dozen stingers on the bare buttocks, from a slag's studded sjambok, which, Frank assured the weeping maids, was a mild taste of slavery, just to break them in. Greta prowled, in designer micro-skirts with nothing underneath, cracking her own sjambok across the girls' bums, and especially Caroline's. Any imperfection in her laundered clothes meant instant flogging of a laundress, with the threat of 'the mangle'. Their meals were taken in bondage and strappado, just as at Furrow Weald, while the 'naked beasts' – as they named the older inmates – stampeded, fighting and clawing, in their huge cage, whenever a slag hurled in a trough of fried locusts and mealie porridge.

Under their filth, the beasts were in superb physical shape, with golden-brown muscles rippling. Despite her enslavement, Caroline was rather smug about her own, frankly, *fabulous* all-over tan. The beasts were filmed boxing, wrestling, fighting for food, pissing, dunging, spanking and gamahuching, or queening a hapless victim, by taking turns to sit on her face and pee, while the victim licked them off; the Furrovians, too, had to practise those sports. Beasts exulted in their feral cruelty, especially in mass buggery, where the victim was tooled by a variety of strap-on dildos, and braying in their Sloaney accents.

'Do lash the cunt harder, Beatrix!'

'Fuck her hole raw, Tara!'

Curiously, yesterday's victim became tomorrow's fiercest dominatrix. Sometimes they sang raucous parodies of the Furrow Weald school anthem: 'Bumholians, Bumholians Tweak your clit While mistress sit Bare your bum Till master come . . .'

Caroline realised that all the girl slaves were Furrovians! Daily, slaves suffered buggery, lashings and full-body whippings, strung from the gibbet that was the centrepiece of the television village, enfolded in lush jungle. Everywhere, video cameras hung out of reach, recording every wank or thrashing, to back up the hand-held cleverness of the cameramen. Frightful punishments for trivial offences were routine: full-body whipping, in suspension from the gibbet; nude burial up to the collarbone, in earth full of worms and beetles; heads bagged in paper or canvas for a sound caning, and a day of stumbling. In full-baggings, the sheath had eyeholes, and enclosed the entire head and torso in a sweltering heat box, down to the cunt gourd, leaving legs and bottom bare for thrashing, while the girl dripped sweat.

Once, as a treat, they crouched and bared up for Frank himself, who, after savage caning and over ten minutes' buggery, rewarded them with fruit gums, peanuts and imported Spanish lemonade. Their future was as beasts, to be released for races, armed only with whips, to fight, lash and gnaw their way across jungle and savannah, with Frank's camera crew in pursuit on their motor-buggies. Caroline mentioned escape; the others shrugged, or pouted.

'It's what *I've* always dreamed of,' Aaliz gasped, rubbing her weals, after taking two dozen on the buttocks with a quirt of lianas from Cow. 'We are all Stingers now.'

'You're from San Fernando – didn't you *know*, Merilee?' Caroline asked bitterly.

Merilee hung her head. 'Yes, I knew,' she whispered. 'I had enough of being a lady. I know myself for girl meat. You will, too, Caroline.'

And now, sweating in the laundry, Caroline did.

Swank or Stinger, I'm a slut for punishment, girl meat to be beaten and fucked. And I love it. My bum's whipped to ribbons, and I want to feel more lashes. My raspberry's buggered to mush, and I can't get enough cock in my bumhole. I'm a female animal, made to submit. Bother, bother and triple bother!

'I don't think you can ever get clothes really clean in the tropics,' she said with a sigh to Samantha.

'Well, a woman's work is never done.'

Samantha's naked breasts glistened with soap suds.

'Doesn't the soap make your quim sting?'

'Why, yes. That's what soap is for.'

Together, the girls rhythmically churned the foaming liquid, stamping on knickers, bras and skimpies, most of them Greta's. The slag Twat lolled in the corner, pink bra and panties sopping with sweat, and smoking a cigarette.

'What wouldn't I give for cock,' Samantha said with a sigh. 'I don't mean these teensy-weensy camera twerps, I mean real cock, young, stiff and huge.'

'Frank's huge.'

'But we're just his hareem. One *bonk de politesse*, and that's it. I went to some Greek island once – Samothraki, that's it – and I never got off the table in the beach bar! They'd feed and water me while I was bummed by Greek studs, and make me sleep chained up in the sand, where I had to pee and dung too. One gorgeous tool after another, filling my bum. What a heavenly week!'

'Total shame,' gasped Aaliz. 'I simply must wank.' Her hand dived beneath the soap suds, and she smiled.

'I've been on Samothraki too,' said Caroline, 'only they fucked my cunt.'

'That's a bit tame,' Samantha said, sniffily. 'How many cocks?'

'Five, I think.'

'Ooh! I'm coming!' Aaliz squealed.

'One after the other?' asked Samantha.

'Of course.'

'My boys *mentioned* meeting an English beauty, and having to fuck her a strange way.'

Stooping under the soapy water, the girls scooped armloads of washing, climbed from the tub and dripped their way to the mangle, to dump the wet things into a drainage sink. Greta strode in, cracking her whip. 'Where are those pink knickers of mine?' she barked. 'Mr Funn's taking me into town for tea with the boss of FernandOil, and I *must* have them.'

'Jiffy, miss,' sang Merilee, wringing the panties through the mangle, and slipping her finger briefly into the gusset.

Caroline took the damp panties to Persimmon, who rapidly ironed them; then presented them to Greta, who grabbed them, lifted her skirt and jammed the tight bikini panties over her minge.

'I'm so thrilled,' she blurted. 'The boss is bound to give me a *fuck d'honneur*. No honours for dirty slaves!'

The afternoon passed, the weary toil broken only by a change of slag, and, once, a languid six cuts on Aaliz's bum for laziness. It was dusk when a fuming Greta burst into the laundry. She rushed to Caroline, wrenched her out of the tub by the hair.

'You've got it coming, slave bitch,' she screeched.

'What – ouch!' Caroline wailed, as Greta began to slap her face.

'You think it's funny to rub chilli pepper in my knickers? My quim was in agony all afternoon. Thank heaven the boss of FernandOil didn't fuck me *there*.'

Slap!

'Ooh! That hurts!'

'*That* hurts? Wait till you take my birch.'

'No! Please, miss. Not the birch.'

'Girls, string her up. Then it's the mangle.'

'Ooh . . . no . . .' Caroline wailed.

She began to cry, as Greta slapped her ankles in a wooden hobble; her friends helped the slag rope her wrists behind her and knot her hair so that her mane was taut, and all were suspended from the ceiling, so that Caroline was on tiptoe in her hobble, inches from the iron mangle. The slag, Bitch, was sent to fetch Greta's Norwegian birch. It came: a fearful crackling sheaf of sharp twigs. Greta stroked Caroline's bare bottom with it, very gently, and Caroline shivered, sobbing.

'Wait till it whips you,' sneered Greta.

'Please – I didn't –' Caroline wailed.

'*You* handed me the pepper panties,' hissed Greta.

Merilee put her hand to her mouth, suppressing a giggle.

'You,' Caroline blurted. 'Oh, Merilee, how *could* you?'

'Told you. I'm tired of being a lady.'

'Feed her nips into the mangle,' Greta barked. 'A full half-inch press.'

'No! Please! I beg you!' Caroline cried.

Bitch pressed Caroline's nipples between the mangle rollers. Smiling, Merilee began to turn the rollers, drawing Caroline's naked breasts into the mangle.

15

Real Stripes

Her proud nipples, pink flowers on the sun-kissed golden breasts, disappeared slowly, *so slowly*, between the iron jaws of the mangle. The pain was excruciating.

But girls have their nips clamped. It's no different. Is it?

Caroline bucked, restrained by the wrenching of her knotted hair, and her arms, above her back in strappado. She watched her teats stretched pale, as her nipples disappeared, crushed by the iron rollers. The buds were out of sight, with only the areolae visible, and the breasts strained white tubes of flesh, when Greta nodded; it was enough. Merilee laughed and stopped, while Caroline gasped, half in agony, half in relief. Her nipple buds were squashed flat, trapped by the mangle, better and crueller than any ropes. She could not move, without waves of extra agony shooting through her wrenched titties, which obliged her back to stoop at just the right angle for the most helpless display of the buttocks. She moaned, her face scarlet in pain and shame, as come dripped from her parted cunt flaps. The Furrovians licked their lips, watching the birch rise over Caroline's quivering bare buttocks. Vap!

'Ahh!' Caroline screamed, her imprisoned titties wobbling, and her buttocks clenching, as the flesh quickly streaked pink.

Vap!

'Ooh!'

Vap!

'Oh! Ahh! Please stop!'

Vap!

'*Ahh! Ahh!*'

Her bare bottom clenched and wriggled violently. The searing of the birch was like no other pain on earth.

'Bet she's going to lose her mud,' drawled Persimmon. 'Birching does that to a chap.'

'I know I would,' said Samantha. 'Dung all over the show.'

Bitch put her fingers down the front of her uniform pink knickers, and began to wank; Merilee masturbated too, cunt wide and clitty frigged, with a big grin at Caroline's face, contorted in pain. Soon, all the Furrovians frigged, staring lustfully at Caroline's squirming buttocks, quivering straight legs, feet dancing on tiptoe and clamped nipples, as the birching continued, and Caroline's bare fesses were suffused by a gaudy blush of crimson twig welts. Vap!

'Ooh! Ahh! Gosh, it's awful! I've never been so sore!' Caroline said, sobbing. 'Have you no pity, miss?'

'None,' said Greta, licking her teeth. 'My bumming by the owner of FernandOil has put me in a whippy mood. He's the real power in this country, and a girl loves to be fucked by power . . .'

Vap!

'*Ahh*! Please tell me, at least, how many cuts I'm to get.'

'. . . his wife masturbated, watching him bugger me, and spanking her own bum as she wanked off. Such a sensuous couple! What? Oh, till the birch is denuded, slut.'

The girls frigged noisily, come slopping from their cunts, and Merilee playing with her nipples, mocking Caroline's clamped titties. Vap!

'Oh! Oh!' Caroline wept, her legs jerking rigid, toes curling and bottom squirming madly.

As she shuddered at each cut, her titties wrenched from their nipple clamp, stretching the quivering udders to pale mottled marrows.

'If ever an arse begged for the birch, it's yours, bitch,' gasped Greta.

Vap!

'Ooh!'

Caroline's birching continued for several minutes, the cuts spaced on the twelve seconds. Her croup was squirming uncontrollably, her hair and titties wrenched against their restraints and her arms in bondage straining in their sockets. Vap!

'Oh, please, Greta! I can't take any more,' she wailed.

'Can't? You've no choice.'

Vap!

'*Ahh! No!*'

The laundry echoed to the crack of the birch across Caroline's buttocks, and the gasps of her friends, masturbating to orgasm. When the birch was bare of twigs, Caroline was helpless and drooling, her bum twitching, while come streamed from her cooze. Greta threw down the wasted birch, lifted her skirt and touched her clit, erupting into a gasping, shuddering climax. Released, her titties springing back to their normal hugeness, Caroline wept, as she patted her hair into place.

'I hate you,' she said to Greta between sobs.

Greta balled come-soaked fingers into a fist. Slap! She punched Caroline hard in the nipples.

'Ooh!' Caroline squealed. 'You filthy bitch.' She sprang at Greta, knocking her over, and grabbing her twat.

'Ouch! Ooh! Let go,' Greta yelped.

Caroline began to slap her face, and punch her titties, while Greta squirmed and sobbed. Bitch stepped forwards to intervene, but Merilee overpowered her with a savage kick to the panties, and seized her cane, then sat on her face, while Samantha pinioned her ankles. Caroline hoisted Greta, plunging her face in the washtub, with her bottom in the air. Caroline ripped off Greta's skirt, and thrashed her naked buttocks with the slag's short cane. Greta's wriggling body whipped the water into a froth of suds. Her pink panties stolen, the slag Bitch squirmed, tonguing Merilee's extruded nubbin, and drinking the come and occasional spurt of piss from Merilee's cunt; Samantha and

Persimmon tongued the slag's clit, while wanking off each other's wet gash. Aaliz observed, masturbating, licking her lips, with drool coursing down her titties.

'Urrgh . . . ooh,' gurgled the crushed slag. 'You fucking cunts! This is mutiny! We'll flog you raw, brand your tits and bury you alive.'

Merilee silenced her with a massive spurt of pee, filling her mouth. Masturbating vigorously, Persimmon and Samantha frotted Bitch's clit with their stiff nipples, while embracing in long, drooling French kisses. Their upthrust bottoms waggled pertly, and Caroline, clamping Greta's legs, while she caned the immersed girl's squirming arse, regretted that she couldn't spank Persimmon's and Samantha's lovely bottoms too. Occasionally, she dragged Greta's head up for air, reimmersing her quickly, to continue her caning.

Come streamed down Caroline's thighs, as her victim's bruised red bottom squirmed, and she frotted her clit on Greta's curling toes, occasionally bending to bite the girl's bum weals. The cane wasn't *quite* the birch, but it would do. She flogged Greta until her bottom was purple with puffy weals, and Caroline had wanked herself to two more orgasms; gasping, her thighs wet with cunt juice, she released Greta, who slumped, weeping, on the floor.

'I shall have your nipples branded for this,' Greta said.

'Merilee,' Caroline whispered, 'I think it's time to escape.'

'Agreed,' Merilee replied.

While the girls gagged and bound Greta and Bitch, Caroline put on Bitch's pink knickers and bra, although they were uncomfortably tight. Carrying the slag's cane, she bagged her friends' heads, and led them outside, into the dusk. The ruse worked. In the twilight, other pink-knickered slags, leading their own slaves for punishment, nodded civilly to Caroline.

'Where to?' she hissed to Merilee.

'Into town, of course. We shan't take the track, we'll go by the swamp and lagoon, where they'll least expect.'

Suddenly, Aaliz ripped off her bag. 'Awfully sorry,' she blurted. 'Jiffy – forgot something –'

She ran back to the laundry, and, after moments inside, rejoined the group, bagging her head once more. She panted that she just had to 'give that beastly Greta a jolly good kick between the legs'.

They got easily away from the village, but Caroline did not permit them to unbag, until they had emerged from the jungle, into the savannah. Ahead stretched a dismal swamp, and glinting waters of a lagoon. Merilee said rather glumly that her cousin Clive *might* shelter them, if they could get into the FernandOil headquarters, beside the presidential palace. They had twenty miles to travel. As they set off, the sound of a hunting horn split the velvet darkness, and then a girls' chorus of the Furrovian anthem accompanied by the growls of motor-buggies. The sounds were approaching.

'Girl hunt!' hissed Merilee. 'Leg it!'

Pursued by the rapidly approaching whoops and whip cracks, the girls ran, squelching and stumbling, through the swamp, until their bodies were slimed with stinking mud. Behind them, there were curses, as the motor-buggies became bogged down, but the troop of beasts, with Frank Funn leading, raced on. They reached the lagoon, glinting black under the starry sky, and plunged in, seizing reeds from the shore. They swam out, and lay motionless in the inky water, breathing through the reeds, with fishes and slimy things crawling over their bodies, and invading their intimate holes. Caroline kept her mouth clamped shut, shuddering, as worms ate through her knickers, and crept into her cunt and anus. After an age, the girls surfaced, to see the posse only yards away, but in retreat.

'They must have taken the track after all,' panted Frank.

'Damn that lying bitch Aaliz,' Greta spat.

'*You* . . .' Caroline hissed. 'Sneak!'

'I'm sorry,' Aaliz bleated, as the girls seized her. 'I didn't mean . . .'

Whap! Whap!

She was silenced by Merilee's slaps to her mouth. Crying and whimpering, Aaliz was strung to an overhanging tree branch, her hair knotted round the branch and her arms folded over it, in a yoke, with a smaller branch jammed in her anus supporting her. Caroline spread the girl's thighs, and filled her cunt with worms and crustaceans, while straining to expel the slimy invaders of her own holes. She stripped off her own filthy bra and knickers, wadded the panties in the girl's mouth and wedged a bra cup over her cunt to stop the crustaceans escaping. Aaliz hung, helpess and snivelling, while Persimmon and Samantha knotted whips from lianas. Aaliz's cunt gourd writhed, as the beasts wriggled inside her slit. Each girl held a whip behind Aaliz's naked back and buttocks, shivering in the starlight.

'Mmph! Mmph!' Aaliz whined, shaking her head.

'No mercy, traitress,' Caroline snarled, raising her whip.

Thwap! The thongs streaked Aaliz's buttocks and the girl moaned. Thwap! Merilee flogged her back, then Samantha and Persimmon her buttocks, the girls taking turns to stripe the writhing bare flesh, until Aaliz's back and buttocks were bruised with glistening red whip scars, and weals criss-crossed her thighs and haunches. Thwap! Thwap!

'Urrgh!' she gurgled under her panties gag.

Tears streamed down her face and rivulets of come glistened in clear channels down her mud-slimed legs, as her buttocks squirmed on the branch impaling her anus. The nude bodies of the whippers, muscles rippling and teats bouncing, flashed in the starlight, as the thongs rhythmically rose and fell on the helpless, tethered girl. Thwap! Thwap! Not an inch of Aaliz's back and buttocks were unbruised, the long whip weals puffing crimson and purple in a quivering mass of blotchy girl flesh. Her brimming cunt gourd seethed with crawling life, yet, as she screamed into her gag, come oozed around the bra cup on her cunt, and streaked her quivering thighs. All the vengeful maids masturbated, spurting come from their frigged cunts, as they flogged their victim. Thwap! Thwap!

Suddenly, a spray of piss burst from the bra cup at Aaliz's bulging twat, drenching her whippers.

'The slut's going to lose her mud!'

Aaliz moaned; a torrent of dung squirted past her anal impalement, splashing Caroline's feet.

'You fucking bitch,' she hissed, and began to whip Aaliz directly on the naked breasts. Thwap! Thwap!

'*Urrgh!*' the tethered girl screamed, titties shuddering.

After half an hour's flogging, Aaliz's whole body was purple with welts, and each whipper had wanked herself to orgasm at least twice. Merilee ripped out Aaliz's gag, and told her she could gnaw herself free.

'Thank you,' Aaliz said, sobbing. 'That was lovely. I've never felt such shame.'

Caroline brutally squeezed the girl's cooze, under the bra cup, and Aaliz jerked.

'Ooh! Ahh!' she gasped. 'I'm coming!'

'See you in Furrow Weald, slut. Mwah!' Merilee said, blowing Aaliz an air-kiss, and the escapees laughed.

Resuming their trek, they made good time across the remaining savannah and jungle, and arrived in the city around midnight. Rows of shanties appeared, and Merilee casually led them along rough muddy tracks, all deserted. As they neared the glittering presidential palace, a few policemen nodded stonily. Merilee explained that nudity was their best disguise – they would be assumed to be presidential slaves, returning to the palace from some errand. They passed a street of raucous bars, with abundant girls, showgirl naked, not jungle nude. Many clung to revelling sailors.

'Gosh!' Persimmon exclaimed. 'HMS *Gunsight*'s in port.'

They crept around the rear of the palace, where, Merilee said, the slaves entered. 'A tunnel links the palace with FernandOil HQ, next door. We just pretend to be returning girl slaves, hop into the tunnel, and bingo! Assuming Clive is there.'

'The president really has *slaves*?' Caroline whispered.

'Of course,' said Merilee. 'He's a cunt hound. Only the juiciest girls, with the biggest tits and bottoms, are chosen, from thousands of hopefuls. It's a bit like *Up Your Raspberry*.'

'So, girls willingly sell themselves into bondage?'

'Caroline, why do you think I was at Furrow Weald? *Learning to be a better slave.*'

Merilee was right. They entered the palace without challenge, surrounded by numerous other girls: some carrying canes and adorned with tight metal or rubber harnesses, some in frilly pink or violet gauze and chiffon, some in the full nude.

'You gels had better wash up for the show,' drawled one girl, nude, but for a rubber snake curling around her cunt basin, 'unless that's an extra-special costume!'

Sounds of gurgling water indicated a washroom. Soon, the escapees were naked in a throng of other nude slaves, showering in warm water.

'We'd better steal some clothes,' Caroline whispered.

'Cousin Clive isn't particular about girls' clothes,' Merilee sniffed, 'unless it's to tear them off.'

'What . . .?'

Merilee giggled.'His job is getting English girl slaves for our sex maniac President Cana. You'll see him: a big, Spanish-looking geezer, who likes to parade in a leopard-skin robe. English is our second language because Queen Victoria owned us for bit. The old Spanish elite prefer hareems to politics, so FernandOil really runs the country, while Cana plays with girls. *Es la verdad!* If we want Clive's help, we'll have to play too.'

Squeaky clean, the nude maids entered a steamy locker room, where gaggles of girls dressed and undressed.

'Look here!' hissed Samantha, eyes bright.

She pointed to a pile of frilly French maids' costumes. Rapidly, they squeezed into the too-tight pink bras and sussies, clinging white low-cut blouses, really nipping pink satin thong panties, seamed black fishnet nylons, frilly black skirts, with starched pleats, and pinching six-inch stilettos. Persimmon uncovered a selection of false tigers' whiskers, so they gummed them on as a disguise. It was a short walk to the tunnel, with Merilee in the lead, no longer quite so cocky, but biting her lip, as she teetered on the narrow stiletto heels.

'Why so glum? You seem to know your way around,' said Persimmon.

'That's just it,' Merilee replied. 'They know their way around me, too.'

'Let's just blend into the background,' said Caroline hopefully. 'Serve as maids, for we're in costume.'

Their situation *did* seem a bit rum. Cousin Clive might not be their rescuer, but some kind of . . . *slavemaster.* They emerged from the tunnel into a lushly carpeted corridor, scented with jasmine and gardenia and girl sweat and with pink tapers burning on the gilt walls, and at the end of the corridor were two massive teak doors. Caroline raised her hand to knock, when the door opened.

'Mr Clive?' she asked.

'Of course. Wherever have you been, you beastly sluts?' drawled the tall svelte young male. 'President Cana, the owner of FernandOil, the captain of HMS *Gunsight*, the television people – why, *le tout* San Fernando is here.'

He did not look at Merilee, but straight at Caroline, or rather, her breasts, almost fully exposed by the tiny uplift bra, painfully smaller than a D cup. He scanned her legs, shiny in nylon, and craned for a peek at her bottom, wobbling under the starched skirtlet.

'With that bum, you must be Frank's escaped slave Caroline,' he said smugly. 'What a lark! Well, you'll do, my bewhiskered sluts. Grab your trays – champagne come, caviar, honey-fried locusts, jellied eels – and start circulating. If guests want to play games, you *must* obey.'

Urgently, Caroline blurted their problem of escape back to England. Clive laughed. 'Fat chance without exit visas,' he sneered, 'and juicy sluts never get exit visas. Get to work, spank maids!'

They crept into the vast *salle*, around the side, to the sumptuous buffet. The décor was of a grotto, replete with nooks, caves and crannies, and waterfalls sluicing red stalagmites and stalactites. The lighting was quite dim, save in spotlit pockets where the television crews were filming, and the salon thick with cigar smoke, from clumps of animated ladies and gentlemen, their conversation oddly punctuated by applause, groans and the unmistakable crack of wood on bare flesh. At the end, adoring wenches clustered around a tall man in a leopard-skin robe. *That must be President Cana. Gosh, he's dishy.* There seemed plenty of frilly maids, except that most were out of service at any moment, playing games. Caroline gulped, as she hoisted a tray of champagne glasses. Around her, air-kisses blew.

'Mwah!'

'Darling! Mwah!'

'Spank my bottom?'

'*Encule-moi, mon chéri!*'

'Mwah!'

'Merilee,' she hissed, 'there's Frank Funn, with Greta.'

'I know. I don't know if our whiskers are much of a disguise – not with that bottom of yours.'

'And yours.'

They giggled. A silver-haired Royal Navy captain, with a jewelled cane at his waist, summoned Caroline with a crooked finger.

'At last, the grog wench,' he said, seizing a glass, draining it, and taking another.

His companion, a young ensign – *dishy bum*, Caroline thought – helped himself shyly.

'*You've* a wench's bottom ripe for spanking,' the captain chortled to her, 'and there's another, with some rations. Over here, gel!'

Persimmon approached, rather timidly, proffering her tray of jellied eels. The sailors tucked in, and Caroline circulated. As Persimmon prepared to leave, the captain cried 'Hold hard,' and tickled Persimmon's whiskers, which came unglued. The young man gaped.

'Why . . . Ensign Pipp!' he blurted.

'Peter . . . I mean, Ensign Warchant,' Persimmon stammered, blushing.

'The gel's a blasted deserter,' roared the captain.

Persimmon put aside her tray, bent over, touched her toes and lowered her panties to her ankles, to receive a loud bare-bottom thrashing from the captain's cane. Caroline scurried away, knowing a spank maid couldn't shirk her duty forever. Knots of guests applauded, as girls bared up for caning, hand-spanking, or whipping, all under the winking purple eyes of the television cameras.

The caves and crannies, as Caroline replenished the thirsty guests, seemed to offer every supplice, from racks to branks, stocks, hobbles, gibbets and simple flogging stools. All were in use, with nude girls whimpering pitifully in bondage, as guests flogged their quivering bares, peed on them, obliged them to suck one cock after another, or accept a sequence of stiff tools in their bumholes and cunts – frequently, an artful girl being fucked by two males at the same time, one in each hole, while she sucked a third, and manually pleasured two more cocks.

Caroline recognised a beaming Samantha doing just that, with the refinement that Merilee, herself buggered from behind by cousin Clive, was whipping Samantha's naked breasts with a gutta-percha ferule. Frank Funn was receiving an energetic tit wank from the glowering, nude Greta; he smoked a cigar, and explained that it was for the Japanese market. Greta's buttocks were parted, and examined by several males, all naked and erect.

'Look at that raspberry,' said Frank. 'Isn't it fine and mushy, shiny with arse grease, and just the right colour? I've been up her scores of times – cured her of being a lesbo! She's a willing animal, gents, so take your pleasures.'

Buggered, Greta grimaced in agony, as she rolled Frank's rigid cock between her quivering teat melons.

There were boy slaves, too – nude, muscled youths, obedient to command. Trying to ignore the come oozing from her tight-pantied cunt, Caroline smiled and curtsied, as lusty boy slaves pleasured ladies writhing on the floor, naked or with skirts and panties aflutter, cock penetrating anus, while distinguished husbands urged their young rivals to bugger their wives harder.

There was a boxing match between a boy and girl slave, both nude, but for heavy gloves, with the boy battering the open-thighed girl in teats, belly and cunt.

'Ooh! Oh! Not fair,' moaned the unresisting girl, come streaming from her cooze flaps. 'Uhh! Yes, do me, do me hard.'

Two naked girls fought with teat scourges; hands bound behind their backs and with short flails of studded thongs pinned to their nipples, they whirled fiercely, each lashing the other's breasts with her teat-flail. The girl with the rubber snake nude-wrestled another, with the snake filling each girl's cunt.

Caroline ran backwards and forwards, restocking her drinks tray, as if fervent activity would spare her. Yet there was no hiding place. A group of whooping English girls, visiting sixth-formers from posh Exmoor Academical, and nude, but for pearl chokers and golden nipple-rings, collared Caroline, and forced her to kneel and lick their cunts. One of them buggered Caroline with a strap-on and, of course, all wanted to try it, after which Caroline's smarting bum was further seared by twenty strokes of a cane. Groaning and weeping, Caroline nevertheless kept her tray held high. She told them about St Radegund's and Furrow Weald.

'Is it true there's a caning club called the Swanks?'

'Yes. I'm a member, and so is Merilee over there.'

Merilee's buggered bum was splashed with spunk, as cousin Clive spermed in her rectum; she groaned, as he led her towards Caroline.

'Your bumhole's still tight, but you haven't really been punished for running away, slave,' Clive said pleasantly.

'I'll see to her,' said Caroline.

'You will? Thanks awfully.'

Caroline took the gutta-percha ferule, while Merilee, eyes moist, took position. Legs apart, she rested her hands on her knees, while Caroline flicked the cane on her pendulous breasts. Merilee winced, as the cane sliced her nipples.

'I've always promised I'd cane you,' Caroline murmured.

'Really hurt me,' Merilee said, come oozing from her wet cunt. 'I've always wanted you to.'

Caroline's cane whistled, cracking across Merilee's bare black buttocks. Vip! The fesses clenched hard.

'Ouch!'

A second stroke followed quickly, and a third. Vip! Vip!

'Ooh!'

Vip!

'*Ahh!*'

Caroline caned until Merilee's face was a mask of anguish, her wealed buttocks squirming fiercely, while the Exmoor girls, wanking off at Merilee's distress, egged Caroline on. Come spewed from Merilee's wriggling cunt, until, at the sixtieth cane stroke, she touched her erect, protruding clitty, and gasped in a shuddering orgasm. She dropped to her knees and tongued Caroline's clit, drinking her copious come, until she too climaxed, while the giggling Exmoor girls masturbated and playfully spanked each other's pink bare bottoms.

'You're a nimble gel,' boomed the captain of HMS *Gunsight*, taking Caroline's arm, 'so I'd like you to attend to a disorderly tar.'

Caroline was given a naval birch, and led to a block, where a kneeling boy's bare bottom faced her. She examined his naked cock, and gasped.

'Yes, I joined up, miss,' moaned Jabez Prestellen.

Caroline stroked the birch twigs, and smiled. 'I'll make you wish you hadn't,' she murmured.

Vap!

His buttocks tightened, as the birch streaked his bare arse red. Vap!

'Ooh, miss . . .'

Vap! Vap!

'Ohh! It's agony!'

Persimmon stood beside Caroline, advising her on the finer points of birching, and masturbating openly, with Peter Warchant crouching naked beside her, his neck in a leash, and his bottom laced with fresh weals. Peter's cock was stiff.

'Up, boy,' snapped Persimmon, crouching, to expose her anus. 'You said you'd have me – remember?'

'Yes, mistress.'

'So have me.'

As Peter bum fucked Persimmon, the captain of HMS *Gunsight* enculed Samantha from the rear, while hand-spanking her bare buttocks. Jabez's cock was rigid; after three dozen cuts of the birch, Caroline crouched, and took his glans into her mouth, then sucked him to a groaning spurt, swallowing all his cream, except for the sperm droplets drooling down her chin onto her heaving bare breasts; she squeezed her breasts up, and sucked spunk from her nipples.

Peter's cock spurted cream into his mistress's rectum, spilling down her thighs, for which Persimmon awarded him a birching at the crouch. Merilee knelt at Peter's face, and presented her cunt for tonguing; when the birched ensign had licked her to a gush of come, Merilee rode him bareback, wanking her clit on his neck, and frotting his cock with her toes. Persimmon completed his birching, and knelt to take Peter's glans between her lips, and, while Merilee wanked off, with her toes stroking the boy's balls, Persimmon sucked him to a new spurt, which splashed spunk over her face. Merilee sprang up, to kiss Persimmon and lick the sperm from her face, while both girls masturbated to come.

'What exciting japes!' said an Exmoor girl, giggling. 'These Swanks are hot.'

'You want a real jape?' snarled Caroline.

'Yes, please.'

Caroline led them to Frank Funn, tit wanked by the scarlet, sobbing Greta, whose arse was buggered by yet another tool.

'She's the perfect female animal,' Frank explained.

With a roar, the posse of eager girls overpowered him. Greta milked her bugger of sperm, then wrenched her bum away, with a plop, and seized a cat-o'-nine tails of nine knotted sjamboks.

'Wait – no!' Frank appealed. 'You can all be on my show – aah!'

Thwap! Vap! Vip! Sperm dripping down her thighs, Greta lashed him with the cat, Caroline with the birch and Persimmon with the cane, while the Exmoor girls, peeing and wanking off, sat on Frank's face.

'Oh! Ah! Stop!' he pleaded, as his squirming buttocks were whipped dark crimson; yet his cock remained rigid.

The girls flogged his bare arse purple, then dragged the sobbing funster to his feet, holding him for Caroline to mount him and penetrate his anus with the biggest, roughest strap-on dildo. Persimmon clamped his nipples, drawing them on a rope up towards the ceiling.

'Oh, no. The shame,' he moaned, as the television cameras whirred.

Caroline buggered him for several minutes, then Persimmon, and finally Greta, who fucked hardest.

'Cripes, it hurts,' Frank wailed. 'Oh, cripes, oh, cripes.'

Caroline looked for Merilee to join in the fun, and saw her on the presidential throne. The president, in his leopard-skin robe, had the black girl over his knee, and was giving her naked bottom a ferocious hand spanking. Smack! Smack!

'Oh! Ah!' Merilee's bare bum squirmed.

'You really are an absolute beast,' drawled the president, sounding rather like Merilee.

Smack! Smack!

'Ouch! Ooh!'

'You've been behaving like a bally guttersnipe.'

Smack! Smack!

'Ohh! Yes, I have.'

'Say you're sorry, you naughty, naughty girl.'

Smack! Smack!

'Ooh! Ouch! I'm sorry,' wailed Merilee; a final spank, and she was released to rub her sore bottom and sob.

'*Ahh* . . . Greta, please . . .' Frank groaned, buggered, as a droplet of sperm appeared at his peehole. 'Ooh!'

Spunk jetted from his bucking cock, while his laughing crew filmed their enculed boss.

'Bit harsh on old Frank,' said a sleek raven-haired man of about forty, nude, and smoking a cigar, his erect cock rising above a shaven gourd.

'And who are you?' snarled Caroline, brandishing her cane.

'Why, I own FernandOil,' he purred.

Caroline stared at him intently. 'Is black your natural hair colour?' she said.

He blushed. 'Well, no, actually, I'm as blonde as you, my dear.'

Caroline ripped off her tiger's whiskers.

'Caroline!' he gasped.

'Yes, Daddy,' she said stonily.

'Mummy will be pleased to see you – when she's finished playing, um, diplomacy, with our president.'

A nude female writhed, bum fucked in missionary position by President Cana, sans robe, his arse pumping, as his massive cock penetrated her squirming anus. Drool flowed from her lips, as she gasped, clutching his buttocks, and pulling him into her.

'Hello, Mummy,' drawled Caroline. 'Remember me?'

'Yes . . . yes . . . *ooh*!' gasped Mummy, exploding in orgasm.

'It's a bit rum for a chap's mummy and daddy to abandon her like that,' Caroline said.

'How ungrateful,' her mummy gasped. 'We're not your real mummy and daddy, you know. You're a complete stranger! Yet we've done oodles for you.'

'Well, I'm going to do something for you.'

Caroline curtsied to the president, who plopped his dripping tool from her mummy's anus. Caroline lifted the gutta-percha ferule.

'Now, just wait,' said her daddy.

'How did you buy FernandOil, Daddy?' Caroline said. 'With a cheque to the president?'

'Bearer bonds, actually.'

'Perhaps from the Citizen New Century Bank of the Cayman Islands? I could have a little word with the president . . .'

'You wouldn't . . .'

'I would.'

The president was distracted, with his cock in Samantha's mouth, while Persimmon licked his balls, smeared with Caroline's mummy's come and arse grease.

'Now, just a minute. This is blackmail.'

'Down, sir.'

He lay beside his wife, and Caroline gave their bottoms a severe caning, until both squirmed, sobbing in agony. Daddy's cock was hard; after fifty strokes each of her cane, Caroline obliged him to fuck his wife's cunt. He spermed rapidly, and Caroline explained a small further task, involving bearer bonds.

'I don't think Mr Funn would want to sell you *both* his schools,' he groaned.

'He will.'

She strode towards Frank Funn, still suspended from his nipples, and placed her cane on his cock tip. She took his balls into her mouth, and sucked.

'Ooh! Urrgh!'

'I've a bone to pick, Frank.'

'Cripes! Not again.'

'It's just a business deal.'

'Name your price.'

Papers were drawn up, and signed, a surprising number of the guests, in cock-clamps, masks or manacles, proving to be corporation lawyers. A glowing Persimmon clasped Caroline's waist.

'Caroline, how super! The captain has agreed to overlook my desertion, and take me back aboard HMS *Gunsight*. Only, I must take a full flogging at the mainmast.'

'Ships don't have mainmasts these days.'

'Well, *you* know. Then, I'm to be chief birching officer. A real officer, with real stripes.'

'Excellent,' said Caroline. 'Mwah!' She blew an air-kiss at Persimmon, who blew one back.

'Mwah!'

Caroline crouched, baring her buttocks, and winking her anus at the president. Within seconds, his massive stiff cock rammed her anus, plunging into her rectum and slapping her colon, to begin a fierce buggery.

'Gosh, you're hurting me, sir,' Caroline gasped. 'That's really, truly the biggest cock I've ever had.'

Come poured from her cooze, as she wanked her erect clitty. While the president bum fucked Caroline, Persimmon slipped beneath, to lick his balls and drink Caroline's come.

'Mwah!' She kissed Caroline's wet cunt.

Samantha perched on the president's shoulders, wanking her clitty with his earlobe.

'Mwah!' Samantha pouted, blowing an air-kiss to Merilee, who watched, hands on hips, shaking her head, with her lips curled in disdain.

'Aren't you going to join in the fun?' Samantha squealed. 'The president has the most fabulous tool!'

'Are you out of your mind?' Merilee spat. 'That's absurd! It's grotty enough, having to watch.'

'But he's *soo* virile,' Caroline gasped.

'I don't doubt it,' said Merilee. 'He's only my *daddy*, that's all. Don't you daft tarts know *anything*?'

'Sorry,' said Samantha.

'Sorry,' said Persimmon.

'*Ooh*! *Ahh*! You're going to split me in two, sir,' Caroline groaned. 'Oh, yes, don't stop. I'm a naughty, wicked girlslave. Bugger me rotten, split my bum . . . I'm coming . . . *ooh* . . .'

Her rectum squeezed the giant cock, milking it. Licking the president's balls, Persimmon wanked off to orgasm, while Samantha's come poured over Caroline's hair. Hot spunk washed Caroline's bumhole.

'*Ooh! I'm there!*' she squealed. 'Sir, can my friends and I all have exit visas? Please, please, please?'

'*Yes . . .*' gasped the spurting president.

Caroline blew air-kisses. 'Mwah!' she gasped, her cunt drooling come, as she orgasmed.

Envoi – School For Stingers

The coal fire glowed cheerfully in the grate. Outside, autumn leaves fluttered, and the Cornish breakers pounded the shore of Furrow Weald. Deputy headmistress Merilee Caine buttered hot crumpets, while the head, Mistress Caroline Letchmount, poured tea. The television set burbled in the corner of the head's study. Sighing contentedly, the two girls settled back in their leather armchairs.

'Samantha's doing terribly well as head of St Radegund's,' Merilee said, with her mouth full.

'Yes,' Caroline replied, dribbling butter down her chin, 'she has a spiffing new regime. If any maid commits an infraction, it's *Samantha* who has to take the bare-bum caning.'

'What a terrific guilt trip. That was a nice postcard from Persimmon, wasn't it? HMS *Gunsight* seems to visit San Fernando quite a lot. I'm so glad she's won her third stripe.'

'She'll be disciplinary vice-admiral one day.'

'Or rear-admiral.'

'I say,' said Caroline, rubbing the crotch of her skirt, 'suddenly, I'm awfully fruity. Have we time for . . . you know?'

Merilee shook her head. 'She'll be here any moment. Business before pleasure.'

'Beast. Bags I be swank, for that.'

'You were swank last time. My bum still smarts.'

'You're one of nature's stingers, Merilee.'

Both girls rubbed their crotches, making a moue.

'I'm fruity too,' murmured Merilee. 'Still, things are jolly good, really, aren't they?'

'Yes,' said Caroline. 'A few little reforms – naval birching, for example – and Furrow Weald is the happiest place in the world.'

There was a knock on the door. Merilee opened it, and bade the entrant remain standing, while the mistresses finished their tea. Squeals of anguish came from the television, where Frank Funn, dressed in pink panties and bra, was being pelted with mud by jeering Exmoor girls, while Greta, dressed as a schoolmistress, spanked his bottom most realistically with a hockey stick. When the teacups were drained and the last crumpet scoffed, Caroline rang for the maid. Vicca Valcul hobbled in, on all fours, wearing a frilly French maid's costume, the tutu up over her naked, freshly caned buttocks, and wearing one sharp stiletto on her stockinged foot, with the other wedged in her anus. She balanced the tea tray on her bottom, and crept out, snuffling.

Merilee and Caroline stood up; Merilee handed Caroline a birch. The girl gasped, and went pale.

'Yes,' said Caroline. 'You know why you're here – it's a shocking offence – you're a prefect, who should set an example to the maids – so it's two dozen with the birch, on the bare, I'm afraid.'

'Oh, please, mistress, won't a caning do?'

'Impudence! You'll take *three* dozen cuts of the birch on your naked buttocks! When will you beastly maids ever learn? Get your panties down and bare up for your punishment. You may bend over the back of my armchair.'

The girl did so, whimpering and sobbing, as she pulled up her pleated skirt and bent over the chair, then lowered her white panties, heavily stained with juice from her cooze. She parted her thighs, baring the twin orbs of her bare buttocks, with the shaven cunt flaps dangling swollen below and glistening with furtive drips of come.

'Yes,' said Caroline. 'Three dozen of my hardest cuts on that innocent bare bottom. Those fesses are going to smart like the dickens, and glow like hot coals, and, you know, I'm going to enjoy every minute of it. A nice, slow birching, with every cut a stinger. Speaking of which, you don't deny your offence – membership of an illegal gang, the so-called Stingers?'

Caroline frowned in disgust.

'No, mistress.'

'Taking part in forbidden practices, like masturbation?'

'No, mistress.'

'*Mutual* masturbation – gamahuching, in the nude, with other maids?'

'No, mistress.'

'Meeting town boys, and . . . and taking their sex organs in your bumhole?'

'No, mistress.' She sobbed. 'But every girl's in one gang or the other.'

'The *other*?'

'Why, the Swanks, mistress.'

Merilee and Caroline exchanged shocked looks.

'*Another* gang!'

'Heavens!'

'The rot is deeper than we thought.'

Caroline lifted the birch. Vap! The birch lashed the quivering bare fesses, and the miscreant gasped. Vap!

'Ooh!' the flogged maid sobbed.

Vap!

'Uhh!'

Vap!

'Ohh!'

Her bottom squirmed, scarlet with welts, the seared flesh wriggling more and more fiercely as the beating progressed past the first dozen, then the second dozen cuts. Merilee's hand wriggled beneath her schoolmistress's gown, between her pantiless cunt lips, as she wanked off, gazing at the flogged bare bottom; Caroline's hand, too, was busy between her legs, with a squelch of come, as her nylons slithered together.

'And which girls are members of these dreadful gangs?'

'Well, Vapula, and Pimella, and Bronwen, and Emma . . .'

'We shall have to beat them all!'

Vap!

'*Ooh!*'

Come dripping from her gash, as she rubbed her engorged clitty harder and harder on the come-soaked leather, the flogged maid continued to gasp out names. 'Judy, Gertrude, Mandy, Victoria . . .'

Merilee's tummy fluttered, and her fingers squelched in her quim, as she frotted her clit to spasm.

'Why, it seems we must punish every girl in school!' cried Caroline, masturbating. 'Oh . . . oh . . . *ooh*!'

'Yes, mistress,' gasped Aaliz. '*Yes* . . .'

NEXUS BACKLIST

THE BOND	Lindsay Gordon	0 352 33996 9	☐
CAGED [£5.99]	Yolanda Celbridge	0 352 33650 1	☐
CHERRI CHASTISED	Yolanda Celbridge	0 352 33707 9	☐
COLLEGE GIRLS	Cat Scarlett	0 352 33942 X	☐
COMPANY OF SLAVES	Christina Shelly	0 352 33887 3	☐
CONCEIT AND CONSEQUENCE	Aishling Morgan	0 352 33965 9	☐
CONFESSIONS OF AN ENGLISH SLAVE	Yolanda Celbridge	0 352 33861 X	☐
CORRECTIVE THERAPY	Jacqueline Masterson	0 352 33917 9	☐
CRUEL SHADOW	Aishling Morgan	0 352 33886 5	☐
DEMONIC CONGRESS	Aishling Morgan	0 352 33762 1	☐
DEPTHS OF DEPRAVATION	Ray Gordon	0 352 33995 0	☐
DISCIPLINE OF THE PRIVATE HOUSE	Esme Ombreux	0 352 33709 5	☐
DISCIPLINED SKIN [£5.99]	Wendy Swanscombe	0 352 33541 6	☐
DOMINATION DOLLS	Lindsay Gordon	0 352 33891 1	☐
EMMA ENSLAVED	Hilary James	0 352 33883 0	☐
EMMA'S HUMILIATION	Hilary James	0 352 33910 1	☐
EMMA'S SECRET WORLD	Hilary James	0 352 33879 2	☐
EMMA'S SUBMISSION	Hilary James	0 352 33906 3	☐
EROTICON 1 [£5.99]	Various	0 352 33593 9	☐

MISS RATAN'S LESSON	Yolanda Celbridge	0 352 33791 5	☐
NAUGHTY NAUGHTY	Penny Birch	0 352 33974 4	☐
NEW EROTICA 6	Various	0 352 33751 6	☐
NO PAIN, NO GAIN	James Baron	0 352 33966 7	☐
NURSE'S ORDERS	Penny Birch	0 352 33739 7	☐
ONE WEEK IN THE PRIVATE HOUSE	Esme Ombreux	0 352 33706 0	☐
ORIGINAL SINS	Lisette Ashton	0 352 33804 0	☐
THE PALACE OF PLEASURES	Christobel Coleridge	0 352 33801 6	☐
PALE PLEASURES	Wendy Swanscombe	0 352 33702 8	☐
PARADISE BAY [£5.99]	Maria Del Rey	0 352 33645 5	☐
PLAYTHING	Penny Birch	0 352 33967 5	☐
THE PUNISHMENT CAMP	Jacqueline Masterton	0 352 33940 3	☐
PENNY PIECES [£5.99]	Penny Birch	0 352 33631 5	☐
PET TRAINING IN THE PRIVATE HOUSE [£5.99]	Esme Ombreux	0 352 33655 2	☐
PETTING GIRLS	Penny Birch	0 352 33957 8	☐
THE PLAYER	Cat Scarlett	0 352 33894 6	☐
PRINCESS	Aishling Morgan	0 352 33871 7	☐
PRIVATE MEMOIRS OF A KENTISH HEADMISTRESS	Yolanda Celbridge	0 352 33763 X	☐
PRIZE OF PAIN	Wendy Swanscombe	0 352 33890 3	☐

THE PRIESTESS	Jacqueline Bellevois	0 352 33905 5	☐
THE PUNISHMENT CLUB	Jacqueline Masterson	0 352 33862 8	☐
SCARLET VICE	Aishling Morgan	0 352 33988 8	☐
SCHOOLED FOR SERVICE	Lady Alice McCloud	0 352 33918 7	☐
THE SCHOOLING OF STELLA	Yolanda Celbridge	0 352 33803 2	☐
SERVING TIME	Sarah Veitch	0 352 33509 2	☐
SEXUAL HEELING	Wendy Swanscombe	0 352 33921 7	☐
SILKEN SLAVERY	Christina Shelly	0 352 33708 7	☐
SINS APPRENTICE	Aishling Morgan	0 352 33909 8	☐
SLAVE ACTS	Jennifer Jane Pope	0 352 33665 X	☐
SLAVE GENESIS [£5.99]	Jennifer Jane Pope	0 352 33503 3	☐
SLAVE REVELATIONS [£5.99]	Jennifer Jane Pope	0 352 33627 7	☐
THE SMARTING OF SELINA	Yolanda Celbridge	0 352 33872 5	☐
STRIPING KAYLA	Yvonne Marshall	0 352 33881 4	☐
STRIPPED BARE	Angel Blake	0 352 33971 3	☐
THE SUBMISSION GALLERY [£5.99]	Lindsay Gordon	0 352 33370 7	☐
THE SUBMISSION OF STELLA	Yolanda Celbridge	0 352 33854 7	☐
THE TAMING OF TRUDI	Yolanda Celbridge	0 352 33673 0	☐
TASTING CANDY	Ray Gordon	0 352 33925 X	☐

- - - - - - ✂ -

Please send me the books I have ticked above.

Name ....

Address ....

....

....

.... Post code ....

Send to: **Virgin Books Cash Sales, Thames Wharf Studios, Rainville Road, London W6 9HA**

US customers: for prices and details of how to order books for delivery by mail, call 1-800-343-4499.

Please enclose a cheque or postal order, made payable to **Nexus Books Ltd**, to the value of the books you have ordered plus postage and packing costs as follows:

UK and BFPO – £1.00 for the first book, 50p for each subsequent book.

Overseas (including Republic of Ireland) – £2.00 for the first book, £1.00 for each subsequent book.

If you would prefer to pay by VISA, ACCESS/MASTERCARD, AMEX, DINERS CLUB or SWITCH, please write your card number and expiry date here:

....

Please allow up to 28 days for delivery.

Signature ....

Our privacy policy

We will not disclose information you supply us to any other parties. We will not disclose any information which identifies you personally to any person without your express consent.

From time to time we may send out information about Nexus books and special offers. Please tick here if you do *not* wish to receive Nexus information. ☐

- - - - - - ✂ -